# About the Author

Paul Waters is an award-winning BBC producer. He grew up in Belfast during 'the Troubles', was involved in cross-community peace groups and went on to report and produce for BBC Northern Ireland, BBC Radio 4, BBC Radio 5 Live, BBC World Service and Channel 5.

His claim to fame is making Pelé his dinner. But Paul has also covered elections in the USA, created an alternative G8 Summit in a South African township, gone undercover in Zimbabwe, conducted football crowds, reported from Swiss drug shooting-up rooms, smuggled a satellite dish into Cuba to produce the first BBC live programmes from the island and overseen the World Service's first live coverage of the 9/11 attacks on America.

Paul has also taught in Poland, driven a cab in England, busked in Wales, been a night club cook in New York, designed computer systems in Dublin, presented podcasts for Germans and organised music festivals for beer drinkers. He currently presents a book and writers podcast called *We'd Like A Word*. He has two children and lives in Buckinghamshire.

# *Blackwatertown*

Paul Waters

**unbound**

This edition first published in 2020

Unbound
6th Floor Mutual House, 70 Conduit Street, London W1S 2GF
www.unbound.com

ISBN (eBook): 978-1-78352-924-7
ISBN (Paperback): 978-1-78352-925-4

Cover design by Mecob

Printed and bound in Great Britain by Clays Ltd, Elcograf S.p.A.

*To Oliver, who told me stories. And to Helen, who
helped me tell some.*

# Super Patrons

Charles Ansley
Rosie Arkwright
J Atmore
Simon Avery
Anjili Babbar
Lia Baker Perera
The Baron, VRM and Bips
Philip Bass
David Bell
My darling Clarie Bell
Amanda Bolt
Gerard Brennan
Stan Burridge
Simon Button
Andrea Catherwood
Jamie Cawley
Edward Chaplin
Ya Chin Su
Stevyn Colgan
Peter Conduct
Karen Court
Sarah Cowen
Basim Basil Dajani
Will Dean
Sophia Dettmer
Samuel Dodson
Alena Doll
Sue Dorrell
Simon Edwards
Melanie Elliott

Lisa English
Steve Fleming
Tim Footman
Helen Foster
Jim Frank
Eileen Fulton
Greg Fulton
Louise Gallagher
Purminder Gandhu
Brian Ging
Lorraine Golli
Christine Gosling
Kimberly Graber
Geoffrey Gudgion
Andy Hardy
Alan Harris
Mary Hatch
Mike Hickman
Emma Horner
Adrian Horsman
Anna and Richard Horton
Liam Howard
David Humphreys
Janet Inglis
Lucille Inglis
Karen Ingram
Máire Ivory
Tim & Kate Jenkins
Dai Jones
Helen Jones

Eddy Joseph
Irene Jovaras
Gertrude Kennedy
Zoya Kensi
Jonathan Kent
Tony Kent
Michelle Knowles
Bee Bee Koh
Lee Kumutat
Pete Langman
Ewan Lawrie
Julinda Lee
Sandra Leonard
Beryl Lewis
Samantha Lloyd
Kevin Lynch
June MacMahon
Jane MacSorley
Arthur Magee
Chenab Mangat
Alison Martin
Frances Mc Aleese
Deirdre McConvey
Graeme McCoy
Judith McCoy
Sophie McCoy
Matthew McGrath
Catherine McGuinness
Clem McGuinness
Nicola McLean
Paul McMahon
Kirsty McQuire
Anna Millar
Aneysha Minocha
Varun, Bipasha and Vansh
Minocha
Veena & Arvind Minocha
Anne Montague
Lee and Debra Mowers
Agatha Murphy
Dorothy Murphy
John Murphy
PB Nagle
Wendy Ng
Adam Nicholls
Roger Noble

Sarah Norris
Martin O'Brien
Sean O'Flanagan
Jake O'Kelly
Julia O'Kelly
Mark Page
Richard Pearce
Melanie Perry
Patrick Plunkett
Anna Richmond
Christopher Richmond
Mark Richmond
Peter Richmond
Ruth Richmond
Fiona Robb
Paul Rocks
Swazi Rodgers
Adam Rosser
Richard Rowntree
Amy Russell
Fergal Ryan
Santhi
Richard Selwyn
Peter Silvester
Robin Silvester
Rosemary Silvester
Tamsin Silvester
Parmjit Singh
Gary Sired
Liam Mark Smith
Bonnie Sneed
Anne Springer
Deepali Srivastava
Janice Staines
Trevor Tall
Alice Tamagni
David Tamagni
Emily Tamagni
Woon Tan
Beverly D Thurley
Barry Turley
Mark Vent
Julie Walker
Catherine Walls
William Ward
Aidan Waters

Andy Waters
Anita Waters
Charles Edward Waters
Clare Waters
Ewan Waters
Joanna Waters
John Waters
Lisa Waters
Orla Waters

Rebecca Waters
Sheila Waters
Stephen Waters
Tanya Waters
Chris West
Heather Willars
Michael Workman
Julian Worricker
Yanfang Wu

This story is set just north of the Irish border in the 1950s. It is based on events that have been recorded by history and some true stories that have not. But it's just a story. The names have been changed to protect the guilty.

What is history but a fable agreed
upon?

   – Napoleon

# Sunday

# CHAPTER 1

Sergeant Jolly Macken didn't want to be a policeman any more. The butt of his hand pressed on the polished handle of his baton, not yet drawn. He felt hot despite the cool air of the Mourne foothills. He hated his job. He hated the crowd pushing at his back. He hated the string of men blocking the road ahead. All of them impatient for his signal – the ones behind muttering his nickname. He hated the verbal albatross that had been hung round his neck too. *Jolly*. Christ!

The stony slopes of fern and heather and gorse would usually lift his heart; the open land a refuge from complication and regulation. He'd feel the tension ebb from his shoulders. The small smile that would quietly creep over his face, unwitnessed. If Macken believed in anything, it was that there was no better place nor way for a man to be at peace than by quiet water, with a rod and line. Alone, but never lonely.

Today was different. Today he was only a hard-faced big man trapped inside a uniform. A stone bounced past his feet. The serenity of this County Down emptiness had been shattered long before. But at this moment of decision, all the shouting and jeering, the drums and the fifes, seemed to fade to silence in Macken's mind. The violence was about to begin –

the striking out at head and body with stone and bar and baton and rifle butt. And he was going to be the one to start it.

The parade was one of those annual territorial pissing contests. Like a dog reminding its neighbours who is cock of the walk. And just as a mutt has its regular lamp posts, so the local Orange Lodge doggedly stuck to its traditional route along the Longrock Road. It was the very long way round from their meeting hall on the Irish Sea coast at Kilmurray to their chosen church service. A long tramp through unprepossessing hill country, inhabited only by incurious sheep. But it had the merit of passing through the village of Ballydrum, which was both the only obstacle and the real objective. For what would be the point of asserting one's inalienable right to walk the Queen's highway if there was no one to object? For the Catholic and stubbornly nationalist residents of Ballydrum were no fans of the Orange, nor any of the other loyal institutions dedicated to celebrating the monarch and damning the Pope.

Usually, Ballydrum and Kilmurray happily went their separate ways. But once a year, every year, the Diamond Star of Hope Kilmurray Defenders, Loyal Orange Lodge No. 1598, had an irresistible atavistic urge to pay Ballydrum a visit. It would have been a dereliction of duty and an affront to the ancestors if they'd failed to remind the benighted Catholics just who was top dog in the valley, and indeed the state.

Ballydrum residents were not required to line the route, cheering for the Queen. It was enough that they tolerated the banners, the kick-the-Pope band and the walkers with their bowler hats, collarettes, furled brollies and unsheathed ceremonial swords. The marchers were content to perform to an audience of gritted teeth, closed doors and empty streets. And most years they did.

But word was it would be different this time. The band's warm-up walk had lingered outside a Catholic church and drowned out the prayers inside with a particularly rousing rendition of 'The Sash My Father Wore', listing past Protestant battle victories. The disapproval that spread through neighbouring townlands had grown into defiance. Ballydrum resolved that the historic victory of King Billy over King James would not be celebrated in their village. Not this year. They fancied a wee break.

But traditions do not brook interruption. Especially new traditions. The police suggestion that Kilmurray Lodge revert to its previous, shorter, traditional route, avoiding Ballydrum, was met with suspicion and scorn. So it was, that Sgt Jolly Macken found himself the miserable leader of the Diamond Star of Hope Defenders, marching as to war.

Macken and his score of constables came first. Behind them swaggered the Pride of the Valley Orange band. The fifes and side drums were littered like piglets round the huge rolling sow that was Big Jim Courtney and his legendary Lambeg drum. Jim's belly was a legend in itself, but he needed his bulk to support the even bigger drum propped vertically in front. Macken was impressed, despite himself, that such a fat, waddling figure could summon forth the strength and stamina to even carry the Lambeg, never mind beat out the dread rat-a-tat-tat on its two faces.

Following Big Jim and the band were the officers of the Lodge, and then the ordinary brethren – respectable types to the fore, bank manager, business proprietors and elected councillors. Macken suspected that many were just as keen as he was to be out of the drizzle. But it was the one day of the year they had to publicly prove their credentials.

Bringing up the rear was a rowdier contingent of younger men, boys and some women. The promise of trouble had swelled numbers. Macken knew that, if challenged, the parade marshal would describe this element as spectators or supporters, absolutely nothing to do with the official walk. But they sure came in handy in a bust-up.

As a child, Macken had enjoyed Orange gatherings. He remembered the excitement of accompanying his father to 'The Field' near Belfast on the 12th of July, the height of the Orange year. Despite the officially sectarian tone of the day, the organisers hadn't been fussy about the religion of the stall holders who kept the brethren fed and watered. It had been thrilling to hawk sweets and minerals to the thickets of black-suited men leaning on their swords and pikes. Back then, he'd drunk in their finery through big eyes. Now it seemed tawdry and pathetic.

Apart from a flourish of pomp as they'd left Kilmurray, the only sounds since had been amiable conversation and the striking of stout shoes and hobnailed boots on the road. One drummer kept time. They were saving their attitude for their captive audience in Ballydrum.

But as they approached the three-mile mark, the walkers' backs suddenly straightened. At a barked command, the drums and fifes were roused, and Big Jim Courtney began to batter the thunderin' bejaysus out of his big Lambeg.

Macken looked up. He'd been concentrating on just putting one boot in front of the other, and keeping the rain off his face. He exhaled sharply in irritation. This year, Ballydrum was not going to mutter under its breath as they passed. This year, Ballydrum had come out to meet them.

Boulders and branches blocked the road. Stern-faced men, some with sticks, stood behind the barricade. Macken saw cairns of smaller rocks piled nearby. He called a halt at what he hoped was further than a stone's throw away.

The shouting began immediately: 'Go home or we'll move you' met 'Aye, you and whose army?' The absurdity of that retort got a laugh from both sides, as the answer – Macken and his constables – stood between them in plain sight.

A hand landed on Macken's shoulder.

'Come on, man.' It was the Lodge's Worshipful Master. 'Fire a volley. That'll clear those Fenians from the road.'

He shook Macken's holster. 'Or are you forgetting who you are?'

No danger of that, thought Macken. What a mess. He politely removed the Worshipful Master's hand from near his Webley 45 revolver. 'I hope firearms won't be needed, sir.'

'Quite right, Sergeant,' Macken's district inspector intervened. 'Madden, isn't it?'

The voice of reason has arrived, thought Macken with sinking heart.

'Macken, sir.'

'Yes, of course.' The DI was off duty, but present as a Lodge committee member. 'We don't like to see guns drawn if it can be avoided.'

He leant on his blackthorn stick. 'Now, what's your plan of action?'

'Sir, if the Worshipful Master has a word with his opposite number,' suggested Macken, 'we may yet persuade the

Ballydrum crowd that it's honours even and find a way forward.'

The Worshipful Master snorted. 'Is this the kind you have in the Royal Ulster Constabulary these days, George? Comparing us to yon rabble? He'd do better to enforce our right to walk the Queen's highway. For if he's not able, or not willing, there are those who are.'

Lodge members cheered the prospect of action.

'Let's stay calm, Sammy,' the DI asserted himself. 'This is a police matter. Of course rights must be upheld. If we can do so peacefully then all the better.'

The DI turned to Macken. 'Go speak to them. Be firm. They've made their point, but they must disperse immediately. I hope they'll listen to one of their own.'

Aye, there's the rub, thought Macken, as he trudged towards the barricade. Someone is taking a perverse pleasure having the likes of me escort an Orange march.

One face at the barrier looked familiar, so Macken headed that way. He paused at the boulders to allow his presence to be felt. Everyone, deep down, has reason to fear the police. Macken slowly looked along the line of faces. Most avoided his gaze, as he willed their anxiety to grow into something he could use to dominate them – to let one man overcome a mob. They just need a nudge, he thought, from overt truculence back to grudging respect and then compliance. Almost there...

'Jaysus, he came all this way and forgot what he had to say!'

Macken heard sniggering.

'Don't worry, we've room for one more round this side,' said the familiar face, mocking him. 'It's about time you deserted that shower of Orange bastards!'

Macken realised his bubble had been burst, lanced by a sharp thrust of ridicule from someone with a nose for weakness. He consoled himself that if they were laughing, it eased the tension.

He opened his hands in a gesture of conciliation. 'Hello, lads. Who's running this show?'

The looks turned stony once more. The answer was another taunt. 'I thought it was you, Sergeant Macken. Are you here to negotiate?'

More laughter. It was the sneering way he said 'negotiate' that reminded Macken of who he was.

They'd met a few weeks before, when he had been playing away for his local football team against some notorious bruisers. Size and toughness are significant assets in the knockabout combat into which Gaelic football can descend. Macken had both. But they had only begun warming up when he had become aware of pointing and discussion on the touchline.

When it came, the tap on the shoulder had been from his own shamefaced captain. The home team were objecting to Macken's presence under Rule 21 of the Gaelic Athletic Association. It barred members of the Crown forces from taking part in GAA events. A gesture of defiance against the oppressor. Macken's job was common knowledge, but no one had made a fuss before. Sure, there was no harm in being on good terms with the local policeman. And if you were on bad terms, then a game of football or hurling was the perfect opportunity to knock his block off.

Macken remembered that it had been the skinny martinet looking down on him from the barricade right now who had clung to the rule book that day. Bottom lip out, finger wagging, he'd rejected any offer to 'negotiate' – a word apparently so despicable that he'd spat it rather than say it.

Macken had departed the field, shoulders slumped, without complaint. He'd not wanted to embarrass his protesting teammates, who'd been decent enough to turn a blind eye to his status themselves. He'd been left on the sidelines, wondering where he belonged, watching a bad-tempered football game quickly turn dirty.

Better get on with it, thought Macken. 'You've made your point, lads. Time to move before things get nasty.'

'That sounds like a threat. Jolly by name, but not so jolly when it comes to his own kind. We know whose side he's on.'

He must be a schoolteacher, thought Macken. Derision is his way of keeping control. But behind the bluster, not so sure of himself maybe? Too keen to pander to the back of the class. Time to find out if he can take it as well as dish it out.

Macken permitted himself a small smile, squared his shoulders and stared the schoolteacher in the face. The man blinked uncertainly, twitching bags under his eyes that sagged with the weight of past disappointments.

'Away and chase yourself,' growled Macken. 'I'm making the rules today.'

His tormentor flinched, suddenly more quarry than hunter. But before Macken could press home his advantage, a stone hit him between the shoulder blades. More clattered off the nearby boulders.

Macken couldn't very well hide behind the barricade, so he ran, feeling ridiculous, arm over his face, back through the hail to the police line.

'I'm afraid they got impatient, Sergeant,' said the DI. 'You seemed to be getting a bit pally with the other side.'

'Sir, you told me to talk to them.'

'Sergeant, your job is to move them.'

The marchers finally had the excitement they'd come for. They bombarded the barricade from behind the police. The defenders popped up to hurl catcalls and a few stones back. These barely reached the feet of the constables in front. Macken suspected the men on the roadblock were waiting till the Orangemen came closer.

'Sergeant, prepare your men to charge.'

'Sir, what about these boys behind us? They started the stone-throwing. They're using us as a shield.'

'Sergeant! Your men are under attack from that mob!'

'With respect, sir, the first officer to be attacked was me, from behind our own line. We can defuse this, but we need to move back out of range.'

But the decision had been made. Perhaps it was the thudding of the Lambeg drum, so loud and resonant it seemed to be inside everyone's head. Or the fear that failure to act would be seen as cowardice. The DI ordered batons to be drawn.

'Sergeant, lead your men!'

Christ, thought Macken, I don't want to be a policeman any more. He drew the polished ebony from its case on his belt, raised it above his head and shouted, 'Charge!'


Macken's cry was the cue for an even bigger volley of stones from the Orangemen behind him. The line of policemen became the shape of an arrowhead. Like geese in flight, no constable wished to reach their destination before the leading bird.

Behind them rushed the delighted horde of camp followers. The bandsmen came too – fifes tucked away, drummers still sounding a ragged rat-a-tat-tat. And on came the sober-suited official brethren. Some had discarded their jackets, rolled up their sleeves and pocketed their precious collarettes, the better to get stuck in. Those still clinging to notions of propriety wore expressions of grim concern rather than glee. They advanced with the air of reluctant school prefects, the stout sticks or umbrellas with which they had tapped out their route now raised as clubs.

At least the penetrating rhythm of Big Jim Courtney's Lambeg had stopped. Big Jim was unharnessing himself, the better to batter rebels with his fists. Two older Orangemen stayed behind to guard the Lodge's fringed banner – its scenes of past atrocities against the Protestants of Ulster a warning never to weaken in future.

The stampede triggered the response Macken had anticipated – a painfully accurate hail of stones into the mob of police and Orangemen.

Here's me, thought Macken, a Catholic, leading a bunch of bigots against other Catholics trying to defend their village. But on the other hand, I'm a policeman and those corner boys on the barricade are trying to take my head off.

Baton aloft, yelling, Macken reached the barrier first and came face to face with the smart mouth who'd taunted him before.

As he leapt onto a boulder, Macken saw the man was holding a bicycle, preparing to flee the battle. No time for escape now pal, thought Macken grimly. The man glanced back over his shoulder, the blood draining from his face when he saw Macken so close. But as Macken scrambled closer, the man lifted and swung the bicycle. Then he let go.

Macken put up his arms to protect himself and became entangled in the bicycle's works. He fell back, his head poking through the triangle of the frame and his baton arm caught in the spokes of the back wheel. The skinny man hared off through the heather as Macken went down hard.

Macken lay there, his face full of pedals and handlebars, as the combined forces of law and Orange Order surged over the barricade, scattering the defenders.

Beefy-faced farmers planted themselves on top of the barrier, leaning forward, hands on their thighs, catching their breath. The backslapping got underway, as they gathered in excited chatter round Big Jim, who sat panting, his vast girth quivering. Macken tried to extricate himself from the bicycle. He hissed in pain as a pedal dug into his side.

The Worshipful Master quietened the war whoops to lead three cheers and a prayer of thanks. He thanked the loyal officers of Her Majesty and drew attention to one in particular: 'Sergeant Macken sadly does not have the stamina of people who are proud to walk the Queen's highway. He's found himself a bicycle.'

Macken staggered, crab-like, to his feet. This delighted his audience.

'Look at the walking deckchair! He belongs in the circus.'

He gingerly disentangled himself and slowly straightened up.

'Stop horsing around, Sergeant!' barked the DI. 'You'll not catch them on that pile of junk. Let's take control of the situation.'

Macken angrily dashed the buckled bicycle to the ground and pushed his way through to where Big Jim stood glaring at the DI, across the Lambeg drum, which sat squat like a broad, round table on the roadway. What now? Macken sighed to himself. Isn't winning enough for him?

The sleeves rolled up over Big Jim's broad arms revealed dull flecks of blood. Looks like he's crushed a few noses, thought Macken.

Laid parallel across the drum like extra-long cutlery were

two malacca canes – tapered and thinly splintered at one end, the fatter ends pointing to Big Jim's brawny, reddened arms.

You have to admire the sheer brute will it takes to lug that beast, thought Macken, to whack it with such furious abandon that the hillsides themselves flinch. Red dots speckled the drumskin. Macken smiled ruefully at his earlier mistake – the blood had come from Big Jim's own wrists, from repeated contact with the rim of the drum. No matter how bad things are, he reminded himself, jumping to conclusions always makes them seem more bloodthirsty than they really are.

Then Macken realised too late that he had just made another, even worse mistake. In some cultures, a smile may be disarming. In Ulster, a nod will do just as well. In fact, far better. You nod in acknowledgement, respect or agreement. A smile may be seen as weak, devious or ridiculing.

'Funny, is it? Now we have this friend of the Fenians rubbing it in too!'

Spit from the irate drummer sprayed Macken.

'Thank you, Macken,' said the DI under his breath. 'I was halfway to persuading them not to worry about it – until your helpful intervention.'

The DI looked up the hillside to where a couple of small figures were jigging about on a rocky platform. Macken cursed silently as he recognised the banner hanging from the projecting rock. It was the green, white and orange flag of the Irish Republic. An affront the Orangemen were not willing to overlook.

'Get up there, Sergeant. Get the bloody flag, so we can get going.'


Macken made slow progress, plunging into holes hidden by heather and filled with sheep droppings. The large, flat rock above was a local landmark. Catholics had used it as a Mass Rock – the site of an altar for secret religious services when their priests risked execution under the Penal Laws. Legend had it that the great shard of granite had been thrown there by an ancient giant, during a duel with a rival across the Irish Sea. It was known to all as the Long Rock.

And on the Long Rock, waiting for Macken, were two more eejits keen to crack his head open. Can this day get any worse? he wondered.

Their first stones missed. Macken lurched sideways under the overhang of the Long Rock.

He slipped a finger inside his collar, feeling for the thin, metal disc on a chain round his neck. He pressed it for a moment as he gathered his courage. Back down the hill they were waving and shouting. He couldn't hear what, but it wasn't difficult to guess. Get on with it. He drew his baton once more and charged.

His charge immediately slowed to a stumble, making him an easy target. But as he scurried up onto the flat, stone shelf, Macken found it empty. Hardly believing it could end so painlessly, he stepped carefully to the edge of the platform and jerked free the Irish flag.

Another shower of stones fell around him. Macken wobbled on the edge. He realised that his attackers had merely retreated to a higher cairn of missiles.

Macken's balance shifted again. He tried to plant his feet more firmly but still he gradually pitched forward. His stomach lurched and it seemed like the stone floor was rising to meet him. He fell onto his hands and knees, baton in one hand and flag in the other. The heather on either side of the Long Rock seemed to be falling away.

His brain could not process the information being registered by his senses. It was as if the ground was moving, and he

15

was tipping further and further backwards. He saw the stone-throwers pointing, mouths agape. He blinked and their gawping faces were further away. It's as if I'm the one moving, he thought, not them.

Macken felt another lurch beneath him and was suddenly lying flat, his cheek against the cold stone, with the hillside moving past. He finally understood that the great granite platform, the Long Rock itself, had tipped and begun to slide down the steep slope.

He heard a faint whimpering from his throat, as if the sound was coming from some other frightened animal. His heart and stomach plummeted far below. His legs and arms shook. His clenched fists pressed into the stone, unable to grip, as the world rushed by faster and faster. Macken rode the Long Rock, crashing and bouncing through the heather, gouging and scraping towards the marchers below – the green, white and orange flag in his fist billowing behind like the tail of a kite.

*Darkness came down on him. Pouring in thick like tar.*

*Each time, before the yellow light vanished, the child resolved to keep watching. To bring her back. To keep her flame living with the intensity of his gaze.*

*But every time was the same. His eyelids closed. The moment of trial had come and gone. He was alone again, in darkness.*

*Each time, the fading glow inside his eyelids taunted him with her echo. His loss.*

*Then that echo died too. The inner glow extinguished. Leaving him sinking through black water. Every time the same. Night, with no promise of morning.*

# Monday

# CHAPTER 2

Macken was up before the top brass the next day.

'John Oliver Macken. Sergeant. Third Class,' the county inspector murmured as he read the report. 'Stand easy. We've been concerned about you.'

It was not the eruption Macken had expected.

'Yes, sir. I don't know that I'm the man for the job any more.'

'Hardly surprising, Macken. You tore a hole in the Longrock Road that'll take some mending.'

The CI shook his head as if at some private joke. 'They say you came downhill like an express train. Flying your green, white and gold!'

Macken had been bucked off the Long Rock into a thick clump of heather. He'd felt the thud as the boulder ripped a great gash in the road below. It had seemed an age before he'd had the courage to look. The Long Rock had scored a bullseye on Big Jim Courtney's Lambeg, a giant, jagged, grey shard sticking up from a wide crater. The marchers had scattered in time, but the drum had gone to glory.

'According to the Worshipful Master, you had them in some kind of mass hypnosis.'

The CI glared at Macken, his jaw tightly clenched. 'A single act of God could have wiped them all out. A single act of Jolly Macken, that is.'

The officer's control cracked. Macken braced himself for the outburst. But when it came, it was a roar of laughter not anger.

'Ah, Macken, that would have been... terrible. We were very lucky. We'll not be hearing from that particular Lambeg again.'

'No, sir.' Macken tried again to spit out what was on his mind. 'But I'm not the same man. I find myself having doubts. About taking sides, sir.'

There, he thought. I've finally said it. Now it would come hot and heavy, with a boot up his arse on his way out of the force.

But still it didn't.

'I wouldn't expect the son of the renowned Declan Macken to be knocked back so easily. Your father was all action. A war hero. But heroes see things in black and white. You think more. And no harm in that.'

No escaping family, thought Macken. I'm following my father's illustrious footsteps as usual.

'But there's no difficulty knowing what side we're on, Macken. The side of order. And order comes from the law.

'We all want a quiet life and the price we pay is sometimes tolerating a bit of showing off. Provided it stays within limits, we let it pass. And pass it does, and we all get back to normal. What we cannot tolerate is any challenge that could spark off something bigger. You see?'

'Sir.'

'Our job is to get everyone through these moments of madness. Then we all go back to normal. We steer people through, with a word, or when necessary, a crack on the head. For their own good.'

'Yes, sir. It's just that sometimes we seem to favour those not entirely deserving of our support.'

'I think you can guess, Macken, how supportive I feel personally towards the likes of the Kilmurray Loyal Orange Lodge…'

The CI pronounced the word 'Loyal' as though, in this case, it left a sour taste in his mouth.

'But that's the world we live in. And they won't be your concern in future. It's time you had a change.'

'That's just it, sir…'

The CI cut him off: 'We're agreed then. Too awkward to keep you here. They're out for your blood. You'll fill a vacancy in Blackwatertown.'

Macken frowned.

'Nasty accident with the young lad you're replacing,' nodded the CI, more sombre now. 'His weapon discharged while he was cleaning it, apparently. Shot himself in the head. Died instantly, I suppose. Small consolation to his family.'

Macken understood the subtext. Talk of suicide was always to be avoided if possible.

'This has just happened, has it, sir?'

'Yes, good timing for us.' The CI paused. 'Sorry. What I mean is that he was of the same faith as yourself, so it gives us a reason to transfer you to fill the gap, without seeming to give in to outside pressure.'

Macken felt deflated. They wouldn't let him resign with good grace now.

'You'll be replacing Constable Daniel McMahon with immediate effect.'

Macken staggered backwards, as though punched in the chest.

'*Constable Daniel McMahon?*'

'I'm afraid so,' the CI shrugged, misunderstanding the reason for Macken's shock. 'He was a constable, and that's what you'll be too. I have to be seen to punish you.'

Macken couldn't breathe. *Not Danny.* Even as he reeled from shock and grief, Macken could sense the guilt growing inside him.

'Don't see it as a step down,' the CI went on. 'More of a new start with a clean slate. A man of your calibre will soon climb the ladder again.'

Macken opened his mouth – nothing came out. But he knew that, somehow, the untimely death of Constable Danny McMahon, his abandoned little brother, was his responsibility.

'I can see you're surprised, Constable, but I actually envy you. Nice sleepy place near the border. Good fishing. Used to be a castle on the river. Only a few stones left now, but I daresay the locals like having them. Please don't wreck them, or any other ancient monuments you encounter. Reckon you could manage that, Macken?'

The CI chuckled at his own joke, but then flinched at Macken's stricken expression. He looked down at his desk, as Macken steadied himself, then left to unpick the stripes from his sleeve.

# CHAPTER 3

They don't know, Macken realised. Different surnames, so how could they? They haven't even waited for the funeral. Though that'll only be for real family. No ghosts like me.

It'll come out eventually, thought Macken. I should tell them now.

But he knew that he'd made his decision when he'd held his tongue. Enough of standing up. Easier to be swept along.

And they're sending me where I want to go now – where I have to go. It was my responsibility to look after him. It's my responsibility to find out what happened to him.

Macken slowly gathered his kit and possessions for his transfer. His limbs were leaden. His heart heavy with guilt. His memories of family were at once more real and more remote than the room around him.

Family can only hurt you if you let them, Macken had learnt. He tried not to think of them much. The memory of his mother was where he turned in times of danger. He supposed he must love her, but he had never properly known her. Not her fault. She had died when he was young. That was the first mark on his conscience. Her premature death was somehow connected to his own arrival in the world, so he'd later understood. He imagined he remembered her alive and holding him.

After a decent interval his father had married again. And more children had followed. Half-sisters and a half-brother. A new family into which Macken never fitted.

He couldn't blame his father. It had been the sensible thing to do. But he and his stepmother had never warmed to each other. Looking back, Macken knew now that he'd probably never given her a chance. What living person could ever live up to the imagined memory of his martyred mother?

When his father passed on, his stepmother had also married again. A man called McMahon. It had been the sensible thing to do. She and her children had naturally taken her new husband's name.

But not Macken.

There had been no sudden rupture, but Macken had drifted away, and they had been happy to let him. Less awkward for them. Or so Macken told himself. Less painful.

Except for Danny. That had always been Macken's job – to look after Danny. *Watch out for your wee brother.* Where Macken went, Danny would always follow. Even after Macken left. Even after all these years.

Macken doubled over with pain, new and remembered. Never mind excuses, he thought. His brother had kept on following him, even into the police. Into danger. And now he was dead.

But surely he would never have killed himself, reasoned Macken. He wasn't much of a believer, but he knew that taking your own life closed the door on any chance of going to heaven. The Danny that Macken knew would never have considered it.

But what about the Danny he didn't know? Even if his death had really been an accident, it was still Macken's failure.

Macken's responsibility. The brother no one knew he had. What else could he do now but take his place and find out the truth?

As Macken left Kilmurray, he knew it wouldn't miss him. Nor he it. The village seemed hollowed out – fishing boats gone out from the quay, children corralled from the sunshine into rote learning. Only shrieking seagulls bickering over territory.

Macken preferred the nearby mountains. He escaped there when he could – a tramp through the Silent Valley and up Slieve Binnian, Muck, Beeragh, curving round by old smuggling paths to Commedagh and the top of Donard.

He was never lost, even if the trail was just a slew of rocking stones or a stream bed. Eyes down, feet up and down. Pause for breath, hands on hips, head up and there it would be – a new vista, a lake shining silver through a gap in the interlocking slopes. Or standing on a mountain shoulder gazing down into the broad bottom of a glacier-cut valley, slopes lined with heather and furze, one side a carpet of embers glowing purple, red, orange and yellow in the evening sun.

No need to move at all. You could lie back in the heather and let the sky do the work. Earth mountains at your back, cloud mountains evolving above – one moment letting the sun through to bathe you in warmth, the next closing to draw the ground's chill up through your bones instead. The quick changing light and shade up there made it feel as if the earth's revolutions had speeded up, squeezing the passage of day and night into minutes not hours. During those moments, Macken felt as if his life was racing by, trying to keep up with the clouds passing faster and faster overhead. He'd stagger to his feet, dizzy, surprised he hadn't been carried away.

Those same clouds could swell quickly to black and dirty

yellow. He had often been caught out when the heavens opened, taking shelter by the Mourne Wall. The dry-stone boundary marked the watershed for the reservoir. The flat slabs on top were an elevated pavement above boggy ground, linking the peaks. Hadrian had his wall. The Chinese have theirs. We've our own, thought Macken.

The difference was that you were more likely to meet sheep than people in the Mournes. That's the real benefit of the rain, thought Macken. Not the greenery, but that it keeps people down by the coast. If only the sea would lap closer to the mountains, he thought, submerging the narrow ground below and the people who fight over it.

The road from Kilmurray ran along the sunny north shore of Carlingford Lough. The south shore, in the Irish Republic, was dark under the silhouetted hills of the Cooley Peninsula. Macken wondered if the people there resented living in the shadows, with the bright greens and yellows of the north laid out before them. Perhaps Unionists would concede that the southerners at least had the better view.

Macken finally got off the bus in Armagh, with its two cathedrals. One for Catholics and one for Protestants. Each on their own hill. Both named after St Patrick. Who says we can't agree on anything? thought Macken. On the rare occasions he attended Mass, he was strictly back of the chapel, or down on one knee outside if it was full.

Macken had an eight-mile walk to Blackwatertown ahead of him, but spots of rain sent him inside a café, seeking refuge from the weather and the dark pit of being alone with his thoughts.

A woman in an apron smiled a welcome. She raised her eyebrows to let him know she'd be with him immediately if it wasn't for these other customers, but what can you do?

Macken hunched over his tea. No one paid him any attention. Not the women with bags of shopping. Nor the elderly gent, smartly dressed – still making an effort – squinting at a newspaper, nodding with approval. Only one section could give such obvious satisfaction – the obituaries. Each entry a victory for the reader still living.

Or perhaps an indictment of the living, thought Macken. He winced at the thought that his own guilty secret could be on the page being held in shaking hands two tables away. The old man felt his gaze and looked up. He smiled to indicate that Macken could have the paper when he was done. Macken nodded back. No, too soon. The story won't have made the local weekly yet. His sense of relief disgusted him.

Outside, the roofs became shiny and the rain-wet road darkened. Macken let the heat from his cup curl round his face. Other refugees drifted in, their heavy coats dripping and steaming.

His mind drifted back to the county inspector's references to his father. Macken was always hearing about him. The unstoppable stormer of the Kaiser's own Hohenzollern Redoubt. A hard man. No belittling nicknames for him.

Macken's father had once explained to him the standard routine for infiltrating German positions. Plug the first man you see. Then the next one who moves. If the rest don't surrender immediately, finish them all. He'd brought the unbending rigour of army life back to Ireland. When partition split the country and meant the end of the old police, Macken senior had stayed north and become part of the new Royal Ulster Constabulary. His impeccable war record and ramrod posture took him to the position of head of drill for the whole force, despite his religion. He was the frontman any time there was a visiting royal to be ceremonially impressed. But he had also built a farm and a family. A grafter always.

It was the farm that had led Macken into the police. One evening during the war against Hitler, he'd been at home with his stepmother when men came calling. Macken senior was away checking on a cow. The men said they were from the Irish Republican Army. The IRA had never completely gone away since winning the South and losing the North. They claimed the first British casualty of the World War just hours after Chamberlain declared war on Germany. Shot in the stomach on Library Street in Belfast. Other squaddies had the uniforms stripped off them.

It might have been a world war, but in keeping with Republican tradition, that meant 'England's difficulty is Ireland's opportunity'. Which brought three IRA men to the farm demanding the guns they knew were there. Maybe they were guessing. Though it was a fair assumption. One of the intruders let them see he had a revolver inside his coat.

Macken's stepmother swore she knew nothing about any weapons. To his surprise, the raiders didn't threaten or even search. Instead, they took them both outside. They made her watch as Macken was put to work, digging a short, shallow trench. They told him to lie down in it and cover his face. He'd clenched his body and screwed his eyes shut as they scattered soil over him – until his stepmother cried out 'Enough'.

Macken had been sent to bed while his stepmother and the men talked quietly. Ever since he'd had a loathing of small spaces. When his father was told, he put his hand on his son's shoulder and nodded. The next day he gave Macken a creel of seed potatoes to plant in the trench.

After that, it had seemed natural for Macken to follow in his father's footsteps, to take his place in the loyal caste.

Macken started slightly when the waitress returned. He realised he'd nodded off and took a slug of tea. Ghastly. Gone cold. She chuckled and offered him a wee heater, quickly followed by sausages, bacon, black pudding, beans, egg and soda farls to insulate him for his trek.

The fug of body heat, cigarettes and cooking enveloped Macken in womby warmth. There was no question of opening his uniform tunic in public, but he undid his collar to let in some air and hooked a little finger round the chain hidden beneath.

A small oval medallion, a 'Miraculous Medal', hung from the chain. Macken gently rubbed the contours of the image pressed out in relief. It had come from his mother. The words pressed out round the edge were the only prayer Macken would ever recite spontaneously. He knew it by heart: 'O Mary, conceived without sin, pray for us who have recourse to thee.'

It was a prayer for protection, he supposed. A Catholic charm. Though for Macken it was more akin to an invocation of his lost mother – a comfort in a harsh world. Lately he worried it was becoming just another physical tic when he wanted to put off something unpleasant. Like getting off my arse right now, he thought, when I feel so full.

A voice broke through his reverie. 'Having a sneaky break from the beat, are we, Officer?'

Macken turned towards a trio of grinning clergymen at the next table, crumbs sprinkled down their black fronts. The speaker, a hollow-cheeked, long-boned, spindly sort, had the look of one of those clerical crows who wield Jesus like a stinging nettle. His smile was like a graip pulled up from a potato field. There was sponge cake sticking to his gappy teeth.

Macken sat up. It was always best to be respectful around the clergy, he had found. By their collars and confectionery, these three appeared to be Church of Ireland.

'No, sir. I'm in transit from Kilmurray to Blackwatertown.'

'Good man. Your tea will be frozen. Let me order you a refill.'

Macken had already had his fill, but his benefactor overrode all objections. The Reverend Snipe introduced himself and explained that the trio were on a daytrip, Monday being their day off. And it was Macken's good fortune, the reverend said, that they'd be passing through Blackwatertown and would be honoured to give a member of the constabulary a ride. After all, they couldn't expect him to walk that far.

'It galls me how people take the police for granted. You're the front line of our defence against the enemy down below,' the vicar nodded sideways to indicate he meant south of the border, rather than hell itself. 'And the enemy within.'

More nods of agreement from the clergy's table.

'If you've come from Kilmurray, were you in that business on the Longrock Road?'

The other two paused in their grazing, expectantly. Macken pressed the oval into the crook of his finger with his thumb and answered reluctantly.

'I was on duty, sir.'

Macken's interrogator clucked delightedly. 'I hear you gave them a well-deserved leathering. If we had more of that sort of policing, we'd have a lot less trouble. Well done.'

Macken said nothing, which they interpreted approvingly as modesty.

The Reverend Snipe signalled for the bill, for both tables. 'Allow me, please,' he said, squashing Macken's protests.

The vicar scraped his chair closer, and with an expression of possessive pride, extended an arm, as if to bring Macken into their circle. Then he paused, his eyes dropping to Macken's chest. The smile froze, then faded, leaving no hint of the previous warmth. The arm was slowly withdrawn.

'Well, suit yourself,' said the vicar abruptly. 'We'll be on our way.'

The clergyman glanced at the two chits of paper and put money on top. Then they were gone, speaking briefly to the waitress at the door.

Nonplussed, Macken rubbed a small circle of the window clear of condensation, to see them hurrying away; three flushed faces turned in towards each other, mouths working in that narrow way Ulster folk impart grim tidings.

Macken sighed and thought, there goes my lift. The waitress presented him with one of the paper chits.

'But didn't the reverend…' he began, then shrugged and reached for his cash.

'That was just what I needed,' he smiled. 'My stomach thought my throat was cut.'

She took his payment, then slowly reached towards his chest, tapping twice on the small oval still hanging there. She raised her eyebrows, checking he had understood.

Macken realised he had let the small medal creep out from behind his tunic, puncturing his image as a loyal son of Ulster. He squeezed it again, feeling the cross and the Virgin, then tucked it back into hiding.


Macken was not officially due to report till Tuesday morning, so he decided to explore the apple orchards and beech woods near Blackwatertown, and to find some of the dark water from which the place took its name.

Outdoor life was the main appeal of policing for Macken. Some officers found their bliss drinking tea in front of a well-stoked hearth. Macken preferred to be outside and out of sight. Ideally by some water, well stocked with fish.

Blackwatertown had the makings of just such a place, he thought, as he picked his way through the woods. There was a lake on the edge of the Brookemartin demesne. That's where he was headed. Strictly speaking, it might be *inside* the estate. However, Macken doubted there'd be much in the way of patrols, even though it was the country seat of Lord Brookemartin, Northern Ireland's seemingly permanent prime minister. From what little Macken had been able to glean, it seemed the local police did not exert themselves unnecessarily.

Macken reached the lakeside and built a hide of branches and foliage under an overhanging tree, the better to fool the fish and any passers-by. He wrapped himself in his bivouac sheet, leaving his arms free. He laid out a small sack for any catch. Then he slotted his rod together, threaded line through the eyelets and tied on a fly and hook.

He prolonged the moment before the first cast, then flicked his rod forward, sending the line floating over the lake. He kept his elbow tucked in, letting the elasticity of the rod do its work, saving his own energy.

The hook and fly set off widening skin-deep circles across the velvety smooth water. Macken let the line drift. There was no urgency. He hoped there were dollaghan moving below. The big, brown fish were like sea trout, but swam upstream from the inland sea of Lough Neagh, to lurk in the rivers and lakes that fed it. They wouldn't be rushed. They were sensitive. Easily spooked at night by a torch or match flare. Sometimes they came quietly. Other times a dollaghan could surprise you with an arm-wrenching tug, then try to free itself with a head-shaking twisting retreat through weeds and snags.

Macken let the world of men retreat. He focused on the depthless surface scum on which the fading evening light shimmered in shifting patterns. It was gently mesmerising. Sometimes he looked deeper into the green shallows, where indistinct, dark shapes moved like faint, floating threads across the liquid of an eyeball.

The warm evening drew in. Shadows hid him. Macken relaxed into a state where he thought and worried about nothing. Not his job, not the world, nor his place in it. He was conscious only of the air and leaves around him, the insects, the birds and of course the water – from which he'd occasionally draw a brown dollaghan. One of them cooked over an early morning fire would do very well for breakfast. In this stillness, Macken passed the hours into night, eventually, imperceptibly, falling into sleep.

*An eye pressed to the slit, he gazed at the flame in the window. Then it shivered and was gone. Now there was only darkness. It brushed past him, stroking his face. It caught in his throat. It tasted of soil. It smelt overpowering. It clutched at him, wrapping itself round him, covering him, making it difficult to breathe.*

*He curled himself into a tight ball and closed his eyes to hide from the strange shapes closing in. He squeezed closed his mouth and nostrils to prevent the tendrils of darkness creeping inside. He blocked his ears against the scratching by his head.*

*The child hummed quietly to himself, and then louder until the sound inside his head overcame the sounds outside. Then the shivering began. From the chill. Or from the familiar fear that the darkness would be never ending. That the light would not return.*

*He rocked and rolled in the dirt to fight the shivering, and to comfort himself. His own arms wrapped around himself where other arms had once held him. Behind the lids of his closed eyes, he* concentrated on the glow of the flickering flame. But soon even that was merely an uncertain memory in the darkness.

# Tuesday

# CHAPTER 4

Macken twitched awake an hour before dawn. He was too canny to draw attention to himself, and so remained still, taking in his surroundings. There was just a hint of moonlight on the lake. If only this were the beginning of time spent here, he wished, rather than the beginning of the end. He'd have to make a fire, gather his kit and set off into town. But the calm and solitude were so comfortable. And the water so inviting. An early swim would be just the thing to get the blood circulating, he thought.

He stripped and slipped into the dark water. Jesus, it was cold. Macken ducked under the surface and swam till he had to come up for air. Then he struck out across the lake, turning at the far bank, moving more slowly now. Beads of water spilt from his fingers like scattered pearls. He turned on his back and smiled, savouring the freedom of the coolness round his body, and nothing but sky above.

If the Longrock Road battlers could see him now, he thought. But then a feeling came over him that someone *was* watching. If he had not been almost just floating, the rush of water round his ears would have masked the rustling in the bushes. Macken sank till only his face broke the surface, treading water slowly. Something, or somebody, was moving near where he had left his belongings.

This could be tricky, he thought. He couldn't lurk offshore till they left, because the cold was seeping through him. And his gear was ripe for the taking. No point shouting an official challenge either. A thief could be away with his uniform, before he was out of the water. Who would believe he was a peeler anyway, naked and dripping in the dark? There was no good hoping it was a bailiff either. Even if his discarded uniform persuaded the bailiff not to shoot, the evidence of the fish in the sack could turn this into a very embarrassing first day in Blackwatertown.

Macken slowly moved nearer, and then sidled through reeds to the shore. He crept up the slippery bank and stealthily towards two backs.

'Watch it!' Macken heard someone whisper. 'Could be a trick.'

'Calm down, Cedric. We know it's not the peelers anyway.' This second, older voice seemed more knowing. 'The fishing gear looks more like someone in the same line as us than the bailiff.'

'Sure you'd never see yon fella at this time of the morning,' said the younger voice, sounding reassured. 'And it looks like our friend here has caught us breakfast.'

'Thank God for that,' said the older man, 'after the night we've had. Lift them and see what else there is before the mystery man returns.'

Macken crouched. This was disastrous. Losing the fish was acceptable, but not the rest. His fingers touched and then curled round a fallen branch. A weapon. But even with the element of surprise it was only a branch, and by the lightness of it, rotten and hollow. It would break if he hit one of them.

And yet, as his fingers travelled to the open end of the wood, he had a crazy idea. Don't think, he told himself. Just do it.

In a moment they'll realise it's a police uniform, thought Macken. He stepped forward silently and placed the end of the branch gently against the bigger man's back.

'Don't move or I'll plug you.' Macken put on as gruff a voice as he could manage. 'Thieving scumbags. Hands in the air.'

This is the moment, thought Macken, where I'm done. Or I get away with it.

Macken could feel the man considering, and then speak.

'Easy now. Let's not get excited.' As he spoke, he began to turn.

'Keep turning,' barked Macken, 'and I'll drop you first, and then your friend.'

The man stopped turning.

Macken continued. 'I'd be within my rights to shoot you with no questions asked.'

'Hold on now, hold on,' said the big man, 'no need for that.'

'Calm down, mister.' The one called Cedric recovered the power of speech. 'You don't know who you're dealing with.'

Good point, thought Macken. Better get on with it. The other man seemed to be thinking the same way.

'Never mind who any of us are. You're not the bailiff, and you can see we're not either.' The bigger man seemed eager to resolve the stand-off.

'We just came for a quiet bit of fishing. You've been luckier than us. Let's shake hands and leave it at that.'

Macken pushed into the man's back as hard as he dared, without snapping the stick.

'There'll be no handshaking nor backslapping with a pair of creeping thieves. You can keep your rods, but I'll blast the first one to look back.

'Now get off. I'm covering you and listening, so make noise as you go.'

'Alright, if that's the way of it.' The big man seemed to be regaining confidence with every second. 'Perhaps we'll run into each other again.' The threat gained power from the pleasant tone in which it was delivered. Macken marvelled at the man's self-control. 'Go before I change my mind about letting you keep your gear. My trigger finger is getting itchy.'

'Alright, Billy?' Cedric wanted to hear from the man who usually issued the orders.

'Shut it! Come on then. We're off.'

Both men crashed through the bushes out of sight. Macken darted behind a tree to avoid being silhouetted if they looked back. He listened to their cursing progress as their sounds dwindled through the forest.

# CHAPTER 5

Once he was satisfied the intruders were gone, Macken broke into a fit of shivering. Adrenalin had carried him through, but now he was freezing. Time to warm up.

Just then, he heard a quiet, but unmistakeable sound of movement from the undergrowth close by. Macken stood completely still, then very slowly turned to investigate. It was coming from low down. He began to breathe again. Some animal, disturbed by their conversation. He stretched out the stick to poke amongst the leaves.

'Why don't YOU hold it there?'

Macken recoiled from this new voice, stunned that he'd missed a third intruder, better concealed than the others. He heard a dull slap from the bushes.

'You make quite the picture,' said the disembodied voice. 'Though I don't know how anyone could ever capture it with you shaking all over the place. Boy with stick, I suppose you would call it.'

Macken turned to the voice, a woman's voice.

'Mmm, man with stick, then. Well, I suppose it *is* pretty cold this morning.'

Macken peered into the gloom and saw the third intruder

he had missed. Peering back at him was an amused female face, framed by a cascade of curls loosely wrapped in a scarf. Macken could still detect faint sounds of movement, a small animal scratching, though the woman herself was still.

'Who are you? What are you doing here?' barked Macken at last – angry with himself for being caught out.

'Now, hold on.' She slapped the side of the suitcase on which she was sitting, as if to emphasise her objection. This time, whatever had been making the scratching sounds stopped. 'You burst in on me,' she continued. 'I was just sitting waiting for daybreak.'

'You were what?'

'Oh, you know,' she opened her hands. 'A bit of early morning landscape sketching.

'But if you insist, I could try for something more classical. 'Adonis at Dawn Bathe'. How does that sound?'

She raised her right hand and made an L shape with a finger and thumb, like two sides of a frame. As she squinted through at him, Macken thought she had completely lost the plot, until he suddenly remembered...

'Jesus!' He made a panic-stricken dive for his clothes, to peals of her laughter.

'I was only joking about the effects of the cold. You were fine the way you were.'

'Give me a moment to get decent,' Macken muttered, pulling on his uniform.

'Oh, it's a policeman!' This revelation seemed to send her off even worse than before. 'I should have realised. Sure didn't you show me your truncheon?'

It was no good, Macken couldn't keep a severe face after that. His dignity marginally restored by his clothes, he stepped over for a closer look.

'I apologise for startling you and for my display. I thought I was alone,' he said. 'Is it always this busy round here?'

She was still chuckling.

'I admit I really *was* impressed back then. No, not with that. I mean the way you handled your stick.'

And she was off again.

'Sorry. Give me a minute… God, I never imagined this morning would be so – so exhilarating. Who are you anyway? You're clearly not on poaching patrol.'

'I'm on my way to Blackwatertown. I've just been transferred.'

'You're lost, then?'

'I was just taking in some peace and quiet before reporting for duty. A chance to think. Or to not think, you know?'

She smiled at him again – a gentler smile. 'Yes. I do know.'

Macken blinked. He did not know her from Adam, but she was easy to talk to. A shadow passed over her, but it was fleeting, and he saw past her bravado to her beauty.

'This is unfair. You know everything about me,' said Macken. 'Far more than I usually reveal on a first acquaintance.' Macken had been about to say *first date*, but stopped himself in time. What on earth was he thinking? 'But I know nothing about you. What's your name for starters?' She tapped the suitcase underneath her again, as if marking a decision, and stood up.

'Aoife Penny is my name. How do you do?'

She held out her hand most politely. Macken hesitated, repeating her name to himself the soft way she said it. 'Eee-faa'. Then he shook her hand.

'Good morning to you too, Aoife Penny.'

She giggled.

'You looked like you weren't sure whether to shake it, kiss it or jump back in fright. Goodness, you've got cold hands. Let me give them a rub. You know what they say, don't you?'

'What do they say?'

'Cold hands, warm heart. I'm not sure what other body parts that works for.'

Macken raised his eyes to heaven, getting used to her now.

'How long have you been here?' he asked, puzzled not to have noticed her arrive.

'Nicer than sitting on the damp ground,' she said. 'I haven't been here long. You must have been over by the far shore.

'I kept quiet when the others came along. Not everyone is such a gentleman as yourself. I wasn't spying. Though if I'd known, I'd definitely have come earlier.'

Macken was not so distracted as to miss the opportunity to get information.

'You know those two? Who else have I had the pleasure of meeting this morning, Miss Aoife Penny?'

'What presumption! Though you're right. There's no ring on my finger just yet.'

She winked. Suddenly being alive was more vivid than before. He could see now that her curls were auburn red. 'You're the only one with jewellery.'

His hand went instinctively to his neck.

'I couldn't help noticing,' she said. 'It was all you had on. Somebody once gave me one the same.'

Macken automatically looked down.

'I mistook it for a romantic gesture at the time, but he wasn't interested in that.' She sighed, suddenly sad. 'I gave it back to him. I thought he needed it more.

'As for the two boys earlier,' she said, perking up again, 'they won't be boasting about your encounter. Not that you'll be either – given your ill-gotten gains Mr Poacher Policeman. Let's just say that I predict you'll see them again very soon.'

The dawn mist was lifting. Macken thought it would be unwise to linger over a fire to cook the fish. Time to make a move.

'Do you only haunt lakesides at dawn, Aoife Penny, or might I see you again too?'

'That's the mystery. But I'll keep an eye out in case you get into any more trouble. Or go parading without your uniform.' She giggled and waved him off.


Macken set off in a happy daze. She had materialised out of the mist like some pale sprite to bewitch him. Her name was Aoife. *Eee-faa*. It sounded like a sigh of contentment. His head was away with the fairies and his heart was beating fast although he had only started walking. She had banished the cold from his body. He felt life pulsing through him.

As he approached Blackwatertown, low hills and hedges and high ditches opened out onto a broad flood meadow. On his right, the snaggly drear-grey teeth of a graveyard were spotted with lichen in shockingly bright orange and white. Their carved epitaphs did not give away whether the occupants were Catholic or Protestant. Like the headstones, they seemed to lean both ways.

I must be nearly there, he thought. A screen of trees hid what Macken guessed must be the Blackwater river. Which means I'm in Tyrone, he thought, looking east towards the old frontier. He breathed in the feeling of freedom beyond the Pale. He felt that he could turn around and keep walking. There was still time. All quiet. Just the tiny sounds of the leaves of the ash trees brushing against each other, and the lowing of unseen cattle. Nobody around. Just us, thought Macken, acknowledging the dead beside him. Must be Catholic, he decided, this far out of town. Wrong side of the tracks. Across the county line. Wrong side of the river.

Macken walked on and noticed a couple of cars on the bridge. There was a policeman at the far end. No one seemed to be in a hurry. It looked like one of those endless chats country people stop in the middle of the road to engage in. Odd to see a checkpoint, thought Macken. Maybe there's been an accident. He looked over the parapet at the peat-brown water flowing underneath. Sycamore branches drooped from the bank, tips dipping into the current, setting swirling eddies corkscrewing downstream. Otherwise, the dark water flowed smooth and supple like the hide of a horse.

There was a sudden ding-dinging behind him. He turned in surprise as the lady of the lake wobbled her bicycle to a halt beside him, her old suitcase lashed precariously onto a rear carrier. Her emerald scarf was stuffed into the basket on the handlebars. Her hair, bright in daylight, was dishevelled from her ride. She brushed a wayward twist of auburn away from green eyes that seemed to be twinkling specially for him.

'Aoife Penny,' he smiled. 'Didn't expect to see you so soon.'

'Ach, when you left you took my artistic inspiration with you. And here you are in trouble again already.'

Macken was puzzled and delighted all at once.

'What do you mean? You're the one having difficulty staying upright.'

'Oh, is that right? Are you ready to flaunt your contraband to your colleague up ahead?'

'Sure, these fish could have come from anywhere. They wouldn't suspect a police officer, would they?'

'For a newcomer, you're very sure of yourself. But in the light of your courageousness with the stick, I'll carry them through for you.'

I find it impossible to refuse her, thought Macken, unsure if he was humouring her or under a spell. He hid the sack of fish under her scarf.

'Will I get them back on the other side?'

Aoife adopted an innocent look. 'I don't know. I'll need compensation for having my morning so shockingly disrupted.'

'And for being drawn into dishonesty and corruption. By a policeman of all people.'

Then her mouth dipped into something between a frown and a pout.

'And for being treated so rudely by someone I thought was a gentleman.'

Macken was lost again.

'You never introduced yourself,' she laughed. 'Unless you expect me to make up a name, based on what I've seen of you so far?'

'It's Macken.'

She raised her eyebrows.

'Just Macken.'


Aoife rang her bell as she reached the sentry. As the policeman turned towards her suitcase, Macken saw her put a finger to her lips and lean forward conspiratorially. She and the sentry hunched over the bicycle's basket, as she whispered in his ear. He waved her on with a broad smile.

Macken walked on. The sentry was rubbing his hands, from satisfaction by the look of it, rather than the temperature. He was a tall young man, pale skin and pale ginger hair. His pointy face hinted at inner eagerness, if only he possessed the intelligence to decide for himself which direction to go. The sharp edge of his jaw was blood-flecked from an early morning scrape of blade in cold water.

He looked Macken up and down. No warm welcome. 'The new man? Thought you'd be here last night.'

Macken came back down from fairyland with a bump. This is what happens when you lose your stripes, he thought.

'I report for duty this morning. It's Macken, by the way. Hello.'

'Well, good morning to you too. You'll find the barracks up the road.'

Looks like he's not had much sleep either, thought Macken. He felt there was something familiar about the slight man trying to make himself seem larger in the uniform.

'Is this the usual thing,' asked Macken, 'to have a checkpoint here?'

'Ah, no. We're very quiet. Not like where you've come from.'

Good news spreads fast, thought Macken sourly.

The sentry carried on: 'We had reports of manoeuvring in the woods. It's just a precaution.'

'And who'd be on manoeuvres round here?' asked Macken.

'Republicans. Free Staters from over the border, maybe.'

'I thought we were done with all that. I hadn't pegged Blackwatertown as a hotbed of insurrection.' Macken cocked his head, as if considering it, then looked the other policeman in the eye. 'Sounds more like poachers to me, Constable…'

'Cedric Andrews,' said the checkpoint guard, reddening.

Macken nodded. One puzzle solved. His guardian angel had been right. He looked for her, but she was gone.

# CHAPTER 6

Blackwatertown was little more than a street, with only a few side roads before you were out the other side and into fields again. The dull corridor of grey buildings managed to impose a grimness despite the green countryside around it. Less of a town than a village, and most likely somewhere he could be forgotten about.

It had been somewhere once, though. The Blackwater river flowed into the vast Lough Neagh in the centre of Ulster. As an angler, Macken knew his rivers. The Blackwater was the county boundary between Armagh and its western neighbour Tyrone. Centuries ago, it had marked the furthest edge of English control in Ulster. Which would explain the ruined castle, thought Macken. Hadn't there been some historic punch-up nearby? Wonder who won? Must have been us, he decided. Because if the other lot had, they'd still be marching to remind us.

All quiet now. No excitement of any kind.

To Macken's left, a huddle of sheds spoilt the view of the riverbank and a small slipway. A small, black strip of wood above its front door betrayed the purpose of the first blank-faced house. In barely legible letters, it read: *The Bridge Bar,*

*Leonard Maginnis licensee*. I've reached the bright lights now and no mistake, thought Macken.

High, windowless storehouse walls faced the dead public house. And from there, the drab lines of Blackwatertown's main road slunk between terraced houses, yard walls, a couple of shops. The colour of last night's ashes, cold and dead in the hearth. But any town is a wasteland compared to fields and forests, Macken reminded himself. Especially this early. Here and there, he caught the glint of the night's dampness on roof tiles or kerbside, like the signs of a snail's passage. Don't do the place down, he told himself, before you've even met the people.

He couldn't see a soul, but he felt the locals watching him. Curtain twitches and door creaks. Suddenly a loud voice commanded him to stop in his tracks. Surprised to meet yet another security check, Macken automatically obeyed. He heard a grunt of effort. Then the opaque contents of a bucket flew through the space into which he had been about to step, to splash over the roadway. A large woman of mature years in a housecoat looked out, taking his measure.

'Just washing the floor down,' she explained. 'You the replacement?'

Without giving him time to answer, she waved him on. 'March on, Constable. March on. Too early an hour for introductions. Drop by later.'

Once again, Macken did as he was told. The police barracks, halfway along the main street, was set back a couple of yards behind a low wall, with bay windows on either side of the front door. Its once-white walls made it stand out a little from the general greyness. The door and windowsills shone glossy black like a policeman's boot. Each downstairs sill held a dark green wooden trough, from which geraniums jiggled in the breeze:

their petals bright Williamite orange, blood red and the light pink of yapping tongues endlessly gossiping.

On the wall by the door were the Royal Ulster Constabulary crest and an official noticeboard with a sliding glass window. A poster warned of a gang of cattle poisoners Ragwort, Dock, Thistle, Ox-Eye and Dog Daisy. Farmers were warned on pain of prosecution to watch out for these noxious weeds and to cut, spray or other otherwise exterminate them.

Another notice drew attention to the Game Amendment Act (Northern Ireland) 1951, which made it unlawful to burn gorse on uncultivated land between the 15th of March and the 15th of July, in order to protect wildlife during the breeding season.

It was what he expected. A life regulated by the RUC code.

He heard a hacking cough. Another woman, same housecoat but skinnier, watching from the door. She made no effort to move out of his way, taking a long drag on her cigarette as she carried out her own inspection.

'You've met Alena then. Looks like you escaped a soaking.'

She eyed his muddy boots and trouser ends. 'Pity.'

'May I come in?' asked Macken politely. She began to answer, then just shrugged, and let him pass.

Macken immediately tripped on the uneven threshold. He stumbled forward onto shiny brown linoleum, scattering flakes of dry mud. He looked back at the doorstep, which was cracked from side to side, slightly higher at the back than the front. The doorway on his left led to the day room, the reception area of every police station, where Macken was again looked up and down – this time by a constable and a man in civilian clothes. Between them, on a large desk, was Macken's bag of fish.

The desk officer shook his head sympathetically. 'Don't worry, that step catches everyone the first time.'

'Why don't you fix it then?' snapped Macken in embarrassment.

'Sure, you get used to it in no time. We don't even notice it's there.'

Macken identified himself. The desk constable said his own name was Bull. Macken had noticed the way Bull's hand had instinctively dropped below the desk when he had entered. As he stepped round to shake hands, Macken noted the usual sawn-off shotgun on an easily accessible shelf, out of sight from the doorway. Bull introduced the other man as Trelford Dunlap.

'Mr Dunlap is the boy we need to keep sweet, so we do. Isn't that right, Trelford?'

'I'm just hoping you'll look after the place better than these boys, Constable Macken,' Dunlap chuckled along. 'I'm relying on you.'

With that, Dunlap became the latest to look pointedly at the trail left by Macken's boots. Macken stammered an apology.

'Yes of course, sir. It was a bit clabby underfoot, having to walk here.'

Dunlap tutted in sympathy.

'That's a hard station, making a man trek to his new posting. What's the police coming to, Bull?'

'A question I frequently ask myself, Trelford,' laughed Bull. 'Don't worry, Macken. Mr Dunlap is not an inspector. Though he does like to inspect us every now and then.'

'Ah, now,' said Dunlap in affable disagreement, 'I just drop by to be sure you boys are getting on alright.'

'Mr Dunlap is our landlord, making sure we're issuing enough fines to pay the rent.'

Macken laughed along dutifully. He was trying not to stare at his bag of dollaghan. A thick register for recording comings and goings had been pushed aside to make room for the fish.

Behind the desk was a row of files and ledgers. Macken presumed they were the usual records of summonses and official notices, the patrol books in which were noted all incidents outside the barracks and the bicycle book that held the frame numbers of missing or stolen cycles. Fixed to the wall were the daily duty roster, some Hue and Cry notices and the standard litany of barrack rules: *'The Undermentioned Regulations are to be strictly observed and enforced.'*

A portable bed was folded in the bay. The duty roster would ensure a twenty-four-hour presence in the day room, though visitors might have to shake the guard awake. Glowing coals in the hearth and the fire-blackened kettle on its holder gave a touch of homeliness.

Bull recorded Macken's arrival and then took him on a short tour of the barracks, holding the bag of fish in one hand and gesturing with the other. Halfway along the hall, steep stairs climbed to the right. Back left, behind the day room, was the kitchen.

'Mind how you go there. That's Molly's territory,' Bull cocked his head back to the front door. 'She also cleans, or so I've heard. But it's mainly the meals. If she's time between fags and gossiping,' Bull held up the fish, 'I'll get her to do something with these. Gift from a grateful public. I bet you didn't get that in Belfast?'

Macken decided it wasn't worth correcting him. Moving clockwise, Bull pointed to the washroom and the old bog outside in the back yard. 'Not somewhere you'll want to linger.'

Carrying on round, the door by the foot of the stairs led to the cells. Bull explained that they rarely used either of them. And finally, completing the circuit on the other side of the front door, was the private office.

'For meetings. Though it's cosier in the day room. We don't

lay a fire in the private office in case some visiting bigwig settles in too comfortably.'

As they tramped upstairs, Bull told him they had room for eight in comfort, two per room, but that one of the back rooms was being used for storage. The barracks sergeant, called Gracey, had the other. Of the three remaining doors, Bull explained that the furthest one led to a small toilet room with a basin.

'It's the only improvement since this place was built,' said Bull. 'Saves you traipsing outside in the middle of the night, so it does.'

He ushered Macken past the door of the first front bedroom and into the next room. Macken guessed he was now standing above the reception area and therefore in the noisiest spot.

'This is you,' concluded Bull. 'I'm next door. Cedric's your room-mate.'

'We've met.'

'Well then. I'll leave you to get spruced up.'


Macken sank down on the free bed. The room was plain. A wardrobe with drawers beside each bed. And a heavy, iron-bound, black wooden box, the size of a tea chest, handles on either end. C. ANDREWS was stencilled on the front. There was space beside it for Macken's own box, which was due to be delivered later in the week.

The butt of a Sten gun poked out from under the other bed, but otherwise the room was tidy. No personal touches. Typical barracks.

Macken felt the bed calling to him. It had been a long and wonderful morning, but the walls around him were squeezing out the space and clarity he had felt only hours before. His boots were filthy too. Not a good start. As Macken unpacked a rag and brush and boot polish, he reflected that life these days seemed to be a constant challenge to avoid putting a foot wrong. Looking down at your boots instead of up at the sky.

The small tin of polish rolled out of sight. Macken sighed and imagined just putting his head down. 'Into action!' he remembered his father would say. So instead he knelt to find the polish. Must have rolled under the other bed, he thought, reaching underneath.

'What's going on?' burst in a voice, surprised and shrill.

It was Cedric from the bridge, and the lake, looking down with suspicion.

'Don't tell me you were saying your prayers, because I've seen your lot praying before, and there was no hoking under other people's beds.'

Macken pushed himself to his feet. Cedric stepped back.

'Thought my polish might have rolled under the bed.' I've got off on the wrong foot with this one, thought Macken, and forced a smile. 'So, we're in here together then?'

'Aye,' Cedric curled his lip. 'No surprise there.'

Am I missing something here? thought Macken. 'Oh aye? How's that?'

'Dead man's shoes. Dead man's bed anyway.'

Macken winced. 'Is this where... Good God!'

Cedric seemed to gain comfort from Macken's dismay. But seeing the grim satisfaction on Cedric's face helped Macken master his own emotions.

'Were you...'

'Aye, I found him. He'd been plugged. It wasn't pretty. And now you're here. The new Fenian. Maybe you'll last longer.'

Jesus, thought Macken, the hostility coming off this fella is incredible.

'Thanks for the vote of confidence.'

But there was something else.

'He'd been plugged? I thought he shot himself.'

'That's what they say.'

'What do you think?' asked Macken.

'I don't think anything,' said Cedric. 'None of your business either.' His eyes flicked to his own wardrobe. 'And stay away from my things, do you hear?'

'Aye, sure.'

It was obvious that Cedric was reluctant to leave him unsupervised, but his desire to end the conversation was stronger. He turned to go.

'But Cedric,' began Macken.

The other man stiffened at the use of his first name.

'Less of the Fenian, Cedric. A bit of civility and you'll get the same.'

Cedric's eyes narrowed. He grunted.

'Anyway, I came to tell you. You're due downstairs.' He screwed up his nose. 'And those boots…'

Macken glanced down and swore to himself. Cedric left and Macken dropped to the floor again, flat this time. He saw the polish under his own wardrobe. As he reached for it, something gently stroked the back of his hand. He reached in again and drew out a scrap of paper. It must have fallen behind the drawers at the bottom, thought Macken. It was torn, but what remained was easy to read.

*'if they knew the truth it would be the end for you, Cedric'*

A whistle came from below. Macken folded the note and hid it in his pocket. Boots on, he clattered downstairs.

# CHAPTER 7

Cedric and Bull were standing to attention in the private office. To one side was a man wearing the stripes of a sergeant. Almost as tall as Macken. Hard looking. No fool. The fourth man, a senior officer, was the only one to languidly turn his head as Macken entered.

'Good you could join us. Macken, isn't it?'

'Yes, sir. Reporting for duty.'

Macken drew himself to attention.

'Glad to have you. McReady's my name. District inspector for this part of God's country. I knew your father. He was a stickler, wasn't he?'

Macken smiled politely. 'Yes, sir.'

'So, he'd be disappointed if I failed to remind you that, though we may be far from Belfast, we do try to observe punctuality.'

'Yes, sir. Sorry, sir.'

McReady peered down over the moustache that gave him a certain Errol Flynn rakishness. 'And Macken? We have certain standards of dress on parade, if that's not too much for you?' He waved his blackthorn stick at Macken's feet, the shine on the polished wood a contrast to the still filthy boots. 'We may have to wade through muck, but we don't have to let it stick to us. Buck up, Macken.'

'Yes, sir,' Macken's cheeks reddened. Wherever he went, his father's illustrious reputation always lay in wait. From the corner of his eye, he detected a glare of renewed suspicion from Cedric.

McReady got on with business. 'Just dropping by to keep you on your toes. Though I'd say Sergeant Gracey is well able for that task.'

The inspector turned his stick slowly in his hands as he spoke. Macken noticed a faint tremor and realised that his constant fiddling with the blackthorn was less affectation than an attempt to conceal a physical tic. He guessed that McReady had been one of the cadet officers commissioned into the RUC from the regular army after the War. Which meant he'd be a bugger about enforcing every regulation, but perhaps more open minded about other things, having swapped the narrow sectarian alleyways of Ulster for the broader killing fields of North Africa and France.

Inspection visits were routine. The DI made unannounced visits to each of the barracks in his patch – Blackwatertown, Keady and Benburb – and surprised constables on patrol, thus ensuring standards did not slip.

He praised them for their quick response to the reports, hopefully groundless, of subversive activity in the area. All that was a thing of the past, he hoped. So he was confident that Sergeant Gracey would be able to keep the statistics on an even keel.

'We run a tight ship here when it comes to law breaking. Especially at this time of the year, isn't that right, Sergeant?' The inspector beamed, and turned to Macken. 'You might even say we're sticklers.'

The DI departed, which put Sergeant Gracey back in charge. He turned to Macken, and mentally weighed and measured him, his bottom lip protruding as he carried out the assessment. Then he stuck out a hand. Macken took it, and felt himself gripped tightly, while the scrutiny continued, this time boring into his eyes.

'Welcome to Blackwatertown. Jolly, isn't it?'

Macken got the message: Don't think you can keep any secrets from me.

'Just Macken,' he replied, cursing once again his nickname.

'Billy Gracey,' said the other, 'but you can call me Sergeant.'

Aha, thought Macken, Cedric's partner in poaching.

'Sort your boots out and we'll get you out on patrol. Help you get the lie of the land.

'Normally, I'd send you beyond the Catholic chapel. Constable McMahon's beat, God rest him. But the rest of us have business there ourselves this time of the year, so you can walk out by the church instead. Not far for your first day.

'Try to keep out of trouble.'

For a moment, Macken thought the sergeant was referring to his unedifying exit from Kilmurray. Then he realised it was merely a standard dismissal.

'What's all this about the statistics?' Macken asked Bull. 'Am I missing out on some private joke?'

Bull was doing a bit of cleaning himself – the shotgun from the front desk. He leant forward to assess Macken's boots.

'I suppose they'll do, so they will,' he tutted. 'Joke? No joke. Harvest time, so it is.'

'What's that got to do with anything?' asked Macken.

'Important time of year. Harvesting the cash,' said Bull.

'Have to cover the rent somehow, keep auld Trelford contented.'

Bull could see Macken still did not understand. 'Ah no, I'm messing with you. The RUC isn't that badly off just yet. It's for the statistics. The DI is a fierce man for the statistics. Very particular.'

Bull looked as though he seldom pounded the beat. He had the bulk of a bull but none of the energy. He explained that Macken's normal beat would be the Catholic townlands across the river, but that he'd be covering the Protestant end of town until the current sweep was over.

'It's the same every six months, so it is. This is a sleepy sort of a place, bar the odd drunk. But we can't have the powers that be thinking we're dozing. They might close the barracks and shift us all to Belfast. We'd be rushed off our feet there.

'Sure you couldn't do better than here. Near the border, true enough, but quiet all the same. The Roman Catholics keep their heads down.

'Though of course,' chuckled Bull, hefting the shotgun, 'this is always loaded just in case.'

'So what am I supposed to do?' asked Macken.

'You don't have to do anything,' laughed Bull. 'A nice easy introduction to Blackwatertown. They'll be pleased to see you up that end, even when they realise you're the new Roman. Oh aye, it'll be all smiles this week. Only twice a year mind, so don't go getting carried away.'

He grinned at Macken's continued confusion: 'Sure they know it means the rest of us are getting stuck in across the river. It's only human to take a mite of pleasure from the misfortune of others.'

Macken picked up a typewritten list of minor offences and fines. There seemed to be an awful lot about bicycles – failure to display a functioning front light, failure to display a functioning rear light, absence of a bell, defective brakes.

He brandished it towards Bull. 'It's a funny time of day to check for lights on bikes.'

'I didn't think you'd be so slow on the uptake,' said Bull. 'As we don't get much criminal behaviour, thanks be to God, twice a year we have a big push to generate some activity. Nothing spectacular to attract unwelcome attention, just a nice even figure to keep us ticking over. Do you follow?'

Macken nodded.

'A big jump in the figures compared to six months ago will make it look like crime is running away from us.'

Bull paused to let that sink in, and then went on.

'By the same token, any big fall and we'll have somebody in Belfast asking questions about our detection rate. So what we're aiming for is steady as she goes. Crime more or less the same as the last time. Nothing to rock the boat.'

'I get you,' said Macken. 'But am I not part of this great effort then?'

'Sure it wouldn't be fair to have you spend this week doling out summonses to your fellow Romans for cycling without a light during daytime, and then expect them to be all pally with you the week after.

'You'll be sent over when we have sufficient numbers clocked up.'

'Someone for them to blame,' said Macken.

'Ah no, they'll be pleased to see you, so they will,' disagreed Bull. 'It'll mean the rest of us are finished with them.'

The day was washed in grey. Not raining, just threatening. Macken's mood was darker. He almost tripped again on the way out and grabbed the door frame. He narrowed his eyes at the cracked doorstep, as if sizing up an enemy. To his left, the street sloped gently down to the bridge. Macken turned right, towards the Protestant church on higher ground. He did not pass anyone as he walked round the far corner of the churchyard, where thick hedge grew over an old stone wall. Tree roots had burrowed beneath and spread under the road like veins on the back of an old woman's hand, rippling the surface. A sign said, 'Rectory of St Aidan's, Church of Ireland'.

Macken took up position in a niche, where the wall was indented round a dead tree stump. Sheltered from view, he re-examined both pieces of paper he had slipped into his pocket.

First, the torn scrap from under his wardrobe. The words looked like a warning.

*'if they knew the truth it would be the end for you Cedric'*

It looked like there was something missing from the start of the sentence. Macken could not tell if there were words missing from the end too.

It was clear who Cedric was, thought Macken. And that he was up to something he would not want the world to know about. But who wrote the note? Danny – his former room-mate? Macken didn't want to think about Danny.

And the truth about what? Arguing over a girl? Unlikely. Danny had never shown much interest in them. But Cedric was definitely behaving as if he had something serious to hide.

Macken rubbed his cheek. Need to shave, he thought.

Of course, there's the poaching, or whatever Cedric and Gracey were up to last night. They would get in trouble for that, right enough.

Definitely something shifty about Cedric, thought Macken. But then again, he considered, I could be reading too much into his bad attitude. Maybe he doesn't like sharing a room. With a Catholic of all people.

The police force was not entirely composed of bigots, but it had its share. Christ, he thought, what more do they want from me? I've sworn loyalty. Even if you were to convert, they'd suspect you for being a turncoat.

However, if the written message was a warning, couldn't it just as likely be a threat? Though you'd have to be a brave man to threaten a peeler, thought Macken. We don't take kindly to it. Unless it was another peeler?

He rubbed his eyes. Too tired to think straight, he told himself. His speculation was getting a bit far-fetched. A way of not thinking about the true awfulness.

Danny. Dead. The little brother who he had left behind – thinking it was for the best. The little brother who had put on the uniform, put himself on the front line, put himself in harm's way – to be just like Macken. The little brother he'd failed to protect. Had as good as denied his existence. The guilt was crippling. Deeper than the shame all Irish Catholics grow up with. Much more personal. No way to hide from it. Not when he'd been sent to Blackwatertown, following in Danny's footsteps for a change.

Odd way for Cedric to talk about it though. Almost as though Danny hadn't plugged himself, by accident or… or on purpose.

But not something you'd boast about, thought Macken. Unless you thought yourself untouchable.

I'm being pathetic, thought Macken. Trying to shift the blame onto anyone but myself. And anyway, I was sent here to keep out of trouble, not to stir things up. I ignored Danny easily enough while he was alive. Accidents happen. It's my own guilt that's making me grasp for a conspiracy.

Macken folded away the scrap and scanned the second piece of paper, the list of minor offences and fines.

This is something I *can* be angry about, he thought. It's not the flags and the fuss and the drum-beating that's the worst, though we'd all be better off without them. It's the easy assumption that the price we have to pay for a humdrum, peaceful society is that, every so often, one lot gets to remind the other lot who's in charge. The small, bitter pills, thought Macken, that we swallow to reassure our masters that they still rule the roost. So they can keep on ruling with a light touch.

It'd be nice if they could do their own dirty work without dragging me into it, he thought. Then Macken remembered that, for once, he *was* being left out of it. But it didn't make him feel any happier.

'Hello there, Constable.'

Macken looked up, startled, to find that a vicar had materialised before him.

'You had me worried, lurking there, ready to pounce.'

The vicar was amidst a clutch of cyclists, whose number grew as more slowed and stopped. Apart from the vicar, they were all women. Macken was thrown to see Aoife among them. She gave him a look of mock severity, as if to say, 'Not now, with all these ones around.'

'Bracken isn't it?' The vicar was enjoying Macken's discomfort. 'I never forget a name.

'Having forty winks, eh? Don't worry, your secret's safe with us, eh ladies?' Macken felt flustered at the tittering and held up the page.

'My mistake,' continued the dog-collared comedian. 'He was reading the paper, ladies. Following the form, were you? Is it gambling that's your vice?

'I daresay there's not much work for you at this end of town anyway.'

Macken began paying proper attention. He realised that it was *the* vicar.

'I beg your pardon, Reverend,' began Macken, 'Nice to see you again, sir. As you see, I made it to Blackwatertown.'

Macken gave a slight nod, as if in gratitude for the car ride he had been offered but not given.

'And, begging your pardon, sir, I was just reminding myself of the latest regulations.' Macken showed them the sheet of paper. The Reverend Snipe moderated his triumphant beam into something slightly more contrite.

'Yes, good man, good man. I'm afraid we had to rush on yesterday more quickly than I expected.' He brightened again. 'What you need to do, Constable, is find yourself a bicycle. Isn't that right, ladies? Healthy body, healthy mind.'

As the vicar turned to his appreciative audience, a door opened in Macken's mind. I want out, he thought, and fate has opened the door. A trapdoor maybe. But it's time I showed more enthusiasm for policing. Meanwhile, the vicar addressed the women.

'Thank you, ladies, for a *wonderful* ride.'

More eye-rolling, mock gasps and giggling from the flock.

'I look forward to seeing you in church, and back in the saddle soon.'

He bowed. Macken tapped him on the shoulder.

'Actually, Reverend, could I say a few words?'

The vicar straightened up, surprised. 'Brethren, the constable would like to address us. Perhaps he fears we've omitted to thank God for this blessed day. I can assure you, Constable, that we're both light in heart and pure in spirit.

'We've given witness to our Lord God this day. And your offer, though welcome, might be better directed to your own sort.'

'Actually, Reverend,' said Macken, attempting an expression

resembling regret, 'it is on more earthly matters that I am compelled to intervene.

'I notice that you and your party are in serious contravention of multiple sections of the Road Transport Act, and I'm afraid I must issue you with penalty notices.'

The hubbub fell silent. Among the shocked faces, Macken could see Aoife's raised eyebrows. She was shaking her head slightly, this time a more serious warning.

The vicar's face, angrier and redder, blocked out the others.

'I think you may be confused, Constable. These law-abiding ladies and myself have been travelling freely along the Queen's highway, as is our right. Perhaps, as a newcomer, you've got lost on your way to another district?'

'I'm sorry, Reverend, but as you know we're doing a big push on road safety. I can see you're in a hurry, so I'll not delay you, beyond noting that your own cycle appears to be without front or rear illumination and that your rear tyre is in a dangerous state. I'm afraid that's three separate penalties, sir. You might want to check that your vehicle is in a roadworthy condition overall. I wouldn't like to have to penalise you further next time.'

Macken dashed down the details in his notebook and scribbled out a summons for the speechless clergyman. Then he moved onto the women, one by one. Having seen the treatment meted out to the vicar, they took it quietly.

This'll help their statistics, thought Macken grimly, as he finally came to Aoife. She, however, made no attempt to suppress her indignation.

'Well aren't you the brave policeman?'

She turned to the rest of the women. 'Some people act big when you stick a uniform on them – but I'd like to see how they fare without it.'

Her defiance prompted a belated rallying of morale. 'That's right! Outrageous!'

She turned back, her face hidden from all but him, and sneaked him another of those winks. Once again he was thrown. She took over.

'You'll be wanting my name, I suppose. Aoife Penny. Here's my address.'

Macken noted it down, but on her summons, instead of any offence, he wrote: When can I see you?

'Well, Chief Constable – I hope the next time we meet that your manners have improved.'

And off she cycled, to admiring gasps from the other women. As they dispersed, the vicar recovered his poise, with added venom.

'We'll have no Papist ruling the roost here, hiding behind a uniform or no. You'll soon learn, Bracken. Or you'll be taught!'

'Good day to you too, Reverend.' Macken strode off purposefully, displaying a blithe confidence he doubted anyone found convincing, least of all himself. Still, the die was cast. That was the main thing.

# CHAPTER 8

Macken rounded the corner and realised that he had no specific destination in mind. Purposeful marching was all very well, but he'd be out the other side of the village before long. The prospect of slinking back to the barracks was not an inviting one.

He slowed down, and finding himself at a shop, went inside. A hubbub at the counter meant the women there did not immediately register his arrival, so intent were they on an outrageous piece of gossip. Macken realised that it featured him in a leading role.

'You never saw the like! Yon minister was speechless...'

''Twas only Aoife Penny had the gumption to put him in his place...'

Over their bobbing heads rose the inquiring glance of the large woman behind the counter, followed by a broad smile and loud announcement.

'Ladies! The villain of the piece is among us. Good day to you, sir.'

The women froze. Then, heads down, they were off. *Must-*

*get-on's* and *Is-that-the-time's* scattered in their wake, until the shop was emptied of all but Macken and its proprietor.

'Have you come to sling me in a cell with the vicar?'

Macken stepped back from the raw force of her personality. It was the woman who had almost soaked him that morning. A fierce red colour spread over her features. She seemed to physically expand. Macken feared she might explode.

Then she did explode. With laughter – so strong, Macken almost ducked.

'Mandear, you should have seen your face! You'd have thought I was about to ate you up! Come in, come in and take your ease.'

Macken smiled with relief as she came round the counter for a closer look. She put her hands on her hips and craned forward. As she came closer, Macken maintained his smile and, hoping it wasn't too obvious, gradually leant back as she leant forward. With a bit of luck she'd stop before he fell over.

Just in time, she completed her inspection and drew back again.

'Call me Lena. Alena Williamson, to be prim and proper about it. But Lena to my friends. And you've given me the biggest laugh since I don't know when. There's been no excitement here since the cotton mill shut down.

'I thought those giddy women were telling me stories when they began twittering on about you and the vicar. But it's high time yon boy was brought down a peg or two.'

'Well…' faltered Macken, not saying anything.

'Let me take off my glasses so I can hear you properly. What do you call yourself?'

'Macken… No, just Macken.'

'Well then, Mr Just Macken. What on earth possessed you to bring down the force of the law on our vicar and his harem? Are the police all mad over there in County Down?'

Macken's face fell as he realised the whole village had probably known who and what he was long before he had arrived.

'There's an operation ongoing against cycling offences...'

She barged over him. 'Didn't they tell you that was reserved for them Fenians out beyond? Oh, it's the funniest thing ever!'

Though tears were flowing from her, she did not miss Macken stiffening. She waved a hand to implore a moment to recover herself.

'Ah now, don't take me wrong. I meant no offence. I have no quarrel with any Roman. Well, no more than with anyone else. I could show you Romans with more honesty than the worshipful master of an Orange Lodge, and more spirit too. Not that that's saying much, mind. Sure take yon Aoife Penny. She's got spirit to bottle.'

She noticed Macken reacting to the name.

'Oh, yes. Did you not realise you scored an own goal with that one?

'But wait now, wait now. What I want to say to you is that any man who wears your uniform, any man who's prepared to hold the line for Ulster – then I do not care whether he's Protestant, Presbyterian, Catholic or... or... or even a Jew. You've proved your loyalty as far as I'm concerned.'

Macken was not used to being so warmly welcomed into the Protestant fold. Everyone accepted that there were schools, pubs, churches, jobs and businesses for Protestants, and the same for Catholics. And each to their own, cradle to grave, most of the time. Shops too. Which led to an awful lot of duplication.

'And I apologise for nearly drenching you, Mr Macken. You caught me at an hour long before I have the power to be civil to man or beast. But I can tell you now, you are sincerely welcome. Especially after this morning.'

Macken was not sure how to follow such an effusive reception.

'Thank you very much. But I may have shot myself in the foot already.'

'It'll blow over. It's just one of those times of year when people get a bit het up.'

She nodded towards a pile of newspapers. The headline on an opened copy shouted about an election. Macken decided to test the waters further.

'Did you know the man I'm replacing?'

'That was a bad business. Quiet boy. Very sad.'

Macken murmured agreement.

'They say it was an accident,' she went on. 'And sure what else could it have been?'

'What do you mean?'

'Ach, too many lonely hours spent with only animals and liquor for company drives some old farmers to hasten their end. But wee Danny? He was too young to know life's troubles. Sure he'd hardly lived. And he had Cedric, his great buddy.'

'They were friends?'

'Aye, surely. I take it you've met Cedric then. Was the meeting not a happy one?'

'Well…' said Macken.

'It's a terrible blow when someone close to you passes like that. Cedric may still be angry about it. And with you for stepping into Danny's place.'

'I thought it might be something else,' said Macken.

'Oh I see,' said Lena. 'You have to understand, Cedric is like the rest of us here, and I daresay across most of our wee country. We have our prejudices bred into us.

'We may seem settled here. But at the back of your mind, there's always that worry. About them. You could have the most trustworthy and decent neighbour who's a Roman, but there's still that fear of them all together. That they're out there.'

Macken shrugged.

'I'd better be on my way. Thanks again for the welcome.'

'Believe you me, I have harsh words to say about people here sometimes – and them me,' Lena smiled. 'But I suppose they're no worse than anywhere else, and maybe better than some. They can be friendly when they get to know you.'

Macken nodded. 'Isn't that what people say when their dog bites you?'

Lena laughed again. 'Aren't you the sharp one? Well, what can't be cured must be endured. Give it a while and you'll soon settle.'

She looked out the window. 'Though your day may hold more excitement yet.'

Macken saw Constable Bull half walking, half running to the door.

'I've never seen that man shift himself so fast,' said Lena. 'Don't forget, you can take refuge here any time.'

Macken knew it must be something serious to have forced Bull from his cosy nook.

'Mandear, have you gone completely off your rocker?' Bull spluttered, bursting through the door. 'Gracey was almost for driving to the nearest chapel in retaliation and dragging out the priest for offences against the state. Get back to the barracks quick.'

# CHAPTER 9

'Where is that eejit?' Sergeant Gracey's voice blared.

'Sir?' Macken tried to adopt a posture that indicated contrition but not guilt. Gracey grabbed him by the front of his tunic and shoved him against the wall. He pointed the rolled-up newspaper in his other hand at Macken's throat.

'Have I embraced a viper to my bosom?'

'Sir, I was given to understand there was a crackdown underway and…'

'Understand *this* Jolly Boy. You came highly recommended, but we've had enough trouble here. Real tragedy. But messers like you… Buck up, or you'll feel my boot up your arse on the way out.'

'Yes, sir.'

'I suppose you'll go running off to your priest now. He'll probably make you a saint for wrecking our wee campaign against his flock of Fenians.'

Gracey's face screwed up as if he had eaten something almost intolerably unpleasant.

'I'll tell you, boy. Don't go getting carried away with your cleverness off the back of this exploit. I'll be watching you.'

After such a disastrous start with the vicar, there was no point in

Macken explaining how little he was looking forward to meeting the local Catholic cleric either. Best to keep your distance from priests, he'd always thought. As the token Catholic in the barracks, he presumed he would be the linkman, but he didn't like being pigeonholed. Nor the prospect of all the unhappiness that would be channelled his way from his co-religionists too wary to deal with other RUC men.

Bull and Cedric were in the day room. The smell of frying fish curled through the doorway. My dollaghan, thought Macken. Gracey informed them all that in the light of 'Jolly Boy's unfortunate episode' that morning, the bicycle safety campaign was suspended. He opened the newspaper he'd thrust at Macken and folded back the advertisements on the front, so they could see the main news page.

'There's other news. We have an election. "Let Ulster Speak", it says. And I am determined that we will play our part in ensuring the smooth running of the democratic process.

'We're joining patrols throughout the district, including along the border, to deter any subversives who might want to take advantage at this time.

'The B-Men have been called out too, so that'll help. But most importantly, it'll get Jolly out of Blackwatertown till everyone calms down.'

Blood rushed to Macken's cheeks. The smell of fish frying was stronger now, and Gracey paused to inhale it, then shake his head in annoyance.

'And that fish will go into the bellies of McReady and Bull while we're out. It'll be fish-bone soup for the rest of us, if we're lucky.'


All in all, Macken felt he had got off lightly. Too lightly. There must be something unpleasant ahead. The first demonstration of Sergeant Gracey's disapproval came as they armed themselves with Sten guns for the patrol. Macken knew he would have more chance of actually hitting something with a Lee Enfield rifle, but he was not offered either option.

'Safer for you to skip the big guns for a while, Jolly,' announced Gracey. 'You just stick with your Webley. Don't want the reverend to think you're coming to finish him off, do we lads?'

Macken sat up front beside Gracey, who was at the wheel. Cedric was in the back. They drove over the bridge and were soon in countryside unfamiliar to Macken.

'You're on a short leash, Macken,' snarled Gracey. 'You've spoilt our fun for a brave wee while now. We'll not be checking tyre pressure on Roman Catholic bicycles for another six months. You've filled the quota.

'Any more good police work by the rest of us would throw our numbers completely out of kilter. Not to mention the complaints.'

'Do people not usually complain?'

'Not at all. They have more sense than some incomers credit them with. They grin and bear it. And at least I don't pick on the parish priest himself.

'Fenians aside, we leave people alone as far as possible. It's not what policing is about, is it? Stirring things up?'

Macken thought the best policy was to keep his mouth shut.

'I haven't made up my mind about you yet, Jolly. If you're a cheeky skelp or just stupid. There's something going on in that head of yours though. I can hear the wheels turning.'

The engine noise made it too difficult for Cedric to join in.

'One thing we need to get settled. I know you used to be a sergeant, but you'll take my orders now.'

'Of course,' agreed Macken.

'As long as that's clear, we'll have no trouble. I don't care about your past misdemeanours. If anything, they're reassuring.

'What was it anyway? Hand in the till?'

Macken looked at the road ahead.

'Confiscated poitín that you forgot to pour away? Am I getting warm?'

'No, nothing like that.'

'What then? I like to know what I'm dealing with.'

'I rubbed some people up the wrong way,' offered Macken. 'It was stupidity.'

'You may not be so stupid though,' said Gracey. 'You managed to take the heat off your fellow Romans today. Was that your plan?'

'I didn't have a plan. I just made a mistake with the reverend.'

'To be honest, Macken,' he glanced back at Cedric, 'I don't give a damn about the Reverend Snipe. We'll get along fine as long as you don't get above yourself. As long as you remember whose team you're on.'


The conversation petered out as they travelled along the quiet lanes of counties Armagh and Tyrone, past apple orchards and weaving round low drumlins, the humps set like racks of eggs. An odd comparison, thought Macken, given that the locals were never prepared to walk on eggshells when they could march over and smash them.

The meandering route took them close to the invisible border with the Irish Republic. Life and habits and farming and trade and families went on much as before the frontier was drawn through their neighbourhoods and farms – and in some cases, through buildings. The major benefit of the border – the locals all privately agreed – was the opportunity it provided for smuggling. However, even if the frontier was invisible to the naked eye, it had been elevated to an article of faith by those many prepared to kill and die to guard it. And it was just as strongly heartfelt to be an intolerable heresy by some who wanted rid of it.

It was a line no Royal Ulster Constabulary member was permitted to cross in uniform, without permission. Officers were discouraged from having contact with their opposite numbers in the Garda Siochana, 'the Guards', across the border. Macken was glad he wasn't driving, because it was hard to keep track of which side you were on, as the line wriggled back and forth across roads, fields and farmyards.

Gracey filled him in on his duties. There'd be the collection of fines imposed at the petty sessions courts (Gracey shot him a sour look), the serving of noxious weeds notices, public house duty, rare traffic duty to check cars for road licence, insurance, lights and number plate illumination and attendance at road traffic accidents.

'And I'm sure we'll find you an Orange Lodge to walk with,' teased Gracey.

The sergeant explained that as far as crime went, they had a shortage. Apart from occasional theft from farms, drink was the main culprit. There were cells at the barracks, but in the interests of keeping them clean, it was simpler not to give drunks overnight lodging. A ride home or a crack on the head with a baton counted as more effective policing in his book. The former good community relations, the latter soon forgotten.

The powers that be had decided patrol cars should not have heaters, in case the men got too comfortable inside. But the warmth of well-wrapped bodies, the hum of the motor and the litany of pointless minor duties dulled Macken's senses and his mind wandered.

Life was a constant challenge to take sides, Macken thought. His family had lived in a watermill for a while. Like all his childhood memories of the time after his mother died, after everything changed, the recollection had a bitter edge. As the eldest child, it had been Macken's job to prevent the mill being overrun by vermin. He remembered that bone-cold winter when the rats were ever more daring, trying to escape the bitter temperatures outside.

He'd had to smash a hole in the ice to kill them. There was no other way once they were trapped, without risking a bite or a scratch. It was tiring work, fuelled by the exhilaration of wielding a great big stick, scything down over your head to smash through the frozen crust – with the fear of overbalancing and following it into the black water below.

It was a rotten job. Macken had to watch for the rats, set the traps, gather them up and hold them under the cold, cold millpond water, until the creatures drowned. Or froze to death. Stopped moving anyway.

And as Macken watched for the rats, Danny followed him around with his own smaller stick. Danny used to say it wasn't fair to kill the rats – *they're just getting food for their wee families*. He always wanted things to be fair. But everything Macken did, Danny tried to copy. He used to beat the ice to help. Hardly made a mark. Macken tolerated him. Made sure he didn't fall in. That was also part of the job. Keeping an eye on the wean. Protecting him from the rats.

Macken screwed his hands into fists in his pockets at the memory. He knew he hadn't protected him. He'd once given him the twin of the medal round his own neck, 'to guard against harm' he'd told him. And then abandoned his trusting little brother to his death as sure as if he'd drowned him in the mill race.

Too painful to think about. Macken forced himself to remember the rats instead. They were never known by their true name. Just like anything awkward or unwelcome, he thought. Catholics were Romans or Papists or Fenians. Is it the venom into which you dip a word that turns it into an insult? wondered Macken. A century ago, the Fenian Brotherhood had risen up against Britain. Nothing to show for it, bar another round of sentimental ballads. And those failed rebels had themselves reached back into myth to borrow their name from the legendary warriors of the Fianna.

But these days, 'Fenian' was an insult. They've not just taken over the country, thought Macken; they've even taken over the words.

So Macken's childhood war was against the Quare Fellas, not the rats. His mother taught him that speaking their true name aloud was a summons. He learnt to talk in guarded tones about the Quare Fellas instead. Even now, just thinking about them roused vague feelings of unease.

Macken considered himself a rational man. He had gradually let fall the leaves of belief. There had been no sudden break with the Catholic Church. Just a gradual drift away. It was only when he encountered prejudice that he felt he was any kind of a Catholic. And that was more a gut reaction against bullying. He was the opposite of a fair-weather friend. Only being under attack brought out the Catholic in him. The rest of the time, he wasn't really interested.

But superstition was different. Visceral. Too deeply ingrained to discard. All he had left of his Catholic upbringing was the guilt. And superstition was all he had left from his mother before that. It was a comfort.

Macken's mind drifted back to that winter at the watermill. Falling temperatures and hard ground had driven the Quare Fellas inside the sheds to threaten the Christmas flour. So Macken hunted them down and drowned them.

They had to be drowned, because his father did not want dead and dying vermin in the Christmas flour. The traps were his father's own invention – humane in that they were not an immediate death sentence. That was left to the son.

Macken recalled setting the wooden cage traps with bait where he spied the Quare Fellas' droppings or holes gnawed in the sacks. In the mornings, clumsy with thick gloves, he would gather the cages into a bucket, heavy now with scratching, squirming, squealing life, for the walk to the pond.

His father warned him not to leave the bodies in the water afterwards. It wouldn't be clean. So Macken and his brother built pyres. On top went the sodden, slick, dead things, to burn in a crackling, fat-spitting, hair-fizzing, hand-warming show for any village kids with nothing better to do than watch. Which was all of them.

Once, Macken had complained about the bitter cold that chilled his core as he smashed the ice. His father had given him a look of disgust.

'You have to choose which side you're on, boy,' he had said. 'Yon Quare Fellas or your family. Do whatever it takes to keep them out and keep them down.'

His father had said they had to save the Christmas Flour. Though it was only the same flour as the rest of the year, with a handful of spices mixed in. The Quare Fellas couldn't get enough of it.

Even now, Macken didn't like to say their true name. It was the same with the wean. Macken felt as if his insides had been ripped out.


He gazed through the windscreen, still in something of a dream. Leaves danced in shafts of sunlight threading through the trees. They looked to be neither falling nor rising, but spinning and skipping ahead of the car like dolphins leading a ship to harbour.

That's how it was, just before everything exploded around them.

# CHAPTER 10

Macken pitched forward into the dashboard, as a deafening staccato of bangs exploded inside the car. He covered his head with his arms.

All was confusion and noise. The engine stalled. Macken heard panic around him. His ears were ringing. Bellowing from his right. Fading in and out. 'Get out! Get out!'

Macken's door was jammed. He leant back and kicked it as hard as he could. It yawned open and he dived out, falling awkwardly into a hole. Adrenalin picked him up and carried him scrambling into the bushes.

He cowered, fumbling with the fastener on his holster, feeling helpless waiting for the next explosion of violence. From across the road, he heard Gracey shouting.

'What are you doing? You fucking nearly killed me!'

He saw Gracey shaking Cedric by his lapels. The constable's gun lay on the road.

Macken was bewildered. The car was nose down into a trench. The windscreen was shattered. But there was no sign of attackers nor any follow-up to the initial shooting.

Gracey threw Cedric to the ground. Exasperated, he turned to see Macken peering from the undergrowth.

'Get up Jolly, for God's sake. It's clear.'

Macken slowly stood up, wincing as pain rushed into the space left by his ebbing fear.

'It turns out Jolly that the enemy within isn't you after all. Or the IRA. That genius Cedric is the man trying to kill us. His gun went off when we hit that hole there.'

Gracey angrily shook his own Sten. 'Listen to that rattle. They're rubbish.' He shouted over at Cedric. 'And he hadn't got the safety catch on, had he? He could have done the Fenians' dirty work for them, fuckin' eejit! The sooner we get those new Sterlings the better. Hopefully before we have to take on the IRA for real.'

Macken pointed to the trench. 'What about that?'

'Ah, the bloody Specials,' explained Gracey. 'We're near the border. They've probably been digging up roads since we heard about the election. You know what the B-Men are like. Anything for a bit of overtime.'

Macken frowned dubiously.

'Standard practice,' the sergeant continued. 'Limit the movement of the enemy. We can't watch every back road over the border. They'll be blowing bridges next.'

'I hadn't realised it was so serious,' said Macken.

'Life on the border, Jolly. It's not like the seaside. There's always a threat. There always will be.'

Gracey kicked one of the tyres.

'The Specials are one of life's necessary irritants. They're clumsy. But they're the prime minister's pets, so you can't kick their arses when they dig holes without telling us.

'And they come in handy when the shooting starts.'

The three men assessed the car. Cedric had shot through the floor and dashboard.

'Still looks driveable,' said Macken.

'What'll we do, Billy?' asked Cedric.

The sergeant glared at him. 'The first thing, *Constable* Andrews, is to shift it.'

Gracey put the car in neutral and the three of them gripped it under the front bumper and strained together, lifting it up and back from the trench.

'Cedric, pick up your gun and the shell cases. Jolly, make sure we've not left any bits of the car lying around. Leave no traces.'

'What about the car?' asked Macken. 'There's no hiding damage like that.'

'Oh, is there not?' said Gracey. 'You leave that to me.'

Gracey started the engine.

'I need a road back to the border, Cedric. Close by. But quiet, mind.'

'Aah…'

'Come on. Quick now.'

'There's a forestry track round the corner.'

Gracey slewed the car round. After a few hundred yards, they turned through a break in the hedge. The dim, dry, earth track was strewn with pine needles. They threaded through a plantation of conifers. Part of the Brookemartin demesne, explained Cedric. He pointed down a slope to a stream, which he said marked both the boundary of the estate and the border itself.

'We're definitely on the right side?' asked Gracey.

Cedric pointed to cuts on the tree trunks. 'Those are His Lordship's marks for which trees are to be took down. We're still in Ulster.'

Macken stared across the stream. It looked no different. He thought better of reminding them that it was Ulster over there too – one of the three Ulster counties left in the South when the border was drawn. Easier for northern Protestants to forget. They might feel embarrassed at abandoning them. Much like how the rest of Ireland felt about the six counties up north, he supposed.

Gracey checked the magazine from Cedric's gun.

'Not much left. Lord God, Cedric, you're an almighty eejit. Jolly, take his gun. I still haven't forgiven him for trying to kill us.'

'What are we doing, Sergeant?' asked Macken.

'Right, this is what happened.' Gracey paused to be sure they were listening. 'As we carried out our patrol with due diligence and attention, I noticed signs of suspicious activity in this wood by the border.'

Macken interrupted. 'What signs?'

'Ah... broken branches. Like a large vehicle had gone through. Cedric, go back and snap off some branches at the entrance. Keep out of sight, unless you have to stop someone coming in.'

Cedric hurried off.

'As we investigated, we came under fire from... from over here. And from in front. Jolly, go over there and when I give the word, rake the front of the car with what Cedric has left you. When that runs out use this.'

Gracey tossed Macken a spare magazine, and stepped back, raising his own gun.

'Hold on,' Macken slung his gun and raised his hands. 'You're not going to shoot up our own car, are you?'

'No, Jolly. *We* are going to shoot up the car.

'You're not expecting me to traipse back into town and say we accidentally opened fire on our own car while we were in it, are you? Would that look good on your personal record?'

'But I...'

'Don't worry, Jolly; I'm not trying to pin it on you. But have you no loyalty to young Cedric? Do you think he'll have a future in the force after that piece of prime stupidity? Whose side are you on?'

'No one will believe it,' argued Macken. 'We'll never get away with it.'

'That's more like it. You're coming round to the idea,' nodded Gracey. 'We *will* get away with it, if we do it here and now. And don't forget to aim high.'

The sergeant raised his gun. 'Now, Macken, I'm ordering you to open fire.'

What was this madness he had stumbled into, thought Macken? It must be a set-up. He was the one about to be riddled with bullets. In these, his final moments, the world around him seemed to grow distant. The sounds of the forest and his companion fading further and further.

Suddenly, the deafening rattle from Gracey's Sten gun slapped into him, like physical blows. Macken began to shake and a dull pain grew in his hands as he squeezed his fists harder and harder. His vision swam and then began to clear as he realised he was still standing. Dizzy. Alive. He looked at the car, windows shattered, rocking back to settle on its wheels.

'Christ almighty, Jolly, it's like waiting for the day of deliverance. Will you be joining the party any time today?'

Puzzled, Macken turned his head to see who had addressed him by his Christian name. A man in dark clothing, like himself he realised. Rough looking. A peaked hat. A gun in his hands. Not pointing at him, but at the car, from which glass was still falling.

Macken looked down at the gun in his hands. He raised it and looked over again to the man. The face staring at him had changed, no longer wearing an expression of complacent control. The eyes were narrowing to slits, then widening. He was pointing now and shouting.

'The car! For fuck's sake, shoot the fucking car, Jolly!'

Macken looked towards where the hand was pointing. The car. It was their car, he thought.

'Shoot the car!'

Yes, thought Macken, as his finger crept slowly onto the trigger, and the gun leapt to life. A great yell burst from him as he raked the front of the car and down the side, bursting the lights, shredding the tops of the seats through the windscreen and plugging the bonnet and the nearest tyre again and again. Release and rage pulsed through him till the bullets stopped. He heard a wailing that made him wince, till he gasped and realised it had been himself shouting.

The car slumped forward on the deflated front tyre.

'Aye, I think you've killed it.' Gracey walked over and put his hand on Macken's shoulder. 'You alright, fella? One minute I thought you'd forgotten what a gun is for, the next I thought you were about to shoot me.'

Macken couldn't speak. Gracey clapped him on the back.

'Oi! If there's to be anybody shooting anybody else, it'll be me shooting you! You hear me, you Fenian bastard?'

Macken nodded.

'Joking Jolly, I'm joking.' Gracey guided him round the car. 'Though, being realistic, Cedric's more likely to shoot the both of us than anything else.'

The sergeant opened both doors on the side further from their firing points. Then he pushed Macken through some low brambles.

Macken moved in a daze, still numbed with the paralysing fear he had felt while waiting for the bullets to tear into him, and then the exhilaration when he had opened fire himself. He had never felt more alive and yet more removed from the rest of the world of people.

Gracey braced himself against a tree and looked at Macken.

'I'm about to pull the trigger. Alright? Don't want you drifting off again.'

What now, thought Macken?

'We wouldn't just sit in the car waiting to be finished off. Our ambushers, being the thick, impatient kind of cowards that you find in the IRA, opened fire too soon. Which gave us the opportunity to jump out, take cover and return fire.'

Macken nodded. Gracey took aim.

'I predict that we'll put the fear of God into them with our accurate response, but sadly not manage to hit any of them before they flee, tails between their legs, back over the border.'

Gracey fired a burst into the woodland opposite. They heard a cry. Saw movement in the bushes.

Macken grabbed Gracey's arm.

The sergeant shrugged it off. 'Aye, I saw it.'

He thought for a moment, then: 'Fuck it.'

Gracey opened fire again. A longer burst, aimed lower, raking the trees and ground from where the sound had come.

'There's someone out there!' hissed Macken.

'Aye, so come on,' growled Gracey.

He ran forward, gun ready, Macken following.

They searched a clump of trees, with the ground sloping down to the stream behind.

'There's no one here,' said Macken.

'But there was,' said Gracey, nodding towards a patch of ground swept clear of twigs and stones.

'So where is he? He must have seen us. Christ, Gracey, did you hit him? He may be lying dead.'

'So shut up and keep looking.'

Macken froze. He'd heard something. There it was again. Faint. More of a whimper.

He raised a hand to still Gracey, then pointed low under a bush at the base of a tree trunk. Slowly and quietly Macken crouched and then lay flat, pointing his gun ahead of him. It was dark under there. But he detected life.

Macken nodded for Gracey to slowly circle round behind the tree. But instead the quiet was shattered again by Gracey's sub-machine gun. Macken hugged the ground as bullets tore into the bush.

Gracey stopped firing and Macken turned to look up at him in disbelief.

'Better safe than sorry.'

'It could be anybody,' protested Macken.

'He won't be telling tales now. Sure no decent person would be creeping round spying on us.'

Gracey pulled aside a branch. 'Let's see who we've got.'

Macken saw him flinch.

'Ah dear,' Gracey rubbed his chin. 'That's a shame.'

Macken looked. The body lay curled up tightly. A small dog, grey and white with darker wet holes in its side.

'It's a dog. Just a dog.'

'Aye, Macken,' said Gracey. 'Just a dog.'

The sergeant turned away.

'Take it across the stream and leave it out of sight.'

Macken went to argue, but he saw the tension in his sergeant's back. He bent down and swept the little animal up in his arms, cradling it as he crossed the stream. He covered it with debris from the forest floor and stepped back over the border.


They tramped back to the car. Gracey pursed his lips.

'Nothing ever goes one hundred per cent to plan, I suppose.'

'The dog, you mean?'

'Well, there's that. But I meant the car.'

Macken didn't get it.

'Didn't I tell you to aim high, you big glipe? Thereby letting us survive the ambush by ducking beneath the windows, safely exiting the vehicle, without having to deal with, thanks to you, that flat tyre. You'll notice I broke a lot of glass but left the doors and the wheels alone.'

'Sorry, I didn't think.'

Gracey sighed. 'Open the boot and see if the spare is still in one piece.'

It was a draughty, quiet drive back to Blackwatertown. They rallied as they reached the village. Cedric was elated. They hadn't told him about the dog. He did not seem to be able to believe his luck. He had faced ridicule, disgrace, probable dismissal and possible prosecution. Now he'd be a hero. Macken couldn't quite believe he was not dead twice over. But by now, and for now, he did not really care. He was alive – the glass crunching under him and the wind in his face told him that.

The sight of their smashed-up car silenced all street conversation. It seemed to Macken that Gracey had grown in stature – swelled inside his uniform, chest out, back ramrod straight. He and Cedric fell in behind as the sergeant led them to the duty room.

Bull looked up and gradually realised that something out of the ordinary was unfolding. It might have been the glass shards glinting on their coats. Or the effort Gracey was making to rearrange his face from glee to stern urgency. He snapped to attention in front of Bull – a sight so unprecedented that Bull leapt up from his chair. The sensation of his own rare physical exertion confused him further, which meant he failed to take in what Gracey was barking at him.

'Do you not hear me, Bull? I'm reporting that we came under attack from subversives. We returned fire and drove them off.'

'What? We're under attack?'

'Christ almighty! Stand easy, Bull. Just get the inspector.'

As Bull clattered off, Gracey calmed himself down and regained his air of competence and long-suffering tetchiness. It would be important to seem normal to complete the most risky part of the charade – securing official approval.


McReady appeared with a look of concern.

'Your report please, Sergeant.'

'Yessir. While on patrol as part of the election security programme, we came under attack from woodland near the border. We were investigating signs of suspicious activity near the Brookemartin estate when gunmen opened fire without warning. We returned fire and drove off a large group of attackers. They fled over the border, at which point I called off our pursuit. If you'd like to step outside, you can observe the damage caused to the vehicle. After you, sir.'

Gracey stepped back and extended an arm towards the door. As suggestions go, it was more of an instruction, but the inspector followed it without quibble. He gasped.

'Heavens above, Sergeant! You certainly took some fire. It's a miracle you managed to make it back. You didn't mention injuries?'

'No injuries, sir. We escaped via the far side of the vehicle. They expected we'd be an easy target. Especially with their superior numbers. But I reckon we gave them an education. I'd like to commend Constable Andrews, and our new arrival, Mr Macken. They rallied well under my direction and behaved in an exemplary fashion.'

'Very good, Sergeant, very good.'

'The IRA will never be a match for RUC discipline. No matter what they throw at Ulster, sir.'

McReady could see Gracey was working himself up into a self-righteous tirade.

'Indeed so, Sergeant. Indeed so. Well done. I'll need a full report. We'll need to mount an immediate response to this threat. Nip it in the bud.'

'I'd like to volunteer to go back on patrol, sir, in case there are more of them around.'

'Yes, thank you Sergeant. Let's get a full picture of what happened first.'

Gracey leant closer to speak confidentially.

'In the meantime, sir: Constable Macken. Bit shaken. Long day for him. If I could send him to lie down for half an hour it might stand to him later, sir.'

McReady's face betrayed surprise at this display of consideration from Gracey. Perhaps the sergeant was maturing into something more than simply the toughest of the gang. These less-educated lads could sometimes surprise you, he thought.

The inspector smiled. 'Good thinking, Sergeant. And good show all round.'

As McReady walked back inside, Gracey turned to Cedric.

'Take the car over to the yard and don't come back.'

'But–'

'McReady will be here till teatime at this rate and I want you kept away from him. Leave the report to me and keep your mouth shut. And Cedric... Don't shoot at anything else, alright? I don't want to hear of any tractors, trailers, livestock or locals with holes that don't belong.'

'What about me?' The first words from Macken since they had arrived back.

'Keep your mouth shut like you have been doing, and you might come out of this smelling of roses. Stay in bed and out of the way.'

With that, Gracey strode into the barracks. Macken felt drained of both energy and initiative. He needed to just stop and close his eyes.


Macken made it to his bed, opened his collar and began to remove his boots. Everything seemed so long ago. The tension, the fear, the adrenalin, the frenzy that had come over him as he shot bullet after bullet into the car. He had been so many people over the past hours – defiant in the face of the cycling bigot, helpless when faced with imminent death, timid in the aftermath. And always the same question in the suspicious looks, and then in a woman's gentle voice: *Who are you really?* Macken had no idea who he'd be when he woke up.


*There was no escape. Every time the darkness claimed him.*

*He tried to spread his wings. But there was no room to stretch, no room to move.*

*He was an egg snug in a box, pinned in place, stuffed under straw. But still he struggled feebly against the tiny nook that held him like a coffin.*

# CHAPTER 11

Hours later, Macken felt he was running. He did not know where his legs were carrying him. He gradually opened his eyes.

'The dead arose and appeared to many.' It was Cedric, shaking his leg. 'You're to get up, Jolly.'

Macken grunted. 'Don't call me that.'

'C'mon. We're in the middle of a major alert, or did that pass you by?'

'I just lay down for a moment.'

'Well, boots on. We're off out on patrol again. See if we can't flush out some more IRA men,' Cedric smirked at him.

We must still be in the clear, thought Macken. Then he shook his head: We – who's we? Are we all in this together then?

And anyway, Cedric's mood was no reliable indicator of the prospect of discovery. Gracey kept his cards close to his chest.

Macken clumped downstairs to where the DI had the men lined up. He was reminding them of the need for stout hearts, steadfastness and judgement too. No good rushing in all guns blazing. They weren't to frighten good, honest, hard-working local people. Nor were they to blunder into other patrols and mistake each other for the enemy. Especially, he said, now that the B–Men had been called out in force.

Macken's spirits took a dive. *The B–Men.* Officially, the Ulster Special Constabulary. The armed volunteer militia. Protestant to a man. The job of the paramilitary Specials was to support the police in border security and at times of Republican attack. They did not lack zeal or energy, though the restraint occasionally exercised by the regular constabulary tended to elude them. God help us, thought Macken, they make this barracks look a temple of tolerance.

Desperate times called for desperate measures. At least, that was usually the justification given by those B–Men who used their legally held guns and authority to remind their Catholic neighbours just who was boss.

Calling out the Specials led to ridiculous exchanges between neighbours on the roads at night. Typically, a car would stop in response to a torch waving from the side of a country lane. Armed men in dark uniforms would surround the vehicle. The driver would be questioned:

'Where are you going?'

'Ah, hello. Is that you, Walter? Bitter night for it, isn't it?'

'Where are you going?'

'Walter, can you not see it's me? It's Michael. Your neighbour, Sinead's husband?'

'Get out of the car and show us your licence.'

All being well, being neighbours after all, there would be merely a few sharp words. Nothing untoward would be found nor planted in the car. There would be no rough stuff. The driver's forehead would not be marked with a small, fading, red circle from where the barrel of a gun was pressed in. There would be no accidental discharge of a weapon. There would be no innocents shot dead in the confusion. All being well.

The following morning, days, weeks, they would still be neighbours. After a while they would be back to nodding hello in the street and, when necessary, guardedly polite conversations. But the one won't quickly forget being in the power of the other. And the other will never lose his deep and abiding fear that those outwardly genial neighbours are inwardly meditating fearful things. He'll clutch to himself the familiar dread that, one night, those smiling neighbours will rise up to take back their land, to murder and drive out the ones who dispossessed them.

Which is the true reality? wondered Macken. Is it the embers of resentment and grievance that glow sometimes into flame, sometimes faintly, but never go out? Or is it the slack poured over to dampen it down – the normal getting on with life – the each to their own – the separate shops for them and us – the accepting of life as it is, them in their place and us in ours?

Not for the first time, Macken wished they could all put it aside and make room for more simple joy in their lives. But he knew that with belonging came certain obligations, certain rituals. And certainty itself. Certainty as to your rightness and their wrongness. And that could justify anything.

The only thing about which Macken was certain was that he did not belong with either side. Jesus, he thought, no point pontificating about the lack of joy in their lives when there's not a hell of a lot in my own. However, as he stood in line, the impudent smile of one Aoife Penny came to mind. He answered it with a small smile of his own.


'Glad you're enjoying this, Constable.'

Macken stiffened as the district inspector glared at him.

'I'm granting you some leeway after this afternoon. Sergeant Gracey tells me you acted with great dispatch. Perhaps you'll also find the prime minister as entertaining?'

'Yessir. I mean...'

DI McReady thankfully interrupted Macken's stammering response.

'I've decided it's important for you men to hear what the prime minister has to say. Not because he is a local, so to speak. But because good people across Ulster will be tuning in to hear him, including your fellow officers preparing to set off on patrol across the country.'

McReady checked his watch.

'Sergeant Gracey, would you be so kind?'

Gracey switched on the wireless. Through the crackles came BBC Radio Ulster, and the tail end of the introduction to Lord Brookemartin, owner of the country estate near Blackwatertown and prime minister of Her Majesty's Government of Northern Ireland.

Then they heard the imperious voice of the prime minister himself. His clipped, anglicised accent had little hint of Ulster in it.

*Ladies and gentlemen. My fellow Ulstermen and women. I was intending this evening to speak of the important decision that lies before us all – namely the election to our sovereign parliament in Stormont. However, just before I came into the radio studio, I was handed a note. The news it contained was most worrying, and I felt it was my duty to share its content with you all.*

*'Earlier today, a patrol of the Royal Ulster Constabulary was attacked by subversives in the vicinity of the border near the village of Blackwatertown. There can be no doubt that the purpose of this cowardly ambush was to kill police officers without warning.'*

Macken's jaw dropped.

The prime minister carried on.

'I am very happy to tell you that our brave officers successfully repelled the attackers and drove them back across the border without suffering serious injury.

'This dastardly attack must serve as a reminder of the ever–present threat our province faces. Constant vigilance is the price we must pay to preserve our way of life. We must always beware of the enemy without and the enemy within.

'Once again our brave defenders have stood firm against those who would destroy us. We all owe them our heartfelt thanks. But mere words are not enough. They also need our help. We owe it to them. We owe it to ourselves and to our children.'

Macken noticed Cedric sticking out his chest and splitting his face with a proud smile. Gracey's face betrayed no emotion at all, neither joy nor anger. And certainly not the fear Macken felt himself.

'Those of you who know me will understand that I am not a man given to great speeches. This is not a time for the cut and thrust of electoral orations. There are those more skilled than I who can perform that role far better. I leave such matters to them.

'I will simply state, from the heart, that the IRA and their Republican friends from south of the border must not – must never – be allowed to overthrow the will of the people of Ulster.

'Now more than ever we must stand together for all that we hold dear. There must be no return to the dark days of Rome rule. Never again will Protestants be massacred on their farms and driven to the hills.

'To that end I have authorised the general mobilisation of the Ulster Special Constabulary in support of the RUC to nip any uprising, invasion or campaign of subversion in the bud.

'*To those who say we cannot stand against the Pope and his legions, I say no surrender.*

'*And today we have a new cry to throw in the face of those who would try to bring down Ulster: Remember Blackwatertown!*

'*Ladies and gentlemen, thank you very much.*'

The district inspector nodded to his sergeant, who switched off the wireless. A sombre McReady gazed along his line of men and felt satisfied. Once again a time for wartime values. The great test had come. He was confident they would acquit themselves well.

'Gentlemen, I'm relying on you now. We're all relying on you.'

He nodded again to the sergeant to dismiss the men, and then left them.

Macken thought: Jesus! It's like he's sending us over the top from the trenches. And then: bloody hell! We did this. It has to be stopped.

He stepped towards Gracey, who guided him to one side and spoke quietly.

'That was a bit of a turn-up for the books, wasn't it? Who'd have thought our wee piece of amateur dramatics would get such a glowing review?'

'We have to stop all this,' whispered Macken. 'It's completely out of control.'

'Is that right? You've thought it through, have you? The effect on morale? The boost it would give the enemy? Aren't they always on the lookout for weakness? To say nothing of what it'll do to all of us here.'

'But it's all a lie,' persisted Macken. 'It's gone beyond covering up for a mate.'

'Oh, Cedric's a mate now, is he? Not very matey to blow the whistle on him just when it's all working out.

'He's had a rough time lately, thanks to your predecessor here. We haven't had the best of luck with the Fenians we've been sent. The way you're carrying on, I can see we're not out of the woods yet.'

'Look,' began Macken, trying to sound reasonable. 'We can still sort this out if we do it now. Before any damage is done.'

'But the damage *is* done, son. You'd only be making it worse. How it would make the RUC look? Then there's me. As the senior man it wouldn't look good for me, would it? And the impact on you would be even more severe.'

'I'll take my punishment. Even dismissal, if it comes to that.'

'I wouldn't, in all conscience you understand, be able to let it get that far. I'm afraid, Jolly, that you might suffer an unfortunate accident. The cause of which, likely as not, would be me putting a bullet in you. Not just in your fevered imagination. For real this time. I'd say disciplinary procedures would be the least of your worries.'

Gracey put an arm round his shoulder, and winked.

'But look on the bright side. If it wasn't this, it would be something else. It's an election. We're bound to be keeping an extra eye out for subversives. Keeps people on their toes to think there's a reason for it. Has it occurred to you that we may actually have done some good by deterring real trouble?'

Gracey warmed to his theme. 'It's not so bad after all, is it? Here you are, walking around on your hind legs, hero of the hour. Quite a turnaround after your run-in with the vicar.

'In these days of world powers and atomic bombs and communism and space rockets, you'd think wee men like us could never make a difference. This is your moment, Jolly. Enjoy it. And for fuck's sake don't keep on whingeing. Today's been busy enough without you needing to be shot too.'

The big sergeant gave Macken one last squeeze, and a smile.

To look at, they were comrades, recently blooded in battle, with an understanding that transcended rank.

# CHAPTER 12

'...*according to the Northern authorities the attackers fled over the border. The Gardai say they are investigating. In other news, the Minister for Industry and Commerce says the government may introduce petrol rationing in the light of the Suez crisis...*'

'Who the fuck was that?'

Sergeant Gracey's amateur dramatics were being reported south of the border too. The appalled listener flicked the switch on the old Philips wireless, cutting off the Radio Telefís Eireann announcer in mid-sentence. Peadar Greenard, owner of the Cross Tavern, searched the studiously vacant faces lined up at the bar. No reaction.

'Right under our noses! Did you hear that? A large unit of men, at least twenty. Prolonged exchange of fire. An RUC car shot to buggery! Jesus, lads!'

As well as being proprietor of the only public house in Tycross, an even sleepier place than Blackwatertown, Peadar Greenard was also the blustering public face of local Republicanism. But he was a businessman with sufficient sense never to get involved in anything that could be mistaken for actual activity. Especially with 'the North' just a few miles up the road.

Rare it was to see Greenard's bulky frame rise from its stool. The spectacle deserved at least some response from the sleepy bunch loitering at the counter. Until the disturbance, they had been contentedly blowing out cigarette fumes to mix with the turf smoke from the hearth.

'Aye, Peadar. A right mix-up indeed.'

'Looks like the boys are back in town.'

'Do they say who it was?'

The fat man slapped the bar. 'They're saying it's the IRA. But how could it be? We've heard nothing.'

'Aye, well, Peadar. Those boys don't always give warning, you know.'

'I'd like to think I know what's happening up the road from my own bar! It's no good them motoring up from Dublin for the day expecting to free the North just like that.'

'Dublin men were they, Peadar?'

'Well, Dublin or wherever. They weren't from round here, were they?'

'Give much of a show of themselves, did they?'

Greenard snorted at the naivety of anyone hoping to find facts in a radio bulletin.

'You wouldn't expect the British propaganda machine to reveal details like that. But by the sounds of it, the boys are bound to have hit a few of them at least.

'If it's what I think it is, we could have busy days ahead, boys. Busy days.'

And with that, Peadar Greenard lapsed into silence. The drinkers relaxed and resumed discussion about the wee jewel of a pig that one had his eye on.

The identity of the Blackwatertown ambushers was preying on minds in Belfast and Dublin too. There were theories. There were always theories. But no one *knew*. From both centres, inquiries, official or otherwise, were proceeding apace. RUC HQ, while pleased with the performance of McReady's men, was pressing him hard for intelligence.

No information was coming from the police south of the border. McReady assessed that this was not because the Gardai were being obstructive. They probably had no idea who the attackers were either. The incident had come as a complete surprise all round. The IRA had seemed to be fading away. They'd flared up during the last war, mainly in Belfast, but barring a few diehard families, the threat had seemed more theoretical than real. Until now.

That's why it's so puzzling, thought McReady. No doubting the holes put in the police car. But there had been none of the usual subtle signals in advance – the quiet distancing of themselves by local Catholics from the police. Neither had they been braced for police reprisals. The B-Men had had no difficulty lifting locals from bars and on the road last night. Good, efficient work, but a sign that the Catholic population had not known to make themselves scarce in time.

McReady doubted anything useful would come from the robust interrogations. He rubbed his eyes. It had been a long night. It was time to get back in touch with an old source.

Greenard was angry, but nervous with it. He was annoyed at being kept in the dark and wanted to let them know they couldn't just waltz into his patch and start blasting away at the Brits. But the IRA leadership in Dublin could be unaccountably touchy, and he was wondering how best to raise the issue.

He need not have worried. They called him. And they were angry too. With the same questions. Who was it? What happened? What are the Brits doing now?

'So it wasn't us then?'

'Would we be asking you, if it was? Do you have any idea what's happening on your own doorstep? It's all kicking off up there. They've mobilised the Specials, roadblocks, gun battles.'

'They've set the RUC running scared alright,' chuckled Greenard. 'Whoever "they" are. Fair play to them though, eh?'

'Anyone hitting the Brits is good news. But we can't allow the freedom struggle to be jeopardised by uncoordinated freelance action.'

'Yes, sir.'

'So find out who they are. Of course we were already poised, waiting for the right moment, but we may bring things forward to take advantage of this new situation. So gather your men, wait for instructions and don't worry. Help is already on the way.'

They rang off.

Jaysus, what a headache, thought Greenard. His days of IRA activism had never extended to actual combat. They gave him a position in local society and helped with a bit of cross-border smuggling. But beyond standing in the rain at a memorial once a year to remember Ireland's fallen, he had not made much effort for years.

Holy Mary! Gather your men? That was a joke. Young farmers fed on old stories. He'd kept the faith alive with bar room tales of heroism and of the poor abandoned North. God forbid they ever do rub out the border, he thought, we'd have to put up with all those hard-faced Belfast men. Never mind the women. And what about all those Protestants? The ones down here were alright, he admitted, but God save us from that dour, miserable bunch up north.

Still, thinking of Protestants, one in particular could hold the answer. The same man had once been a quiet source of cash in exchange for information. Maybe this time the information could come the other way, thought Greenard, if he played his cards right.

# CHAPTER 13

The B-Men on patrol were keyed up for action, nervous that the adversaries they could meet might be armed this time. They were full of questions, but Sergeant Gracey brushed aside any talk of their heroics, warning that they should keep their eyes peeled for the next attack, not waste chitchat on old news. This made Gracey appear all the more heroic. Every now and then he'd tip Macken a conspiratorial wink, as if it were a great lark.

For the B-Men, however, every car they stopped that did not contain the IRA was a disappointment. Farm work is drudgery – cold, dull, damp and repetitive. The B-Men welcomed the change. There was some sneaking resentment at Gracey and Macken and Cedric, that perhaps they had grabbed all the glory for themselves, that the ambush had been a flash in the pan. At the back of every auxiliary's mind was the calculation of their duty pay, depending how long the emergency lasted.

All along the northern side of the border that evening, armed men bumped around on the backs of trucks, lingered at crossroads, checked cars, sized up isolated humpback bridges with a view to dynamiting them and felled trees to block so-called 'unapproved roads'. The main cross-border routes had customs posts on both sides. But there was a web of small lanes criss-crossing the frontier with no official presence. Handy for the locals and for smuggling contraband either way, or for people with more sinister intent. There were far too many to guard, so the routine at times of threat was simply to block them. Inconvenient if your farmland was on both sides. But needs must.

There were also the usual house calls to be made on the usual suspects. Like every policeman, Macken knew the value of the fear his uniform could instil. Fear got you a listening ear and obedience.

The truck threw up gravel as it stopped in front of an isolated Catholic hamlet huddled in darkness. A handful of homes. A scattering of outbuildings, drab and run down. Muddy underfoot beyond the gravel. The place might have had a name, but Macken did not know it. There was no sign of anyone, but Macken could feel their presence as he jumped out. He knew they would be inside, shoulders hunched, waiting for the knock on the door – or for it to be booted open – depending on the whim of the uninvited visitors.

Gracey directed the B-Men to check the outbuildings. He posted sentries to guard against any surprise attack.

'Gives them something to do,' said Gracey quietly, 'and lets us carry on in peace.'

Macken raised his eyebrows: Why are we here?

Gracey shrugged. 'Once upon a time maybe, the granddad would've taken an interest in politics. But these days...

'Just routine. Lets them know we've haven't forgotten them.'

Gracey knocked on the first door and went in. He had a greeting for those within, but did not wait for a response. No time for an exchange of pleasantries. Nor to worry about the muck he tracked over the threshold. Moving quickly. Keeping up the momentum. Getting in and getting out.

Gracey asked to see everyone gathered in the kitchen. It was phrased as a request, and politely done, but was tantamount to an order. They were all there already, as keen as the police to get the incursion over with. Macken paid little attention to the conversation. They all knew it was a formality. It was unlikely the people had any information. If they had, they wouldn't give it.

Does that make them the enemy, Macken asked himself? Does that mean they could be harbouring the men involved in the ambush? Macken mentally corrected himself – the faked ambush. It was easy to become carried away with these things once the ball started rolling. So who are they, wondered Macken – these defensive, closed faces, with hooded, downcast eyes? Unwilling bystanders, trying not to be dragged in by us, by the IRA or by anyone else stirring up trouble.

Gracey led Macken round the house, giving it a cursory search. It was the same routine in the next house and the next one – pointless questions and a futile search for concealed weapons.

Macken realised that, apart from Aoife, these were the first fellow Catholics he had met since coming to Blackwatertown. Of course, to these ones, he thought, I'm just another uniform, to be given a wide berth and handled with care in case I explode.

How angry they must feel, thought Macken, to have us hector them in their homes. And how much more angry, that they dare not show it. But there's no getting away from it. They do look guilty, like they're hiding something. Their rage perhaps. Maybe playing the guilty party is simply their traditional role in a state that automatically brands them as disloyal.

Gracey and Macken reached the last dwelling. This time the sergeant did not receive the same grudging deference as before. The old man of the house remained sitting when they entered. Feebleness, wondered Macken, or a small sign of defiance? He was twisted like a gnarled piece of driftwood, brissling his shins at the fire. His face in shadow, but the eyes sharp, calculating, jaundiced yellow as a duck's foot.

'Hah, Sergeant, sure what knowledge of world events are we likely to have stuck out here at the edge of your empire?'

The man spat into the flames of the fire, to signal his dismissal of any further interrogation.

'Bring that lamp over till I get a decent look at yer man here,' ordered Gracey to one of the family.

'Ach, let it sit,' the man waved it away. 'What need of light for an aul' done man?

'I've seen you come and go before, and now you're here again. There's nowt to see, and nowt to tell.'

Macken sensed that Gracey was thrown by this refusal to cooperate. A boot up the backside would have been the usual reaction, but in this case, it would be like kicking a bag of bones. Gracey held back from lashing out, for the moment.

'I'll be the judge of that. There's something afoot here, and somebody knows it. And somebody's going to tell it.'

The old man snorted and held Gracey's stare. When he spoke there was no sense he'd backed down, despite being first to break the silence.

'Forbye that, for any soul who blabbed to you is likely to come to the same end as young McMahon. Am I right?'

Gracey looked as if he had been slapped across the face. He seemed to shrink back for an instant, then grabbed the old man, lifting him from his chair. The room tensed. Macken dropped one hand to his holster, at the same time laying the other on Gracey's arm.

Gracey lowered the old man nearly all the way back down, then dropped him the last few inches.

'What are you talking about, you poisonous aul' eejit?' hissed Gracey, almost spitting in the man's face.

He was sunk back in the chair like a bundle of worn-out clothes. Macken could see fear now in the man's eyes, but still no submission. He could almost hear a collective growl round the kitchen from the other family members. He increased the pressure on Gracey's arm. The sergeant looked pointedly at where Macken's hand rested. Macken let go and Gracey eased back from the seated man. He'd seen the old man's fear and had decided it was sufficient.

'Go on then,' snarled Gracey.

Macken took over and spoke to everyone gathered there. 'We know we're visitors in your home, and we don't want to disrupt you any further. You know we have men outside. Let's leave them there and complete our business.'

Macken took the silence as permission to turn back to the patriarch.

'Now, sir, if there's any information, anything at all, you can give us – well, it would be a great help, and would see us off out of here on our way.'

What can he tell us, thought Macken. That's it's all a con? That somehow, there's a change coming anyway, and that all our guns will be powerless to stop it?

Macken had noticed that none of the houses had a radio. Couldn't afford one, he supposed. So how would they even know about the ambush that morning? Unless it was in the way all significant news spreads in these parts, like an invisible virus. Like the ice cracking in a frozen canal, low twangs under the surface, echoes of the nudging of a barge pushing against it upstream. Nothing more noticeable than the fleeting shadow of a cloud passing, or a downturn at the side of a mouth.

For all Macken's efforts to see inside the man's mind, nothing was given away. Gracey was casting about for some inanimate object on which to vent his frustration. He began poking with his baton into folded blankets and the dresser, as if afraid of contamination if his skin came into direct contact.

Macken noticed the old man's lips were moving, and he bent closer. 'Yes, go on, I'm listening.'

'I know you,' whispered the old man.

Macken frowned and thought – unlikely.

'I know what you are, and I know who you are.'

Here we go, thought Macken, preparing himself to be impassive in the face of whatever insult was coming next.

'You try to run with the hounds and hide with the fox.'

Macken felt the man's spittle on his ear.

'Choose sides or you'll die alone,' the whisper continued. 'Your father knew the score.'

Macken recoiled. What was this auld bastard doing bringing up his father? The old man jerked his head slightly, to let Macken know there was more, if he wanted it. Reluctantly, Macken bent down again.

'Make your choice. You may turn your back on your own, but those others will never take you in. No smiles nor sweet words nor blind eyes turned will ever keep you safe.

'Your Da learnt that,' he rasped. 'He was a fair man. All duty. And he would do a kindness to a neighbour in hardship without telling the world. No fuss. But his card was marked all the same.

'He smiled at me once, your father, just before I stuck a gun in his face and pulled the trigger.'

Macken gripped the arm of the man's chair to stop himself

falling forward. Something as light as a spider crept lightly over the back of his hand to rest there like a claw.

'He was a lonely man, your Da. He chose his path. Hard-working. Alone. You'll be like him.

'I'm happy now the gun jammed.'

The whisper faded to nothingness, and Macken suddenly became acutely aware of the pressure of the old man's fingers. He pulled his hand free and straightened up quickly, feeling disorientated and angry.

'Well?' Gracey was smirking beside him. 'Had he anything to confess? You looked like a priest crouched there.

'A lot of sins to get off your chest, had you?' Gracey addressed the old man, from whom all spark of life seemed to have vanished.

The chance to dish out ridicule expunged from Gracey's mind any lingering sense of personal humiliation.

'I'd say that aul' fella has been running round with every young thing from here to Armagh,' said Gracey, nudging Macken.

'What did you give him? Three Hail Marys and a How's Your Father? The dirty bastard.'

Gracey slung a convivial arm round Macken and guided him towards the door, all thoughts of further investigation apparently gone.

They paused at the door. Gracey looked from face to face, marking each of them. He slowly scraped each boot on the doorstep, as if removing dung from the heel. Then he propelled Macken back out into the night, signalling to the rest to get back in the vehicles.

'Who was that old one in the chair?' asked Macken.

'A nobody. Did he get to you then?'

Macken grunted.

'Calling you a traitor? Ah, Macken, you're one of the good guys now. Watch me. Look and learn.'

They set off down the rutted track with a clattering din.

'Yon fella,' shouted Gracey. 'They make out he was once someone in the so-called struggle. Never saw any evidence of it myself. If everyone who people say was involved back then really had been, well... We might really have been in trouble. But as with most things, it's more talk, less action.

'And if he ever was the great hero, where did it get him? A bog hole in the back end of nowhere.'

Gracey settled into his seat.

'See me? See him? I would have tipped him into the fire and plugged the rest of the vermin.

'That's if I wasn't so polite and well behaved.'

They motored off into the darkness, Gracey laughing over the roar of the engine – Macken wishing, for the first time in a long time, that he could talk to his father.

# CHAPTER 14

Back at Blackwatertown, District Inspector McReady summoned Macken for a private interview. Macken had not made up his mind whether he should resist or crumble under interrogation, but the 'incident', which he was trying to think of it as, was only mentioned in passing.

'Sergeant Gracey spoke very highly of your enthusiasm,' said McReady. 'He won't mind me repeating a little of what he told me. He said you were so keen to get at those subversives that he thought you would take a bite out of them.

'I've seen action myself. Not something I tend to discuss. But it's reassuring to hear of such a lively response under fire. Not all men cope so well.'

'It happened so fast, sir. The sergeant is being generous.'

'Well, he may be, he may be. Though that's not usually his style.

'But your behaviour is also reassuring in a deeper sense. I hope you won't be insulted if I tell you that it shows much more than oaths or uniforms where your loyalties lie.

'It also gives me the confidence to allocate to you a rather unusual duty. It's no less vital to our safety than your courage yesterday. But it calls for a cool head. I need you to be able to tread softly when the occasion demands it. Can you promise me that?'

'I hope so, sir,' replied Macken, still completely in the dark.

He realised that the DI was nervous. His false bonhomie gave it away.

McReady asked Macken to sit, and apologised for being so cryptic. He explained that the surprise attack had rather caught everyone out. More embarrassingly, the police still had no idea who was behind it. Neither, it seemed, did the authorities down south. There had been no claim of responsibility from the IRA in Dublin. It was clearly their work, of course, but they were keeping their cards unusually close to their chests. HQ wanted answers. Local intelligence was urgently required.

'Where do I come in, sir?' asked Macken. 'I'm very new here. I wouldn't know where to go digging.'

'I'll point you in the right direction. In fact, I want you to go south. There's a man I want you to meet. I'd worry about sending a more well-known face across the border. Plus, you're a Catholic. So you'll fit in better.'

'Not sure what difference that'll make, sir. The IRA didn't check what religion police officers were when the bullets were flying in days gone by.'

'I'm well aware of your family's history of service, Macken. The point is, you're the right man for the job.'

'Yes, sir. Who do you want me to meet?'


The fat man was perched behind the counter of the Cross Bar, smiling and nodding and fretting. He was waiting for the knock on the door.

It came as a tug at his elbow instead. His son Tomas, eyes shining.

'They're here. Slipped in the back.'

Greenard closed his eyes for a moment. So soon.

'Mind the bar, Tom.'

He hoicked himself off his stool and pushed both hands over his face to mould it into a mask of hospitality. So it begins, he thought. He picked up a clutch of shot glasses and a bottle of Jameson. One last look over the smoke and chatter of the public bar, then he went into the back to meet the first of the night's arrivals.

After being dismissed by the district inspector, Macken gulped down some bread dunked in fish and vegetable broth. Then he escaped upstairs, the better to brood in peace. The old man's comments about his father had thrown him. In a way, they confirmed his belief that the job wasn't right for him, nor he for it.

But Macken knew he had more immediate problems. The mission across the border the following day felt like trouble – but orders is orders. He still could not come to terms with the faked ambush and its results. And then there were his growing suspicions about Danny's death.

There's no doubt that Gracey is a bad 'un, he thought. Dark hearted. The way he handled the so-called ambush showed quick wit. No scruples to hold him back. But killing a comrade in cold blood? That's a huge jump. And why? Macken couldn't see it somehow. There were plenty of ways of getting rid of people without killing them. Hadn't he himself been got rid of from Kilmurray without need of a bullet?

Gracey was a law unto himself and capable of just about anything. But killing a policeman just because of his religion did not seem credible.

However, there was definitely something not right. Cedric was jittery. And that scrap of paper. Danny had discovered something. Maybe he had threatened to reveal it. Macken knew that Gracey wouldn't hesitate to defend himself.

But what could be so damning that they'd kill to conceal it? The poaching? Disciplinary proceedings if caught. But surely not so they'd kill someone.

Unless Danny was blackmailing them? Macken shook his head. You're getting ridiculous now. Blackmail? In a place like Blackwatertown? Get a grip.

Still and all though, they're suspicious of me. Because I'm new? A Catholic? Sent to snoop? It dawned on Macken that he had never really questioned why he had been exiled to Blackwatertown in particular. Maybe I was sent to stir things up. As bait. That would explain why Gracey was so keen to suck me into his little ambush charade, he realised. I'm as dirty as they are now. They're safe from me.

He sighed in relief.

But Danny was still dead. Macken suddenly felt no wiser, and no safer.


I'm getting nowhere, thought Macken. He took off his boots and tunic and lay down. He tried to recapture that moment at the lake when he was floating, propelling himself with long, slow sweeps with both arms, calmly drifting in space…


*He was buffeted from all sides, his only escape to screw tighter the curve of his tiny frame and tuck his face into the crook of his rake–thin arm. All around was bumping movement, no space to raise his head. If he faltered, they would rip his skin with their claws, or stab at his eyes, zeroing in on their gleam in the blackness.*

*They had no names, the beasts that populated the darkness outside his head. Nor did he. They existed together in an unceasing industry of scratching survival until they fell or disappeared. He outlived them all to return here again and again to the fearsome dark.*

# CHAPTER 15

Shouts from downstairs roused Macken from his reverie. It was still dark. He did not feel refreshed. Nothing was sorted out. And never will be by lying here, he chided himself. He fumbled for his boots and clumped downstairs, buttoning his jacket.

Bull was snug by the fire in the day room as usual.

'Lord God, Jolly! I thought I was going to have to get up and fetch you.'

'That would have been a tragedy,' said Macken drily. 'What's the big emergency?'

'You're on the knock at the Bridge. We're making sure you get value for money from your first day.'

A few windows still hinted at life on the dark main street. From this one, a flickering fire glow filtered through curtains. From that one, weak light shone through a gap to guide home a late drinker. Macken's shadow escorted him – an unreliable, skittish companion – now growing in stature in front, now darting away behind, thin and nervous. His indistinct reflection in the windows was not much more encouraging – a dark, walking cadaver, hurrying to catch up with the hearse.

Macken's job was to roust out the regulars from Blackwatertown's only public house. Standard duty. The main thing was not to rush in and catch people unawares. Live and let live. There was a routine to be gone through, to give those inside time to gulp down their dregs and exit out back. That way law and order was preserved, and the drinkers got home before they became too incapacitated to walk, or work in the morning. For they were, most of them, hard workers. And for all their complaints, they were happy for the constable to ease them from their cosy snug into the night and back towards home. And Maginnis, who ran the Bridge Bar, was pleased to be able to blame the police, rather than having to personally evict and risk offending his tipsy regulars. Otherwise he would never get to bed himself.

The only specific instruction Bull had given Macken was to be sure not to catch their barracks' landlord, Trelford Dunlap. After the incident with the pedalling vicar, Bull had made sure Macken was paying attention.

'There's no profit in stirring up bad blood with him. He'll only bump up our rent to pay any fine anyway,' warned Bull. 'And watch you don't trip over him accidentally, for he has more money than many, and drinks more than he can hold.'

'But if he's too drunk to shift himself?'

'They'll move him out back. So take a wee dander round to check. Once you've given the rest a chance to disperse.

'And, Jolly...'

'What?'

'Don't bring any lost drunks back to our nice clean cells. Use your powers of detection to find out where they belong.'

The Bridge Bar looked dead when Macken got there. It was not a serious attempt to deceive, more a tactful and traditional aid to policemen turning a blind eye. Macken listened at the door and detected an undercurrent of conversation.

He smiled despite himself. It was like a baby napping in the afternoon. As the oldest child, Macken had helped with the younger ones. You couldn't let them doze all day if they were to sleep at night. But looking down at your baby brother, lying warm and safe from the cares of the world, you felt it was a shame to disturb him. And you watched over him as he slept on a little longer. But that was before Macken was squeezed out of the picture.

He looked towards the bridge, with the dark water flowing beneath. He could just make out the trees on the other side. It would have been an uneasy night watch in years gone by, he thought, waiting for the Irish to come rushing back from the darkness into which they had been driven. Wondering if they were out there. Plotting to turn your fortress into your funeral pyre.

What about now, Macken wondered? He paused for that eerie, prickling feeling that meant someone was spying on him from the blackness. Nothing. He shrugged and checked his watch. Fifteen minutes after time. He knocked on the front door. It had been quiet before, but suddenly it seemed as if even that quiet had been stuffed into a sack and the neck drawn closed.

Macken hammered harder. 'Who's there?' came from inside. As if he doesn't know, thought Macken, and him still downstairs rather than in his bed. No doubt he'll tell me he's just tidying up.

'Police on Public House Duty,' answered Macken loud and clear. Then he waited. From inside came sounds of chairs scraping back, boots on floorboards and a sudden hubbub, which gradually diminished as the drinkers left by the back door. Accompanying this were occasional placatory comments from the landlord, letting the officer know he was just coming, just getting the keys, just trying to work this stiff lock, was sorry to keep him waiting.

The door opened and Macken was hit by a warm, sour blast of alcohol and body odour, peat and cigarette smoke.

'Come in now, come in,' said Maginnis, in a show of effusive hospitality. 'I've not yet had the pleasure. Leonard Maginnis. Or Lenny,' he winked, 'if you prefer.'

'Macken. Constable Macken.'

The publican nodded, as if in appreciation of some sage point. There were wet rings on the tables and fag ends smoking in ashtrays.

'Just tidying up,' said Maginnis, wiping a table. 'No rest for the wicked, eh?

'I could offer you a drink perhaps? By way of a welcome to Blackwatertown.'

Macken was not really listening. He frowned at the sounds of raised voices from out back. Just go home, he thought. I don't need more trouble this week.

'No?' Maginnis carried on, misinterpreting Macken's expression. 'Not now, of course, we're past time, I'm afraid. But tomorrow, surely?'

Macken drummed his fingers on the bar, distracted, hoping the noise outside would die down and whoever it was would go home. He felt wetness on his fingertips. Beer dregs on the bar. Macken sighed in annoyance and flicked the liquid from his fingers.

He nodded to Maginnis.

'Goodnight, and be sure to secure your doors, front and back.'

Macken heard the door close behind and the bolt drawn across. He trudged resignedly down the alleyway beside the bar. The shouting grew louder. Excitement, cursing, some kind of activity. They're either dancing, thought Macken, or...

He rounded the corner and saw a ragged ring of men, their broad backs blocking his view of what lay within. A small lamp over the pub's back door illuminated the alternately thrilled and pained expressions dancing over the faces of the spectators. It was clear to anyone who had ever spent time in a school playground that a battle was in progress.

Macken pushed his way through to the centre. Jesus, he thought, it's no sham fight they have going on. None of that 'Hold me back, hold me back' procrastination. One man was on his back in the dust. Macken saw he was a game wee fella, wiry, no weakling. But his flailing was making little headway against the heavy man sitting astride him, pinning him down and raining what should have been great, clobbering blows. Macken winced with the rest of the crowd, as another rock-like fist connected with the body below. It was puzzling. The wee guy should be pulverised by now, but the punches he was soaking up didn't seem to be having the expected impact.

'Had enough?' snarled the man on top.

'Never!' was the squeak from below.

Macken's sympathy was not automatically with the smaller man. He knew from bitter experience that skinny skelps were just as likely to start trouble. But no matter how this fight had started, his job was to stop it. He felt a hand on his shoulder.

Macken turned, prepared for trouble, but found only understanding.

'I know what you're thinking, Constable,' said the ruddy face under a hat squashed into the shape of a cabbage. 'But I wouldn't bother. Let them wear themselves out.'

The face seemed familiar. Macken nodded to acknowledge

the advice. Then he stepped into the ring and shouted: 'Police! Stop your fighting! That's an order!'

Neither combatant gave any sign of having heard him, nor that they would pay him the slightest attention if they had.

There was a hand again on Macken's shoulder. He saw Cabbage Hat shake his head. His sad expression suggested he knew that his advice would once again be ignored. Macken realised the well-intentioned slurring was coming from his new landlord, Trelford Dunlap.

'I know you want to help, Constable, but you'll be taking your life in your hands. Big Penny came in looking for trouble and the wee guy started goading him about his lost dog. They'll only turn on you if you get between them.'

Macken realised that there was no longer just one show in town. He had pushed his way into the limelight too. And there were only two roles the audience expected of him. The foolish blow-in, who receives a good hiding despite his uniform. Or, more likely, the coward who turns tail at the sight of real men slugging it out.

Macken knew that either fighter alone might be more than a match for him, never mind together. But it was a different fear that drove him to draw his polished ebony baton. Fear of humiliation.

The smaller man's nose flattened under a piledriver from above. Fist and face were washed in red. The arm drew back again. Macken raised his baton. It was fear again that gave strength to his arm – fear that he might prove inadequate to the challenge.

The hardwood struck the big man at the top of his punching arm. The result was instant. The arm spasmed. The big man screamed in agony, then sagged sideways like a stunned bull. Macken raised his baton again to deal with the smaller man, but saw he was beyond resistance.

Macken's tunnel vision had blocked out the spectators, but now they rushed back into focus, whistling in appreciation, laughing and clapping. Clapping him on the back too, so that he had to steady himself.

'You're some boy!'

'Yon pair bested. That's a sight I never thought I'd see.'

'Two in one, eh, two in one…'

Macken prodded the big man with his baton and ordered him to pick up his duelling partner. He cowered, trying to protect his injured arm, but then staggered fearfully to his feet and helped up his enemy of a moment before. The two leant into each other to prop each other up. Macken could see what looked like blood seeping through the sleeve of the big man's shirt. I hadn't realised I hit him so hard, thought Macken, as he shepherded the hapless pair to the barracks.


No one was asleep. The sounds of the disturbance had reached them, and they had been unenthusiastically preparing to investigate.

'Good Christ, Macken! What have you brought?' asked a shocked Bull. 'I told you not to drag in any drunks.'

Sergeant Gracey peered at the bloodied faces. The flush of the fight had drained out of them. They looked worn out and sorry for themselves. Gracey looked back at Macken in surprise.

'Not a mark on you, Jolly. Jesus, what did you do to them?' Gracey nodded towards Macken's baton case. 'Give 'em a taste of the timber, did you?'

'They did most of it themselves,' said Macken. 'But yer man would have killed the wee fella.'

Macken evaded further questioning by dragging his own weary carcass back to bed.

# Wednesday

# CHAPTER 16

Macken stepped out of the barracks. Last night's gladiators were long gone, slung out sobered up and shamefaced. News of the late-night dust-up had already galloped round the town and knocked other gossip into the ditch.

Macken realised he was attracting sidelong glances and some outright stares. He did not want to imagine the poison circulating behind the hands shielding the whispering mouths. A pair of wee boys put him at ease.

'Hey, mister?'

Macken looked down. Two faces looked up, cheeks shining in the mizzle, hair licked down into place. Mini men, in worn work clothes they would someday grow into.

'Is it true? You clobbered the both of them?'

Macken looked from one earnest face to the other. The whole street was waiting for the answer. He crouched down till his face was level with theirs.

'Boys, is it the business behind the Bridge Bar you're inquiring after?'

They nodded.

'Police business is a serious matter. Not for idle street-corner gossip.'

Their faces fell.

'However, seeing as how you look such responsible boys, working hard at school?'

They nodded again.

'Then I can tell you this. You'll do well to remember it.

'The law does not speak, but to command. And does not command, but to be obeyed.'

He gave them what he hoped was a significant look. He could tell they were thinking so hard it was almost hurting. Ach, stop teasing them, he thought. And added just loud enough for them to hear.

'Two in one, boys.' Macken winked. 'Two in one.'

They raced off, wide-eyed, frantic to share their news while it was hot.

There's nothing like the adulation of small boys and a secret mission to make a man feel like Alan Ladd, thought Macken. Strong, silent, self-contained.

'A man happy in his work,' said a warm voice. 'That's what I like to see. Though I'm surprised you let that pair of rascals slip through your fingers.'

Macken found himself face to face with the woman who had been in his thoughts every rare quiet moment. He realised from her smile that she was teasing him about the schoolboys.

'Struck dumb, are you? Would the hero of Blackwatertown like to join me under the arch? Or are you as impervious to raindrops as you are to bullets?'

Macken gazed at Aoife. The fun she was having with him shone in her face. She was a fizzing pot of delightful mischief, with magic sparkling in her eyes.

'Less of that hero nonsense,' smiled Macken. 'How are you? Where are you off to?'

'I find myself under interrogation,' said Aoife. 'Are you never off duty? Alright, after how you handled those eejits behind the bar, I suppose I'd better confess. I'm fine.' She paused. 'All the more for seeing you.'

He sensed her breasts rising and falling with every breath. Her lightness and freedom infected him.

'It's great to see you too. During those moments when I haven't been confused, scared or dead to the world, I've been wondering when I'd see you again.'

'Ah, that'll teach me not to get ideas above my station. He freely admits to not dreaming of me. What kind of a poor impression have I made at all?'

They laughed.

'Sorry about my Da,' said Aoife. 'The drink caught him more than usual. He was upset about our dog.'

Macken clapped a hand to his forehead. 'That was your father! I'm so sorry. I didn't realise. I think I hurt his arm.'

'Ah, don't mind that,' said Aoife quickly. 'Where are you off to, anyway?'

Macken tapped his nose conspiratorially: 'Ask no questions, I'll tell you no lies.'

Then he had an excellent idea. 'But I'm going for a drive, if you'd like to come?'

Aoife raised an eyebrow.

'Curiouser and curiouser. How can I resist being drawn into your web of intrigue?'

Macken begged for five minutes' grace to nip to the shop.

'Pick me up across the river so,' agreed Aoife. 'Past the chapel. We might avoid a few prying eyes. We can't have them thinking I've been arrested.'


Macken crossed to the shop with no idea what he wanted, but his conversation with Aoife had not gone unnoticed.

'No need to be a detective to know what's going on with you!'

'Mrs Williamson…'

'Lena!'

'Lena. Sorry, I was miles away.'

'Aye, well I suppose you were duty bound to follow up on the cheek she was giving you the other day. The authority of the law and all that.'

Macken opened his mouth to reply, but realised he was, once again, completely in the dark.

'My word! For a policeman, you're awful slow on the uptake. Though being a man could account for that.

'Was it a good ticking off you were giving young Aoife Penny, for that business with the bicycles?'

Macken felt warmth creeping up from under his collar.

'There's little escapes you, Mrs Williamson. Lena.'

'You're right there, Mr Macken. It's like that fillum *Rear Window*, with me sitting here watching the street go by. Everything and everyone passes here sometime or another.

'I saw it at the pictures in Armagh a wee while ago. I wouldn't have been as slow on the uptake as that James Stewart. Then again, he had Grace Kelly distracting him. They say she's lovely. She your type, Mr Macken?'

'I wouldn't really know, eh, Lena,' said Macken, puzzled at the turn in conversation.

'Ah, but sure blondes aren't your thing, are they Mr Macken?' said Lena. 'You'd have a preference for a fiery redhead, I'd guess.'

Macken stammered: 'I'm just getting to know the locals.'

'Is that right? Well, I don't have time to gossip about fillum stars all day. Or was it a purchase you came in for?'

Macken gave a weak grin. 'Something to eat on the road. I'm not really sure…'

He felt her beady eye weigh and measure him. Accurately, but not unkindly. 'I'll put together a few things, or you'll be all day trying to think for yourself.' She cut him a sideways look. 'You'll need enough for two. Big fella like yourself.'

The food and drink gathered and bagged, Macken paid for the provisions.

Lena removed her spectacles. 'That'll keep you soldiering on. Here's your change, and a wee warning too. I've a fondness for that Aoife Penny. She's a wee dote, with a spark in her too.

'But if you've an interest in her, or if she's set her hat at you, well, you'd want to have your eyes open before rushing into anything. That's all I'd say.'

Lena held his stare a moment longer, then perched her glasses back on her nose. Macken wasn't sure how to reply. He thanked her for the groceries and left the shop.


As soon as Macken picked Aoife up, and she leant in to him – protection from the wind, she said – he forgot Lena's cryptic warning. All was right with the world.

'Are we heading to Tycross?' asked Aoife. 'I didn't realise you were taking me across an international frontier. I'm not sure I'm ready for such a jet-setting lifestyle.'

Macken realised he had acted on impulse. He had not thought how to combine his mission with the unexpected company.

'I've to drop in on the way. Just briefly.'

'What a relief. For a moment I thought your idea of treating a girl was an afternoon in the Cross Bar. Though it's easily the equal of Paris or Monte Carlo, and much more convenient.'

'So you know Tycross well?'

Macken sensed her hesitate.

'My father sometimes drinks there – on farm business. It's not my cup of tea.

'But you still haven't said where you're taking me. It being such a lovely day and that being some manner of picnic in the back, I deduce that you have the open air in mind.'

Macken smiled.

'All in good time.'

But she already knew him too well.

'Just as I thought. You haven't thought that far ahead. But that's fine; I like a man who seizes the moment. Better than planning everything to extinction. And I might just have ideas of my own.'

She nestled back into him as they slowly zigzagged through a series of shallow trenches – a reminder from the B-Men that they were about to cross the border.


Aoife roused herself as Tycross church steeple came into view and asked to be dropped at the edge of the village.

'If I didn't know what a fervent churchgoer you are,' teased Macken, 'I'd think you didn't want to be seen with me.'

'It's not that. I could do with a wee walk to mull a few things over. Pick me up when you've finished your business.'

'You're awful sombre all of a sudden,' said Macken. 'You look like you're heading for confession.'

She brightened up.

'Why would I need confession? Sure we haven't done anything yet.'

And with a wink she was away.


Aoife's 'yet' sent Macken the rest of the way into Tycross and to the threshold of the Cross Bar without another thought. He opened the door and his shadow stretched across the floor to the counter. His nose wrinkled against the sour, stale trace of last night's porter slops. The sunlight over his shoulder picked out dust motes stirred up by his arrival. The room looked cool and dim and empty.

'Born in a field, were you?'

Macken realised a seated figure was considering his silhouette from behind the bar. He let the door swing closed behind him.

The figure lowered its newspaper and made an effort to appear more hospitable.

'That's better. I can see you now. Would I be right in thinking I'm welcoming a first-time visitor?'

Macken walked to the bar.

The fat man moved little and slowly, but his eyes betrayed a mind working to a quicker tempo.

'What can I get you? Or should I say – how can I help you?'

Macken considered.

'A glass of stout would do well on a day like today.'

'Nothing better,' agreed the fat man, as he turned away to lift a glass. 'And would there be anything else?'

His eyes met Macken's in the mirror behind the bar.

'I'm looking for Mr Greenard.'

The fat man nodded to himself, as if in confirmation. He held up the glass to examine it and then filled it.

'You've found him. But who might it be that's looking for him? And for what?'

Macken could not help looking round the room, to confirm that apart from them it really was empty.

'My name is Macken. An old friend of yours asked me to look you up. McReady.'

'Ah, yes, my old friend McReady. Mister McReady is that?' Greenard emphasised the 'Mister' and gave Macken a searching look.

'That's right. Mister McReady.'

Greenard nodded again. It seemed Macken was passing muster so far.

'So how is *Mister* McReady? And how can I be of assistance?'

'He's very well, thanks.'

Greenard waited.

'It's just that, lately, he's been a bit concerned. About recent events.'

'Has he now?'

'He thought you might be able to shed some light,' Macken paused. 'For old time's sake.'

The stout had settled. Suddenly angry, Greenard banged it down on the bar. 'You crowd never change. You want what you want and you don't give a damn about anybody else. McReady sends you waltzing in here...'

Macken went to speak.

'Don't interrupt me. I notice he didn't come himself. Too risky? But he's not bothered about the risk to me. Who are you anyway? Somebody dispensable?'

The jibe hit home.

'It's not like that. He sent me because I'm not known. Better for us both.'

The fat man settled back on his stool and some of the tension drained away.

'So what is it – exactly – that you want to know?'

'Who ambushed the patrol from Blackwatertown?'

This is true craziness now, thought Macken. I'm investigating something I know never happened. Or, to be strictly correct – it did happen and I already know who did it. Me.

'Don't go slinging accusations,' retorted Greenard. 'You're not in the Six Counties now. You're out of your territory and out of your depth.'

Macken put up his hands to placate him.

'We're not accusing you. Far from it. We know it wasn't you. I'm told it's been quiet here for ages.'

'Oh, is that right? You have an insight into the freedom struggle, do you? What makes you think that we weren't just biding our time till the right moment? If you know so much already, what business do you have with the Republican Movement in Tycross?'

Macken took a long drink. He tried again.

'Look, we don't want this happening. It stirs up all sorts of trouble. The B-Men have been mobilised. We can do without those head-the-balls digging up the roads. And if... *if* the IRA were not responsible, I imagine they wouldn't be too delighted about new boys muscling in. Sure where would that leave you? Am I right?'

'The Crown forces never need excuses to harass innocent Catholics,' growled Greenard. 'And as a proud Republican, I would never condemn anyone taking up arms to strike at the oppressor. No offence.'

'None taken,' said Macken, belching slightly, then taking another sip.

'Obviously, I have no personal connection with anything you might term as operational,' said Greenard, stretching out his arms to encompass the empty room. 'I'm just the humble proprietor of this hive of activity. From time to time gossip does reach my ears.

'But know this,' he grasped Macken's arm tightly. 'I'm no class of informer.'

The grip eased.

'But for an old friend in need... Well, I might keep an ear open. Especially if we're talking about cowboys upsetting the natural order. It's Óglaigh na hÉireann who are custodians of the national destiny, not some Johnny-come-latelies.'

'So? The ambush?'

'Well, early days, early days. McReady will have to give me a little time. Did he mention anything about appreciating the risk I'm running here? Not everyone would understand that this is just something between old friends.'

Macken slid over an envelope.

'We're in business then,' said Greenard. 'How will I get in touch? You can't hang round here. Much as I welcome the custom.'

The publican looked pointedly at Macken's glass. Macken put some coins on the counter. It's all business, he thought to himself. Then he had what he considered a brainwave. Maybe the undercover life was for him after all.

'Do you know the Pennys' farm?'

Greenard sat back, reassessing Macken.

'The big fella and his daughter? An interesting choice, Mr Macken.'

'Why's that?'

'Their land straddles the border, as you obviously already know.'

Macken hid his surprise.

'It should work for both of us then, Mr Greenard. Midday tomorrow suit you?'

'What reason will you give to be visiting the Pennys?'

'I thought the likes of me didn't need an excuse,' said Macken. 'But I'm sure one can be found if necessary.'

Greenard leant across the bar.

'You're a most uncommon example of your kind, Mr Macken. Conversation here is not normally what you'd call scintillating, so your visit has been an unexpected pleasure. I'd be giving you that drink on the house, if you hadn't already paid for it.'

He put his hand back on Macken's arm and spoke quickly and quietly.

'You should brace yourselves for more and soon. I'll know more tomorrow.'

The fat man reached for Macken's glass. It wasn't quite empty, but it was clear that Macken was being dismissed.

'There was something else.'

'Oh yes?' Greenard raised his eyebrows.

'I'll take two bottles of stout with me, if you have any that are cold.'

'I can't tell if you're on duty or not, Mr Macken. Maybe you find the line blurs sometimes?'

Macken put more money down and left.

The door banged closed. Greenard hid back behind his newspaper. After a moment he slipped off his stool from where he lorded it over his regulars and, insignificant-looking now, moved uncertainly around the room, passing a cloth over tabletops, touching chairs and ashtrays.


Macken was surprised it was still bright outside, though he had been only minutes in the bar. He forced himself to pause. Pretend you're taking in the sunshine. Stay calm. Move slowly. Above all, commit to memory what was just said in there.

He went over it quickly in his mind. Not much. Except for the warning. Hard to tell if there's any substance to Greenard or not. Still, McReady must know what he's doing. And I've managed to fix another meeting. Macken smiled at how he had set Aoife's farm as the rendezvous.

He felt the chill of the bottles and wished they were in a bag. It was as if everyone could see through him. Not that he was an RUC man on the wrong side of the border, but because his desire for Aoife was so strong it felt like a beacon.

She was sitting on the church gate, holding flowers, swinging her legs.

'You haven't forgotten me after all.' She tucked a long-stemmed daisy behind his ear.

'So where are we off to?'

'I was thinking somewhere quiet...'

'We both know just the place then, don't we? As long as it doesn't bring back embarrassing memories for you?'

Macken realised she meant the lake. He was grateful she was helping him take the lead, despite the shyness he felt and that she could so clearly detect.

For all his nervousness, he felt comfortable with her. As if he could trust her. It was as if she could see into him and already liked what she saw. There was no need for pretence.

'I've never met anyone like you,' he said. She smiled back as they set off north again.

# CHAPTER 17

Greenard's mind was working. Money had that effect on him. No need for anyone else to know about the cash, he thought. Money's money. The Cause is something else entirely. Best kept separate.

A tidy amount all the same. They must be very shaken up north, he thought.

But who was behind it? Not locals, that's for sure. We've not been active for ten years. Twenty, if he was honest. And Greenard was always honest. To himself.

The door behind the bar opened a crack. Greenard answered the unspoken question.

'He's gone.'

A tall, fit-looking, fair-haired man appeared from the back room.

'You heard?' asked Greenard.

The man nodded once. He considered Greenard and slowly tapped the surface of the bar with a finger. He radiated a calm confidence. It was only the eyes, hard, glistening, that hinted at the pent-up violence within. Eyes like guns, thought Greenard. He shivered. The silence was too much for him.

'Who do they think they are?' he blustered. 'Thinking they can just come in here…'

'Do you know him?' the other interrupted.

'Of course I don't. He's McReady's man. McReady sent him.'

'So they don't know either.' It was a thought said aloud, not a question. 'Peadar?'

'Yes, sir,' answered Greenard before he could stop himself, silently cursing his weakness in front of this so-called commandant sent up by Dublin.

'Are you McReady's man?'

'Dublin knows all about me and McReady. I use him, not the other way round. I use him!'

'It's an opportunity then,' the commandant continued. 'A chance to redeem yourself.'

Greenard shrank back into himself aghast.

'There are many like you, Peadar,' said the commandant with the air of a teacher explaining, yet again, a concept he considered perfectly obvious. A teacher with an underlying menace.

'We've grown soft. Docile. Fat.'

He paused. Then his gentle south-west accent, which could almost have been American, coiled round Greenard again.

'There are those who close their eyes to what's happening in our country. To what's being done to our abandoned countrymen in the Six Counties.

'What kind of man can live like that? Who could be so base?'

Greenard shook his head. 'Things have been on the slide all over, Peadar. Disappointing to see it so close to the border though. Harder to turn a blind eye to the Brits when they're just up the road.

'But still,' the eyes of the commandant drilled into him. 'Information is gold.'

He opened his jacket to reveal a revolver in a shoulder

holster. He tapped it and then made the shape of a gun with his hand, aiming at Greenard.

'You can't storm the castle without guns,' smiled the commandant. 'But the right intelligence lets us walk in the door. We've made a good start, thanks to you.'

Greenard clutched at the happier-sounding turn of conversation.

'What do you want me to do?'

'Nothing. Leave it to us. We'll make some noise on the border, then visit an old friend.' The commandant winked: 'And there's a man I'd be proud to take along.'

'Who's that?' frowned Greenard. 'They're not the brightest round here.'

'Ach now, no false modesty. You know rightly who I mean.'

Jaysus, thought Greenard, this bastard plans to get me shot.

'I'd be honoured,' stammered Greenard. 'But wouldn't I hold you back...'

The commandant spoke over him.

'You've raised a fine young man. You've not neglected your national duty there. He asked me himself and I'm pleased to take him on.'

'You mean Tom? Tomas? Sure he's never fired a gun. He's only a boy. Into sport and childish things.'

'Aye, but you can see the man he'll become. Good head on him. Fit. He may need time to get his shooting eye in, but he's got a strong arm for throwing grenades.'

The commandant laughed. 'The lads have given him a nickname. Tom Grenade. I've no doubt he'll live up to it.'

He clasped Greenard on the bicep. Greenard was not used to being manhandled. He was the one who usually dealt out the slaps and kicks. He felt his eyes welling up from the pain in his arm. Or maybe for his son.

All those years of talk about the struggle and the glory days. Jaysus, that's all it was. Just talk. It wasn't... I never...

The commandant seemed satisfied by his show of emotion.

'Stirring times. We're waking up again.'

Greenard could only nod as the commandant instructed him to tip off McReady about a raid on the arsenal at Armagh garrison planned for the next night.

'Are you sure? Wouldn't it be well protected?'

'It will be after you warn them.'

'But... you're not going to Armagh, are you?'

The commandant shrugged.

'Which will leave me in the shit with McReady. Passing dud information.'

'I think we can live with that,' said the commandant. 'Better than a bullet.'

Greenard got his bluster up again. 'That sort of insinuation is totally uncalled for.'

The commandant raised his palms. 'Calm down, comrade. I'm talking about the Northern police. You don't want them cooking up a warm welcome for myself and Tom, do you?

'McReady won't cut you off. He needs you. And it'll be thanks to your information that the attackers were forced to change their plans at the last minute. At least that's how I'd tell it afterwards, if I were you.'

'Alright. What about tonight's operation?'

The finger tapped the bar again. 'Give the credit to the cowboys who kicked this all off. They deserve it. It'll keep the peelers guessing. Sow confusion.'

'But I don't even know who they are. Is it definitely not us?'

'Dublin says not, and Dublin knows everything. Eh, Peadar?' The commandant winked again. 'Some of us have been pushing for this. Especially with the election in the North coming. We shouldn't be sitting on our hands letting them get away with it. The fellas in Dublin would debate till the cows come home. But those cowboys, whoever they are, tipped the balance.'

'Is it really starting?' Greenard suspended his usual cynicism for a moment. 'Are we ready? It's one thing hitting them. But once they're roused, they'll hit back.'

'Don't worry. We'll be light on our feet. They'll not see us coming.'

'But when they get riled they're not fussy who they take it out on,' persisted Greenard, displaying a rare concern for anyone other than himself. 'We could make things very hot for our own up there. When the B-Men start burning people out of their homes again, will we be able to stop them?'

He winced as the commandant slapped him on the arm he'd gripped before.

'We'll be ready. We *are* ready. The people are ready. Soloheadbeg. Right here. This is where the war started again. The genie is back out of the bottle.'

Left alone, Greenard deflated. I pity those poor bastards in Belfast, he thought; they'll be the first the Protestants turn on. And even if we drive the Brits from the border, what then? Will we be able to hold the ground? And we'll never take the whole North, even if we do give the peelers a hiding. There are just too many Protestants.

Still, he reflected, if they were open to charm or persuasion there'd be no border in the first place. And Lloyd George thought he had us beat in the Tan War, and we won that one, against the might of the British Empire. So why not? Who's to deny us the chance? At the very least we may push back the border and spare some poor unfortunates the prospect of another thirty years of Stormont rule.

Greenard filled a glass, as he warmed to his own internal rhetoric. Yes, he thought, there's no harm taking the war to the North. And no need to upset the applecart down here. '*Tiocfhaidh ár lá*,' he said aloud, and toasted himself.

'You've heard then, Da?'

Greenard coughed as his drink went down the wrong way.

'The commandant is taking me with him. *Tiocfhaidh ár lá.*'

'Aye, that's right, Son, our day... *your* day... will come.' Greenard nodded vigorously. 'But you wouldn't want to be a burden. The commandant is very kind to offer. But it's important business. It wouldn't be fair to put yourself before the cause.'

'Ah, Da...'

'Hear me out. You're still young. Plenty of time to do your bit. Ireland'll not be freed in a week. He'll be relieved he won't have to look after you.'

'But Da, what age was Kevin Barry? What age were you when you took the oath? You're always saying we need new blood.'

'But, Son,' Greenard smiled gently at his boy. 'They hanged Kevin Barry. We sing about him. But they still hanged him.

'I've brought you up to be proud of your history. But God gave us just the one son, and now there's just you and me. It's too soon for me to give you up to the commandant or the IRA or anybody else.'

The boy stepped back from his father's outstretched hand.

'You're not keeping me stuck here while the rest of them go into action. You've said it yourself often enough. Everyone has their part to play. The commandant thinks I'm old enough. This is my chance.'

'But, Son...'

'Sure it's only up the road.' The boy took his father's hand. 'You'll be proud of me.'

Greenard squeezed his son's hand back: 'I am, Son. I am already.'

Greenard sat in the gloom. He heard the cars starting out back. He tried to resurrect his optimistic defiance. Nothing came. This is where my years of bar room bollocks and posing as one of the secret army has got me. Seeing my son walking away with the wild men. With that mad, Yank-sounding commandant. Must be mad to believe that rubbish. Mad but not stupid, thought Greenard. He knows me, or knows the likes of me at least, and the temptation. But he has Tomas, so what can I do?

The front door banged open. The outside world crashed back into his consciousness.

'Ara Peader, how's the man?'

Greenard swivelled his ample backside on the stool to confront this latest intrusion. The man in wellingtons and dusty suit halted inside the door. 'Are you not open?'

Greenard realised he was staring wide-eyed at a regular.

'No, yes, come in,' gabbled Greenard. 'We're open. You startled me is all.'

He fell into the easy, inane patter of the publican nursing a reliable source of income. The clatter of coins reminded him of the envelope in his jacket. He would have to earn it now, which was irritating. Still, payment in advance was not to be sneezed at.

Greenard faked interest in his customers as he thought what to give McReady.

The RUC say it's a new organisation, thought Greenard. Dublin agrees. So who is it?

I wouldn't put it past yon commandant himself, he thought. Maybe that was what the slippery new peeler was fishing for.

Could the RUC have sniffed out our bold leader already? Greenard wondered. That's the problem with the struggle – it's always been bedevilled by informers.

The whole thing was hard to credit, he thought.

Except somebody did shoot up the patrol. No getting away from that. So if McReady wants a new group I'll give him one.

No betrayal in that, surely. No harm in passing information about an organisation that doesn't exist. In fact, thought Greenard, it appeals to my sense of creativity.

He smiled benevolently at the clutch of men across the bar sheltering from their responsibilities. I'll have to chuck in a few real names to keep things looking authentic, thought Greenard. Fair's fair.

# CHAPTER 18

Macken smiled nearly all the way to the Brookemartin estate until he remembered his first unsavoury encounter there.

'Are you not worried we might have extra company? I might not be ready for poachers next time. And His Lordship must have a bailiff.'

Aoife giggled. 'Is that how you prepare for battle then, my Celtic warrior? I suppose the sight of you naked would scare anybody off.'

'You're obviously fearless.'

They laughed some more.

'I'll call in on old Kenneth in the gate lodge,' she reassured him. 'He's the man you have to worry about. He's eighty if he's a day, but he knows the estate back to front. He doesn't mind me coming in for a bit of peace.'

As they approached the back entrance to the estate, they passed a huddle of men round two cars at the side of the road. Macken stopped just inside the gate.

'Do you mind walking on to the gate lodge yourself and I'll catch you up? I want to have a word with the boys we passed back there.'

'You're not deserting me, are you?'

'God, no. They just caught my eye.'

'Did they? That's why you're the great detective and I'm not.'

She walked on. Macken had stashed his tunic and cap in the boot, so as not to attract attention south of the border. He put them on and walked back to the parked cars. The men were intent on their discussion, but looked up as he crunched over the gravel. Macken noticed them all glance at a tall, fair man who was folding up a piece of paper – a map maybe – and tucking it inside his jacket. Was he the leader? Macken wondered. But it was a younger man, a boy really, who stepped into his path, smiling.

'Grand day, isn't it officer?'

A local accent anyway, thought Macken. Could be from either side of the border though. He kept his response just as friendly.

'Aye, surely. How are you all doing yourselves?'

'Oh, grand,' said the young man. 'And yourself?'

'Not so bad.'

Macken let the silence continue, to see what would emerge. They've been here a while, he thought, noticing a scattering of cigarette butts. Northern cars, or at least the licence plates were.

But they're tense, thought Macken. Strange to let a boy do the talking. And no one has spoken to fill the silence. Why would that be? he asked himself. Fear? Or discipline? Well, here goes…

'I was wondering to myself what you gents were doing parked by Lord Brookemartin's back door?'

'Is that where we are?' It seemed the first speaker had a monopoly on the group's speech. 'We just stopped to get our bearings.'

The boy gave what to Macken seemed like a forced laugh.

'You're not from round here then?' asked Macken, already knowing the answer. Because if they were, they'd have commented on him being a newcomer himself.

'No, not too far off track though. We're just on a day trip from Armagh.'

Macken remembered why he was there himself and hurried the conversation to an end.

'Well, lads, I'll ask you to hop back on-board and continue your tour, if you don't mind.'

A new voice intervened. With the flatter, harder tones of Belfast city. 'No law against it, is there? Have we not the same right to enjoy the countryside as anyone else?'

Facing the eight of them, Macken sensed he still held the power. Or that they were not yet willing to seize it from him.

But he just wanted them gone. He would not be able to relax if there was a prospect of them disturbing him and Aoife. He wanted rid of them and the rest of the world.

'You're as welcome to enjoy it as anyone else, but not to ruin it. I see you've been having a wee smoke. Maybe giving the car a bit of a spruce-up. I'll leave you now, but if I come back and find your rubbish, I'll prosecute you under the Litter Act.'

The Belfast man's eyes bulged, but he restrained himself when the blond man touched his arm. The official spokesman resumed his duties.

'Sorry about that, officer. Some people, eh? You can't take them anywhere. We'll clear up and be on our way.'

Macken graced them with a perfunctory smile. 'Enjoy your day.'

His grin became real as he walked away, hearing the Belfast man complaining that he hadn't come here to pick up after the effing peelers.

They were an odd bunch, he thought. Especially the way they held their tongues. Except for the fella from Belfast. He couldn't help himself, smirked Macken. Temper often gave people away. Still that nagging question though. Who were they? Too late to find out now. And what a fool, he thought. He'd even ordered them to clear up after themselves and remove any clues. At least he had the licence plates. That should be enough to find them if there was any vandalism or stupidity.

But all that fled his mind as he saw Aoife.

'Sorted them out, did you? Follow this track. I told old Kenneth I didn't want to be disturbed. Like one of those signs you get in a hotel. Or so I've heard.'


It was a perfect day, thought Macken. They lay in the sun looking out over the lake, a screen of reeds curving behind. It would be perfect in any weather, he thought. That's the effect Aoife has on me.

'I'm not sure whether I know everything about you, Macken, or hardly anything.'

'Does it matter?'

She shrugged, but happily.

'Well, that jacket you wear.'

'Is it in the way?'

He had already undone the top buttons.

'I don't know. Do you like being a policeman?'

'No. I don't like it.'

'Your jacket's definitely in the way then.'

He sat up and felt her breasts against his back as she helped his jacket off his shoulders.

'This is where I feel at home,' he said. 'Away from people. I get annoyed when people resent me because of the uniform. But I resent it the same when they like me because of it. I don't fit anywhere.'

He turned to her. 'I don't know why I'm telling you this. God knows, I've little enough reason to complain. Decent job. Roof over my head.'

Macken lay back. They were close enough for the hairs on their forearms to touch. He closed his eyes and felt the sun's warmth on his eyelids.

'It's a relief in a way, being a blow-in. Nobody knows me. No ties. It's a kind of freedom. I'm on my own.'

Aoife traced the line of his forearm, her fingers barely touching his skin. He felt the small hairs becoming erect, rising up on goose bumps despite the sun. He shivered. He knew something was happening.

'Sssh.' She kissed him on the forehead, her hair spilling over, shading his face. 'I know what you mean about not belonging.'

She kissed his eyelids. 'And you're not on your own.'

'Sssh.' She kissed him on the lips.


Afterwards, Macken felt righter than he'd ever felt.

'Is it magic? You transform the world whenever I see you.

'You know the way if you pull a face and the wind changes direction you're stuck with it? Can you make the wind change direction now so we can stay stuck like this?'

'I'll see what I can do,' she smiled.

'When you're here, time slows down,' said Macken. 'I feel everything. Every touch, every murmur you make – they stay with me, building up, until I feel everything from you all at once. I can't explain it.'

She gazed back, her eyes sometimes gently connecting with his, sometimes ranging over his face, drinking in his features as if to commit them to memory.

'For me, it's as if time speeds up. Back then, when we…'

She touched his face. 'When you hold me, I feel everything

start to race by. I want to grip you so tightly so you can't be swept away. It's as if this... this happiness is rushing by so fast it'll be used up and gone before we know it.'

Macken put his hand on her chest. 'It's your heart that's racing. I can feel it. You're too late anyway. I've already been swept away. By you.'

She put her hand over his and pressed it against herself.

'Another strange thing,' said Macken, after a while. 'I never want to tell people things. They're always asking, but I never want to tell them anything. But I want to tell you.'

'You don't have to.'

'But I want to. Why is that?'

'I don't know,' said Aoife. 'What do you want to tell me then?'

'Well, I am on my own.'

'Not married? That's a relief!'

'No, I'm not married. I meant other family.'

'I'm sorry.'

'I'm not doing this very well,' said Macken. 'My mother... Well, she passed on a long time ago.'

'Mine too.'

'I'm sorry. Here I am going on like no one else in the world has troubles but me.'

Aoife squeezed him. 'What happened?'

'She died when I was young. Something to do with having me,' said Macken. 'My father married again and had another family. He's gone now, and she's married again. I don't have much to do with them. It's not their fault. They used to look up to me – the second lot of children. Especially my wee brother.'

Macken looked away. Aoife stroked his back. He breathed slowly in and out.

'I never seemed to hit it off with my father's second wife. I felt she resented me. Maybe I was a reminder of her predecessor. A hard act to follow. After a while it was easier for me to go my own way.'

'So you never knew your mother?'

'I find it hard to even picture her.'

'I can tell she's in your heart though. She must have been beautiful to have a son like you. Your father must have been a big, handsome bloke too.'

'I don't know about that. He was also a policeman. So I haven't fallen far from the tree.'

'He must have been proud of you.'

'I'm not sure I knew him very well. Is that unusual? Fathers and sons? What about you and your father?'

'Oh, we know each other well. Too well.' Aoife paused. 'But I'd have thought you and your Da would have a lot in common with the job.'

'He was always busy. Hard working. I'm sure I'm the reason he married again so quickly. To have someone to bring me up.

'If you knew her, you'd say my stepmother was a good person, a good mother and kind enough to take on a widower with a child already. And that's all true.

'But my own memories are darker. She never took a shine to me. He wasn't around a lot. I ended up resenting him for it.'

Macken was comforted by her arms around him.

'To be honest, I probably never forgave the poor man for marrying again or for my mother dying. But what could he do? He did his best.'

'You can still go back,' said Aoife. 'Take your brother out for a pint. Never too late.'

'No,' Macken shook his head. 'I should have. I don't know why I didn't. I just knew I couldn't have a real family and I didn't want to give in to the grip of a substitute. But that wasn't fair on my brother. And now it really is too late.'

155

He shuddered, then pushed himself up on one elbow and turned to Aoife.

'There's my tale of woe.'

Aoife shook her head slowly, in mock disbelief.

'Isn't it amazing that you'd uncover your life like that...'

Macken shrugged. Aoife went on.

'...to someone who doesn't even know your first name?'

He grimaced. 'You're after my secret then?'

She raised her eyebrows. 'More secret than all that? You're not one of those boys named in honour of the Blessed Virgin, are you?'

Macken laughed. 'No, it's not Mary, thank God. My first name is John.'

'So...'

'And my middle name is Oliver. Though my Da used to call me Jack.'

'Jack Macken? Sounds very manly. What's wrong with that?'

'Nothing. It was only my Da used that though.'

Aoife considered the options.

'I like John better. It's softer. Everyone else can call you Jack. You can keep John just for me.'

She kissed him again.

'But why the big secret? Nothing wrong with Oliver. Unless your partner is Stanley?'

She put on a goofy expression and scratched the top of her head.

'Stan and Olly? Laurel and Hardy?'

'I get it,' said Macken. 'He acts like Laurel. But it's not that. And Olly works fine on both sides of the fence. Oliver Plunkett, martyr for the faith. That's who I got it from. The other Oliver... Cromwell. He's a bit trickier. The ones who approve of him massacring Catholics aren't so sure about him chopping off a king's head.'

Aoife wouldn't let it go. 'You're trying to divert me from the original question.'

'Guilty. It's more a nickname. If you run John and Oliver, Olly, together, you might come up with Jolly.

'You know, like a happy, laughing person. Jolly Macken.'

Macken shrugged, as if to indicate it was a matter of no importance.

'Maybe they thought it suited me back then.'

He felt Aoife's hands on his neck, pulling him down towards her.

'No wonder you look like such a crestfallen wee boy. It's enough to make the sunniest soul miserable.'

She held him to herself.

'There, there, don't worry. I'll stick with Macken in public.'

He snuggled in more comfortably.

'But when you think about it,' she went on, 'it could be a lot worse.

'They could call you Smiler. Or Laughing Chops. Or...' and she poked him playfully in the side as she listed alternatives.

Macken struggled free.

'You can talk, with a name nobody can spell!'

'You cheeky pup.'

They wrestled playfully, till their lips met again.

# CHAPTER 19

Unchanged on the outside, Macken was transformed in spirit. No longer the outsider consumed and viewed with suspicion. He had become swashbuckling, intrepid. Nature sang to him as he drove back into Blackwatertown. He had accomplished his confidential cross-border mission. And somehow, he had stepped across another far more significant border, into a life he had never imagined possible. His senses felt heightened and the world seemed more vivid. That was the effect of Aoife. He realised he was careening down a slope very near to losing control. But if he just let go, he felt he would not fall, but fly. The stooped, narrow lanes of his past had opened up into glorious light and space.

Aoife had wandered home across the fields. Hard to believe they'd first met only yesterday morning. He didn't mind that she was still wary of being seen with him in the village. Early days. Nothing could spoil his mood.

'The prodigal returns. Finally decided to grace us with your presence again, Jolly?'

'Aye, so you can slaughter the fatted calf... Bull.'

I'm over the threshold and they still cannot touch me,

thought Macken, pleased at his swift retort. He had also remembered not to trip on the doorstep.

'Or maybe your lady friend wasn't as hospitable as you expected?' Bull continued.

Macken's jaw set, but he allowed his momentum to carry him on to the private office. Bull was small fry, he thought.

District Inspector McReady was waiting. 'From what you tell me, Macken, we're not dealing with the IRA itself, but a completely new organisation. It's hard to see how such a large assault force could have been trained and armed without the likes of Greenard getting wind of it.

'Did you notice anything unusual? More Gardai or the Southern military even?'

'Nothing, sir. It's even sleepier there than here.'

'I wonder if there's more to this than meets the eye. You can never rule out desperate measures from the Free State government. But would they be that stupid?'

McReady thought for a moment. 'Some of what Greenard says will be true. But keep your wits about you. It's not a game. He and I go back a bit, but we're not friends. He's not your friend either, don't forget that.'

'No, sir.'

'They struck the first blow, but we hit back harder.' McReady sat back. 'You may have done enough for us to nip whatever this is in the bud before it turns into something serious. Good work.'

Macken went upstairs. If spying out non-existent subversives meant days like this – long may the illusion last. Maybe Gracey was right. No one was hurt, and it wasn't doing Macken any harm.


Macken's certainty that all was right with the world lasted until he almost collided with Cedric, who was just leaving their room. Cedric looked as if he had been caught in the act. And that in turn made Macken feel that his own inner thoughts had been exposed. He had an uneasy sense of being caught red-handed thinking that life was good, that he could be happy. Guilty of naivety or an odd disloyalty to the real, everyday world of pursed lips and calculation.

Cedric misinterpreted Macken's discomfort as silent accusation.

'No, you've got it wrong. I was just looking.'

Macken considered Cedric anew, and wondered what on earth he was talking about.

'Don't start accusing me. You were hoking around my stuff. Why can't I look at what you've got?'

'Like what?' asked Macken, hoping to hurry Cedric towards whatever point he was trying to make.

'Like nothing. Search me if you don't believe me.'

Macken opted for sarcasm instead.

'I'd search your head if I thought I'd find anything.'

But Cedric had not quite given up.

'So where is it? Your holy stuff?'

'This is a barracks, Cedric, not some sort of temple. Would you give my head peace?'

'Danny had one. A Roman Catholic holy picture. He didn't hide what he was. He wasn't ashamed of it.'

Macken waved him away. He didn't trust himself to speak. Guilt rolled over him in full force now. In his selfish joy, he'd forgotten about Danny.

Macken sank into his bed. He contemplated the only picture on the wall. A dull watercolour of a nondescript river nowhere in particular. Odd, he thought, that anyone would go to the effort, however slight, of trying to brighten up a police room.

Macken wondered what Cedric had been after. The room had little scope for concealment. It's like a monastic cell, but with worse conversation, he thought.

The picture was askew. Macken unhooked it to set it straight. He saw it had been covering an untidy gouge in the plaster. A bullet hole.

A chill crept through Macken's core. They said Danny had died in an accident with a gun. But no one had said exactly where. Suddenly, Cedric began to seem like someone more sinister than a trigger-happy buffoon.

Macken was not the sort of Catholic much given to rosaries and holy water. Given how rarely he attended Mass you might say he was not much of a Catholic at all. But he understood that, under tribal rules, he was as permanently labelled as anyone more fervent. So he had not been expecting a gushing welcome from his Protestant colleagues. That was normal.

However, this was getting out of hand. Though he may not have shared Danny's religious enthusiasm, they did have two significant things in common. Both Catholics. Both on the receiving end of bullets.

Of course, they'd missed him, conceded Macken. And Cedric opening fire had been an accident. A big difference.

Except that Danny had apparently been shot by accident too. So what is really going on here? thought Macken. Whose finger was on the trigger? And what was that note about? Am I being paranoid? Or am I next?

A shrill whistling from downstairs broke through Macken's deliberations. That's what I need, he decided, a wee cup of tea.

He clattered back down to where Sergeant Gracey was filling a large teapot.

'Finally, we have proof that you're a real policeman. The ability to sniff out tea the instant it's made.'

He held out the kettle: 'Stick this back on the stove for me.'

Macken reached for it, but Gracey jerked it back.

'Watch it! Get yourself a rag.'

Macken noticed Gracey had a cloth wrapped round the handle. He picked up one for himself.

'That's better. Don't want you to burn your fingers, do we?' said Gracey. 'Especially that trigger finger, eh? Never know when it'll come in handy round here.'

'Expecting more trouble?' asked Macken.

Gracey set a big mug in front of Macken and lifted up the sugar. He answered Macken's nod with one, two, three heaped spoons.

'Now then,' said Gracey, raising his mug in salute. 'The cup that warms.'

Gracey let the steam from the mug bathe his face. He looked up again, redder and shinier.

'Trouble? Hope not. The main risk to our sleep tonight is a farmer imagining things and firing off his shotgun at a shadow. Times like this, people get carried away.

'Before you know it, his wife has raised the alarm, the whole thing gets blown out of proportion. It wouldn't be the first time I've had a farmer trying to explain to me why we're both standing out in his yard in the rain for no good reason.'

'What do you tell him?' asked Macken.

'It can go either way. Some people try to blame you for their embarrassment. Poor, defenceless Protestants being left unprotected by RUC men tucked up in warm beds. Intruders long gone by the time you lot finally arrived.

'Usually though, they save their anger for the wife. We have a cup of tea, and he tells us what great lads we are. I tell him you can't be too careful these days. That's for the wife's benefit. Might save her from getting the back of his hand. I seldom leave empty-handed. Eggs, bacon, maybe a chicken.'

'That's generous,' Macken admitted.

'A wee present to stop the story of the eejit who shot up his own farmyard doing the rounds,' Gracey nodded. 'There's nothing they enjoy more round here than someone else's misfortune.'

Macken added: 'Especially if it's self-inflicted?'

'You're learning fast. Maybe you'll fit in here after all. The chorus goes up: "Oh, he brought it upon himself." Sure that's meat and drink round here.'

Macken drew himself up.

'What about Constable McMahon? Did he not fit in?'

Gracey's smile faded. The room temperature seemed to drop, despite the heat from the stove. Macken tried again.

'Some accident, wasn't it?'

'That's right,' said Gracey coolly. 'Some accident. A bad episode. But life goes on.'

'Cedric was poking round my room. Looking for Catholic things, he said. What's going on?'

Gracey held his gaze, then seemed to come to a decision.

'Don't mind Cedric. He's just curious. He was pals with McMahon. Probably saw him as an exotic creature. Though God knows why, he was just some Taig from the city. Sorry – a Roman Catholic from Belfast. Nothing special.'

Gracey took a sip.

'But to Cedric, he held an air of mystery, with his religious medals and his holy pictures and his rosary beads. Cedric was pretty shaken up when he died.'

Gracey shrugged again, signalling an end to his story. No you don't, thought Macken.

'What happened?'

'A round was discharged accidentally. Maybe he was cleaning his gun and hadn't made it safe.'

'Bit careless.'

'I wasn't there, Macken. No one really knows for sure.'

'It happened in his room, didn't it? My room. On my bed. I knew this job was dead man's shoes. I didn't realise I was sharing his sheets.'

'Did Cedric tell you?'

'Are you joking? Get sense out of Cedric? Get information out of anyone here?

'I found the strike mark. At least someone had the decency to cover it up. I'll sleep much easier with a wee picture the last thing I see before I close my eyes, rather than a bullet hole over my head.'

Bull breezed in, rubbing his hands.

'Mandear! Tea on the go and you haven't told me! What's the world coming to, eh?'

He poured himself a cup and turned to the other two. 'A wee heater, either of you? No? If there was a biscuit or two we'd be set rightly now, so we would.'

Bull looked at them both, hope not quite extinguished. Neither responded.

'No harm in asking. So, what's happening? You both hiding from work?'

Suddenly, the room felt too warm and too crowded for Macken. He put down his mug and opened the door. He felt Gracey's hand on his arm as he stepped out.

Shielded by the door, Gracey whispered.

'That's where McMahon had his Holy Roman picture hanging. Not appropriate in a police station. Jesus holding up a heart with a crown of thorns. The bullet went through it. Shot through the sacred heart.'

Macken walked away without looking back.

# CHAPTER 20

Macken stopped at the front door. He looked down at the doorstep. You've been waiting for me, he thought, haven't you?

Then he set off in what he hoped was that calm, rolling, reliable policeman's gait towards Lena's shop.

He saw the newspaper front page through the window. As usual, it was mostly advertisements. Dips for livestock – hoose, roundworm, tapeworm; cattle feed; new fashion at a ladies' boutique in Armagh; and, just what I need, thought Macken – Carnegie's course on How to Make Friends and Influence People.

The headline was about the election. Some local event in which he had no interest. A picture of a dog caught his eye. He gets my vote, thought Macken.

'That's some pup, eh?'

Macken looked up to see Lena, leaning in her doorway.

'Dogs in space. What'll they think of next?'

Macken looked again at the newspaper: the picture was of a Russian dog, which had indeed been blasted off in a rocket to orbit the planet. He shook his head in wonder.

'Do you ever feel, Mr Macken, that the world outside is

moving on and here we are stuck in Blackwatertown, stuck in the past?'

'Aye, it's hard to believe we're in the same world sometimes.'

'Och, I know. Blackwatertown? They should rename it Backwatertown.'

She laughed: 'I can say that because I'm a fixture. I know you'd be too polite.'

'It's odd to think,' said Macken, 'that yon dog will see more of the planet than either of us will ever do.'

They shared a moment of wistful contemplation.

'Still an' all,' said Lena, 'there's much to be said for the quiet life. Too much rushing around these days. People would be happier if they did their work, saw to their family and said their prayers. That's enough to be going on with for most people.'

Macken nodded along. 'And I can think of better people to blast into space than that dog,' he said, pointing to the election headline.

'Can't argue with that,' agreed Lena. 'Send *them* off to annoy the men on Mars. It's sad though. Poor wee dog. Going round up there all alone.'

'Sure he'll be the world's most famous dog when he gets back,' said Macken. 'Dog biscuits and treats for life.'

'Oh, no. One-way only for that poor craitur. They know how to send them up, but they haven't invented a way to get them back safely.'

'That's a shame,' said Macken, 'but I stick to my alternative suggestion even more then.'

They laughed. Then Macken heard a rattling from ground level.

'I know who that is,' muttered Lena.

Macken followed her gaze. A scrawny, brown and white mongrel was bothering a chain hanging loose below the shop window. The chain was there to secure a canvas cover that protected the boxes of vegetables on display during downpours. The dog was entertaining himself by pushing the chain with his snout and biting the links.

'Get the hell outta that, Cúchulainn!' shouted Lena, then muttered under her breath, 'What a name to give a dog.'

The dog looked at her calmly and trotted off. She harrumphed.

'Ah, Mr Macken, I'm bate. That's the difference between young pups and ourselves. They're full of energy. They always want to find out. Will it be the same the next time, or the next time? Bang, bang, bang. Poke, poke, poke. When you get to my age, you just want it to stop. To have a bit of peace.

'Though maybe you've still got some adventure in you? Not ready for pipe and slippers just yet?'

'We'll see,' answered Macken.


He tramped the streets of Blackwatertown, past small windows where lights were beginning to come on. From some homes, Doris Day on the wireless, sweet and clear, counselling 'Que Sera, Sera'. From others, fragments of family conversation trickled round doors left ajar. He detected the aromas of potatoes boiling and meat cooking.

The lives of others took on a rosy, cosy glow. Surely it wasn't so far out of reach for him too? Not now that he and Aoife could share the future?

Somehow he could not suppress the nagging fear that it was still as far away as the lonely dog on a one-way ticket into the unknown.


Gracey caught up with Macken at the bridge, staring into the black water, letting his mood darken with the evening.

'You know your trouble?' There was an undercurrent of

genuine sympathy in the older màn's voice. 'You think too much.'

Macken kept looking down.

'Sure I know life is shit,' Gracey went on. 'It's a bad joke. But there's fun to be had all the same.'

'If you say so.'

'I do say so, Macken. I do say so. Do you think everyone in those houses back there is slumped in front of their fires pondering on life's miseries? They're getting on with it. They're even enjoying it sometimes. There's satisfaction in working hard and raising a family.

'I'm sorry about what I said earlier, about the holy picture. We don't like talking about what happened before. But for God's sake, you can't go taking everything to heart all the time. Life's too short.'

He turned to look at Macken, forcing him to respond.

Macken nodded. 'Aye, sure.' His shoulders slumped.

'There you go. There's hope for you yet.' Gracey paused, and then continued with a note of mock innocence. 'Though, from what I hear, I don't know why you're so gloomy.'

'What are you on about?'

'Mandear, keep your hair on. It's only the gossip. And you know what they say about gossip.'

'What do they say?'

'That it's usually true. Or have I got that back to front?'

Gracey raised an eyebrow.

Macken scowled back. 'It's not official business. My private life is my own.'

'Hark at yon. Nothing's private here. All the same, I notice you didn't mind using official police transport for your so-called private business. Hmm?'

'I had orders from McReady. She was good cover.'

Macken realised he had said more than he had intended. He

also felt suddenly guilty, as if a cock had just crowed over his denial.

'Fair enough,' said Gracey, putting his hands up to placate him. 'She'd be an interesting proposition all the same. Not a match for just anyone. But for the right man... maybe.'

Macken's idea of himself as a free agent was fading. It seemed the world and his wife knew as much, if not more, about his life than he did himself.

'Still, it's good to get out and appreciate the evening. Get a break from the non-stop hurly-burly of Blackwatertown.'

Macken couldn't help smiling at that.

'Though I'm more of an early morning man myself, Jolly. Quiet, crisp air. More chance of catching the fish unawares.'

Macken recalled their first encounter. He took hold of the thought that, just maybe, there *were* things that only he knew. They did not have him entirely laid out and dissected just yet. He breathed deeply of the twilight. From sycamore and laburnum, willow and hawthorn bush, birds were calling out their evening chorus.

'Not much peace with yon racket,' said Macken.

Then came the low toll of the Angelus bell from the Catholic church beyond the river.

Gracey laughed at Macken's embarrassment. 'Didn't used to be so peaceful. This is the old border, not so far from the new one. Blackwatertown was the front line. There used to be a fort by the river. Only a few stones left now, but it was an important place once upon a time.'

'That must have been donkey's years ago. Not much sign of it now.'

'Ach, it was Spanish Armada days. The Irish over there, rebelling as usual. And us lot over here. They used to come over and burn down the fort. And the bridge. There were some big battles near where we are standing right now.'

'You make it sound like Hadrian's Wall,' said Macken.

'Well, the barbarians are still out there. No offence, Jolly.' He touched Macken's arm by way of apology.

'Strange we don't hear more about it,' said Macken. 'The powers that be are usually keen on that sort of history.'

'The result went the wrong way. The barbarians used to win some back then.'

'It happens,' said Macken, suppressing an unexpected sense of satisfaction. 'So how did all that glorious heritage end up like this?'

'You needn't sneer,' said Gracey. 'We can't all be like Belfast. Dear God, we wouldn't want to be.'

He leant on the parapet.

'There was more life here before the mill closed. And a fair bit of water traffic between Lough Neagh round through Monaghan into Lough Erne. The border and the railways killed it.'

'That's progress for you,' Macken chimed in. 'You should dredge up those old war stories. Put Blackwatertown back on the map. Day-trippers. There's a lot of business in anniversaries.'

Gracey responded sourly. 'I don't think we'd want to be remembered for that. And it might attract the wrong sort, if you know what I mean.

'Anyway,' he brightened up, 'isn't it enough to celebrate the Battle of the Boyne without harking back to every other bust-up since the year dot?

'And speaking of that particular triumph for liberty, I didn't come to admire the evening with you. I need you at the election meeting in the Orange Hall.'

'Would I be welcome?'

'Dear God, Jolly! You don't ask much, do you? Of course

you'll not be welcome. You were still a Papist the last time I looked.

'But they're dying for a look at the fella who helped fight off the IRA. And you've an even greater claim to fame that that.'

'You've lost me completely,' admitted Macken.

'I daresay there may also be a sneaking regard for the man who embarrassed that preening peacock of a vicar who has their wives won over.

'Though officially they're cross about the insult because you're a Fenian. So don't get carried away thinking it's going to be all cups of tea and how-do-you-do.'


The noticeboard announced that 'The Honourable Sir Basil Caitiff will address Brethren on Ulster's Peril' on the occasion of the impending parliamentary election. There was no real battle to be fought in this constituency. The official candidate for the ruling party would be elected comfortably, whoever he was. But as the previous member for the Stormont parliament was retiring, the voters wanted to see who they were getting. It was the one time he would have to make the effort to court them. Once installed, the Protestant majority meant the new man would be able to take re-election for granted for as long as he wanted the job.

'But isn't this the PM's patch?' asked Macken. 'He's not giving up the ghost just yet, is he?'

'The PM lives here, right enough, but his constituency is next door,' explained Gracey. 'His ancestral seat is only just over the line from his parliamentary seat, so the voters are happy enough just to let it...'

'Sit. Yes, I get it,' Macken stole Gracey's punchline. 'So where is he this evening?'

'He's probably excused himself on the grounds that it's a matter for the local party.'

'The local Orange Lodge, you mean?'

'Naturally,' confirmed Gracey. 'And because it would test anyone's patience sharing a stage with a buck eejit like Caitiff.'

According to Gracey, Sir Basil had only the most tenuous connection to the area – a small parcel of land, most likely bought specifically to establish said connection. But the party bosses saw him as a coming man, and Lord Brookemartin hadn't publicly demurred. That meant all Sir Basil had to do was to reassure the burghers of Blackwatertown that he would not give scandal and would vote the party line. Business as usual.

Macken took up position at the back of the hall, as Gracey glad-handed the suited and booted men inside. Aware of the florid faces blatantly sizing him up, as you would livestock, Macken mused that Loyal Orange Lodge No. 1641 was clearly no temperance outpost. The sergeant had explained that their role was to ensure order, but that there was little likelihood of bother. More importantly, Macken was to simply stand there, keep his trap shut and not offend anyone. He was there to be looked at. Ornamental.

'So what's your part in all this?' Macken had asked.

'I'm just curious to see if this new boyo is as awful as they say. We're policemen, remember? We're supposed to know what's going on.'

The hall was packed as Orangemen mingled round trestle tables laden with tea and platters of cakes and buns and sandwiches cut into triangles. All displayed on white paper doilies. Enough to feed a regiment, as Macken's father would say. The few women present were doing a fine job pressing sticky confections on feebly protesting men. Credit where credit's due, thought Macken, they put on a good spread.

'Brethren! Please be seated. Brethren, please.' The Grand Master of the Lodge harangued the Orangemen to their seats. 'And ladies,' he nodded graciously.

The brethren's dismay at leaving so much food uneaten was obvious. It was matched by furrows of concern on the women's faces that their menfolk should be so deprived. Macken could see they felt it was downright rude to leave any platter uncleared – especially when so very much had been prepared. However, for once, LOL No. 1641 had business to get through. Third helpings would have to wait.

They began with prayers. They were prayers unlike any Macken had heard before. They were simple, plain-spoken and seemed to be from the heart, before wandering off into a long, meandering discussion of neighbourhood happenings. There was none of the hypnotic Latin chanting with which Macken was familiar. No rhythm and hum, just a seemingly haphazard relay of hope and affirmation.

After the first few invocations of the Lord, Macken forgot it was any form of prayer at all. Only the occasional 'Lord God' or 'Lord Jesus', dropped into a statement about struggling livestock, moral lassitude or civic pride, reminded him that the conversation had any religious significance at all.

So it was a jolt when he realised that they had begun praying about him. Amidst the Lord Gods and Lord Jesuses a public discussion of his presence was underway. The cheek of it staggered him.

From one side would come: 'Dear God, take to your heart our brave police officers. May they continue to uphold your righteousness, and not stray from the true path.'

To be answered thus: 'Yes, Lord God, we commend to you

those officers who defend us, whoever they may be, whatever their background.'

From somewhere else, a coded rebuttal: 'Please Lord, keep your forces of law and order strong and pure. Help them resist those pernicious influences that would threaten Ulster, or corrupt our loyal deliberations.'

Hang on, thought Macken, that's me they're praying about.

Again, a voice of moderation: 'We welcome, dear Lord, all visitors with your hospitality. We know you have room for all who are willing to follow your path.'

Back and forth. Jesus, thought Macken, if you want me out the door just say so. No need to bring God into it. They must have finally agreed to differ, because they eventually moved on to pray about the new candidate, and some of the qualities God might be so kind to reveal in him, or provide if necessary. However, as far as Macken could see, Sir Basil already had everything he needed. He was a walking, talking, Protestant man. That is, he corrected himself, we'll find out about the talking shortly.


By the time the Honourable Sir Basil Caitiff rose to speak, Macken's stomach was protesting. Would it have killed them to have given him a plate of sandwiches? A saucer even? Gracey was impassive on the other side of the doorway, at ease. But Macken had seen him tuck in earlier while he worked the crowd. This had better be short and sweet, hoped Macken.

It turned out that Sir Basil certainly could talk. Throughout the prayers he had sat head bowed, eyes modestly down. Now he used his rich voice to fill the room. He began well by thanking them for their gracious hospitality – particularly the ladies, as he bowed in their direction.

'Now, brethren, ladies, good people of Blackwatertown,

citizens of Ulster,' he began to warm up. 'I use that term advisedly. Citizens of Ulster.

'We are all free people in a free Ulster. At this time of danger, we should never forget that our freedom was hard won and demands constant vigilance.

'What does that freedom mean? It means freedom from the dread grip of Rome. Freedom from the priest-ridden superstition south of the border not many miles from where we stand together tonight. It means freedom to raise and educate our families, to tend our farms and businesses in prosperity. Free from the suffocating backwardness of the so-called Free State of Dublin.

'You men of the border know well that we can never relax our guard against the insidious tentacles of Rome. I salute your steadfastness, especially those brethren in the B-Specials who give of their time to guard our children. I have a special thank you for one man here tonight. I understand that he's a modest, retiring sort. Like myself.'

He paused, to allow appreciative chuckles and a smattering of applause.

'Like myself, he's a modest man. So he won't thank me for drawing attention to his exemplary heroism. For putting himself in harm's way to defend Ulster. For personally thwarting the murderous IRA cowards who seek to slither under cover of darkness into the farms of decent Ulster men, women and children.

'Brethren, please show your sincere appreciation for Sergeant William Gracey.'

Gracey bowed his head to acknowledge the applause, his posture suggesting he felt he was far too humble to deserve such attention. Being so easily ignored made Macken feel all the more conspicuous. Gracey winked at him. By then, Sir Basil was wresting hold of his audience again.

'Brethren,' he bellowed. 'Such bravery reminds us what this election is about. The men who protect us do their good work quietly and without thought of reward. They do the right thing, because it *is* right.

'So should it be with the rest of us. We want prosperity and progress. And Ulster has always been in the forefront of both. At this time, however, we put such lofty aspirations to one side. More weighty matters prey on our minds. The threat of rebellion and sedition and dark forces once more focuses our thoughts.

'In this hall dedicated to liberty and free thinking, we remember how the Orange Order began. To defend Ulster Protestant values. We celebrate the victory of enlightenment over Romanism at Londonderry, Aughrim, Enniskillen and the Boyne.'

The orator paused to mop his brow and nod in agreement with himself. Macken saw the audience nodding along with the familiar litany of triumph and fear. His stomach growled, as if in disagreement. Shut up, stomach, thought Macken, or I'll have to arrest you for causing a riot.

'Orangemen have won these precious freedoms. We remember 1698. But we also recall the horrible events of the years before, when Irish hordes massacred Protestants in their beds, and drove women and children off bridges to drown.

'Even here, the rebel O'Neill destroyed the fort and very bridge over the Blackwater, and then wiped out the Queen's army in dastardly ambush.'

He's researched his local history, Macken realised.

'Dark days indeed. But as the Lord guided the Israelites through the desert, neither did He desert Ulster. Our God, which helped Saul destroy the Amalekites, was with us. Our God, which gave strength to David to smite the Philistines, was with us. We defeated our enemies with His help.'

And a bit of the Old Testament always goes down well with Orangemen, thought Macken.

'These past days remind us that the enemy is still there, stealing envious looks across the border at our proud, free land. And can anyone doubt that the enemy is among us too? Who can deny the existence of that fifth column in our midst?

'You may see them in the street and greet them with the good manners and dignity of an Ulsterman. But never forget that Home Rulers are a dark, subtle and dangerous race. They may act genial and friendly. We cannot tell from their faces at what moment they will choose to rise and wreak murderous havoc. What warning will there be before they try to possess themselves of your farm, and once again drive your children to perish on the hillside?

'Their poverty and duplicity are the deep stain of their Irish race and Romish creed.'

The temperature of the hall seemed to Macken to be rising as the speech became a tirade. You weren't fussy about my religion when I was defending your border, thought Macken bitterly – until he remembered the fakery of it all. That was the trouble with rousing words, he reflected, they pulled you away from reality.

As Sir Basil paused once again, there was an undercurrent of supportive muttering. Or were they just eager to polish off the remaining refreshments?

Was he finished? Macken saw the Worshipful Master trying to catch the orator's eye. But no, there was more to come. The speaker clearly felt there was still some small room for doubt about where his loyalties lay.

'Finally, fellow men of Ulster. We can never relax our vigilance. For if we do, Ulster is doomed.'

Macken suspected it was the word 'finally' that prompted the chorus of 'hear hears'. But Sir Basil took it as encouragement to more extreme plain speaking. He raised his voice above the hubbub.

'I speak to you frankly at this moment of peril. The Roman Catholic Irish in our midst are traitors. And have always *been* traitors to the government of Ulster.'

Sir Basil was fairly lashing his audience with his words now. Macken imagined they'd be feeling the shpits of him four rows back.

'When all we hold dear is at stake, one can say that the only good Roman Catholic is a dead Roman Catholic.'

There was a sudden silence. Macken felt a twisting pain in the pit of his stomach. The room seemed to recede. Blood rushed from his face.

One of the ladies at the trestle tables replaced the cup she had been holding onto its saucer. The chink of china was the switch that unleashed a wave of feet-drumming, clapping and cheering. Evidently, many in the audience were delighted to find that at least one of the posh politicians was not afraid to say things as they really were. However, to this din of approval was added the scrape of chairs and shouts of dissent.

'Simply outrageous! Uncalled for!' A cadaverous figure bellowed his disapproval, his cheeks the only two bright spots on his waxy features. A significant minority of the audience was rising and striding in disgust towards the exit, with others marching towards the stage. They in turn were enveloped by larger numbers of men standing up because everyone else was.

Macken looked at Gracey, who seemed unsure what to do. The Worshipful Master took Sir Basil's hand, both to shake it and to steer him away from the podium. The noise level rose as he tried to assert control over an increasingly ill-tempered gathering. Factions collided. Fingers wagged in purple faces. The mob simmered.

Macken saw Gracey's hand move to his baton. There was

no way the two of them could take on this crowd. Too big, thought Macken, and too Orange. The candidate was now at the centre of a tug of war at the foot of the stage. Macken saw fear on his face as solid, angry Orangemen surrounded and argued over him.

'Fuck,' said Gracey. 'This is about to be a riot.'

# CHAPTER 21

The new, young Queen gazed at Macken over the tumult from her portrait over the stage. Don't look at me, he thought, it's you they're loyal to.

Then it came to him. He gave a single shrill blast on his whistle. For a moment, everyone stopped and turned. Macken did not hesitate.

'Ladies and gentlemen, the Queen.'

He began to sing the national anthem. As loud and clear as he could manage.

Thankfully, before he got to 'Send her victorious', the Worshipful Master had overcome his surprise and joined in. Everyone was already standing. And out of respect, force of habit or relief at being offered an alternative to a punch-up, they all sang too.

Macken caught the Worshipful Master's eye and jerked his head towards the exit. He then looked at Gracey and together they walked towards the stage.

By the time the anthem ended, the Worshipful Master was at the podium thanking the ladies for their fine spread and the police for their attendance. Macken and Gracey reached Sir

Basil as the Worshipful Master was wishing the brethren a safe journey home.

'Could we escort you to your vehicle, sir?'

The Honourable Sir Basil Caitiff looked wan and shaken. 'Yes, yes, thank you Sergeant.'

Colour was returning to his cheeks. 'Dashed good thinking. Just the ticket to round off the evening.'

Macken could see Gracey chewing this over.

'Actually, sir, that was my colleague here.'

Sir Basil turned and gave Macken the full benefit of his political smile.

'Good man, good man. Quick thinking, Constable, eh?'

'Macken, sir,' said Macken.

'Macken, eh?' Sir Basil couldn't help frowning. The Worshipful Master joined them.

'Time we were going, gentlemen. Sir Basil and I are due at the Big House.'

The prime minister's country seat was known locally simply as the 'Big House'.

'Is Lord Brookemartin here, sir? I didn't spot him earlier,' said Macken, earning a stern look from the Worshipful Master, though the candidate pointedly ignored him. 'I only ask to be sure we get you all away together.'

'Oh yes, I see,' said the Worshipful Master, satisfied that no jibe had been intended. 'No, His Lordship felt it would be polite to let the coming man have the stage to himself. We're on our way now to avail ourselves of his hospitality.

'So if you'd be so good as to walk with us to the car. My friend here has woken the place up, and I wouldn't be surprised if some want to carry on the conversation. But that's for another day.'

The two dignitaries strode outside with a confidence they

did not feel, bolstered by a uniformed man in front and another behind.

A renewed but less intimidating ripple of applause met them. A few backslappers got past Macken and Gracey's outstretched arms, but the severest critics had gone or at least gone silent. Though Macken detected a new thread of anger, this time directed at him.

'Isn't that the Fenian?'

'What's Gracey doing bringing that Papist to the Orange Hall?'

Gracey indicated to Macken that they should escort the car as it navigated its way through the crowd and onto the lane. As the crowd thinned, the car picked up speed till the faint gleam of its rear lights disappeared round the corner of a hedge.

'Just keep walking,' said Gracey.

They continued towards Blackwatertown.

Macken broke the silence. 'The PM missed a treat tonight. Is Sir Basil the norm round here?'

'His Lordship was well shot of it,' replied Gracey. 'Happy to leave glad-handing the lower orders to someone else. And he might include Caitiff in that category. New money. No roots.'

'A blow-in?' asked Macken.

'A blow-in. Like yourself,' smirked Gracey. 'But the party chose him, so His Nibs in the Big House has to officially back him, even if he can't stand him.'

'So why's he having him over for tea?'

'Ach, he'll have yer man stuck in a big leather chair with a brandy, and he'll let rip at him about the state of the place, standards on the slide, no respect for tradition and position, going too soft on your lot. All that auld guff.

'It means he doesn't have to put an arm round him in public, but people can presume that it's all mates together behind closed doors.'

'The old guard doesn't have much to worry about if Caitiff is what's coming up,' said Macken. 'He doesn't *sound* like a fella about to go soft on my lot.'

'Never mind that business about the only good Fenian is a dead one. You know politicians. They say what they think you want to hear.'

'Some of them liked what they heard.'

'Half of them loved it, half of them didn't and the other half were half-asleep. Just because they don't like you, Jolly, it doesn't mean they want to see you dead,' said Gracey. 'Not all of them, anyway.'

'Thanks for setting my mind at rest.'

'Sir Basil was expecting a bloodthirsty crowd. He misjudged them, that's all. I've heard he's a bit liberal, if anything. He probably laid it on thick so he didn't look soft.'

Gracey barked a laugh. 'Having a Fenian come to the rescue will really upset him! No wonder he wasn't falling over himself to thank you!'

They carried on between the high hedges, with trees darker blotches against the darkening sky.

'Some others weren't happy to see me either,' said Macken.

'Aye, I heard.'

'So why bring me?'

'You saw yourself,' said Gracey. 'You can never tell when meetings like that will take a turn for the nasty. Especially when someone's determined to stir them up.'

'So why not bring someone more palatable?'

They flattened themselves against the ditch as a lorry rasped past. Macken hoped the driver would go slower past any Orangemen and women straggling behind them.

'I suppose you deserve an explanation. Especially after your stunt with the anthem.' Gracey shook his head. 'If you were worried about attracting attention, you've a funny way of keeping your head down. It was a clever move, but people don't like cleverness like that. Especially from a body like yourself.'

'From a Catholic, you mean?'

'It's the world we live in, Jolly. But that doesn't stop us having a poke at it every now and then.

'Sure I brought you mainly to annoy them. They're a sanctimonious bunch. Happy to prosper off the back of others doing their dirty work for them.

'But it's one thing me messing with them. Don't you try it. They might not see the funny side of a Papist lording it over them at an Orange gathering.'

Macken realised that Gracey was glaring at him intensely as they walked. He seemed gripped by some powerful emotion, like incipient rage. Macken tensed.

Suddenly the evening's peace was rent by a crack of laughter. Macken jumped.

'Still and all, it was a cracker!' Gracey adopted a pious tone. 'Ladies and gentlemen, the Queen.'

He bent forward laughing, hands on his thighs. 'You, Jolly, are one of a kind. Thank God, says the rest of us.'

'I'll take that as a compliment.'

'Do that. I doubt you'll get many more.'

The faint lights of the village were now visible. There was activity on the bridge.

'Joking apart, Jolly, try to be more Ruby Murray in future.'

'You want to hear more of my singing?'

'Definitely not. Your rendition of 'God Save the Queen' was bad enough. But next time you hear Ruby on the wireless singing 'Softly, Softly', listen and learn. Stop blundering about. You're ruffling feathers.'

As they approached the bridge, they were challenged by Bull, on sentry duty. Gracey turned to Macken instead of answering the challenge directly.

'Dear God, Jolly, it must be the Second Coming if Bull is so far from the kettle.'

'Ah, you're very smart,' blustered Bull. 'There's been more attacks while you've been out hobnobbing.'

'Where? What's happened?'

'Hit and run along the border. Ambushes. Customs posts.'

'What about round here?'

'There was reports of something out the back road. False alarm or long gone before our lot got there. The B-Men are out looking.'

'You're holding the fort then?'

'Aye, lucky me.'

Though they all knew it was preferable to searching bogs and woods in the dark.

Macken chipped in. 'Don't be too quick on the draw.' He pointed to Bull's rifle. 'There's a bunch of the Orange coming along behind us.'

'Right enough,' Bull agreed. Then he grinned. 'Don't worry, Jolly, I'll hold them off until you get to safety.'

Gracey laughed. 'You joke about these things, Bull, but...'

'Oh, I see. Went down well, did he?'

'Like you wouldn't believe.'

As they walked into the village, Gracey put a hand on Macken's shoulder.

'You know, it's terrible news about the attacks, Jolly. I didn't see you eating at the meeting. And now I don't know *when* you'll get to sit down for a bite.'

He barked out another laugh.

McReady was in the barracks. He told them he was coordinating with the reserve force, and that he had called out Lord Brookemartin's detachment from the Big House to cut off any IRA gangs trying to escape over the border. Armagh was handling operations further in.

'Information is patchy about the overall situation. At least two customs posts burnt down. There have also been explosions. A B-Special training post, some electricity pylons and a BBC transmitter apparently. So far, nothing to that extent locally.'

'Should we check the village perimeter, sir?' asked Gracey. 'Or perhaps take a run by the Orange Hall?'

'Constable Andrews is out the far end of the village. You'll have passed Bull on the bridge. Yes, why don't you drive by the hall. Just in case.'

The district inspector looked up.

'Oh yes, I'd forgotten. Go alright this evening? Sir Basil safely on his way?'

'Yes, sir, he's off to the Big House for drinks. There may still be people at the hall, clearing up.

'It was a big spread they laid on, wasn't it Constable?' said Gracey mischievously.

Macken muttered a 'Yes, sir' without glowering too obviously. But the DI had already moved on.

'I was just on the telephone to check His Lordship's B-Men had set off. But I couldn't get through.'

Macken contributed for the first time.

'Would that have been them in the truck that flew past us?'

'Now you mention it,' said Gracey, 'I think that was an estate vehicle. I'd say it was the stable man behind the wheel. I've had words with him before about his speed.'

'That's good to hear,' said McReady. 'Take a car. Check on the Orange Hall. You'd better both go.'

Some shapeless thought was squatting in Macken's head. It was connected to the night's events, but it was mixed up with everything else.

There's too much going on for me to hold inside this one head, he thought, as they crossed to the car. Whatever happened to the long stretches of boredom? he asked himself. The slow dull plodding to predictable confrontations and occasional bursts of violence, followed by a slow sink back into stolid inactivity. That's what life had been like. But this so-called backwater was hitting him with one thing after another, with not enough time to think through any of it.

'Wake up and get in.'

Gracey broke through his meditations and Macken swung himself up and in. They juddered under the arch and turned towards the river.

'Let's see if Bull has shot any straggling Orangemen,' said Gracey, opening the throttle.

The constant action at least stops me brooding, thought Macken. He would just have to accept that life was not all bad, and enjoy it. Gracey once again harangued Bull at the bridge before driving on. Macken smiled as he thought of Aoife and their time by the lake. What she is doing right now, he thought? And then: what would His Lordship say if he knew that the likes of them were using his grounds to meet in? The prime minister had publicly declared he would never have a Catholic about the house. Did that go for his forests and lakes too, Macken wondered?

Suddenly it dawned on him.

He slammed both hands on the dashboard.

'Stop the car!'

# CHAPTER 22

Gracey stood on the brakes. The engine stalled.

'Bloody hell, Jolly! What?'

'It's the house. It's the Big House.'

'What the fuck are you on about? I nearly drove into the river!'

'It's not the Orange Hall. There's no one there.'

'Exactly,' Gracey shot back. 'No point in trying to torch it with hordes of Orangemen milling about, is there?'

He put the car in neutral.

'No, wait,' Macken grabbed Gracey's arm. 'They're not going for the Orange Hall. Everywhere else, they've been hitting easy targets. Nothing like that here.'

'Well, let's keep it that way.'

Gracey turned the key in the ignition.

'I saw them,' said Macken.

'You what?'

'At least, I think I saw them. On the edge of the Brookemartin estate. That's why this area has been so quiet. They're planning to hit the Big House.'

Gracey spoke slowly and deliberately.

'You saw the IRA preparing to attack the prime minister and you didn't think to mention it till now?'

'I didn't realise at the time. They were parked by the side of the road. Just having a smoke. I sent them on their way.'

'Are you out of your mind?'

'We don't have time for this.'

'You're right there,' said Gracey, sticking the car into first.

'Look, do you want to hang around an empty Orange hall? Or go to where Lord Brookemartin, Prime Minister of Northern Ireland, is meeting the Honourable Sir Basil Caitiff, future Member of Parliament for West Armagh, in the company of the Worshipful Master of Blackwatertown Loyal Orange Lodge and stop an attack which could be happening right now!'

There was a knock on the driver's window.

Gracey and Macken both jumped. The car jumped too, and stalled again.

'Fuck me,' said Gracey, stamping his foot back on the clutch, too late.

Bull looked in: 'What are you two nancy boys doing blocking the road?

'Oh, did I disturb you?' he asked sarcastically. 'These cars can be a devil to drive, right enough. All those gears and levers…'

'Fuck's sake, Bull!' exclaimed Gracey, recovering from his surprise.

'Not had much luck with cars lately, have you?' smiled Bull slyly.

'I'll put your head through this windscreen, Bull! Creeping up like that.'

'Calm down,' said Bull, more sourly now. 'I was just checking you were alright.'

'Bull to the rescue?' scoffed Gracey. 'You'd run to your kettle the moment there was trouble.'

Bull waved dismissively and turned away.

Macken opened his door and stepped onto the road. 'Wait Bull, you have to come with us.'

'Jesus, Jolly! Catch a grip,' called Gracey.

'What do you want now?' asked Bull at the same time.

Macken looked Gracey in the eye. 'The B–Men from the Big House have been called away. We're guarding the barracks and the village. Or off on a wild goose chase to the Orange Hall. There's no one defending the PM.'

Gracey thought about it.

'We should call them on the telephone to warn them. And alert the inspector.'

'No time. Call him from the Big House. We have to go now. And we need Bull's rifle.'

'Hold on a minute,' said Bull. 'I'm not deserting my post.'

'And we need to go now,' said Macken. 'Right now.'

Gracey returned Macken's stare. 'Right, then,' he said quietly. Then he yelled at Bull. 'Get in and quit whining or I will personally run you over!'

Macken grabbed Bull and pushed him into the back, still protesting. Gracey accelerated away from the village.

'I hope you're right, Macken, or we're in big trouble,' Gracey muttered.

'No ifs or buts, you're done for now, Gracey,' piped up Bull from the back. 'Leaving the bridge open, taking me from my post.'

'Shut up, Bull,' Gracey snapped back, and then, more measured, to Macken: 'How many of them did you see?'

'Eight or nine. In two cars.'

'I'm only here under duress,' Bull hadn't given up. 'You've kidnapped me, so you have! This is all your cock-up, Gracey!'

'Shut up back there and listen,' Gracey yelled again. 'And

make sure you've got your weapon on safety, I don't want you shooting me if we hit a bump.'

Macken looked at Gracey and received the ghost of a smile in return.

'See any weapons?' asked Gracey.

'No, but they could have been in the cars.'

'Were they Free Staters?'

'One was from Belfast. Another from round here, I'd say. The rest held their tongues. Like they didn't want to speak. For fear it would give them away.'

'So what did you do with them?'

'There was something not right about them, but they weren't committing an offence. I made them pick up their litter and sent them on their way.'

'And they did that, did they? Picked up the rubbish for you,' Gracey was incredulous.

'Aye, and without much fuss. Harking back to it now, they seemed... disciplined.'

'You're some pup, alright. So we've nine disciplined men with guns waiting for us. I hope you're wrong, Jolly.'


Gracey stopped at the gates to the Brookemartin demesne and switched off the headlights. They listened. Macken could hear the creak of branches, but nothing out of place.

'Doesn't sound like a battle to me,' said Bull. 'D'ye reckon His Lordship will welcome us at this time of night?'

Gracey drove slowly through the great gates and past the lodge.

'No lights,' said Gracey.

'Are you surprised? The poor man is in his bed,' said Bull.

'With important guests staying?' asked Gracey. 'Though I

suppose they may have settled in for the night themselves too. Bloody hell, Jolly.'

'Switch the headlights on again,' said Macken. 'Full beam. The engine will give us away anyway. The lights might help scare them off. Keep your eyes open, Bull. You look right. I'll take this side.'

Neither saw anything but the rushing darkness. As they emerged from the tunnel of trees, their lights swept across a broad lawn and the façade of the mansion.

'Jolly, I'll drop you at the front. Take cover inside the porch. I'll drive round to the service entrance. Bull, you cover the back door while I go inside and see what's what.'

The car crackled over the gravel and crunched to a halt by a domed portico and steps to the grand front entrance. Macken ran up to the door, and began hammering on it.

The car, which had begun to move again, immediately lurched to a halt.

'Jolly, what the hell are you doing?' hissed Gracey.

'You go round the back if you want,' Macken answered over his shoulder. 'I'm going in the front door.'

'Good God,' murmured Bull. 'You can take him nowhere.'

Gracey swore as he realised that Macken had begun using the butt of his weapon to pound harder on the big wooden doors.

'What did I tell him about 'Softly, Softly'? C'mon, Bull. Let's get up there before he breaks a hole in it.'

Macken heard bolts shifting and stopped banging. The door opened just enough to reveal a worried face.

'Yes?'

'Police business. Is His Lordship in?' asked Macken, stepping forward as the door opened wider.

The man, some kind of servant Macken presumed, noticed his uniform and the other two policemen coming up the steps.

His body relaxed, and Macken noticed he had been holding an iron bar behind his back. A poker from the fire maybe. The fear left the butler's face, to be replaced by annoyance.

'Do you know what time it is? Are you trying to wake the dead with thon racket?'

Macken didn't answer. He was too distracted by the vast entrance hall. His gaze took in gilded furniture reflected in the polished marble floor, and a chandelier so elaborate it seemed to disprove gravity. Stern faces glared from glistening frames. A bewildered peasant stared open-mouthed and idiotic from a tall, gold-edged glass opposite him. Macken realised it was a mirror. He closed his mouth.

Through a doorway on the right came the smoke–scent blend of tobacco and turf. Macken saw wavering shadows on the inner wall and the reflected pink of a hearth. He heard a voice raised in exasperation.

An elderly man in formal dress strutted out to confront them. He appeared tightly wound, embarrassed at having to deal personally with the disruption. His head bobbed forward aggressively like a chicken.

'Mowers! Mowers, what's all this bother, man?'

'Very sorry, sir. It's the police.'

'The police? I see no officer here,' said Lord Brookemartin, waving his hand back and forward in front of him.

Gracey manoeuvred himself in front of Macken, who was suddenly unsure of himself.

'Sir, excuse me, sir. Your Lordship. Sergeant Gracey from Blackwatertown. We had reports of trouble, sir.'

'Yes, yes. Don't you have the basic good manners to use the correct entrance? Absolutely appalling. I'd be obliged if you would leave immediately.'

'Yes, sir... But, sir,' stammered Gracey.

'If you wish to continue this conversation, please pass a

message by the service entrance. Mowers will see to it that I am apprised of the necessary information. Now I must return to my guests.'

The three policemen stood at a loss, out of place and clumsy in their big coats, boots and hats. Their guns felt like crude clubs. The butler inclined his head towards the door. Gracey rubbed a hand across his face in defeat. 'Let's go,' he said quietly.

Macken saw Mowers wince as Bull too sighed and turned, scraping his hobnailed soles on the polished floor.

'No,' said Macken. 'It's not enough.'

He walked after Lord Brookemartin, beyond Gracey's grasping hand, to the internal door, which lay ajar.

He pushed it open and immediately his face was bathed in heat from the fireplace. The prime minister was at a delicate side table charging his glass from a broad-bottomed decanter with a long, slender neck.

'They gone, Mowers?'

'Your Lordship, I really must insist...'

'What the devil?' Lord Brookemartin swung round to face him.

'I say,' came a voice from one of the high-backed armchairs by the fire. 'It's that clever policeman I was telling you about.'

It was Sir Basil. Macken also saw the Worshipful Master stand up from where he had been sitting, slightly further from the glow of the flames.

'Hello again, Constable...' Sir Basil hesitated.

'Macken, sir.'

'Yes, yes, Macken. But what are you doing here?' intervened the Worshipful Master, at once moving in to smooth over any unpleasantness. He put a hand on Macken's shoulder, leaning as if to share a confidence.

'We're all fine here, as you can see. Why don't I get Mowers to sort you out with something warming? Just the ticket on a night like this, eh?'

To his fireside colleagues he added heartily, 'Very dedicated officers we have here. Very enthusiastic.'

Macken felt himself being ushered gently, inexorably, to the door. No, he thought, not before I have a chance to speak. I'm in deep enough trouble; I may as well carry on. Macken let the butt of his gun bang on the floor.

'Your Lordship,' he began, 'and Sir Basil. I have to tell you that a series of IRA attacks is underway. And with you being such prominent figures...'

'Yes, yes, Constable, we're already well aware,' interrupted the prime minister.

Then in an aside to Sir Basil: 'I think he means targets.'

Sir Basil harrumphed out some appreciative laughter.

'Yes, sir, but we've had reports of activity right here, sir.' In for a penny, thought Macken. 'Inside your grounds.'

'Reports? What reports? McReady said nothing about intruders.'

'Well, sir. Suspicions rather than reports. Some men were spotted.'

'Here?'

'Yes, sir. That is, on the road nearby, earlier today.'

'I see.' He turned to Sir Basil and shrugged as if to say: Ridiculous, isn't it, and it's what you'll have to put up with when you join the parliamentary club. Sir Basil reciprocated with a world-weary smile.

The prime minister turned back to Macken, to focus on finally dismissing him.

'We thank you for your concern, Constable. We're well protected by my own company of Specials, and of course, the stalwart men of the RUC, like yourself. For which we're most grateful.'

The PM finished with a gracious bow.

'But your Specials have been called away, sir.'

Lord Brookemartin's eyes flashed with anger.

'Quite right. At the request of your superior. Which should suggest to you that he feels the threat, if any, is more pronounced elsewhere. But I'll be sure to inform him of your... your dogmatic insistence on disturbing us, while ignoring the gunmen apparently marauding round the countryside.'

He went to the desk and lifted the telephone handset.

'Perhaps you might address yourself to catching those same gunmen. If you've no more pressing business?'

Macken lowered his gaze. No way out down there. Polished wooden tiles, the colour of caramel, in a herringbone pattern. The frayed edge of a rug from some far-off imperial outpost. Deep crimson. Like the colour seeping up his neck.

He looked up again and stared past the expectant men towards the large window. In daylight, the view would be of manicured lawn, giving way to wilder open space, then trees, from which a deer might emerge, blinking into the sunlight. Now, with darkness outside, Macken could see the room's inhabitants clearly reflected. The host and his guests with the fire's oranges, reds and yellows playing over them – his image dimmer, less distinct.

I've gone too far this time, he thought. Lord Brookemartin was trying and failing to get a connection on the telephone. That's probably McReady he's calling, thought Macken miserably.

'Good night, Constable,' said Sir Basil, raising his glass.

'Bally thing,' said the prime minister. 'Can't seem to get a connection.'

Suddenly the reflected figures exploded towards Macken.

Flashing glass filled the room like sparkling drops of water from a wet dog shaking itself dry.

Macken fell backwards behind a sideboard, shielded from the shards cutting through the air and slicing into chairs, cushions and a mounted stag's head. He lay winded for what seemed like an age, before he made sense of the sounds of shattering, smashing glass and gunfire from beyond the dark hole where the window had been. There was shouting. Cries of alarm. Confusion and pain.

*Sunk in darkness, he would press his tiny body against the rough planks, rubbing his skin over the grain, bobbing up and down, up and down, like the rest of them. Each time he stole a glimpse through the crack between the wooden boards. Up and down. Looking for a flicker of the yellow gleam she kept lit, over where there was warmth and softness.*

*He could not stop and stare. Stillness would be out of place, abnormal. In here, the only unmoving bodies were corpses.*

# Thursday

# CHAPTER 23

Macken scrambled to his hands and knees and fumbled for his gun. He heard a loud bang to his right. The door to the hallway swung open, knocking him sideways.

Christ, they're inside the house, thought Macken.

He raised his gun, but saw Gracey peer round the bottom of the door.

'Jolly! Are you alright?' Gracey did not wait for an answer. He shouted above the noise to anyone else still alive. 'Get down, get down!'

Gracey began firing through the spaces where the bay windows had been, moving his Sten gun in a narrow arc back and forth. Macken recoiled from the deafening rattle.

'C'mon, Jolly! Give them something to keep their heads down!'

Macken rested his gun on the padded leather arm of a chair. No need to aim, he thought, I can't see anything anyway. Just so long as I aim high enough to miss anyone inside. He began firing in short bursts. The wooden window frame uprights finally disintegrated, leaving one gaping hole into the night.

Macken saw the room's three original occupants on the floor. Lord Brookemartin was closest, and bleeding from the head. He was crawling towards the doorway in a jerking fashion, dragging one leg. Macken could not tell whether the prime minister was deranged or enraged, as he looked up and bellowed. 'Turn that bloody light out!'

The Worshipful Master was crouched beside Sir Basil Caitiff, who was holding his arm. Blood was seeping through his sleeve.

Macken and Gracey ceased firing. No one stood up to reach the light switch. The attackers outside began again, filling the air with bullets, smashing the lights, plunging them into the leaping shadows cast by the fire.

'Let's get out of here, Jolly. We're too exposed. Your Honours – can you move?'

Lord Brookemartin was already crawling through the doorway, cursing in a constant monotone. Macken heard him calling for Mowers the butler.

Macken looked at the other two men. The flickering shadows and firelight on their wide, frightened eyes and their pain gave the scene a hellish cast. The gunfire from outside seemed diminished, but glass and wood splinters were still falling like light snow. The pair seemed paralysed.

Here goes, thought Macken. He fired again towards the unseen attackers, and then ducked and walked in a low crouch to the men on the floor.

'He's hurt. He's been hit,' said the Worshipful Master. Sir Basil smiled in a fixed, manic way, but said nothing.

Brave bugger, thought Macken. More likely he's in shock.

'What about you?' asked Macken.

'Yes, I... I'm alright. But we can't move. They'll hit us.'

'We're sitting ducks here, we have to go. You'll be fine if you keep your heads down. Keep behind the furniture. They're not shooting so much now. They weren't expecting us to fire back.'

Macken fired blind over the back of a large leather sofa. He waited. The answering fire was less than before. He swore. It meant the attackers were moving elsewhere, closing in.

He grasped Sir Basil's jacket on what appeared to be his uninjured side.

'You push, I'll pull. Let's go.'

Macken led them over the debris to the back wall and behind the heavy sideboard he had used as cover before. He was conscious of Sir Basil's moans but did not acknowledge them or look back.

They made it through the doorway, and Gracey slammed shut the door. It was damaged but still intact. Macken saw Bull kneeling by a side window at the front of the entrance hall. He smashed the glass and let loose a burst into the darkness at the front of the house. Of Mowers and Lord Brookemartin, there was no sign.

'Where's the PM?'

Gracey shouted at Bull. 'That's enough. Save your ammunition.'

'Where's Lord Brookemartin?' Macken shook Gracey's shoulder.

'They've gone to the gunroom. What state are these two in?'

'He'll do,' answered Macken, nodding towards the Worshipful Master. 'He wasn't in the inner circle. They missed him completely. But His Nibs took one in the arm.'

'Bloody hell. We need to call for help.'

'I think the phones are cut. We couldn't get through before the shooting.'

The men looked at each other. They heard more bangs from outside.

'Who's guarding the back way, Gracey?'

A hoarse whisper came from a side corridor.

'Is the coast clear? Constable? Are you there?'

'Yes, sir,' Macken shouted back.

Lord Brookemartin and his butler appeared round the corner. The prime minister had a rifle in one hand and a shotgun in the other. The butler had two rifles under one arm, and a box of ammunition under the other. The master of the house seemed re-energised.

'Let's get these bastards! Sergeant, how are you for bullets?'

Gracey shook his head.

'Mowers, give him a rifle. Plenty of bullets in here for you. They're trying to get in the back. Let's lay on a welcome.'

The lord passed the butler his rifle and limped off clutching the shotgun. Macken could see his jacket pockets were bulging – presumably with cartridges.

'Are you alright, sir?' he called.

'Just old age,' he slapped his thigh. 'But I feel it loosening up by the minute.'

He looked like an ancient warrior with the glass fragments winking in his hair, and the dust and blood drying like ritual patterns on his face.

'I'd better…' said Gracey, handing Macken his almost empty Sten gun. He followed Lord Brookemartin and the butler.

Macken pressed the gun into the hands of the Worshipful Master.

'But, I can't…'

'You might have to. Just point and fire. Bull will keep you right.'

'Where are you going, Macken?'

'You watch the front. I'm going to have a look from upstairs.'

As Macken ran up the grand staircase to the dim upper floor, he heard firing from the back. And the boom of the shotgun.

He peeked cautiously over the bottom of a window overlooking the front lawn and driveway. No sign of anything or anyone. They're clever, thought Macken. This side faces the road and ultimately towards Blackwatertown. But they might have someone out there watching for the cavalry coming. Maybe to ambush them too.

He ran round the upper corridor, darting into bedrooms to peer outside. At last, he caught his first sight of trouble. The outbuildings were on fire. Macken saw a figure leading horses from the stables. He took aim through the glass. Then he saw the man release the horses and slap their flanks, waving his arms as they ran into the darkness.

Macken lowered his gun. Calm down, he told himself. It's an estate worker saving the horses, not stealing them. Just a lad by the looks of him. And a brave one, whoever he is.

As Macken watched, the shadowy figure stopped and stooped. When he stood up again, there was a glow in his hand which grew and then arced towards the stable.

'Jesus!' exclaimed Macken. 'He's torching it.'

He swung up his gun and fired through the windowpane, sending glass crashing outside and around his feet. When he stopped firing, the figure was gone. No, there he was on the ground, holding his leg.

Got him, thought Macken. He saw the figure point up at him. A bullet hummed past him. Macken heard the shot as he ducked too late. Then the figure was up and running awkwardly away from the firelight.

The gunfire from the back of the house was more sporadic now. Macken ran round and risked a look. There did not seem to be much incoming, though it sounded as though His Lordship was rattling through his own ammunition.

Macken ran back downstairs.

'How are we doing, gents?'

'We're fine,' answered the Worshipful Master. 'But this man needs a proper doctor.'

Sir Basil shook his head in disagreement. He showed Macken a brave fixed smile, as if to apologise for being so troublesome and useless.

'They're looking for you out the back,' Bull chipped in.

'Anything out front?'

'Nothing at all.'

'Right so, you carry on here, and I'll join the shooting party to the rear.'

Macken moved cautiously through the servants' corridors to the dark kitchen. The butler, Mowers, was sitting exhausted by the big kitchen table. His hand was on a rifle amidst empty cartridge cases. Spent ammunition lay scattered round his feet. He started up when Macken entered.

'Stay there,' said Macken, waving him back down. 'Where are the other two?'

'Just outside, sir. I think we've driven them off.'

Macken heard his name being called. He crouched by the kitchen back door and risked a look outside at waist height.

'There you are at last, man! Are you hurt?'

Macken stood up to face Lord Brookemartin, who was using a rifle as a subtle crutch, and waving a shotgun in his other hand.

'I'm fine, sir.'

'Then why are you creeping around?' boomed the prime minister. 'We have put them to flight!'

He seemed oblivious to the fires taking hold of the outbuildings around him. With the dirt and the sweat and the ecstasy smeared over his face, he looked like some ancient god renewed in the blood of battle.

Gracey joined them.

'Aye, they're gone or going. Hit and run. They wouldn't want to linger. Bad luck for them running into us, but they'd be expecting opposition to arrive fairly quickly regardless. Especially with the fires.'

They looked at the burning outbuildings, knowing there was nothing they could do to save them.

'At least the house is safe,' said Gracey.

'What happened back here?' asked Macken quietly.

'His Lordship was in full cry,' said Gracey, nodding over to where Lord Brookemartin was hopping round his rifle-crutch in a jerky dance of victory or released battle nerves. The destruction did not seem to bother him. Or perhaps he had not come down sufficiently from his war high to notice it yet.

'I don't know if we actually hit anyone,' continued Gracey. 'It was too dark to see.'

'I hit one. At least, I think I did. In the stable yard.' Macken exhaled loudly. 'The same boy nearly got me. He was some shot. I think I caught him in the leg. He'll not be making such a quick getaway as the rest of them.'

'He was firing the stable, was he?'

'Aye. I thought he was a stable boy at first, saving the horses. Until he chucked a bottle of petrol inside.'

'What about inside and out front?'

'All clear according to Bull.'

'Aye, all quiet on the Bull front as usual. He has a talent that man…'

'Sir Basil, though,' interrupted Macken. 'He needs medical attention.'

Gracey nodded to himself. 'We can't leave here yet. Mowers can take a car to Blackwatertown for help and a doctor. I'll send Bull out to check the outbuildings with you. You might be able to save something. Or find something.

'In the meantime, we should be able to find a drink somewhere in a house this size, until the cavalry comes. Or a cup of tea at least.'

'Won't you need the butler for that?'

'Ach, the Worshipful Master can do it. Orangemen drink tea by the bucket. He can surely *make* a pot for once.

'But, Jolly… Take it handy when you're looking round out here. In case they've left any nasty surprises.'


Macken stood alone in the half-darkness. He did not expect Bull to be eager to leave his secure position, so he wandered over to the stable while he waited for him.

The heat was terrific. Macken crouched and shielded his face. He saw a dark patch on the ground. It felt damp. So he *had* hit him. Which way had he run off? Macken squinted against the heat as he replayed it in his mind. He looked up at the Big House and saw reflections of the flames dancing round the jagged edge of the window where he'd been standing. A lucky shot maybe, shrugged Macken to himself. Lucky for me anyway.

He swivelled round on his haunches to face the corner of the yard where the shooter must have run. Or hobbled.

Macken paused at the corner of a shed. No movement, apart from the licking, cracking and spitting from the blaze behind him. Looking round the corner, he saw rakes, hoes and a long-handled brush strewn across the ground. He also noticed a scattering of small-calibre bullets. Suddenly feeling exposed, Macken dropped low.

He looked at the tools. The shooter must have run into them, stumbled and spilt the bullets.

No sign of a gun. Maybe he threw it aside further on when he realised he'd lost his ammunition. Macken walked slowly along the side of the shed. It was quieter here. And darker, Macken realised. His eyes had not quite adjusted to leaving the gleam of the flames. He could not see much ahead. There was no point going further.

He looked to his right. That was where the main group of attackers had been. His shooter would have been cut off from them once Gracey and the others had begun firing back so furiously. He would have had to work round through the trees to avoid being seen. And he'd have to move fast not to be left behind, thought Macken.

He listened out for Bull. No sign of him yet. No surprise either. Ah well, time to get back.

As he turned, Macken heard an exclamation from somewhere in the trees. He tensed. It sounded like a cry of pain. Or a curse, maybe.

Macken walked towards the sound, finally beginning to see more clearly in the dimness. A thin hedge bordered the lane. Someone had torn a man-sized gap in it.

He may not be far ahead, thought Macken. We could nab him now and get to the bottom of this whole thing. But how long will it take to drag Gracey and Bull away from the house? We could lose him.

Macken crept forward, looking for signs of passage ahead. More broken branches, scraps of clothing. But no sign of the fugitive. Just the trees and bushes and leaves and branches ready to hit him a clout if he didn't watch where he was going. Aye, and a bullet in the chest if I make enough racket, thought Macken.

Just stop and think…

He's not going to leave me a trail of shining pebbles. He's just trying to get away as quickly as he can, without bumping into every tree. He'll take the easy route. Or whichever way *looks* easier.

So all I have to do is take the path of least resistance too, thought Macken, skirting round a tangle of brambles in front of him, and stepping through the gap between two trees. If I just keep up a steady pace, I should gradually gain on him. He's bound to make some noise.

Unless he's behind that next big tree, waiting and listening for me to blunder past, so he can put a bullet in my head. Or the tree after that. Macken contemplated the forest ahead and swallowed with difficulty, his mouth suddenly gone dry.

# CHAPTER 24

The undergrowth quickly blocked out the sound and the flickering light from the fires at the Big House. It was an odd feeling, travelling into the dark wood in pursuit of a quarry who was, as yet, unseen. The journey began to be an end in itself.

Ducking under boughs at head height, climbing round the base of a tree, carefully pushing between bushes, feet skidding in the troughs between the roots reaching up through the earth. Tripping, but catching a tree limb that gave way under his weight, he listed badly but did not fall. The sharp end of a broken branch scraped his neck. Macken swallowed in surprise as a painful weal reddened across his throat.

He felt as though he had entered some endless, solitary game, the only point of which was to keep on. He sensed himself being lulled into a trance, as if moving under water. There was nothing solid to the touch, only yielding leaves or branches, soft soil and tree trunks mailed with shifting scales of ivy.

He could not see far ahead, or back. There was no sense of distance covered or destination. Only that he was moving over and through and round and ahead. Any sense of real danger faded. There was no sign of anyone ahead. Maybe no one *was* ahead. Maybe he had lost the trail long past or gone wrong from the start. His immediate mission was to protect his eyes from the branches in the dark. His enemy was the low bough that would jar his shin.

It was a dream world through which Macken began to feel he was fleeing, not chasing. That he was the one escaping the coarseness, the violence, the narrow alleys and suspicious glares. Swimming through a dark sea with no end in sight.

Wading through the black night, Macken wondered if this was where he really felt at peace. The long nights of loneliness as a boy, shut away from human warmth. Was that what he had wanted from the police – company? The cold-shouldered, sharp-elbowed, narrow-eyed security of barracks and uniform and us against them?

However, he could no longer deny that when it came time to close ranks, they also closed against him. There was no point in him blaming religion and prejudice, it was surely that they could sense the boxed-in little boy he had once been and perhaps still was. How long could he hide the hatred he felt for the prison of rules and restrictions and invisible lines that had grown up around him?

That was why he loved the fields and forests and the space of the world away from people. Especially wrapped up in the familiar darkness. A weight lifted off Macken and his lungs filled with the loamy air. He was glad to be out in the night. Dry and warm enough from his exertions. It reminded him of that other night. The night he had found the lake. The night Aoife found him.

Macken smiled as he saw a lessening of the dimness ahead. He was happy to be missing the commotion back at the Big House, to be out alone with his thoughts of Aoife. Aoife, who was strange and wonderful and would transform his life. Of that, he was certain.

He reached the edge of the forest and stepped out. It was all fields ahead now. Macken's heart was pounding. His fingers were tingling. He reached back till he felt rough bark against his hand, and let the tree take some of his weight.

The shooter was gone. Long gone. If he had ever been. But that wasn't important, thought Macken, looking around. If anything, Macken owed him thanks for leading him here, to this moment of respite, where he could throw open his arms and throw back his head and open his eyes to the vast night sky and the memory of her touch.

The bullet zipped past his ear. Macken crumpled and rolled onto his front. His nerves jangled. His ribs ached where he'd hit the ground. He was not sure which way he was facing. He was pumped full of pent-up energy ready to burst, but rooted to the spot, like the trigger of a gun still seeking a target.

He unclenched his jaw as his mind crashed back into the here and now. The shooter must have been waiting for him to make an easier target out in the open.

Where have I been? thought Macken. Away with the fairies.

He lay flat, cowering, waiting for the next shot. His fists locked round clutches of dock leaves that edged the field, green juice escaping between his squeezing fingers. Should he move? Or would that draw another shot?

Time passed. Nothing happened. Nothing other than the tips of the grass lightly pricking his face. Nothing except the single tear of sweat that ran down his cheek. Had the shooter moved on again? Or was he waiting to eliminate his pursuer once and for all, to shake himself free? The miniature world around him became more individuated as he focused on the plant fronds and soil inches from his face. Rabbit droppings like scattered shot.

Macken became conscious of how tense he was, every muscle poised for an explosive rush. Easy now, he told himself.

Don't panic. No rushing off and getting yourself plugged. He felt the faint tickle of an ant cross the back of his hand. He forced himself to unclench his fists. Had it been minutes or merely seconds he had being lying there?

Well, the chase was real alright. But it seemed turned around now. Macken was the one at bay. He remembered how close the shooter's first attempt had been. That was twice Macken had been lucky.

The second shot had missed him just as he had been filled with thoughts of Aoife, he realised. If it hadn't been for her he'd have a hole in his chest. His eyes widened. Yes! He could just lie here. The shooter had seen him fall. He'd think him dead. Just so long as he stayed still. The shooter would never risk coming back to check. I should just let him go, reasoned Macken.

His neck hurt. He slowly moved his fingers over his throat. He could feel where the point of the broken branch had drawn a line – raw but not bleeding. Macken hooked a finger under his collar to extract his Miraculous Medal. It would be a comfort to rub the small piece of metal between finger and thumb. Both medal and chain were gone. Ripped off in the wood and replaced by the shallow cut that was beginning to burn.

Back to the present then, sighed Macken. He knew there was another life on offer. One where he turned away from this dark pursuit. He had only to let go of his gun, turn towards Aoife and leave. The shooter had brought him here and given him this insight, and left him with his life.

Why squander the opportunity? he thought, as he squirmed sideways on his elbows and knees. Why stumble onwards to the slaughterhouse like a helpless bullock? Macken asked himself as he began zigzagging across the field.

Every now and then he paused, braced for the shot, listening for movement from ahead. He heard nothing but tree creak, owl hoot and accusations of cowardice in his head. He ran on to shut them out.

The pain in his chest became a clenched fist round his heart as Macken reached the far hedge. Then the ache gradually subsided, as the bullet did not come. He swept his eyes across the open ground beyond, catching sight of a dark figure fading ahead.

Macken felt the pull of his disappearing quarry take him through the hedge, loping across the next field, trailing along once more. Following rather than chasing. Macken was not trying to close the gap any more. Not out of fear, but out of uncertainty as to how it might end. He knew he had to keep in touch with the shooter, that it was important somehow. It was as if they were in some strange partnership. However, he couldn't picture himself standing over him, as the mystery man twitched and died. Nor did Macken feel now that a bullet would take his own life. The prospect did not seem relevant.

They traversed dark fields in curious pursuit. The shooter did not pause to look back. Maybe he had run out of ammunition.

Macken realised he was gradually catching up. He was used to being outside and keeping going. He recalled grimly his father dispatching him over the hills to do the rounds of their neighbours. Loaded with a bucket to collect blood and slops and waste to feed their own pigs at home. He had learnt then not to think of the splash and smell, nor the weight of the bucket, growing heavier and heavier, burning the small muscles in his arms and shoulders. He had learnt then not to think of anything beyond keeping moving forward.

Macken could tell that the man ahead was tiring. He was listing to one side. There was no doubt that Macken would overhaul him. He could be seen more clearly now. It was as if someone was drawing back the darkest velvet sheet from the sky, revealing imperceptibly lighter shades beyond.

They had been running for – how long? Not running any more. Walking. Slowing all the time. He knew the key was to keep a small part of his energy in reserve, ready for that decisive moment. In the meantime, just keep on. Don't squander energy on anger or fear.

Dawn was coming. Macken was not sure where they were, except that it was darker ahead. They were both fleeing the sun and chasing the night.

Except that there was now a light ahead, winking from a patch of deeper darkness. Which meant a house. And help. The shooter would have to go round it, surely. He would not risk a shotgun blast from a jittery farmer at this time of the morning. Unless it was his intended destination. Macken speeded up, as he saw the shooter's silhouette disappear.


*Hunched in the dark, it was almost impossible to believe in light. Too painful.*

*Yet he knew it existed. His memory was confused, but the intensity of the sensation had left an indelible impression. That feeling of being swept up and wrapped up, bathed and dabbed, cosseted and spoon-fed, immersed in warm glow and warm touch.*

*And if he pressed his face up against the wooden wall, an eye to the crack, he could detect the golden gleam – the beacon of that other world.*

*But each time it faded. Till all that remained was a lonely, keening melody. Whether it came from outside his head or within, he couldn't tell. Each lingering note carried to him on the breeze like a dandelion seed. He hoarded each one in his heart, hungry for more. Each one a thin thread linking his underworld to the light.*

*Then both light and sound were gone.*

*He treasured the memory, scared it would break his heart before the dark place smashed his body.*

# CHAPTER 25

As Macken crept forward, a clear, plaintive woman's voice carried across the air. It had an otherworldly quality – a banshee lamenting the disappointments of life. But there was gentleness in it too.

The song and the light and the hint of warmth came from an open window in the farmhouse. Suddenly, the shutters were slammed closed and the window shut behind them. He heard raised voices. Macken moved quietly round to the front door.

He knocked loudly, and then again, calling out that it was the police. He was acutely aware that he was announcing his position to the shooter. But there were people inside. They had to be his priority.

'Who is it?' came a woman's voice from inside. He could hear her fear.

'Police! Open up quickly.'

A pause and then: 'How do I know? Who are you?'

Macken swore under his breath. 'Either you open the door immediately or I shoot a hole in it!'

'No, no. Don't shoot! I'm opening the door.'

Macken stepped back to avoid being caught in the wedge of butter-yellow glow spilling into the yard. A frightened, wild-eyed woman stood half shielded by the door. She was in a nightdress, her hair falling in dishevelled curls over a shawl.

Macken was struck dumb. She was beautiful.

She was Aoife.

There was no answering recognition in her eyes. It was his gun she was opening the door to. No one saw far beyond the barrel of the gun when the RUC came calling, he realised. And who was he? Only a dirty, bedraggled, armed stranger in a uniform invading a peaceful home.

Her eyes narrowed. She peered closer. 'John?'

Then an involuntary twitch as she went to look over her shoulder, but caught herself.

'Come inside. Look at you. What are you doing here?'

Macken stepped in and closed the door, looking round the big kitchen.

'Is there anybody here?'

'No,' Aoife blurted out immediately. 'What is it? What's wrong?'

'I've been chasing a gunman. I followed him here.'

'What? What gunman?'

'Look,' said Macken, putting his hand on her arm. 'Don't worry. I'm here.'

She looked down at his hand. He became aware of how filthy he must be, noticing the dirt on his hand and on her sleeve where he was touching her.

'Sorry,' he said, withdrawing his hand. 'I've been through a few hedges.'

She shook her head, dismissing his worries, but too scared to speak.

'Aoife,' said Macken slowly, 'is he here? Have you let anyone else in?'

She shook her head again.

'Have you a telephone?'

'No,' her voice little more than a squeak.

Macken found it hard to focus. He was all thrown about inside, meeting her here like this. The sight of her. The warm smell. For once, he did not want to escape from inside enclosing walls. He did not want to leave her and stalk through the dim barns and byres.

But, what else was he to do?

Aoife was shaking. He wanted to reassure her she was safe. But he was not yet sure that she was. And he felt as though *he* had been the one to bring fear into her home, not his quarry.

There was a door ajar in an internal wall. Macken presumed there were stairs behind it. He was also becoming more and more convinced that there was someone hiding behind the door.

Aoife took a half step back as he raised his weapon, eyes widening again.

'Are you absolutely sure, Aoife?' asked Macken quietly. 'Certain sure you're alone?'

He was stone calm. Everything had changed. No doubt or scruple would impede him from stopping or killing anyone who threatened her life. He would extinguish them without hesitation.

'Wait! No,' she grabbed his arm, 'don't shoot!'

And then: 'Daddy!'

# CHAPTER 26

Macken stepped back with his gun still raised. Aoife hung onto him, incoherent and babbling. The door opened wider, revealing first a hand and then an arm.

'I'm coming out.'

A large man stepped forward, dark, unshaven and aggressive. He had a face on him that would look suspicious in his sleep. It was a face Macken had seen before.

'Come right out,' ordered Macken.

'I'm coming. Don't get jumpy. I've got a shotgun in my other hand.'

'Drop it,' barked Macken, bracing himself to open fire if he had to.

'Of course. I'm telling you so you don't get a surprise.'

The man stepped out fully and laid the firearm carefully on the floor. Unlike Aoife, he was dressed in day clothes. Trousers held up with baler twine, stuffed into muddy boots. Laces untied. An old, collarless, calico shirt. He looked worn out, one arm weakened somehow – but no sign of a leg wound.

Macken knew he wasn't the man he'd been chasing. He recognised him as the big fella he'd clobbered behind the pub and slung in the cell. Which also meant, Macken realised, that he was Aoife's father.

'It's me own gun. I'm allowed to have me own shotgun in me own house.'

'What were you doing hiding?'

'I was hiding behind the door of me own house with me own shotgun in the middle of the night because some gunman was threatening me and me daughter. That gunman being you.'

From the corner of his eye, Macken saw Aoife nodding frantically. He was not sure. It didn't feel right.

'Is that it? Any other surprises? Other family members you forgot to mention?'

Aoife immediately let go of him, as if scalded.

'Sure who would there be?' she pleaded, then turned her face away. 'It's just us.'

'Have a seat,' said Macken, nodding towards the table. He picked up the shotgun.

Aoife's father stuck out his chin, still defiant. Aoife looked more frightened than ever. She sat down beside her Daddy, and gripped the seat as if she wanted to crush it.

Macken ducked through the doorway, sweeping his gun back and forth. He stashed the shotgun behind the door, freeing a hand to climb the steps. He paused at the top. Nothing else for it, he thought, and stuck his head through the gap, glancing quickly around. A sparsely furnished space. Nobody hiding.

Nowhere *to* hide. A small bed. Just one. For a moment, a quiet scuttling sound. Macken froze. Then he crept along under the low roof. A faint scraping sound came from a box under a folded blanket. He relaxed. Kittens, he thought. Or chicks. Not what I'm looking for.

Back downstairs, Aoife and her father had not moved.

'Aye,' said Macken. 'It's clear. There's no one.'

Aoife slumped in her seat and covered her face. She was sobbing. Macken was stricken. Had he frightened her so badly?

Aoife's father looked distressed now too. He went to stand up, then looked at Macken as if for permission. Macken nodded and the man put his hand on his daughter's shoulder. She stiffened at once, and he took it away. He stayed close though, murmuring to her.

Macken watched them.

'I'm sorry.'

Aoife's father looked at him and then at the gun. Macken swallowed and lowered it.

'I'm sorry for scaring you. There was a man. I saw him come this way.'

'You're sure about that?' asked Aoife's father.

'Of course I'm sure,' said Macken sharply. 'Didn't he shoot at me on the way!'

'Ah well,' said the man, looking at Macken strangely, 'it must be true then. He didn't come here anyway. You've seen for yourself.'

'I came to warn you,' Macken faltered. 'When you were hiding, I thought it could be him. You know, holding a gun on the people living here.'

'Right, so. Fair enough,' said Aoife's father. 'No harm done.'

Macken was surprised his explanation was accepted so readily.

'I wasn't going to let anyone harm Aoife.'

A broad, beaming smile emerged from behind Aoife's hands and hair, as she gave another tiny squeak and rushed over to Macken, throwing her arms around him. Still sobbing a little.

'Ah now,' protested Macken, embarrassed. 'You'll get dirty.'

'Aoife,' her father spoke out, almost an order. 'You're

distracting the poor man. Put some water on the stove. He must be gasping.'

Then more softly. 'Go on now. He must be dead on his feet.'

She released him, still smiling.

'So you're the one I've been hearing about. I should be sticking my boot up your arse on your way out that door,' said Aoife's father, though his tone was not as hostile as the words. 'And not just for the way you came in. You're the fella who's been passing the time of day with my daughter, without so much as a how d'ye do to her father. Is that how they carry on where you come from?

'Where *do* you come from anyway?'

'Belfast, or thereabouts.'

'Aye, there you go. Big city, no manners.'

Macken stammered out another apology.

'Ah sure, don't worry, we've met now. You're Macken, then? I'm Patrick Penny. Paddy.'

'Yes, sir.'

They shook hands. Paddy Penny winced slightly.

'Sorry, caught my arm on a nail the other day. Still tender. But good to be properly introduced. So, you have an interest in my daughter?'

Macken was finding it hard to keep up with the pace of this conversation, and with how the balance of power seemed to have shifted.

'Ah, no need to answer,' said Penny. 'I think that's fairly obvious by now.'

Macken welcomed the warmer atmosphere, but he couldn't dispel a suspicion that there was calculation behind the bonhomie.

'I shouldn't tease him, should I, Aoife?' asked Penny. 'He must like you. Sure, wasn't he about to shoot me in front of you to prove it not two minutes ago?'

'Daddy! Stop it now.'

Aoife lifted a big sooty pot off the flame, and poured boiling water into a battered, black teapot, itself hardly smaller. She brought it to the table, set out some cups and bread and butter and invited them both to sit down. Macken wrapped both hands round his mug, and bent his head over to let the steam bathe his face.

'Thank you.'

He squeezed his eyes shut as he felt the heat. Aoife excused herself to get dressed.

'Sorry to disturb you this early, Mr Penny. Though I see you were already on the go.'

'Huh, there's no early or late when you've a farm to run. There's just work, and that's all there is.'

Macken maintained eye contact while trying not to suggest any doubt with his body language.

'But, you're right,' said Penny.

Aha, thought Macken, raising an eyebrow.

'I did hear something. I was on the settle.' The farmer nodded at a wooden bench against the wall, which could open out into a bed. 'So I got the gun. Usually the dog would scare anything away. But we lost him.'

Penny looked down. Macken remembered.

'Yes, I heard about your dog when we met earlier in the week, behind the Bridge Bar.'

'No need to mention that to Aoife, is there?' said Penny quietly. 'I was upset at the time.'

'No harm done,' said Macken. 'So did you see anybody tonight?'

'Not till you came kicking... knocking on our door.'

'So he could be hiding somewhere still?'

Penny shrugged, as Aoife returned – calmer now.

'What's he after doing?'

'There was an incident at Lord Brookemartin's...' began Macken.

'An incident?'

'You'll hear anyway, I suppose. The Big House was attacked.'

'Was anyone hurt?' asked Aoife.

'There was quite a bit of damage.'

'And Brookemartin?' Penny had difficulty cloaking his curiosity as concern.

'His Lordship is fine. The new fella though, Sir Basil Caitiff, he took a bullet.'

Aoife interrupted. 'Oh God, John! Are you alright? I couldn't bear it if you were shot.'

'Ah now. I'm fine. Thanks to this,' Macken raised his mug and smiled. 'And a sit down and a friendly face. The boy I was chasing had a wee go at me but...'

'Oh, no!'

'But, sure here I am. In one piece. Though I have the legs run off me.'

Penny wanted more detail.

'Sounds serious. Did you get any of them?'

'Ach, I don't know. I maybe winged the fella I was chasing.'

'Mandear, you've run all the way from the Big House.' Aoife put a hand on his arm. 'No wonder you're exhausted.'

'Aye, well,' Macken stood up. 'I'd best look for that boy outside.'

Aoife gasped.

'He's armed,' said Macken. 'You could still be in danger.'

Penny took over: 'Now Aoife, don't worry. And neither should you, Macken. Yer man is long gone.'

He drew back a curtain. Dawn had arrived. 'He'll be away over the border for sure.'

Penny could see Macken was unconvinced.

'Do you not know where you are?'

'Not exactly. I came by the scenic route.'

Penny beckoned Macken over to the window.

'See the hedge at the back of that field? You're in the Free State soon after. You missed him. Sorry, but there it is.'

Macken's shoulders slumped. He was dog-tired. His body was saying 'No' much louder than his mind was able to persuade it to keep going. He felt Aoife's eyes on him. She was smiling but her arms were crossed and he could tell she was still anxious. For all her independence and devil-may-care, she's only a wee girl inside, thought Macken.

'Here's what we'll do,' said Penny. 'I'll give you a ride back to Blackwatertown. You can meet up with your buddies and have a spruce-up and a rest.' He steered Macken towards the door. 'You're welcome to stay, but I know you have to make your report.'

They reached the door. Macken turned.

'Aoife…'

At once she was upon him for another tight embrace. This time he did not try to fend her off.

'Sorry about all this.'

'Would you shush. Go on, they'll have a search party out if you're not back soon.'

They laughed, though Macken realised she could be right.

'I'll see you…' he began and then paused. He never did know when they'd meet.

'When you least expect it,' she finished the sentence for him.

'And most want it,' he whispered.

She gave him another squeeze. An engine coughed into life outside. She kissed him, eyes moist, then released him, turning away as he walked outside.

Macken sucked in the fresh air. He saw trees, drumlins and

fields emerging from the early haze. Penny tapped a cigarette on the packet as Macken got in beside him.

'Beautiful spot,' said Macken.

Penny lit his cigarette. He drew deeply, held it and then exhaled, his eyes narrowing to slits. He answered in a tone of intense bitterness: 'Isn't it sick I am, day in, day out, lookin' at them bloody auld hills and ditches!'

Macken wasn't sure how to respond. The car bumped out of the yard and along a lane.

As they rolled along, his eyes gradually closed.

She'd been singing, remembered Macken, smiling to himself. Singing a lullaby. A beautiful song of peace and love and safety. He imagined she had been singing to him.

*Sometimes, during a lull in the squawking, twitching cacophony, the child remembered her voice. Low, gentle sweetness soothed him from the inside out, easing his clenched body and hooked claws. Far from the other claws that scratched and tore. Softly swaddled. Protected. Warmed and soothed.*

*But the memory brought only brief relief. He never heard how the song ended. Each time it was the same. She would lull him into drowsiness with the beautiful safety of her melody. No matter how hard he strove to prolong it, his eyes would close. When next they opened, he would be back here, adrift in the dusty darkness.*

# CHAPTER 27

Macken opened his eyes.

'The dead arose and appeared to many. This is your stop.'

Macken stumbled out of the car, rubbing sleep from his eyes.

'Here,' came a voice from behind him. 'You'll be wanting this too.'

His own sub-machine gun pointed towards him. Macken took hold of the barrel.

'Thank you. And for the ride.'

'Aye,' Penny nodded and drove off.


'Hey boy, where have you been?'

It was Cedric, straining to hold a heavy sandbag in both hands. Macken was not quite back in the land of the living, but he couldn't resist a jibe.

'Not good. Not good at all,' tut-tutted Macken, shaking his head.

'What do you mean? It's to fortify the barracks.'

'Aye,' said Macken, sucking air through his teeth in a hiss. 'But look at it.'

Cedric glanced down. In that instant, the sandbag slipped from his grasp and landed on his feet.

'Bet that hurt,' said Macken, nodding in mock sympathy. 'You should take care, Cedric. In inexperienced hands a sandbag can be deadly.'

Macken pursed his lips to avoid smiling and walked inside, taking care not to trip, leaving Cedric contemplating sand spilling over his feet.

Macken paused at the district inspector's door to assess how creased, dirty, wet and smelly he was. Then he shrugged and knocked.


'Where did you vanish off to, Macken? You look wretched. Are you alright?'

'Yes, sir. Sorry, sir.'

'Hold on,' McReady gestured at him to stop and picked up the receiver of the phone. He dialled, and then: 'McReady at Blackwatertown... That constable... Yes, he's turned up... Yes. Yes, I'd say so.'

McReady sat back. 'So?'

'I was pursuing one of the attackers, sir.'

'And?'

'And, well, he got away. After a long chase.'

McReady stared at him some more. Macken waited, swaying slightly.

'You're dead on your feet. Sit down before you fall down.'

Macken took him through the events. McReady sat up when he heard that Macken might have hit one of the attackers. Then there was the pursuit.

'Did you ever get a good look at him? No?'

McReady tapped a fast beat on the desk with one finger.

'So was it luck getting to the border or did he know his way? Unless it was the farm he wanted?' McReady pondered. 'Do you know Paddy Penny?'

'I'm acquainted with his daughter Aoife, sir.'

'Well let's stick to Paddy Penny for the moment. How did he react?'

'Very hostile at first. I had to disarm him. Just a shotgun. But he was within his rights, I suppose. He gave me a ride back once things calmed down.'

'Did he? Probably couldn't wait to get rid of you. He's no friend to the RUC.

'We were concerned about you, Macken. Disappearing like that. Sergeant Gracey said he ordered you to wait for Bull. Bull found no sign of you.'

'That's right, sir. I did wait, but I was worried we might lose our man. I'm sorry, sir.'

'Alright, Macken. You used your initiative. We'll leave it at that. Next time, let someone know. It causes people to be... anxious. And it's a distraction we don't need.

'And none of this talk about losing our man. You're our man, Macken, and we don't want to lose you. Teamwork, right?'

'Yes, sir.'

'As for Paddy Penny. He's your proverbial *bad* penny. Always turning up where he's not wanted. He hasn't been caught at anything much. But he's slippery. Always lurking round the edges of subversion. Watch out for him.'

'Actually, there was an incident at closing time at the Bridge Bar, sir.'

'Was that him? Well, there you are. His daughter...'

Macken stiffened. 'Yes, Constable, it *is* a small place. Regardless of her father, I have nothing against her. But as a constable, you must be careful about whom you associate with, and with whom *they* associate. It can look bad. And it can be bad.'

Macken nodded once.

'I hear she's a… a sparky girl.' McReady rubbed his stubble. 'But you're new here. You might want to get the lie of the land before you rush into anything.'

'I say that as a friend, not as your commanding officer. Watch out for yourself. And get some sleep. You have that meeting with Greenard this afternoon. Back at the Penny farm, didn't you say?'

'That's right, sir.'

McReady massaged his temple for a moment. Then he stood up. Macken followed suit and took the hand McReady had stretched towards him.

'Good to have you back, Macken. Well done.'


Macken took off his boots and uniform. He took out a stiff-bristled brush and began brushing the dried mud from his trousers. It dawned on him that his disappearance after the attack – and the gossip would be that it was *during* the attack – could appear cowardly. Or worse.

He started on his tunic. Not as bad as the trousers. Then his boots. Probably pointless, he thought, as they'll be mucked up again in no time, but he didn't want another episode of dirty boot disapproval.

He assessed his position after the night's excitement. His decision had been vindicated, thank goodness. But there had been no witness to his part in the battle. Nor had he any wounds. He could have made it all up. And to top it off, a cup of tea and a ride home courtesy of Bad Paddy Penny. What a mess, he thought.

And there's having to maintain the charade about the fake ambush, though that seems to be blurring into something real, he thought. It was all getting too confusing. Not to mention Danny's very real death. Could it have been just an accident?

I don't know whether I'm imagining things, he thought, or if I'm next.

Boots done. Uniform done. Macken stretched out on his bed.


He had always seemed destined for a police career, given the service of his father, and previous generations. But Macken remembered clearly the day it was set in his own mind.

It began with the sight of a crushed skull, the brains squeezed out and mixed with hair and blood like a dark sponge. A tram had run over a man at the terminus where the Catholic western wedge of the city narrowed to a point at the centre of Belfast. It had been shocking and gruesomely fascinating to witness, but Macken retrieved the memory with a detached calm.

That evening, there had been a telephone call to the house. The dead man had been identified by a letter in his jacket. He was from their hilltop townland, beyond the city's edge and bright lights. Because of Macken's father's job, because he was a person of note locally and simply because he had a telephone, it fell to him to break the news to the dead man's family. It was not an order, nor even a request. It was simply understood. He could have avoided it or postponed it – it was already late on a cold, wet night, for what was sure to be a cold, grim mission. But that was not something to even be considered.

It had never been explicitly laid out to Macken what drove his father. It wasn't duty. He'd bend the rules when he judged it right. It was a private moral code to which he held himself. The one rule appeared to be that he should do no less than he would hope another to do in the same circumstances. And yet Macken senior never really expected others to live up to the code he set himself. Maybe that accounted for the stoicism he invested in his hard graft, or his isolation from other people's drinking and forced cheer.

On that night, Macken had been able to connect with his father. 'I saw him, Daddy. I saw him lying there at Castle Street. The tram hit his head.'

Macken had asked to accompany his father, and was surprised and delighted to be allowed to do so. It was a sign, he later realised, of the weight of the errand on his father's shoulders.

The young Macken's motivation had been a confusing mix of curiosity, of wanting to see the story through to its conclusion, and of a desire for his father's company. He would not have been able to explain it, but somehow he also wanted to be there as a comfort to his father – that big, strong, mysterious man.

Up over the mountain, through the drizzle and wet grass they had gone. Along puddled tracks, ducking under trailing strands of bramble. They saw the prick of light in the window, still lit for the man who would never come home. When his father broke the terrible news, the woman of the house collapsed onto the lino. But there was no scream, no wailing. Macken had been stirred to his core by the way she raised herself to her hands and knees and then used the table to climb back upright.

The searing inadequacy of his father's patently sincere words of consolation was brutally exposed. Yet that was irrelevant. The woman grasped that it was only her own strength that would preserve her family now, and that despair was a luxury none of them could afford. The nobility of someone for whom there could be no comfort had moved Macken.

'Is there anyone to tell?' Macken's father asked.

She selected a boy from the confused, protective knot of children. He was grave and reluctant to leave his mother with these strangers who had hurt her so, who had broken down the powerful woman he had known all his life. Without fuss, however, the boy ran off into the darkness to break the news of his father's death to his uncle, the dead man's brother and the rest of the family. To gather living reinforcements against the thievery of death.

Then there had been the long, almost silent walk back to their own farm. As they crested the last rise, with the lights of home just visible, Macken had touched his father on the arm. He had felt his hand taken in a larger one, rough and gentle. And a murmur.

'That's the worst. May you never…'

The hillside was chilly, but in the clasp of hands was a warmth and a rare intimacy, conveying both vulnerability and gratitude.

Macken's stepmother had been waiting, flushed with anger and strain. What have we done? Macken had thought. But his anxiety had come second to his thrill at the spontaneity of the 'we' in his internal dialogue. He and his Dad. Together.

It turned out her anger was on her husband's behalf. There had been a mistake. The man they had thought was dead had been seen since, sitting out the rain in a bar down the hill. A constable had called in for a drink and gone pale at the sight of a dead man enjoying a pint. The policeman had had the self-control to merely order the man home immediately, without saying why. There had been no protest from the living dead man that he was not at all drunk. Only a nod and a weary inquiry about the weather. He had lent his brother his overcoat that morning, which was why he had been sheltering from the downpour.

Macken's stepmother looked at his father. 'They want you to tell them.'

For the first time in his life, Macken had felt he was truly seeing the sympathy between the two of them. Maybe he had been too caught up with his own hurt to notice what had always been there.

But he had also realised that he was back on the outside, as his father and stepmother communicated with each other, wordlessly. His father had used the telephone to get confirmation, to double-check that there was no chance of another mistake.

'Absolutely sure? Sure certain? No doubt at all this time? You're not going to tell me about some other brother an hour from now, are you?'

His father had explained that an envelope inside the borrowed coat had initially misled the police. The dead man had been with a friend when he died, but the friend had been in shock, and had been taken into a bar to calm down. By the time the true identity emerged, the wrong name had already been passed on.

Macken had fastened up his coat again. 'I'll come with you,' he had reassured his Daddy.

But this time his father had said no. This time he would go on his own. Back to where he had first brought the message of death. The death knock. He would be knocking there again, not to undo it nor turn back time. He would not be bringing good news. His destination was the same because that's where the real widow would be by now, comforting her sister-in-law over the loss of the husband who was now making his way home. Late, because he'd been sheltering, because he'd lent his brother his coat.

Macken had seen in his stepmother's gaze, in the whole way she held herself, a willingness to share, an effort to take some of the awful burden from her husband. He'd seemed to be shutting down inside as he'd closed his coat, his face grey, his expression raw. He had put a hand on Macken's shoulder and left without a word.

They had stayed like that for a while. She facing the closed door, as if looking through it over the dark, wet mountainside, watching the diminishing figure of her man toiling uphill. Macken sitting, watching, wondering what she'd do next.

Presently, she had become aware of him again. Macken had felt that, right there and then, she was looking at him anew. There was no dam bursting or embrace, but it felt as if a truce had been declared, as if each had decided they could accept the other.

She had brushed her fingers over the back of his hand.

'You're cold. Your Daddy was glad to have you with him before. But this time he had to go on his own.'

She had paused at the thought of what lay ahead for her husband.

'Let's get you warmed up and into bed.'

His father never spoke of the second death knock. All he would ever say was that it was just something that had to be done.

Macken knew that people could find his father hard to pin down. As a police officer, he would turn a blind eye to a spot of illegal distilling, but never touched spirits himself. Macken suspected that it was hard for his father to conceal his contempt for the weakness of alcoholic overindulgence. He was a strictly observant Catholic, but had never been heard to utter a dismissive word about other faiths. He could turn on the charm in large groups, but in unguarded moments his face betrayed his true belief that neither the world nor its people were sources of much joy. He was of the 'vale of tears' school of thought, reflected Macken. Life is hard work, and more hard work and then you die.

So Macken knew now what his father had known back then.

That news of life would not make up for the first death knock. That it would poison the outpouring of sympathy between sisters-in-law. That the new widow would feel a helpless, aching hatred in her heart for the woman whose husband was returning. That they would all turn their inchoate, despairing rage on the bleak-faced man who had twice torn apart their lives that night. That the messenger would have to accept the blame for their crumbling lives without demur.

Is that what makes us who we are, thought Macken? Are we each the sum of all we keep silent, locked up out of sight? Are we truly alive only as long as we can add to the concealed burden, without cracking?

Or is it only when we stumble and put out a hand to another, to let them share the weight, that we become fully alive?

Macken wondered too about part of the story that had never struck him before. The friend who had caused the confusion by leaving the scene of the accident. He had always presumed it to have been a workmate, but had never heard a name mentioned. He realised now that his father had never actually said it was a man at all.

Had it been a woman? Had she allowed herself to be led away not from shock, but fear of scandal? And knowing that her sorrow would have to remain secret. No wonder his father had kept him out of it when the mistake had come to light. It had been a bad business.


Macken's introspection drained him. He pulled over a blanket, closed his eyes and let thoughts of Aoife take over. He hadn't realised how vast the gap in his life had been, till she filled it. Now he knew he had been longing for someone to lift him up and take his life in hand. He wanted it so badly. And it couldn't be anyone but her.

Sleep crawled over him, but this time there were no soft lullabies, only a succession of corners beyond which Aoife disappeared each time before he reached her. Sometimes she would be rising from lake water, slick like a seal, wetness running over the bare skin of her shoulders, her arms, her breasts, clothing her nakedness in a shimmering phosphorescent glow. Tiny flickering lights in her eyes, like myriad fireflies, switching on and off. Then she'd bite her lip and look aside in shyness, the outlines of her body shimmering, as if the night's darkness was vibrating inside her. And he'd know that, whatever she asked of him, he'd agree to do.

But each time he got close enough to touch her pale skin, or to gently move a lustrous coil of auburn hair aside from her enigmatic smile, Macken found himself looking into the unfamiliar face of a lost young man. As they locked eyes, Macken would gradually become aware that it was the waxy face of Jesus looking back at him, reaching out with one hand, the other holding a grotesque, pulsating heart crowned with thorns with a large bloody hole through the centre. Each time Macken half woke. But exhaustion sank him back into the dream pursuit again, with the tap-tap-tapping of running feet. And waiting for him each time, the wide, wounded eyes of the young man who seemed to know him.

*Scuttling, always scuttling in the darkness. Heads darting down into the brittle crust of dust and dirt, shit and body parts, feather and scurf.*

*By day, the wire outside was visible. They strutted back and forth, but he remained inside – only emerging when she drew him out.*

*By night, the dimness around him became pitch. How long was it since she had last lifted him from the darkness?*

Tap-tap-tapping finally penetrated the fog of sleep. Macken jerked upright, shivering and frightened, his fist closed tight over his breastbone. He was alone. He looked up at the wall to check for the face in the dream. But in its place was the dull, dark river. He remembered that the portrait had been removed. And why.

Macken had always found it bizarre that the serenely pained face of Jesus hung over so many Catholic marital beds. Still, the prospect of having him catch them in the act didn't seem to put people off, given the size of their families.

The tap-tap-tapping continued. Outside his head. On the window.

He drew back the curtain, disturbing a blackbird pecking at the pane. It flew off, and Macken watched it soar over the main street and out of sight.

The window was jammed tight. The wood was swollen with old damp and he strained to lift the bottom half. It finally scraped upwards as if it had never been opened before.

Immediately, the fresh air slapped his chest and the scent of turf smoke curled into his nose. The street was busy. He heard his name called. The skreek of the window had alerted Gracey below.

'There you are, Macken,' the sergeant shouted up. 'You're exactly the man he wants. Come down quick.'

# CHAPTER 28

The crowd had grown by the time Macken reached the street.

'Would you look at yon sticking up Fenian hair? Been diving through hedges again?'

Macken ran a hand through his hair to flatten it.

'Lost cause, Jolly. But then that's you all over,' said Gracey. 'Just stick your cap on.'

'What's happening?'

'The Honourable Sir Basil Caitiff has specifically requested your presence. You and me both. And Bull, of all people.'

Gracey nodded towards the east end of the village, to where a horseman and retinue were approaching.

'Would you look at the bollocks on yon horse?'

Macken squinted.

'Looks more like a mare to me.'

'Y'eejit, I was talking about the rider.'

Macken slapped his forehead at being caught so easily.

'Oh aye, Macken, the crazy man is back.'

The horseman was decked out in a red frock coat, liberally sprinkled with buttons and braid. Macken also saw breeches, high boots, a sword and a pair of sashes – orange over one shoulder, white over the other. Smiling from beneath a broad-brimmed hat, which was itself perched on a tumbling mass of brown ringlets was – Macken craned forward to check – yes, the self-satisfied face of Sir Basil Caitiff.

Macken turned back towards Gracey, mouth agape.

'It's yer man alright,' explained Gracey. 'He's not John Wayne any more. He's King Billy this time. White horse. Curly wig. The works.'

Macken looked again and realised that only the orange sash was tribal. The white one was actually a sling, supporting Sir Basil's left forearm. His right was holding a sabre. The hand at the end of the injured arm rested on the reins.

Odd that he's wearing a sling, thought Macken, when he was hit high on the shoulder. The sling made it difficult for Sir Basil to properly direct the horse. But it was Constable Bull, walking alongside with a hand on the bridle, who was really in control.

The candidate smiled down at them. 'Glad you could join me, gentlemen. We're becoming quite the team, eh? I'm relaunching my campaign. Getting the tone right. Got off on the wrong foot before. So I'm particularly glad to have you with me, ah…'

'Macken, sir.'

'Yes, indeed. And we have to show those Fenians, don't we Gracey? They'll never keep a good son of Ulster down, eh?'

'Indeed so, sir. Indeed so.'

Macken and Gracey parted to let Bull lead King Billy on his white steed between them. Then they fell in at a safe distance behind, followed by what seemed like the entire population of Blackwatertown, and other parts besides. Macken shook his head in disbelief at the whole spectacle.

'Aye, it's not the same without a band, is it?' said Gracey, misunderstanding. 'I think his near-death experience has put ideas into his head. He's been having second thoughts about the whole "only good Fenian is a dead one" thing.'

'Really?'

'Sure why do you think you're here, you Fenian, ye? And maybe he wants an escort after last night.'

'You have to hand it to him,' said Macken. 'He doesn't give up. No sign of His Lordship again though.'

They chuckled. Just then, a passing bird unloaded a thick white smear down the back of Sir Basil's red frock coat. He twisted in the saddle, trying to see over his shoulder. He winced, in pain and annoyance.

'Good luck, sir,' said Macken. 'That's good luck.'

Sir Basil brightened. He waved his sword and cried: 'Good luck everyone! To the river!'

'You're the smoothest-talking bastard I've ever seen,' muttered Gracey.

Macken smiled back: 'Well, it is good luck. So they say.'

He wondered if it was the same bird which had woken him from his nightmares.


The triumphal procession swaggered to the bridge. Bull led horse and rider and many of the followers down to the grassy space by the river.

On quiet days, anglers and courting couples found havens here. Today it was thronged. Spectators hung over the edge of the bridge. Macken noticed more on the far side of the river.

He raised his eyebrows at Gracey. What now? A hubbub of excitement was building. The spectators didn't know or really care what was going to happen next. It's like when a dog slips into a school playground. The teacher can't stop the children from pressing their noses to the windows to watch it leap and pant and run around. Most people were just enjoying the diversion. Even Lena Williamson had been lured from her shop to cast a sceptical eye over proceedings.

Gracey sent Macken onto the bridge in case of traffic. He was happy to oblige, having spotted Aoife in the crowd. She gave him a small, quick wave, instantly wiping all worries from his mind.

Macken watched Bull lead Sir Basil onto the slipway at the water's edge. The horse stepped forward cautiously on the damp stones. Well, this beats everything, thought Macken; the crazy man looks as if he intends to go into the river. It was at this point that the limitations of relying on Bull became apparent.

The policeman did not want to get his feet wet. Fair enough, thought Macken, he's not high and dry on a big horse. But this meant surrendering control of the nervous animal to its rider. Sir Basil hesitated, then took hold of the reins with the hand of his injured arm. He nudged the horse's flanks till it stepped into the gently flowing water.

There was a murmur of appreciation. Encouraged that he had their attention again, Sir Basil raised his sabre and struck what he hoped was a regal pose. The tip of the blade disappeared amongst the hanging foliage of a great willow arching over the water from the far bank. There was a ripple of applause.

The horse took a few small quick steps, searching for firm footing. Sir Basil lowered his sword and gripped the reins till his mount settled. Then he began:

'Good people of Blackwatertown. We celebrate King William crossing the Boyne to defeat tyranny, to defend the crown and to confound the machinations of popery. We thank him for our liberty today, hard won and jealously guarded.'

He paused for applause, but his audience was too distracted by the prospect of the born-again King Billy slipping off his perch. Macken caught a whisper of odds being offered. He hoped his uniform and stony expression would deter any attempt from the bridge to hasten such an outcome. Sir Basil was blissfully oblivious and in full modest martyr mode.

'This river is a symbol of the line the men of Ulster have held against the foreign invader. I too vow that I will be ever vigilant in defending your interests.

'I wear the Orange sash of liberty. But I am also proud to wear this white sling, evidence of the small injury I sustained this very week at the hands of Fenian assassins. They failed in their cowardly purpose, as they shall always fail as long as good men hold the line against them.'

He bowed his head, seemingly overcome at the emotion of the occasion. Some people had the good grace to clap this time. He's not bad, thought Macken, not bad at all.

'So far I have spoken in rousing terms, as befits this time of peril. Some may find my words too strong. Some of you felt I spoke too frankly, when I was a guest of Blackwatertown Loyal Orange Lodge.

'If I caused offence, I offer sincere apology. I am neither orator nor public speaker. I speak only from the heart.

'But I will add this. Just as King William crossed the Boyne to preserve liberty for all, so do I cross the Blackwater as a symbol of my vow to speak up for every honest loyal subject of our Queen, regardless of where they worship.'

There was no applause for this unexpected promise, but Macken noticed approving nods from a group of older men. They'd been amongst the senior brethren who had stormed out of last night's meeting.

Right so, thought Macken, he's shown he won't embarrass them and can take orders. Thank goodness it's all going quietly, he yawned. Macken had had enough excitement for one day. He looked around to see how best he could bump into Aoife when the theatricals ended. She was watching the horseman. She has a way of doing things, thought Macken, of simply being, that draws your eye. She has no idea of the effect she has on people. Of the effect she has on me.

He drank her in, the way she stood, easy in her own skin. The way she moved, more gracefully, more perfectly than anyone else could ever move. Then, without taking her eyes from the river, she stooped, reaching down to scratch the neck of a scrawny brown and white dog that had sidled up to her through the forest of legs. Ah, it's the wee pest again, smiled Macken to himself. He felt a momentary tightness in his chest as he contemplated the beautiful fluidity of Aoife's movement. Is this what love feels like, he asked himself?

A whinny prompted him to tune back in to the speech. The horse looked uncomfortable in the current. Sir Basil was winding up with a loyal toast.

'Three cheers for Her Majesty!'

The sort of thing that gets everyone on your side, thought Macken. He must have been paying attention to me last night after all.

People patted their coats and raised eyebrows at each other, sensing the show was nearly over. The dog had slunk away already, past the senior Orangemen and behind Lena Williamson. She was firmly planted, eyes almost closed, arms folded. It looked as though she was enjoying the sunshine on her face, rather than paying any attention to Sir Basil.

The dog – Cúchulainn, Macken remembered – paused at the boxes of vegetables in front of her shop. This time he ignored the chain and, as Macken watched, lifted a leg and began to relieve himself over a crate of King Edwards.

Macken's jaw dropped, but it was his pointing hand that caught Lena's eye. She turned to see Cúchulainn coming to the end of his flow.

A great yell erupted from her.

'Yeeargh! That mutt is pissing over my potatoes!'

She rushed at the animal, kicking out at him. Cúchulainn darted aside and her foot hit the crate instead, overturning it and sending the spuds wobbling across the street. The dog raced through the clutch of older Orangemen, who grabbed at each other for balance as the potatoes rolled between their feet.

'Catch the wee toerag,' cried Lena Williamson.

Macken crouched, opening his arms. Others on the bridge, alerted by Lena's histrionics, turned, pointing, laughing or themselves trying to block the dog's escape. Faced with this mob, he swerved sideways, towards the slipway, pursued by Lena and a band of gleeful children.

The crowd on the riverbank had meanwhile struck up 'God Save the Queen'. Sir Basil could not help conducting them with his sabre, keeping the tempo as accurately as a happy baby with a spoon.

Cúchulainn skittered and skidded to a brief halt at the top of the slipway, confused by the mass of singing people. The only clear passage was down the slipway itself. So, with the formidable Lena Williamson and the baying pack of children closing in, he dashed to the edge of the water and leapt in. He half swam, half scrambled through the shallows through the archway formed by the legs of Sir Basil's steed.

'Catch that wee mongrel,' shouted a red-faced Lena Williamson. 'I'll wring his neck!'

As 'God Save the Queen' faltered in the face of this new entertainment, Sir Basil tried to rise to the challenge by twisting in his saddle and slashing back and forth with his sabre. But he couldn't stretch down far enough to connect with the escaping dog splashing under and out the other side of his mount. He then twisted the other way to slash at his hindquarters.

The horse whinnied in distress. The treacherous footing, the barking dog between its legs and the shifting, twisting, slashing bulk on its back all became too much.

For a moment, it was glorious: the handsome white charger reared back, front legs in the air, teeth bared. Sir Basil Caitiff proud in the saddle; his hat, curly wig and head thrown back; his sword arm flung out as if ordering the charge. But his sling meant he couldn't keep a firm hold on the reins, and by the time he realised he had to drop his sword to free his other hand it was too late.

The crowd saw their very own King Billy slide off backwards into the river. Afterwards, everyone agreed that it seemed to take an age for him to hit the water.

Sir Basil landed on his back, arms and legs waggling, disarmed and bareheaded. Macken saw Bull with his head in his hands, and Gracey shoving through the mob to rescue the fallen monarch. As they dragged him out, a cry went up from the bridge.

'There he is!'

Everyone looked to see a brown, curly haired animal swimming under the bridge. A small boy in the mud under the arch struck out with his stick to clout the dog where Sir Basil had failed. He caught it square on the back, raising a cheer from the crowd. However, as he brought his stick back up from the water, it became apparent that the apprehended dog was none other than King Billy's dislodged wig.

The boy brandished it aloft nonetheless, to renewed cheers from the crowd.

# CHAPTER 29

As he drove to the Penny farm later, Macken was still mildly amazed to have merely witnessed a disaster, without having been its cause. He hadn't even got his feet wet. It was turning out to be a good day.

He made slow progress, having to keep checking the map, whilst avoiding dogs, walkers, riders, sheep, cows crossing, cows sitting in the lane, tractors and the ditches on either side. To an outsider, the lanes all looked alike. Macken knew he would end up in the Republic, if he didn't pay attention. The winding roads pre-dated the frontier, criss-crossing it without even a nod towards national sovereignty. No wonder people didn't take it seriously, he thought.

Except when they were deadly serious.

He turned off the route to the nearest 'approved' border crossing, up yet another pleasant, anonymous lane. Just beyond the mouth of it, he noticed the bushes were littered with rubbish. Someone had dumped a load of rags, leaving them clinging to the branches and thorns.

That's us, thought Macken. We can't see beauty without spoiling it.

He examined his own motives. He and Aoife had managed

only a quick hello in Blackwatertown. She had been with her cycling party, who had twittered with excitement and mock fear at being accosted by the vicar's nemesis.

It had been a pleasant surprise for Macken to be treated as a man by them. A man with whom one could harmlessly flirt, rather than being defined by religion. He had just managed to get in a 'Might I drop by…' and receive her 'Mmm…' of assent.

The official and secret purpose of his visit was to meet Greenard. His cover story was that he was calling on Aoife. So was he using her to cover his back? Or was he only sticking with the whole spy game to get closer to her?

He had persuaded McReady that Aoife was useful camouflage, and heard that internal cock crowing a second time. They had joked about King Billy's dip.

'He'll not be back in a hurry,' Macken had said.

'Do you not think so?' McReady had then enlightened him as to how things really worked. 'The plunge at the river will be the making of him. That boy is fast establishing himself as a legend.'

'How's that, sir?'

'He's always been an arrogant so-and-so. Though as the anointed successor, he'll be elected here regardless.

'But now he's been brought down a peg or two in front of everyone. He's shown he's only human after all. He may feel like a fool round here today. But by tomorrow, he'll be *our* fool. And woe betide any outsiders who belittle him.

'The gunfight at the Big House gave him substance. Unassailable credentials. But his swim today will make people like him. Love him even. It doesn't take much.

'Just wait,' nodded McReady. 'If he has the wit to laugh at himself, they'll be hailing him back at HQ as the MP with the common touch. The ideal man for the top job.'

'So all he has to do is stay standing till polling day?'

'No more, no less. Which brings us to what the IRA are up to. If it is them.'

Macken had explained how he would be calling on Penny's daughter, so as to not draw the wrong sort of attention.

McReady had sighed. 'No doubt your discreet meeting with the young lady will be common currency by tomorrow. Still, people won't be happy till they've detected some ulterior motive, so that may keep them satisfied.'

Macken had felt McReady was both pleased with him and disappointed.

Well, who was he to judge? brooded Macken. Didn't he warn me off her before? And he doesn't mind using *me* when it suits.


Macken stopped in the farmyard and jerked back the handbrake with a loud creak. No sign of Greenard. No welcome from anyone.

In daylight, the scattered outbuildings spoke of past or hoped-for prosperity. But there was an air of current neglect. He heard faint moans from animals penned nearby. The dungy brew of cattle and something more pungent filled his nostrils. Pig shit probably, he thought, narrowing his nostrils. Clegs and midges buzzing over stagnant puddles were the only visible signs of activity.

Then Aoife hurried round from the chicken run behind the barn. She smiled at him. Macken felt a momentary helplessness, as if his limbs were not under his control, as if there was a gap in his chest he was gasping to fill. She called out and danced a few skipping steps towards him. Then she reached into the car to take his head in both hands and kiss him.

Macken marvelled. It's as if she's from another planet, he

thought, where happiness pulses through her so strongly she can't help but express it with every movement of her body.

'Hello again.'

'Hello to you too. What are you so happy about?' asked Macken.

'Seeing you. What else?'

Macken just smiled. She squeezed both his cheeks and gently shook them, as you might do to a child.

'Oh, these people who keep their feelings all wrapped up and hidden away. If you're happy, what's wrong with showing it? Eh? Eh?'

And she kissed him again. Macken got out and she put her arm through his, leading him towards the house and the scent of something good.

'Are you on your own?' he asked.

'Sure who else is ever here? Apart from my Da – and he's away.'

'Can we wander? I fancy stretching my legs. And you haven't shown me round yet.'

Aoife seemed to tense for a moment, but then looked up brightly. 'Alright so, if you prefer sniffing pigs to the smell of my baking…'

'Ah now…' began Macken.

'No, come on.'

Arm in arm, they strolled to a row of low brick pens that backed onto the yard. The first one looked empty, till Aoife pointed out a great hulking mass slumped on hay in the shadow of the far corner.

'She's enjoying her last few days of peace before she drops.'

'She's pregnant then?'

'Oh yes,' said Aoife, cooing to the sow. 'You'll be glad to get them out, won't you? But they'll soon be back on top of you.'

She pulled him along.

'This is what she has to look forward to.'

Planted in the centre of the second sty was another large sow. There were hints of her pale freckled skin visible through thick coarse hair, where patches of dried mud had cracked off. She looked like a boulder cemented into place by the thick sludge.

Macken and Aoife leant on the gate watching piglets nosing around the pen, sinking belly deep into the mixed-up mire of mud and shit and hay and kitchen scraps. It was comical seeing them strain to extract their little trotters from the sucking mattress of muck, and then wade forwards, plunging them back into the mess. Like apprentice clowns miming walking through a swamp, they seemed to be tiptoeing round their mother. Gradually they moved closer and closer, till they were scrambling on her broad back, squealing, bickering, nudging and butting her side to get at the submerged teats.

Macken leant forward. The sow lay immobile. Eyes closed.

'What a racket,' he grinned. 'But they're cute wee things, aren't they?'

Aoife snuggled into him. Macken put his arm round her. Suddenly, the sow exploded into action, lifting her strong shoulders and shaking her head and snout, broad ears flapping, sending orange sludge flying over the flailing piglets, the pen and the watching couple.

Macken staggered back, as Aoife burrowed into him even more.

'Aagh, I'm covered!'

As the sow slowly settled back down, Aoife reappeared from under his arm.

'Is it safe to come out now?' she giggled.

'You knew, didn't you?' Macken accused her.

'How cute they are, you mean?'

Macken looked down at his muck-speckled uniform. Aoife ceremoniously pinched her nostrils closed.

'There's really no accounting for taste. Some men would appreciate freshly baked wheaten. But you obviously have different tastes.

'I think we'd better cut the tour short. Now you've witnessed the joys of motherhood, let's get you looking presentable again.'

As they walked towards the house, Macken heard a high-pitched screeching from behind the barn.

'What's that? It sounds... I don't know. Odd.'

'Oh that,' she said, pulling his arm. 'That's just the chickens. They can be aggravating devils. A noisy bunch.'

'There wouldn't be a fox spooking them, would there?'

'They're fine. I fed them just before you arrived. There's always one looking for attention. Probably heard us tramping around.'

She tugged him harder.

'You get used to them. Come on, Doctor Doolittle, let's get you inside.'

Macken smiled in surrender. They passed the open-fronted barn which sheltered stacked hay bales. Tarpaulins covered other heaps inside. They looked to Macken more like machinery than fodder.

Aoife dragged him towards the house again.

'I've heard the sight of a man in uniform can turn a girl's head,' she said. 'But the prospect of getting him out of it... Well!

'Of course it could just be your extra layer of decoration.'

She put a finger to her chin in mock deliberation.

'It looks a little bit orange. Could be a whole new image for the police.'

Macken let her lead him into the kitchen.

# CHAPTER 30

Aoife ordered him to strip and to borrow a pair of her father's trousers.

'It's fine,' she reassured him. 'He's away for hours.'

When he re-emerged, she had rolled back her sleeves and set a stool by a basin of hot water on the floor. Slices of wheaten bread and a brick of butter were on the table.

'That's for you,' she said, indicating the food. 'And these are for me,' as she sat by the basin to sponge his uniform.

'Ah no, there's no need,' protested Macken.

'Believe you me there is. I can't send you back looking and smelling like a pig, can I? Besides, you've got that grub to get down you. Unless you're going to refuse me twice?'

Macken thanked her and sat down to eat. 'I feel like a wee boy. I've done nothing but get myself dirty since I came to these parts.'

She laughed, and he watched the water turn orangey brown as she scrubbed. It splashed over her forearms, slicking back the small hairs like a glistening, shimmering seal pelt, and turning her skin darker. The bread was warm and fresh and delicious.

'This is lovely. Where do you get your butter?'

'Are you asking in an official capacity, or have you not got your uniform on?'

Macken stuck out his arms, as if to say, *what you see is what you get.*

'Well, the answer is: don't ask,' said Aoife.

'We got ours from the same place when I was young,' said Macken. 'My stepmother used to smuggle it over the border during the war. Hidden in her knickers, I seem to recall.'

Aoife laughed.

'I know, the last place anyone would look,' continued Macken. 'Seems unlikely, thinking about it now. It was probably in her bag. At least you don't have so far to go.'

'No, the border's much handier here,' agreed Aoife. 'Even when you've cows of your own. Or should I say, especially when…'

Macken was struck by the unselfconscious beauty she radiated as her hands danced and dived in the suds, the liveliness in her eyes, the promise of sunshine in her face.

'You have a lovely singing voice.'

'Is that right?' she said, turning down the corners of her mouth, though Macken knew she was smiling.

'No really. It has a haunting quality.'

Macken was pleased he had found the right words. Aoife carried on scrubbing, but he knew he had her attention.

'I wonder,' she said, as if to herself. 'When would he have ever heard me singing? I don't recall giving a performance. Your flattery needs to be more convincing.'

'Ah, but I have heard you, though you probably never knew.

'Last night when I followed that fella from the Big House? It was your voice, cutting clean through the darkness that led me to the door. It sounded like a lullaby. Clear and strangely sad.'

Macken had let himself drift off at the memory. When he looked back to Aoife, his wistful smile died.

She was staring at him stony-faced, transformed. Something terrible in her expression.

Macken recoiled, scraping his chair on the stone floor. He opened his mouth to stammer out what might have become an apology, when she interrupted.

'You must have imagined it.' She looked down at the basin. 'These are done. I'll hang them outside.'

Macken didn't trust himself to speak.

'If you can spare a few minutes,' she continued, gradually softening and seeming to return to normal, 'we can take a stroll while they're drying. I'll show you the border, if you like?'

She smiled once more, and he could almost forget the bewildering past few seconds.

'Aye, that would be great,' said Macken, wondering where Greenard was, not daring to look at his watch.


A gorgeous day, thought Macken. Still plenty of time. Hand in hand, they brushed through the long grass beyond the farmyard. Aoife pointed out where he had come from the night before, that morning really. They looked for the trail taken by the fugitive to the border, but found nothing definite.

'You know?'

'Yes?'

'Yes.'

They sat with their backs against a gentle slope. Around and above them all was quiet.

'It's over there,' she pointed.

'Hmm?'

'The border you're so interested in. We're well into the Six Counties by road. But if you're walking, or on a tractor I suppose, it runs through that field.'

'So how do you tell? If you've livestock?'

'Which state they're in, you mean?'

'I've a feeling I've just asked a stupid question.'

'Well, in the absence of passports for cows,' she explained, 'or indeed a border post in every field, there's only one sure way.'

'What's that?'

'Listen carefully to them mooing, and if they have a hoity-toity English accent they're northern cows. Otherwise...'

Macken shoved her over. She closed her eyes and smiled and stretched, feline and content. Macken watched a small, gleaming drop of moisture run slowly over the skin below her neck, disappearing between her breasts. His shadow shaded her face.

'I suppose what side of the border they're on at any given moment depends on where you want them to be,' said Aoife.

'And sure I was forgetting that the rain stops at the border too,' added Macken.

Aoife put on a deep, stern voice, mimicking one of the fashionable young firebrand preachers: 'We will nevarr, nevarr surrender the blue skies of Ulster for the grey skies of an Irish republic.'

She touched his face with a fingertip, just beside his mouth. 'I've a question for you.'

'Go ahead,' said Macken.

'Have you got me where you want me to be?'

He bent down, putting his lips on hers. After a while, a more troubling question crept into his mind. She sensed it and pushed him gently away.

'What is it?'

He shook his head.

'Tell me,' she demanded in a playful gruff voice.

'I keep getting the feeling that people around me know more about what I'm doing than I do myself.'

She frowned, not understanding.

'Take you and me,' he said. 'People…'

She sat up and interrupted.

'People, is it? What have "people" been saying that you've been listening to?'

'It's not that I want us to be a secret.'

'Fat chance of that round here.'

'I don't mean I want to shout about us from the rooftops.' Macken smiled. 'Well, sometimes I do. But I'm not going to skulk around like we've anything to be ashamed of either.'

Aoife tutted in mock disapproval. 'What kind of a Catholic are you at all, at all, John Oliver Macken? No shame? You'll be saying no guilt next, you heathen.'

She covered her mouth in horror. 'Or, could you be, even worse, a Protestant underneath it all? Your soul is saved already, so you've nothing to worry about. Is that it?'

'Seriously,' persisted Macken, 'it feels like people are interested in us. Not necessarily disapproving. In fact, I haven't heard a word said against you.'

'That's a nice change.'

'It's as if they wonder how I'll measure up. That's it. It's not *you* they're judging, it's *me*. And I can tell that the jury is still out. It's not exactly a vote of confidence.'

'Well, at least they haven't written you off yet,' said Aoife. She stroked his face. 'Maybe they're wondering if you'll write *me* off. Maybe I'm wondering too.'

'No chance. No way.'

'Maybe they know something you don't,' said Aoife. 'You judge me on what you see.'

'Not just that,' said Macken. 'Gorgeous though you are.'

They laughed.

'Alright, you fool. But I had a life before you came along.'

She put a hand out to cover Macken's mouth to prevent him from speaking.

'No, wait. It's difficult enough to say this.'

She looked away.

'Some might say that I'm damaged goods.'

'No,' Macken said, more loudly than he had intended, almost a shout. 'That's impossible. I cannot accept that. You're perfect. To me, you are perfect.'

Aoife shook her head.

'Listen to me, Aoife. Aoife. I love your name. I love saying your name. I love you. I love everything about you. For the first time I can imagine having a family. You and me. That's all I need to know.'

'You say that...'

'Because it's true.'

'But as time passes, you'll wonder. Somebody's bound to tell you. It may as well be me.'

'You don't have to tell me anything.'

'I do. I knew it would come. I'm scared because I don't want to lose you.'

'You know me better than that.'

She was silent for a few moments, biting her bottom lip.

'Here goes. If you're ready?'


It began, Aoife explained, when she was a teenager. She and her father were very close. They spent a lot of time together. He delivered coal back then and would take her on deliveries in the big truck. She laughed. She'd always thought of it as 'the big truck'. It was probably just a van.

Being an only child... Yes, pretty unusual. It meant there was no one to be compared to. And she was not brought up to fetch and carry for boys.

'I was a tomboy. As I got older, I'd help him load and unload the truck.' She stuck out an arm. 'Feel those muscles.'

He made an exaggerated expression of being impressed.

'It was nice. Driving round together. Chatting. I suppose he treated me as if I was a boy almost.'

Macken nodded encouragement.

'I didn't know how happy I was, how soon it would be torn away. We didn't have much money. Looking back, I can see that now. But it was never a worry. Maybe for my father, but he never complained in front of me. We just lived simply, I suppose. Ignorance is bliss, eh?'

She laughed with a bitterness Macken had never detected before.

'There was this one day, we swung by a decent-sized farm I hadn't been to before. My Da was giving it the aul' spiel and chatting up the owner. Trying to flog him a few sacks.

'The place didn't seem well looked after, but you could tell there was money somewhere. Country folk don't like to show they've got cash. They'd rather squirrel it away and live in a tip.

'The farmer was one of those pointy-faced bony aul' men. Hard. Like a shard of rock you'd throw away when you're building a wall.

'I unloaded the sacks. It was only when I opened my mouth that he really noticed me. I remember him asking my Da if I was a boy or a girl. I was in trousers and a sweater and a cap. 'Oh, she's as good as any boy,' said my Da. He was proud of me. It felt good to be useful.

'I didn't like the aul' fella's eyes on me. But when I was done, he offered my Da a drink. I was surprised. He didn't look the generous sort.

'When they came out, my Da had an odd expression. He waved me over to join them, then he told me to take off my cap and let my hair down.

'Well, yer man... His eyes were popping out like some kind

of hungry bird on either side of his beak. Says he: "Oh, she's a girl alright. She's some girl." The next thing, he's grabbed hold of my arm and is squeezing my muscles. Like you'd size up livestock. I couldn't make head nor tail of it.

'The two of them walked off and put their heads together, and I saw them spit on their hands and shake. I was relieved when we left. Until my Da told me the farm was going to be my new home.' She stopped and looked down.

'Go on,' said Macken.

'I didn't want to leave my Daddy. Not so soon.

'I knew I'd have to live on the farm if I was to be labouring there. I wasn't scared of hard work, but I didn't want to be so far from home. It seemed such a long way.

'But I had it all wrong, didn't I?'

It was a warm day, but Macken felt the chill from her past that made her shiver.

'Says my lovely Daddy: "Oh no, Aoife. That man's going to be your husband."'

Macken jolted. 'But sure you were a child. What did your mother have to say?'

Aoife wrapped her arms round herself and swayed slightly.

'She died soon after I was born. It was just the two of us. My Da brought me up. He never made a fuss. So it was a shock when he said he couldn't look after me forever.

'I never thought he would. I thought I'd take over and look after him. Just the two of us.

'But he was thinking of my future, he said. The farmer was a very good prospect. I was lucky to find someone so well off and sensible. I complained that he was so old. But my Da said it was an opportunity not to be squandered. After all, we'd no money. Who else would want me? He agreed that it was a bit soon, and that I was young, but he told me that was the way life is. Sometimes it comes at you in a rush.'

'Jesus,' whispered Macken.

'He said I'd be well looked after and not to worry. The farmer was just looking for companionship, a housekeeper really. Nothing physical. He was beyond that. He was four times my age, I don't know…'

'I can hardly believe this,' said Macken slowly. 'For your father to give you away like that.'

'Oh, he didn't *give* me away,' said Aoife. 'I was bought and sold. Bought and sold. I was never let forget that. Two hundred pounds and an old Morris car.'

'Your father did this?'

'How could he? Is that what you're asking? How could a father do that to his daughter? His only daughter? In this day and age?

'Well, he did. He told me he was doing it for me, that it was best for both of us. That if I loved him, I'd not let him down. This was what he'd been struggling for since my mother died. He could die contented knowing he had me settled.'

Macken slowly shook his head.

'What could I do? Run away? Break my Daddy's heart? Throw all those years he'd looked after me back in his face?'

'But you were only a child.'

'I was nearly sixteen. They decided it was near enough. Especially, they said, as it was not a love match. That wasn't a consideration.

'So that was me married. Quiet ceremony. Just me and my Da, and yer man and one of his workers. I don't know if it was even legal. But that was that.'

Macken shook his head again.

'At first it wasn't too bad. He left me alone. He wasn't used to children, or women. It must have been a shock to his system, having a noisy wee girl running around.

'In some ways, there was freedom. I had a room of my own.

I wasn't hauling sacks of coal. There was the farm for me to explore.

'But I was lonely. I missed my Daddy. I missed him so much. I hardly ever saw him after the marriage. He said I needed time to get to know my new husband. Maybe he felt guilty. Maybe it was part of the deal.

'I didn't really see anybody. My best friend… My *only* friend, was a big, bouncy sheepdog. Patch. Patchie. I used to hug him tight. I would smuggle Patchie up to my room and fall asleep with my face burrowed into him.

'I'd run around in my shorts and gutties, with Patchie bounding along happily beside me. I was married, but it was more like the childhood I'd missed. No responsibilities. No work. Just me and Patchie, the two buddies.'

She sighed at the memory. Macken stroked her back.

'That's what yer man used to call us. The two buddies. He hated Patchie.'

Aoife took Macken's hand. 'Of course it was too good to be true. It couldn't last. It didn't.

'One night I was in bed when he came in. Patchie barked. The aul' fella kicked him out of the room. He came over to the bed. He was shaking, angry. I had never seen him like this before. I was hunched up with the covers pulled round me. I was frightened.

'He wore a tatty old dressing gown, which he let fall open. He'd nothing else on. I was terrified. I had never seen anyone naked.

'He ordered me to throw off the covers and lie down. I was too scared to speak. I just shook my head.

'He said I had to do my wifely duty. I shouted at him to leave me alone. To get away from me. I probably shouted for my Daddy.

'He shouted back that he would tell my Daddy himself what

kind of a wife I was. But I wouldn't give in. I was screaming for Patchie. All this time yer man was screaming back at me like some long, scrawny bird, trying to plunge its beak into me. He was pulling at the covers, and I was pulling back. All the time his tackle was waggling in my face as we tugged back and forth.

'Eventually he let go. I thought he'd given up. I was strong, as I told you. He was tough and wiry, but still an old man.

'But he wasn't away long. He came back with reinforcements. There was a middle-aged big fella who used to do work around the place. Bit slow witted. And there he was in the doorway with lengths of rope in his hand. He didn't seem at all put out by the commotion. He said nothing. He just came over, ripped the covers off me, picked me up and threw me back down on the bed.

'The two of them roped me up like some animal. They put ropes round my wrists and my ankles and lashed me to the bed. I couldn't move. The big fella left the room. Yer man pulled up my nightie.'

Aoife paused. 'And then he fucked me.'

She was squeezing Macken's hand very hard now.

'I couldn't speak. I think I let out a wail that just went on. It was...

'It was horrible. He kept snarling at me how I was a slut. That I had been bought and sold. That he owned me. I thought I was going to die.'

Aoife was quivering.

'But I didn't die. You don't die like that, do you? I didn't know then. I was too young.'

They sat in silence. Then Aoife carried on.

'He was shaken too. I could see it. But I could tell he had got some satisfaction out of it. I don't even know if it was, you

265

know, sexual. Maybe it was pride. It had probably been eating away at him.

'That was the first time. Every now and then, he'd take me. I didn't fight back. I tried to disappear to somewhere far away in my mind. I'd turn my head and close my eyes till it was over. I wished I could close my ears so I wouldn't hear the cruel things he spat out at me while he was doing it.'

'Aoife,' said Macken. 'Aoife, why didn't you leave him? Surely your father would have taken you back?'

'But wasn't I his wife? I'd been bought and sold. Run back to my Daddy? He would have sent me right back. Yer man taunted me with it.'

'You were just a child,' said Macken. 'It wasn't your fault.'

'I had nowhere to go. I saw no one. That was my life. Life went on. Just me and Patchie. Like I said, Patchie was my only friend. And that's why he did it.'

She looked long at Macken. The tears she'd held back began to break through. Her eyes shone in her misery.

'I couldn't find Patchie one morning. He'd always come bounding up if he hadn't spent the night in my room. Yer man's beady eyes were on me as I wandered about the yard, calling, calling. He had a knowing sneer on his face. And then...

'Then I found him. In the barn. He was hanging from the rafters. Swinging gently above wet straw. Yer man had strung him up. Patchie must have followed him quite innocently and let him put the noose around his neck. He'd have been struggling and kicking for ages as the life was slowly strangled out of him.

'I took him down and cradled him in my arms. We just lay there together. With yer man, watching, cackling.

'He'd been jealous of the love I had for Patchie. A dog!

Jealous of a dog. He killed him so I would have no one to love. So I'd have to love him.'

Blood rose to Macken's face. He wanted to take Aoife in his arms and comfort her. But he also felt an almost overpowering urge to wreak havoc.

'Who was he?' asked Macken hoarsely. 'Where is he?'

'I'll never say his name. He's gone.'

'And your father. How can you share a house with him?'

Macken felt his chest swell, and his fists clench tighter.

'No,' she put a hand on his chest. 'He took me back. I can't hate him.'

'I can.'

'You don't understand. He made a terrible mistake. But when I finally ran… I told him, and he took me back. My Daddy was so sorry. He didn't know what to do. He just sort of went into himself for a while. He'd been regretting it since I went away. But, well, he really did think he was doing the best thing. To get me settled. You don't understand. You haven't raised a child, a girl, all on your own.

'He's all I have.'

Macken put a finger to Aoife's lips.

'Not any more. You have me. You'll never have to feel alone like that again.'

'I wanted to tell you before, but I was frightened in case I lost you.'

'Shhh. That's fine. It's fine.'

'I'm like a leper. I'm shunned by my own. I have no friends.'

'Ah no, no…'

'That gaggle of women you see me with. They only put up with me for curiosity value. I play up to it with my cheekiness.'

Aoife burrowed her face under his arm, her voice just a mumble.

'They don't even bother trying to save my lost soul. They

parade me about as an embarrassment to every Catholic in the district. Meanwhile, the vicar and his ladies cluck around shaking their heads at my waywardness and egging me on to worse.'

She tensed against him, as if bracing herself against a physical blow. 'I said I had secrets,' she said in a small voice. 'What'll you think of me now?'

'You were a child then. It was shameful what happened,' said Macken. 'Now I know everything about you. I already knew the best. And now I know the worst too. We'll leave here. Leave all those memories. Leave your father.'

'But I'm all he has. I'm all he ever had. He'd be devastated.'

'Aoife, he ruined your life. He sold you into some kind of slavery. We'll make a fresh start. Without him, without anything from here.'

'What are you saying?'

'I'm saying that you and me are going far away. To somewhere where you can be the beautiful, wonderful woman that you are, without snide bigots holding you back. The world is out there. Blackwatertown is a small, narrow place. Who cares about it? Who cares about the whole of Ireland? We'll throw it off our backs and be gone.'

'Gone where?' asked Aoife.

Macken swept an arm through the air. 'Anywhere. England, America, wherever we want. If a dog can go into space, we can surely get on a boat.'

'Just the two of us?'

'Just you and me. No baggage. Nobody else. No ties. Nothing. Freedom. A new family that will start with just us.'

Macken looked her in the eyes.

'Will you do it?'

He was excited and convinced of the rightness of everything

that had just rushed out of his mouth. But everything hung on her answer.

Aoife's eyes flicked back and forth. Scared of the unknown, thought Macken.

'Do you mean that?' she asked. 'Nobody else? Just us?'

He grabbed her by the shoulders: 'Yes.'

'Then, yes,' she said. Then in a stronger voice, her eyes still shining, but now with defiance: 'Yes.'

Macken squeezed her till she gasped for breath.

They held each other. Then Aoife pushed him away.

'But what about you? Your family?'

Macken shook his head.

'And your job?'

'I'm sick of it. I want out. They want me to referee between a bunch of thrawn knuckleheads determined to dance a jig on the back of another lot of equally bitter diehards. Except, every now and then, I'm expected to stick a boot in myself if it ever looks like the red, white and blue brigade isn't getting its own way.

'The rest of the time it's deadly dull or poking into people's secrets. Winkling out their weaknesses. Just so you can swank around like a big man.'

Macken slowly shook his head. 'Even before I was sent here I was getting sick of it. I hate that business of escorting bandsmen round Catholic streets the night before parades. What's the point of drumming at people's doors waking up their children after bedtime? It's pathetic.

'I faced down an angry father in Kilmurray one night. The bandsmen would have loved to see us get tore into each other. But he backed down when I threatened him with the law. No place for decency when it interferes with tradition.'

He felt Aoife's hand stroke his own.

'I'm sure you did your best. Better someone like you than one of those other types.'

'Maybe,' said Macken. He gently pushed back her hair and moved his fingertips lightly over the taut skin behind her ear and down the soft curve of her neck.

'Actually, there is someone.'

He felt Aoife stiffen.

'Not like that,' Macken forced himself to continue. 'You know the lad I replaced? The one who was found dead in the barracks?'

'Not really,' said Aoife, her hand going to her neck. 'I heard he was a nice fella.'

'He was a Catholic.'

'You're not the only one.'

'And they needed me to fill the gap. Another token.'

'That's how it works,' shrugged Aoife, more relaxed now. 'Your last boss must have wanted rid of you.'

She stroked her chin in mock concentration and put on a deeper voice.

'What can I do with this troublesome policeman? I'll banish him to Blackwatertown, where he'll sink without trace forever.'

She switched back to her normal voice.

'So much for you sinking without trace. We're turning into Chicago here.'

Macken put his hand on hers.

'It may seem silly, but I'm worried I could end up like Constable McMahon.'

Macken hated that he couldn't bring himself to tell her the truth about him and Danny.

'They say it was an accident. I'm scared another "accident" could be arranged for me.'

'I know you can rub people up the wrong way, but seriously? If it was the Reverend Snipe gunning for you, I'd understand,' said Aoife. 'Ah, c'mon now. I'm not making a joke of it. But it does sound crazy.'

'You don't know these guys. They're not shy about bending the rules and bringing out the guns whenever it suits them. And… Look, you have to keep this to yourself.'

'Of course.'

'You know that heroic battle on the border?'

'Hark at his modesty,' said Aoife. 'But, yes, of course I remember it.'

'It was a fake.'

'What?'

'There was no attack. We staged the whole thing.'

'But it was in the news and everything,' protested Aoife.

'It was Gracey's idea. The sergeant,' said Macken. 'We faked it to cover up a gun going off accidentally when we hit one of those bloody trenches. We riddled the car ourselves.

'And I thought I was going to end up riddled myself. To make it more convincing. Gracey doesn't deal in nudges and winks. He's told me what will happen if I open my gob. That I'll go the same way as my predecessor.

'You've heard of dead man's shoes? They've even put me in his bed. With a bullet hole over it, in case I forget.'

'Can't you tell someone? Somebody higher up?'

'Do you think they'd believe me? That my colleagues murdered the last Catholic you sent here, and that I'm next. By the way, I also personally faked an ambush that sparked off a massive security operation.'

'Are you sure about all this?' asked Aoife.

'I'm in it up to my neck. I think that's why I'm still breathing. Gracey's not sure what to make of me. Maybe my corruptibility makes up for me being a Fenian. I could be useful to him.'

'And that's why they killed Danny?'

'Why else? It's officially a tragic accident. But one of the others, Cedric, a right gormless eejit, as good as admitted that the trigger was pulled deliberately. And that the same will be in store for me if I rock the boat.'

'John, you have to get out,' said Aoife. 'Even if you're right, it's not your fight.'

'I can't just drop it.'

'But you've said yourself there's nothing you can do about it. We can just go.'

There *is* something I can do about it, vowed Macken to himself. I won't abandon you a second time, Danny. They'll get what they gave you.

'You could be right.' Macken pretended to be persuaded. 'But they might worry about me keeping my gob shut once they can't keep an eye on me. Running off suddenly might spook them. There are procedures.

'I doubt I'll get a discharge until things calm down with these latest attacks. Real ones. And there's more trouble brewing.'

'Then keep your head down till it's over,' said Aoife. 'I've been waiting a long time. I don't want to wait a day longer, but I can, if we have to.'

'As long as I don't get a bullet in the back in the meantime,' said Macken. 'Another accident. Or maybe they'll chalk it up to the IRA.'

'Don't say that, John. Don't even think it. We've found each other. We'll get through it.' She hesitated. 'As long as you really mean it? About us. Are you not even a little ashamed of me?'

Macken smiled and shook his head. 'I could never be ashamed of you. You're the best thing that's ever happened to me. I was lost, till you found me.'

'Then let me take your mind off everything else,' she said.

They lay together watching the clouds idle by. Macken realised why he was still holding back from telling her who Danny was to him. He was ashamed of *himself*.

Maybe all this time Danny had been ashamed of him too. Or too hurt to reveal he had a brother who'd deserted him.

But what was *her* motive? There had definitely been something between her and Danny too. Why would she hide it?

And what about Cedric? Had he worked it out, Macken's bond to Danny? Or was he just suspicious by nature? Would Gracey and Cedric discovering the truth save me, wondered Macken, or put me in more danger?

So many secrets all round, he thought. I can't let them get in the way.

Aoife broke the silence. 'You see the cheeky side of me, John. All smiles, jokes. Because when I see you I feel like smiling. But most of the time Blackwatertown is a coffin.' She closed her eyes. 'I'm inside. The lid is propped open with a stick. I keep on day after day, but I can never get out. I'm just waiting for someone to kick away the stick.'

'Is it your father who's the problem?'

'No, not really. You wouldn't understand.' Her eyes looked paler, as if hopelessness had leeched away the colour. 'I can't explain.'

'I want to help...'

She forced a smile, which settled in and became genuine as she considered him.

'I know. Maybe you will. For the first time, I feel that there could be a road out of here.'

She leant over to kiss him. Macken felt wetness on his cheek.

'You're crying...'

'Just happy.'

'Or sweating?'

She reared off him. 'Have you no manners at all, you great galumph? Only horses sweat. Ladies, such as myself, merely glow.'

'What about men?' asked Macken.

'Apparently, men perspire. Though I've never seen one work hard enough to prove it. Though if you think you might have it in you to produce some perspiration...'

She lowered herself back onto him.

# CHAPTER 31

The skreek of a handbrake made them sit up suddenly.

'That'll be my Da,' said Aoife.

They straightened themselves out and walked back towards the yard. She linked her arm through his.

'Don't say anything now. Leave it for the moment.'

Macken nodded. Her father was calling her.

'He'll be worried because he's seen your car. Let me go on, and you just slip away.'

They stopped, and Macken gently held her face and smiled into her eyes smiling back. They kissed briefly.

'For goodness' sake,' said Aoife, jumping back. 'I completely forgot! Your trousers.'

'And my jacket.'

'Hide in the barn till I bring them to you. Getting caught like this would not do wonders for your reputation.'

She skipped off to her father. Macken watched, letting his happiness grow to leave no room for the anger simmering beneath. Life will never be boring, he thought.

Then another thought. Her father's trousers... I'll fill these, and then some. More than he ever did.

Macken tramped across the field, following the groove she

had cut through the grass. He gave the pigpen a wide berth, and snuck behind the tarpaulins in the open-fronted barn. Soon he heard Aoife come humming towards him. She whispered.

'Where are you?'

He stepped out so she could spot him, feeling embarrassed. She skipped lightly over the wheel ruts cut into the earthen floor, whisked first his jacket and then his trousers out from under a pile of washing and threw them to him. As he caught them she winked, and blew him a kiss.

Macken stuck his arms into his jacket, then stepped out of his boots and dropped the stand-ins. He could tell Aoife was suppressing a giggle, when they heard the farmhouse door opening. Macken ducked back behind the tarpaulins, trousers in hand.

Jesus, thought Macken, if Penny catches sight of me like this... He gingerly ran his fingertips over the floor to find his boots. It was damp. He stifled a groan of surprised revulsion as he touched something soft. Looking down, he was relieved not to see a slug or a dead field mouse, just scattered fag butts. He picked up his boots and listened.

Paddy Penny was calling Aoife. She turned to answer. 'I'll sweep here in a wee minute. I'll just hang these out to air first.'

She began to saunter off, drawing her father's eye away.

'Sure carry on,' he replied. 'I'll sweep the barn myself.'

Macken waited.

'Quick, get out,' she whispered. 'He's ducked inside the house. He'll be over in a second.'

Macken dashed from his hiding place round to the pigpens. He crouched behind the wall and listened again. He heard Aoife and her father talking, getting clearer as her father reached the barn.

'The broom was in the kitchen,' Macken heard Paddy Penny say. 'I see the car. Is Macken back poking around?'

Uh-oh, thought Macken, he does not sound pleased. Better get out of here. He stood up to pull on his uniform trousers, to find a pair of curious eyes fixed on him.

Ah no, not again, Macken silently pleaded, as he looked back into the eyes of the large sow who had showered him with muck before. As pig and policeman stared each other out, Macken heard Aoife explaining to her father that he'd returned to look for evidence along the border.

'Sure Macken's harmless really,' said Aoife. 'He's one of us. And he's sweet on me.'

That seemed to mollify Paddy Penny, who grumbled that he would have a dander down to see how the visitor was getting on.

Shite, thought Macken.

'Shite,' said Macken.

He'd better not find me standing in my drawers. He'll think I've been at his livestock. Shite, shite, shite!

The huge pig bestowed upon Macken a gaze of the utmost sympathy and understanding. Then began to lift itself off the ground. Macken stared in horror. Then he ran, trousers in one hand and boots in the other. He made it round the corner of the pigpens just in time to hear Paddy Penny cry out in dismay.

'Ach, you great big dirty beast ye!'

Shite, he saw me, panicked Macken.

'You've covered me,' Penny carried on, more exasperated than angry. 'You big mucky bastard.'

Right, thought Macken, still a chance. Quick. He ran to his car. From the corner of his eye he saw Aoife, basket in hand, mouth agape. He started the engine and swung the car round. Aoife was rooted to the spot, hand over her mouth. He lifted his trousers from the passenger seat and waved them. Dark patches on his fingertips. Oil, thought Macken. That'll mark them. Then Paddy Penny appeared in the rear-view mirror and Macken pressed the accelerator.

He drove round a few bends and then pulled over to make himself decent before reaching Blackwatertown. He yanked on his trousers to a chorus of unimpressed bleats from over the fence. He was just buttoning himself up when the sheep bounced off – scared away by the rattling squadron of bicycles appearing round the corner.

The Reverend Snipe and his harem are back on the road, thought Macken. He caught the look of pure poison directed his way from the man of God, and realised he must cut a ridiculous figure for the women whirring past. It dawned on Macken that they would assume he had been in the act of relieving himself. He opened his mouth to explain. Then closed it. The truth would be worse. It usually was, he thought.

He heard a muttered 'Disgusting' from the vicar, amidst giggles and tuts of disapproval. Macken restricted himself to touching his cap respectfully. He raised his eyes to heaven at his unerring talent for making himself look a fool.

Then he realised that each bicycle had had a light fixed on front. Just the thing for such a blazingly sunny afternoon. Macken threw back his head and laughed.

He was still laughing as he drove off. No sign of Greenard, he thought. But who cares?

Suddenly, Macken stamped on the brake. The lane was blocked by a delivery van on a blind bend. No driver in sight.

He cursed and ducked down to unfasten his holster. He felt the seconds racing as he drew his gun and peered round, braced for the shots.

'Jaysus, no need for that, Mr Macken, is there?'

He snapped round to face Greenard, who was leaning over the fence. Slowly swaying branches above cast a shadow curving over his face like Death's scythe. There was no hiding the mockery in his tone.

'I was expecting you at the farm,' barked Macken, tying to reassert himself.

'I thought you'd appreciate a more confidential setting,' said Greenard.

Trees on either side of the lane shielded them from any distant observers. Macken re-holstered his weapon.

'And it saves discussing things in front of Paddy Penny. Or his daughter.' Greenard raised his eyebrows meaningfully.

'So, what have you got?'

'Hey, I'm the one doing you the favour, remember?'

Macken reminded himself that he shouldn't be offended if the likes of Greenard took his cover story about Aoife at face value. Especially as it happened to be true.

'Right so,' began Greenard. 'It wasn't us. Don't get me wrong. They've got the right idea. But you can't have people going off half-cocked. There are proper channels.'

'Like yourselves?'

Greenard shrugged modestly. Macken leant comfortably out over the car door. They looked like country folk passing the time of day.

'Bit embarrassing to have these new fellas waltz in ahead of you,' he continued.

'When we hit you, you'll know you've been hit,' retorted Greenard. 'We haven't gone away, you know. When these flash-in-the-pan merchants burn out, we'll still be here.'

'And so will we. Do you never think we should all call it quits while we're ahead?'

'Aye, you'd like that,' growled Greenard. 'There's always a

few willing to take the king's shilling, but you know this'll not be settled till partition is got rid.'

Macken screwed up his face, as if considering the weather. 'And in the meantime…'

'Aye, well, in the meantime,' said Greenard, bringing the conversation back into a more productive vein. 'It'll not be got rid by this bunch of amateurs. Which is why we have a common interest for now.'

'So who are they?'

'They call themselves *Saor Phoblacht*,' said Greenard. 'There's not many of them.'

'So the hit on the Big House wasn't you then?'

'No, though I tip my hat to them for that. Almost got two birds with one stone.'

'Three,' said Macken, 'if you count the Worshipful Master.'

Greenard adopted a smile bereft of sincerity. 'Let's not bring religion into what's a purely political discussion.'

'And the ambush before that?' asked Macken.

It's rare, he thought, to be able to question a suspect and already know the whole truth. He tried to keep his expression blank.

'They were announcing themselves. All flash. Not much bang.'

'We'd a car badly shot up.'

'A lot of trouble just to send a car to the garage. And it was an odd place for an ambush. Almost like they had information.'

Greenard paused, as if to consider and then dismiss the idea. 'But where would they get the tip-off? You're the only left-footer in Blackwatertown. And you've already been bought and paid for by the British.'

'Greenard, I'd hardly set myself up to be plugged, even if I did share your politics. Which I don't. But more importantly, what's coming next?'

Greenard shook his head. 'You aren't seriously asking me to turn informer, are you? We've only been clearing up a potential misunderstanding.'

'Don't come all cute on me. I'm not going back to McReady with that. If there's nothing else, you can tell him to his face.'

'Not going to happen,' said Greenard.

'See that border you were going on about? You're on the wrong side of it,' said Macken. 'So if I need to take you in, I will.'

'Is that how McReady taught you to cultivate a relationship?' said Greenard. 'You're a big man Macken, but a small coat fits ye.'

He considered Macken through narrowed eyes.

'You know that taking me in would finish me. You'd hold me till Sunday morning and give me a uniformed escort back to the nearest chapel as Mass was ending. An audience to see me getting a slap on the back and a big thank you from the RUC.'

Macken didn't deny it.

'You're maybe not the type to shoot me yourself,' continued Greenard. 'But you don't mind setting me up for someone else to do it.'

'So?'

'So I'm only telling you this because of the disruption those fly-by-nights could cause to the rightful forces of liberation. The word is, they're getting cockier.'

'Where?'

'While you're sniffing round the border, they're going to Armagh. The aggravating devils plan to clean out the armoury at Gough Barracks.'

'Taking on the army? You're joking.'

'If you think so, you've a strange sense of humour. When

people feel safe they let their guard down. I daresay that even applies to the great British Army.'

'Do I detect jealousy that your lot didn't think of it first?' jeered Macken.

'I'm not jealous of the reception that'll be waiting for them. No doubt you and your friends will cook something up.'

'I'd say we might,' answered Macken. 'When should we expect them?'

'Late tonight. Wee hours.'

Macken offered Greenard his hand. He pretended not to notice and looked away.

'It's a rotten business.'

'Yes,' agreed Macken. 'It's a rotten business.'

Greenard moved his van to let Macken pass. As he drew alongside, Greenard held him with a question.

'Paddy Penny wasn't there, so it must have been Aoife keeping you occupied.'

'What of it?'

'You're an unusual man, Macken. Hard to place.'

'Sure it keeps you guessing.'

'The thing is, people like to know where they stand. Uncertainty makes them nervous.'

Macken waved and drove on. Mission accomplished, he thought. He felt smug at having bullied the information out of Greenard. But that nagging feeling was back that other people knew something important about his life that he was yet to discover.

Macken dismissed it and concentrated on Greenard's information. Some of it was lies. But the attack on the Big House was real. The IRA must be smarting at being upstaged, thought Macken. But was that enough for Greenard to turn informer?

He had heard stories about the Civil War viciousness down south. There's no fighting as bad as infighting, he thought. This feels the same, except this time the IRA want the RUC to do their dirty work for them. So much for Greenard's holier-than-thou attitude about setting people up.

Still, it made sense, supposed Macken. Eliminate the competition, while creating new martyrs. The IRA would ride the wave of sympathy, hijack the funerals and remind the faithful of the tried-and-tested channels for kicking out the Brits.

Macken shuddered. He had jumped ahead to visions of mass turnouts at funerals. We'll be lying in wait to shoot them down in Armagh, he thought, not to arrest them. Greenard was right about one thing. It *is* a rotten business.

As he drove on, other misgivings surfaced. Greenard's hints about an informer in the police had to be false because there had been no ambush. But if Greenard suspected a spy in our ranks, others may feel the same. At least Gracey and Cedric knew the score.

Macken snorted at his own naivety. Gracey was probably the one spreading rumours against him. That would be rich, thought Macken, fighting off an imaginary ambush only to be blamed for causing it. A difficult accusation to defend against, given the truth.

Back at the barracks, the district inspector drank in the information like a man parched. He produced a bottle and two glasses. Macken raised an eyebrow but said nothing as McReady tipped amber liquid into both and pushed one his way.

'You've earned it,' McReady reassured him. 'We'll settle this tonight in Armagh. Hopefully, once and for all.'

Macken wasn't a great man for whiskey. He winced as it went down. McReady misinterpreted this as squeamishness.

'It's the only way, Macken. Unless there's something you haven't mentioned?'

Macken thought quickly.

'It occurs to me, sir, that the IRA will be using us. To settle scores.'

McReady raised his glass in salute. 'You could have put it more delicately, but you're essentially right. I prefer to see it as our interests temporarily coinciding.

'The IRA has been disappearing up its own arsehole since we hanged Tom Williams during the war. Down south, they're too busy keeping the Dublin Special Branch off their backs. They're growing used to the quiet life.

'If wiping out this gang encourages the rest to stay quiet and cosy south of the border, all well and good.'

'Perhaps it'll not come to that, sir, and we'll be able to make arrests.'

'Macken, we've had enough cowardly ambushes from… What do you call them?'

'*Saor Phoblacht*, sir. It means the Free Republic.'

McReady exhaled loudly in exasperation. 'That's what we need to move on from. All that childish, backward Irish language, myth and legend. These are modern times. We've gone through bloodbaths twice this century. I served shoulder to shoulder with Irishmen from north and south. The world is moving on.

'Up there, Macken,' said McReady, pointing a finger to the ceiling. Or maybe to Bull's bedroom above. 'That's where people are looking now.'

Macken frowned, puzzled.

'Space, Macken. Rockets! New energy. Progress.'

Macken let his expression show he'd understood.

'It's time Catholics in Ulster embraced the future. Embracing the present would be a start. No offence, Constable.'

'None taken, sir,' said Macken. Though the day people round here got hold of rockets, he thought, would be a good day to keep your head down.

Before setting off to join other units in Armagh, the men of Blackwatertown barracks were briefed that recent outrages, not least the attempt on the prime minister's life, meant they were fully justified in snuffing out the perpetrators.

Bull volunteered to hold the fort.

'Hold the kettle,' muttered Cedric.

Macken, Cedric, Gracey and the local B-Men were to make their way discreetly to Armagh and take up position, without attracting the attention of any Republican spies watching in advance of the raid.

Gracey collared Macken while Cedric was fetching the car.

'If I have to stick my boot up your smug, conspiratorial, Fenian arse to loosen your tongue, I will. What the fuck's going on?'

'Information received. You delivered the briefing yourself. I just follow orders.'

'Information received by you, if I'm not mistaken. You continue to impress me,' growled Gracey. 'I hadn't realised how treacherous you could be. Turning on your own like that.'

'They're not my own!'

'Easy now, I'm impressed,' laughed Gracey. 'And we'll finally see if you're really ready to put your money where your mouth is, and plug a few of those bastards, eh?'

Gracey rested a hand on Macken's shoulder as they walked outside.

'You're the man of the moment and no mistake. As long as there *is* no mistake.'

Gracey let that ride for a moment. 'The DI says it may not be the IRA we're dealing with. He thinks some new group ambushed us by the border.' Gracey winked. 'Well done finding out so quickly.'

Macken bridled: 'If you've something to say, spit it out.'

'No complaints from me, *Constable*,' said Gracey, emphasising the rank. 'I'm just happy in my work. As long as you provide the sitting ducks, I'll join the fun. Whether they're IRA, GAA or the Legion of Mary. As long as they turn up on time and aren't just figments of your imagination.'

'You're the one with the imagination round here, Sergeant,' said Macken, with bitterness that would have earnt a rebuke at any other time.

But for now, Gracey was concerned only with the shooting party to come.

'I'll take that,' he replied, 'as a compliment.'

# CHAPTER 32

Armagh garrison was in the centre of the city. Only the size of a small town, but the city status was ancient. The grounds of its Catholic cathedral held the remains of St Patrick. Though he had a second grave in Downpatrick. A miracle, presumed Macken. Though the saint had never managed to be in two places at once while he was alive.

The army base was a daunting target, but it offered the prize of weapons and ammunition in large quantities. It also offered British soldiers, who were more impressive targets than local policemen in any war of national liberation.

It tended to be lightly guarded. The military lacked the visceral suspicion of the Catholic population that kept the police on their toes. They were complacent.

When Macken's intelligence had reached the higher echelons of the RUC, the soldiers themselves had come under suspicion. The Irish Fusiliers, the 'Faughs', who were garrisoned in Armagh drew many recruits from south of the border, so the police and army top brass had agreed that there might be some element of an inside job.

Even so, the defence of the old walled base from inside was left to the military, who had been woken from their small-town sleepiness. The surrounding streets were the preserve of the RUC and B-Special reinforcements. In recognition of his role in uncovering the plot, McReady was in command outside.

Macken was on the roof of the Ritz Picture House, with a view of the garrison's main gate. He and Gracey were near the edge. Cedric and some trigger-happy B-Men crouched further back.

As the murk of the evening thickened, Macken sensed a spark behind him. Gracey hissed an order to stub out the cigarette. The smoker, a B-Man, protested that it was early yet, till he noticed Gracey's gun pointing at him.

'No one, son,' said Gracey quietly, 'is going to muck this up before we riddle these boys tonight.'

The streets grew dim and empty. The workers long gone home, the drinkers still putting it off. Macken could not see the men with guns, hidden behind parapets, at upper windows, in offices. But he knew they were there. Like him. Waiting.

Am I the only one dreading this? he wondered.

The first hint of action was a can kicked from a side alley. How had they got so close without giving themselves away? thought Macken.

He sensed bodies around him rising and settling into firing positions. From the edge of the roof, Macken could see almost the whole killing ground. Now he became acutely aware of the men behind him, guns pointed at his back. He was between them and any target. They were no longer bored, but eager to let rip.

One extra dead Fenian will hardly matter, regardless of my uniform, thought Macken. I'll be safe as long as Gracey is beside me. No one will risk hitting him. But if we're separated, Macken realised, all bets are off. I don't know if I'll get through.

Then that fear was pushed aside by the other creeping dread that Macken had been trying to ignore. It'll be a bloodbath, he thought. I don't know if I can be a part of this... this evil. There'll be no challenge, just a massacre.

Maybe I should be pointing my gun the other way, he thought, as he surreptitiously glanced back at the men behind him. Get them before they get me...

Gracey finally has me where he wants me, realised Macken. And I made it happen. The best place to lose a needle isn't a haystack, but in a heap of other needles. He might even plug me himself when the bullets start. Another tragic accident.

Or even better, a bullet in the back, so they can say I was hit by the other lot while running away.

Macken couldn't see Cedric, but knew he was close by. He'll be watching me to the exclusion of all else, thought Macken. Gracey the puppet master and Cedric the dog he sets on you. Is that how it was with Danny?

Have I signed my own death warrant by poking my nose in? fretted Macken. No one believes Danny shot himself by accident. But why kill him? Because he was a Catholic, or did he find something out? Surely not just the poaching?

Macken's mouth was dry. He tried to swallow. At least they didn't realise that he knew about their poaching. But what if they suspected he did?

Jesus, you're a fool, Macken told himself. You know about the fake ambush. That's reason enough. More than enough.

His mind in turmoil, he reached for the medal inside his collar, then remembered he'd lost it. The night was cool, but he was sweating. It was irritating the scar on his throat.

He weighed up the odds. There's no way I'll get both Gracey

and Cedric before they get me. Even if I do, the rest will think I've gone crazy and shoot me down.

A hopeless madness crept over him. He felt dizzy from the choice racing towards him: to bathe his hands in the blood of mass murder or to outrage all normal decency by turning on his comrades. But what if those comrades had surrendered all rights to be considered civilised? he argued with himself. Perhaps my job here is to even the balance for the poor fools who'll be arriving down below. And if I'm already in my comrades' firing line, maybe better to avenge Danny and go down fighting than be meekly snuffed out by a bullet from behind.

He felt himself tipping forward, slowly and inexorably towards the edge, like a drunk who sets his world spinning every time he risks lying down. I have to get off this roof, thought Macken.


He heard the can being kicked again. It dinked across the road. For Macken, it seemed as if an age had passed since his mind had begun to run out of control, but it had hardly been seconds. The real world snapped back into focus. The clattering from below was like an echoing shout in the empty street.

Gradually, a slouching figure could be distinguished in the gloom. Slump-shouldered, not looking right or left, meandering slowly towards the garrison's gate.

'Hold fire,' whispered Gracey, 'it's the scout.'

The whisper passed along the rooftops, as the man shambled along. He's playing his part well, thought Macken. It was clever, disguising him as an old drunk. A brave man.

The scout neared the big wooden doors, then stopped and seemed to conduct a muttered conversation with himself.

Macken knew that the soldiers inside would be watching for any sign of a mine being set, or a grenade being thrown. They wouldn't wait for the main attacking group if that happened. Macken was impressed that they were managing to hold fire so far.

Suddenly, the scout pulled himself erect and looked around. Macken sensed gun sights zeroing in from every shadowed vantage point. Then the man shouted. There was a collective flinch round the rooftops. From the mouth of the scout flowed a stream of curses, insults and snatches of rebel songs – all directed at the soldiers inside – to the accompaniment of waving fists and challenges to come out and fight.

Macken was nonplussed. It was if a great communal ache ran round the rooftops. A furious desire from the hidden watchers to let loose and obliterate the jerking, dancing, staggering clown abusing the blank wooden doors.

Macken heard Gracey curse under his breath. Then the sergeant hissed his name.

'Get him out of here, Jolly.'

Macken did not move.

'That's all we need. Some drunk fuckin' Fenian fucking it all up. Go down and get him out of the way.'

'Are you mad? There's no way I'm going down to be shot,' Macken hissed back. 'The slightest thing will set these boys off!'

'Macken! *I* couldn't care less if that stupid Fenian fucker gets his head taken off, but I thought you might have some Christian concern for one of your own.'

'Give him the chance to let off steam, Gracey, and he'll be on his way.'

'Do you think our lads will be able to restrain themselves? If he starts up with 'The Soldier Song' someone's bound to plug him. And then everyone will open up.'

Gracey waggled his sub-machine gun at Macken, as if to

shoo him away. 'I'm ordering you, Constable, to shift him before he ruins this operation.'

'Alright, I'm going,' muttered Macken, creeping back from the edge. 'But tell everyone what's happening. I don't want them to shoot me either.'

Gracey took something shiny from his pocket and stuffed it into Macken's hand.

'You should probably have this. If you don't get yer man out of the way quietly before the Indians arrive,' replied Gracey, his gun now aimed steadily at Macken, 'it'll be the both of you in the hot seat. You get me?'

Macken swallowed hard and retreated further from the darkness in Gracey's eyes.


Macken set off downstairs. This is where it ends, he thought. Will they paint me as hero? A police casualty to justify the massacre? Or will they write me off as a traitor who got what he deserved?

The hero angle will look better for everyone, thought Macken. Loyal, decent Catholic. Shot down by men so base that they even kill their own. Should prompt a round of condemnation of Republicans from the pulpits. Kinder for his family too.

He reached the bottom and opened the hand that had been clenched round what Gracey had given him. It didn't make sense. It was the medal he had lost in the forest. But the chain was intact.

A huddle of men in greatcoats were looking at him. They seemed to be almost vibrating – from cold or tension or fear. Jesus, he thought. Any one of these boys could be the one to shoot me. Macken stuffed the chain into his pocket.

'Look, lads, it's only a drunk making a nuisance of himself. I'm going to shift him before the trouble starts. Alright?'

Macken could discern no hint of comprehension in the staring faces.

'Hi, this is important. Don't get carried away and open fire while I'm still out there. I'm one of the good guys.'

He was suddenly conscious of how useless his gun would be. As soon as one man fired, even by mistake, everyone would follow. He'd be safer without it. He offered his Sten to the nearest policeman, who drew back in surprise.

'Ah, so there is someone in there,' said Macken, trying for humour. 'Mind this for me, till I get yer man. I don't want to scare him.'

Macken received a nod. Progress, he thought.

'And I'm serious about not shooting till I'm in the clear. If you jeopardise this operation because you couldn't wait…'

That's more likely to stop them, thought Macken.

He stepped outside. The door was immediately pulled almost closed behind him, leaving just a crack, through which he could feel eyes on his back.

As soon as I step out of the shadow, I'm going to have every other eye on me too, he thought.

Across the square, the swaying man had turned down the volume to an indistinct mutter. Macken looked up around the dark windows and rooftops. He saw no one, but felt the weapons bristling.

'So, then,' he said to himself, stepping forward on legs suddenly numb, but carrying him onwards nonetheless.

His footsteps seemed uneven. The rhythm of his boots striking the hard surface sounded odd. One boot louder than the other. The sound echoing, bouncing off the hard surfaces. One leg longer than the other. His gait unsteady.

If that drunkenness really is an act, thought Macken, we could both end up dead. Christ, I wish I was back on that roof.

He felt the urge to touch the small medal missing from his neck. 'O Mary, conceived without sin, pray for us who have recourse to thee.' Suddenly he understood. The medal Gracey had given him wasn't the one he'd lost in the forest after the attack on the Big House. How could it be? It must be the one that had belonged to Danny.

And the only explanation for Gracey having it was that he'd killed Danny. The message was obvious. He was about to kill Macken too.

Macken was too close to the drunk to turn back – still unnoticed, but in the crosshairs of all those unseen others. He felt a lump in his throat and worried he was about to vomit. He fought back the gagging and rested his hand on his baton.

The drunk appeared to sag. He really is stuthered, sighed Macken in relief. I'd better grab him before he collapses or I'll never move him.

Then the man fumbled at his waist. Oh Jesus, thought Macken, this is it. He's getting something out. Macken could almost sense the hidden soldiers, policemen and B-Men tightening their fingers on their triggers. I have to take him now.

Macken stepped beside the cursing, slurring figure.

'Bit late for a wee dander, isn't it?'

The man, his hands still at his waistband, turned in surprise. Macken saw his expression turn to anger and his mouth open to shout. Macken drove his baton into the man's stomach, like a short sword.

He folded forward with a muffled 'oof'. Macken caught and held him. He looked down for whatever weapon the drunk had been fumbling for.

Quickly, quickly, Macken urged himself. Where is it? Then

he saw it, peeping out from the groaning drunk's flies. A small, wrinkled penis, still dribbling.

Macken detected dampness on his own legs. He had caught the drunk just as he had begun to relieve himself towards the garrison. The stream of piss had zigzagged across Macken's trousers as the man turned.

Macken almost wanted to shove the man aside and throw up his own arms to challenge them all. To turn and shout: 'Come on then, come on!'

But the drunk was showing signs of life again, so Macken began to drag him away.

'Hey, wha? Whaz zis?'

The drunk began to resist. Macken fought down panic. A scuffle will be just the excuse Gracey needs to put bullets in both of us. Macken had replaced his baton in its case, so he quietened the man with a vicious punch to the kidneys. Huddled together, they staggered and sidestepped back towards the alley.

'I should charge you with being drunk and disorderly,' muttered Macken, to give himself the illusion of control. 'But if you go home nice and quiet, I might let you off with a warning.'

They were nearly at the alley. A hand reached out as they made it to safety. Macken felt pain in his chest and panted as if out of breath.

'Fuck sake, Jolly!'

It was Gracey, down from the roof to welcome him back. Or to cut off any escape.

'Have you pissed yourself or what?' hissed Gracey, recoiling.

The sergeant collected himself, and apologised. But not to Macken.

'Begging your pardon, sir.'

'That's alright, Sergeant.' It was McReady. 'Well, Macken, what have we here?'

'False alarm, sir.'

'Oh yes, I see,' said the district inspector, wrinkling his nose in disgust at the reek of urine. Macken hoped he couldn't see the source of it still dangling. The drunk sank onto the kerb.

'I'm afraid I caught him in the act, sir, and unfortunately...'

McReady was exasperated at the distraction and wanted rid of it.

'Get this fellow out of here, Macken. And, eh, sort yourself out too.'

Macken realised that McReady was embarrassed on his behalf.

'I think the element of surprise is intact. Good job, Constable. Take yourself back to the rendezvous point.'

'Yes, sir,' said Macken. He saw Gracey slowly shake his head in disappointment or revulsion. Macken moved closer and produced the medal on its chain.

'What the fuck is this?' he snarled quietly. 'A threat?'

'Well excuse me for trying to help,' said Gracey, in amused umbrage. 'I noticed you'd lost your own one. I thought a replacement might calm your nerves.'

'Aye, you just happened to have it, did you? Which Catholic in particular did you pinch it from?'

'Back off, Jolly. I took it from...' Gracey paused, annoyed at himself for rising to the provocation, but decided it would be better to continue. 'I took it from Cedric, if you must know. He's fascinated with your Papist mumbo-jumbo, for some reason.'

Macken turned away and hauled the drunk up and along the alley. He was still on edge, and conscious of the pent-up violence within him.

'Officer, ah now, please.' The drunk had regained the power

of speech. 'Take me to the cells till I get the run of myself. Don't be sending me home.'

He grabbed Macken's sleeve. Macken shoved him round the corner and against a wall. He pushed his baton into the man's neck, the ridges on the handle digging into his hand, he was gripping it so tightly. Macken needed to lash out. If ever someone deserved a beating, this was the man.

'I left me bike at the Star,' he slurred. 'Let me get my head down. I'll be as good as gold and as quiet as a mouse.'

Let it go, Macken told himself. Let him go. He's only a poor misfortunate in the wrong place at the wrong time. Cedric is the man I want.

He rummaged in the man's pockets till he found a set of keys, then sent him home, pointing his baton in the direction he wanted him to go.

Macken contemplated his own sodden trousers. Still, he thought, better than a bullet. I wonder, will he remember any of this in the morning?

Macken watched the man stumble off the kerb and weave off into the night, muttering: 'Ah Jaysus, I've pissed meself.'

# Friday

# CHAPTER 33

Macken putt-putted out of the city. He had stolen... No, make that commandeered, the motorbike from in front of the Northern Star, where the drunk had been kind enough to abandon it.

It was a risk, Macken knew, disobeying McReady's order. But he reckoned he'd get away with the theft, and that McReady's instruction had been politely dressed dismissal. He wants me out of the way. They aren't planning on taking prisoners. And I'm not hanging round for that. Not with trousers stinking of an old drunk's piss.

Macken went north first, to avoid the insurgents expected to arrive from the south or south-west, the shortest routes from the border. It felt good to be taking control again, however briefly. He had been jumpy taking the bike, as though he was being watched, but presumed it was his nerves still jangling from his two-step with the drunk.

Macken felt reprieved. Being sent away meant his death sentence had been lifted for a while. He must have looked like he was about to snap or smash someone's head against a wall, again and again. So it was sensible of McReady to remove him from the equation. Macken realised the irony that, for all his fear of being shot in the back, he had been the one expelled for fear of being trigger-happy.

But if his own execution had been postponed, he still bore responsibility for the fate of young men who could even now be walking into the trap he had helped lay. I'll never be able to wash that away, he thought bleakly.

The motorbike was not fast, but Macken had to squint into the wind, following the wedge of weak visibility sent out by the headlight. He paused where he knew there were B-Men hidden by the side of the road, to make sure they didn't shoot him. Their instructions were to let anyone through towards Armagh, but to catch Republicans fleeing the city, if any escaped the killing ground in the centre.

He hunched over the handlebars. The strap from his cap was tight under his chin. He knew he would have a second red line when he took it off.

Trees like giant, grasping hands loomed and then just as suddenly disappeared into the gusting darkness on either side. Every now and then, deeper blackness where a drumlin curved against the night sky, or a whitewashed gable end smeared yellow by the headlight.

As he sped onwards, Macken brooded on the real reason he been sent away. The operation was an act of faith, of McReady's faith in the information brought by the Catholic under his command. Every minute that passed without action weighed on the district inspector, Macken knew. All the organisation, the coordination with the army, the reinforcements, the overtime for the B-Men, the police gunmen in the shadows – it was all on the say-so of McReady. Macken's presence was a reminder that it could all be an embarrassing damp squib. By banishing him, McReady was trying to banish doubt.

I'm well out of it, snarled Macken to himself.

He knew that as the time passed, seconds, minutes, quarter-hours, hours, with nothing happening, the men in hiding would fidget, adjust their positions to avoid cramp, become more tired and tetchy as they tried to maintain alertness. McReady would be well aware of the unspoken question coming his way: 'Is it a bust?' He'd be getting more and more wound up, even as he tried to stay relaxed and focused on the sudden outburst of violence that might yet come upon them.

I'm well out of it, he told himself again.

But fleeing the scene of the crime would never absolve him. He tucked in his chin against the rushing air, as the name of Judas crept into his mind. He couldn't block it out. The only uncertainty was, how many? How much blood?

However, there was still time to assuage his other guilt. He might have squandered his best chance to settle with Cedric, but Danny would be avenged.

He throttled down to take a sharp bend, and glimpsed springing movement. The bike wobbled, but stayed upright, as a barking dog was choked short by a chain.

I wonder how long he was listening, waiting for me, thought Macken. For some reason the futility of the dog's action, and his determination to do it all the same, consoled Macken. The world is what it is, he thought, and you just have to go on. And if you can see a path, then what possible reason is there not to follow it?

Through the darkness, in the distance, two lights, tiny pinpricks. Impossible to tell how far away. Like stars come to earth, thought Macken. Distant embers carried by galactic zephyrs, to land as gently as moths, to cool and wink out amongst the drumlins of Armagh and Tyrone.

He felt suddenly awed that, despite everything, there could be something wonderful in his life. That he had Aoife, and that they had a future together. How could it be possible in this squalid life? It was as though he was living in two different worlds at the same time. One of them drab, bitter, colourless and barren – with only the promise of blood. The other a kaleidoscopic garden of the senses, where sight and smell and touch were on a higher plane.

I can't make sense of it, he thought. He decided just to trust it.

Macken rode over the bridge and into Blackwatertown, mentally armoured against the dark walls and windows. You can't touch me, he thought.

But another worry pushed forward. Would Aoife still see in him what she had bizarrely, mysteriously and wonderfully seen in him before, after the carnage in Armagh? It could be happening right now.

No more of that type of thinking, he told himself. It's us against them. Me and Aoife against the rest. That's the side I'm on. That's the war I need to be strong and shrewd for. Nothing else matters.

Macken abandoned the bike on a side street and walked to the barracks, his footsteps echoing. No traffic, bar the dull drone of a truck somewhere in the night. It was as if the invisible damp fields around the town had sucked in all other sound like a sponge. As if somehow word had leaked out and all nature was keeping its head down to avoid the crossfire.

He slipped inside. Door not even locked. Back to normality, he thought. Bull's asleep, no doubt, and who could blame him?

For the first time, the empty rooms and corridors seemed free of the baleful malignancy Macken had sensed since his arrival. He noticed that the cushion on the chair behind the duty desk had a permanent dent. He hadn't seen it before. It was usually filled with Bull, ready to reach for his troublesome back when summoned by anyone or anything other than the bubbling kettle.

The kettle sat cold by the remains of the fire. A camp bed was folded up in the corner. There was a smell of damp. No wonder Bull preferred his bed upstairs.

Macken breathed in the atmosphere. Three bare walls. On the fourth wall, the noticeboard. On that, a warning about subversive activity. A list of agricultural and veterinary regulations from the Department of Agriculture. And – Macken leant forward – aha! Peeping out from under the subversives, the rules on motor vehicle and bicycle safety. Another episode best forgotten, thought Macken.

Was it really only days since he'd clashed with the vicar? It seemed like another era, more innocent somehow.

No, not more innocent, he decided. Just not so far down the road to disaster.

I'll be gone from here soon. Best to remember it like this, he thought. Quiet. Calm. Without rancour.

There was the sound of a heavy engine slowing nearby, then the creak of a handbrake. Must be the truck I heard earlier, he thought.

'Is that you, Gracey?' called Bull from upstairs. 'I just nipped up for a moment.'

Macken smiled at how unconvincing this sounded, with the day room cold and the fire long dead.

'Don't worry,' he shouted back. 'It's Macken. Your secret's safe.'

I won't have to wake him then, thought Macken. He can deal with the truck himself. He's supposed to be on watch anyway.

Macken started up the stairs, his mind fixed on his bed and the poor man's pleasure of removing his boots. Not to mention his stinking trousers. I'll deal with them in the morning, he thought, his mind already slowing down in anticipation of sleep.

At that moment, he was lifted off his feet by a deafening roar.

# CHAPTER 34

Macken collided with the staircase wall and collapsed a few steps from the bottom. He heard the loud, staccato blam-blam-blam of a heavy machine gun, thick slugs thudding against the front door, splintering it and ricocheting past where he sat in a stupefied heap. Next, the downstairs windows shattered, and shells dug into the inner walls beyond.

He clawed at the stairs to find purchase to escape from the hail of bullets, his feet slipping so that he was scrabbling on the spot. The staircase shook beneath him as an opaque wave of dust swept over, filling his mouth and nose and stinging his eyes. He curled into a ball as he felt more shaking and crashing around him. He was enveloped in a cloud of noise. When he opened his eyes, he could hardly see his own quivering hands in front of his face, grey-grimed with powder that only moments before had been wall, floor, ceiling. He tried and failed to find his bearings as gusts from the blast blew gaps in the swirling fog. The wall across the hallway was gone. The ceiling in front of him was gone. Rubble and collapsed beams filled the corridor.

Where the room he shared with Cedric should be, he could see nothing. Just darkness. Nothing about the internal geography of the barracks was where it should be. He was not sure which way was forward and which back.

Turning his head, he found the jagged boundary of the world he knew. There was still an upstairs at the back of the house. But it looked as if some giant beast had taken a huge bite out of the building. Wood and roof tiles and bricks and plaster were falling from the edge of the great gash. Macken could see into the back room upstairs. The internal wall was barely there. And clinging to the edge of it was a large, white-rimmed eye, the black pupil glaring balefully down at him as he lay in the dust and debris. Macken thought he must be hallucinating, or dying.

From the great eye came a loud screech. It jumped up and away from the edge of the splintered floor. Suddenly, through the billowing murk, Macken saw the great eye for what it really was. He realised it was Bull's arsehole, framed in what remained of the upstairs toilet, winking down at him.

Macken scrambled up the stairs. That side of the barracks seemed relatively intact. The corner which had housed the day room and his bedroom was simply gone.

Bull appeared at the top. He was crawling too and fumbling with the snake clasp of his belt at the same time. His face was white, wide-eyed. Blood dribbled from the side of his head. He looked dead, except for the violent shaking.

'We're under attack,' snapped Macken. 'Raise the alarm! Wake the rest of them!'

He knew he was babbling. Anyone needing to be woken after that onslaught would be beyond waking.

'Jesus, Jolly! There's only me here. Where are the rest?'

'I was sent back early on my own.'

They looked at each other helplessly, then winced and ducked as rifle fire pinged through what was left of the upstairs.

'They've an army out there,' moaned Bull. 'We're done for.'

Macken instinctively grabbed for his weapon. It was gone. He remembered handing it over in Armagh.

You'll be the death of me yet, you drunken bollix, thought Macken.

'Are you armed?'

'Just this,' said Bull, producing a pistol in a shaking hand, which he thrust down towards Macken.

Macken cowered to the side.

'Point it at them, Bull, for Christ's sake!'

Bull looked at the gun in his hand. He was still dazed. He pointed it away from Macken.

'Most of the guns are away to Armagh. What about under Cedric's bed?'

'It's gone, Bull.'

'Gone?'

'His bed and the whole room with it. All gone. Any other ideas?'

'Gone? The day room and all?'

Macken nodded impatiently.

'Jesus, Jolly,' said Bull slowly. 'That was the luckiest shite I ever took!'

Macken shook him.

'Guns, Bull! Guns! Where are there guns?'

He could almost see the cog wheels turning inside what was left of Bull's brain.

'Gracey... Gracey has it...'

Macken realised he would not get any more sense from Bull. Officers in barracks near the border usually kept their weapons handy. But Macken doubted Gracey would have left his behind when he went to Armagh. And anything stored downstairs was buried.

There was a lull in the firing. A voice called from the street.

'This is the Irish Republican Army. Come out now and you

won't be harmed. Throw down your weapons and come out with your hands up.'

The two policemen looked at each other.

Macken hissed at Bull: 'Get up there and fire back.'

'With this?'

'Draw their fire so I can scoot round to Gracey's room without getting riddled.'

'We're outgunned. They've heavy machine guns out there.'

The southern-accented voice with a hint of America called to them again.

'This is your last chance before we destroy the building. Come out now and you'll have safe passage. You have my word. Otherwise we'll bury you where you stand.'

Macken hissed again.

'They're bluffing. They don't know how many of us there are. We just need to hold them off till help comes. Which won't be long with all this racket.'

Bull lay still, not responding.

'Bull! I'm going now. So if you're planning on surrendering you're on your own.'

This is it, thought Macken. He scuttled over what remained of the upstairs hall floor to Gracey's bedroom. He didn't look back or down to the gaping hole at the front, nor towards where the shots would come from. As he scrambled towards the breach punched through the internal wall, Macken felt that he was moving more and more slowly. His back seemed to be spreading into a wider and wider target. The back of his head tingled in anticipation. And then he was through the gap and amidst the chaos of the sergeant's bedroom.

The wardrobe had fallen onto the bed, which had collapsed in the middle. Clothes had spilt out of the drawers. The door had been blasted off its hinges. There was broken glass and dust and plaster and shattered lathes of wood scattered over the

room. Macken crouched, scanning for anything he could use
as a weapon.

He lifted the door to see if a rifle had been hanging on the
back. No, nothing. He could not open the wardrobe enough
to see, so he groped inside. His heart leapt. He felt small-calibre
shells running through his fingers. He began stuffing them in
his pocket. They would fit Bull's Webley.

There was another shout from outside. Macken could not
understand how that imperious voice was able to pierce the
rushing noise inside his head that made it so hard for him to
think.

'Right, you've had your chance!'

Suddenly, he realised how useless his attempts to gather
ammunition were. They'd never hold them off with Bull's
pistol. The shooting started again. Macken instinctively
flattened himself on the floor, though he knew it was little
protection. The same deafening reports and thud-thud-
thudding of the heavy machine gun outside, ripping through
the downstairs. Macken felt each impact as a catch in his
breathing. He was vaguely aware of other firing too, from
smaller-calibre weapons.

He tried to slither under the broken bed, but it was squashed
too low and the space was occupied by a large canvas bag.
Macken pulled at it, but it was wedged between the wooden
slats bulging under the mattress. He grabbed the bag with both
hands and worked a shoulder under the bed. Then he lifted and
heaved and strained till the sack shifted and slowly slid towards
him. It had not just been jammed tight; it was also heavier than
he expected.

He frantically tore at the cord sealing the sack. Then the
heavy machine gun began another traverse of the barracks,
cutting a jagged line along the downstairs. The sound and
vibration were almost unendurable. His hands shook so

violently they were useless. He clamped them over his ears and curled into a ball. The firing stopped for a moment. Macken knew he had been on the verge of complete surrender to panic. He opened the neck of the sack and looked inside.

He was puzzled at what he saw. It was the butt of a gun, but bigger than anything normal. Then he realised it was Gracey's latest acquisition. The sergeant had his heart set on a Ferret armoured car, but it had been allocated elsewhere. Somehow, he had got his hands on a Bren gun instead, even though they had no appropriate vehicle to fix it to. Macken delved into the bag and his hand closed round a magazine. Bingo, he thought.

There was another crash from the front of the building. Macken looked down through where his bedroom floor had been, and saw the splintered front door of the barracks slide down the collapsed wall of the day room. Through the dust he could just make out a crouched figure moving cautiously over the rubble.

They're coming to get us, he thought. That's why the shooting stopped. And what about the back way? They could be coming in there too. He realised he had heard no answering fire from Bull. Maybe they got him?

Macken raised himself to a crouch and dragged the sack onto his back. The floor creaked. Jesus, he thought, will it take the weight of me and the bag together? Then he launched himself forward, bent double, humping the Bren gun in the bag through the hole in the wall, stepping over the gaps in the floor, till he passed the top of the stairs. He dumped the sack down beside Bull, who was curled up in a corner.

Bull recoiled in fear when the bag landed, so Macken saw he wasn't dead. He grabbed him by his jacket and shook him.

'Are you hit, Bull?'

Bull looked blank, but Macken could not see any obvious

injuries. The Webley was still locked inside Bull's right hand, so Macken peeled his fingers back and took it for himself.

'There's a gun in that sack, Bull. Set it up for me.'

Bull showed no sign of understanding, so Macken took hold of his collar and threw him over to the sack. He crawled to the top of the stairs and fired blind, three times. Then he dived back into Bull's bedroom.

Immediately, a swarm of bullets flew past where he had fired from. He heard cries of alarm and shouted instructions from below, but he couldn't tell what was being said. He heard movement, boots slipping in the rubble. And then a dull thunk as a hand grenade skittered across the bare boards beside him.

The door to the back storeroom had been burst open. Macken kicked the grenade through the doorway and pulled closed the door, throwing himself sideways. The explosion shook the walls and blew the door off its hinges. Inside the room all was devastation, but Macken, ears ringing, had been shielded from the blast. He shoved the broken door over to the top of the stairs and, using it as a barrier, fired down again until the pistol was empty. More shouts, but he didn't think he had hit anyone. He had glimpsed faces peering up. They had looked young.

Well, young or old, he thought, they'll be more careful coming upstairs now. But he realised that he had confirmed there was still life inside the barracks. And had fought back. He knew there would be no more offers to surrender.

Bull had the Bren gun out of the sack. He was trying to screw in the legs near the front of the barrel. The heavy gun was usually fired from a prone position. The bipod stand was designed to keep the barrel up and let it pivot, allowing an arc of fire. No time for that, thought Macken.

'I'll do it, Bull. Reload this instead.'

He gave Bull back the Webley and the ammunition he had

found. Then he took a curved magazine and slotted it into the top of the Bren. Running away was not an option. Nor was surrender. Where before he had had pity and sympathy for the night-creeping rebels, he was now overcome by adrenalin-fuelled rage at this unprovoked aggression.

He suspected the attackers were withdrawing to give their heavy weapon free rein. Which meant he had only seconds to prepare. He checked the Bren. No time to attach the legs. He was ready.

The energy that drove him came from deep inside. It was not the urge to defend his comrades, because he wasn't sure he had any. And anyway none, bar Bull, was standing with him. And Bull hardly counted. Nor was it the uniform he wore, nor hatred of the ideals of the men outside. It was simply that Macken had been pushed and pushed into a narrower and narrower space, till he could be squeezed no further.

But he was too late. The gun outside began to rake the remaining façade of the barracks. Macken dropped the Bren and covered his ears. Bull was curled in his corner, ammunition littered around him. Macken's body glitched in time with the crack of firing still not quite high enough to penetrate the floor or walls around them, mangling the remainder of the ground floor. The rage Macken had been suppressing for so long propelled him to his feet. He hoisted the gun and poked it through a hole where a window had been.

The Bren gun was heavy, but he could rest it on the bricks and point it downwards. Without really even looking, he pulled the trigger.


Macken's arms and shoulders fought against the jumping gun, struggling to control it. He heard shouting and screams from below, but did not look to see what he had hit. One long burst. Then he hoisted the Bren back inside and ducked behind an intact section of wall. The heavy gun below let rip again. Macken hugged his weapon and ejected the magazine, as he felt the wall at his back flinching. Bullets pinged and whizzed through the holes in the wall, inches from where he was shaking uncontrollably. He was aware of the little clouds of dust they puffed up when they dug into the plaster across the room. As he waited for the moment when he would be swatted aside, he watched fragments of brick and ricocheting bullets fill the air and dance before him.

There was angry shouting from below. An argument, he realised. It reminded him that time had not stopped. He was still here. Still alive. He snapped in a full magazine.

'Shift it up!' someone shouted outside. 'Point it up more!'

What are they doing? thought Macken. He was almost irritated they were prolonging the agony.

He rose again and, bracing himself, opened fire. This time he watched as bullets flew from his juddering gun barrel and tore into the arms and legs and bodies of the men now scattering below. It was his first proper look outside. There was a dumper truck on the road, with men around and on top of it. They skittled about behind and under the vehicle. The bullets that missed first time went glancing and bouncing off the truck and roadway amongst their legs. The men in the back of the truck slammed themselves into the sides of the tipper for cover. But they had no protection against attack from this height. No shield against the snarling wraith spitting death at them through swirling brown dust clouds.

Macken ducked back inside to reload. The return fire was high enough this time, but panicked, poorly aimed single rifle shots. Or short bursts from light weapons. He barked out a laugh. For all their firepower and cockiness, they'd let fear hold them back. They'd been scared of who might be inside. If only they'd known, the eejits. And now they can't even elevate their great big gun!

There were more shots from outside, enough to keep Macken's head down. And more shouting from the Yank. The heavy machine gun remained silent. Right, me lad, thought Macken, we have you now. He crawled to a different gap to wait for a break in the firing. When the lull came, he was back on his feet.

He pulled the trigger and spat out a short burst to keep their heads down. Then he quickly took in the scene on the road. There were men crouched amongst pieces of brick and glass, bracing themselves against his latest burst of fire, but without cover. There was a knot of men at the back of the truck, but he could not tell whether they were trying to push bodies on or pull them off. The floor of the tipper was dark, glistening, awash with blood. A body was splayed across the big gun, which was itself lying across the back of another prone man. A third man was ineffectually trying to pull the body off the gun. He seemed to have the use of only one arm, his other hanging uselessly. Beyond this picture of chaos, a figure hammered on the cab door, as the truck's engine repeatedly turned over and died.

You had your chance to blow us to kingdom come, thought Macken, and you botched it. He squeezed the trigger again.

But nothing happened. He squeezed harder, his knuckles white, his biceps quivering. It's jammed, he realised. And then, looking down the smoking barrel, he saw a figure leap onto the back of the truck. Just a boy, thought Macken. As if in slow motion, Macken watched him pivot, stretch back one arm and then throw it forward. The boy's body seemed frozen, with his arm outstretched. His face looked puzzlingly familiar, though Macken was sure he'd never seen him before. Macken was almost hypnotised by the gracefulness of his movement, and followed the trajectory of the missile as it arced towards him and in through the broken window.

It bounced across the floor between him and Bull. It was as if everyone, inside the room and on the street, was for a moment united. All holding their breath. Macken looked at the home-made fragmentation grenade lying deadly at their feet. The jangling in his nerves subsided. A wave of serenity washed over him. Endless moments passed.

'It's a dud,' gasped Bull, shocked back into speech. 'Thank you, dear Lord God.'

Macken blinked. Then he slammed the Bren gun on the floor, hoping for the best, and hefted it up into a firing position again.

The boy who had thrown the grenade was the first one Macken hit, sending him spinning off the back of the truck. After that, he was not aware of individual targets. He raked up and down the roadway, the side of the truck's cab, and then poured lead into the back, where the heavy gun was mounted. Without mercy, Macken transformed the chaos into carnage.

The truck jolted forward. A man, or a corpse, slid off the back. The engine caught and the truck began to creep forward slowly.

Something whirred close before his eyes. Like an unusually fat insect. It distracted him for a moment. Then a loud double crack just by his head sent him falling sideways. A shower of brick splinters stung at his ears.

Macken shook his head to clear it, and tried to push himself back up. Pain burned in his left arm.

He gasped and fell onto his right side, clutching the wound on his left. The pain was searing. Sharp and piercing, unlike the knocks and bruising he had suffered in the explosion. He pulled his knees to his chest and rocked in a ball on the floor. More shots dug holes in the remains of the ceiling above him, or knocked shards from the shattered front wall.

He saw a slug-like shape humping and scraping slowly towards him.

'Oh God, he's dead,' wailed the anguished Bull, head down, arse in the air, still gripping his pistol.

With a yell of pain, Macken pushed himself up. Bull jumped back a little in surprise.

'Not dead yet, Bull.'

Bull stared back, unsure of how to react.

'Are you going to fire that gun today?' asked Macken.

'You're hit, Jolly!'

'Aye. And it bloody hurts. But I'll live.'

He sighed and gritted his teeth. Tears were running down his face. He let go of his arm and pulled the empty magazine from the Bren.

'We have them on the run, Bull,' he rasped, fumbling for fresh ammunition. 'Their big gun is out of action. It's a shambles. They're clearing out.'

Macken saw he wasn't getting through.

'C'mere,' hissed Macken, nodding to the space beside him. Bull crept forward.

'Now, let's see,' said Macken, trying to smile reassuringly. He peeled Bull's index finger off the pistol grip and moved it to rest on the trigger.

'Gently...'

He held Bull's gaze. 'On my signal, we'll hit them together.'

Macken nodded slowly for emphasis. He thought he could see some flickering response. It would have to do.

'Now!'

Macken twisted to his feet and heaved up the Bren gun,

screaming against the pain in his arm. He fired just a few rounds, not sure of how much ammunition was left.

Through the gloom, it looked like the attackers were trotting alongside the truck further up the street. They were struggling or fighting with each other to climb on-board. A heap of bodies groaned inside the tipper. Blood ran from them towards the lip at the back.

Macken did not want to present an easy target, so he fired one more quick burst and bobbed back behind cover. But he flinched in pain and surprise as several loud cracks came from behind him. He was stunned that the attackers, who he had thought were retreating, had somehow sneaked upstairs and caught them unawares. Then he saw it was Bull, jaw set and lips pursed, joining the battle. Bull emptied his pistol and then cried out in frustration.

'On the floor,' called Macken.

Bull crouched and reloaded from the bullets scattered at his feet.

'There's something wrong with their truck,' said Bull.

Macken risked a look. As the truck moved away, its back seemed to gradually rise, protecting the cab, but sending the men inside slowly sliding towards the back, as if to dump them back on the street.

Too dangerous with all the houses to blast them from this distance, thought Macken. As he watched the truck picking up speed, the tipper settled back down, before starting to rise again.

'The tipper mechanism is banjaxed,' said Macken. 'They'll not get far. C'mon.'

He stuffed a new magazine in each pocket and then, using the Bren to steady himself, clumped down the stairs. He heard Bull objecting loudly, but coming all the same. Macken was not sure what he would do when he reached the bottom. Run after them? He put his boot through a weakened stair and pitched forward, dropping the gun.

'Slow down, Jolly. Sit tight and wait for the cavalry to come.'

Macken jerked his boot free and stamped down the remaining few steps. He lifted the Bren and picked his way over the rubble to where the front door had been. No day room and no doorway left. No doorstep either, Macken noticed with grim satisfaction. But about half the building was still standing. Then he heard a loud crack and the staircase collapsed behind them.

'D'ye think...' asked Macken, catching Bull's eye and looking over the destruction. 'D'ye think Trelford will raise our rent?'

# CHAPTER 35

Macken and Bull heard the screech of tyres from the bridge end of the village. The headlights of a large police car jiggled up and down as the wheels bumped over the debris on the street.

'This must be the cavalry.'

The car skidded to a halt on fallen shell cases. Cedric emerged, eyes darting between them and the shattered barracks.

'Macken! I thought I'd find you here,' said Cedric. 'What happened, Bull?'

Macken stepped forward to pull him in to safety. 'Safety first, Cedric. The bad guys are just up the road.'

The new arrival pushed him away and pointed his revolver at Macken.

'Cedric, what's going on?' said Bull. 'We've no time for this.'

'That's what I'd like to know,' snapped Cedric, keeping the gun trained on Macken. 'This character slipped away from Armagh, disobeying orders. Gracey set me to watch him in case he turned traitor, and look what I find.'

'You've got it all wrong,' said Macken.

'Have I?' sneered Cedric. 'You think I'm stupid. But it was on your say-so that we cleared out of here to Armagh. Very convenient for your Free State pals. I ought to plug you right now. Gracey had you pegged alright. Forever poking and prying.'

'Cedric, for dear's sake.' Bull could not contain himself any more. 'I haven't a clue what you're about. We've just been hammered by those IRA bastards up the road, but we're still standing.

'Isn't that right, Jolly?' said Bull with satisfaction, smacking him on the shoulder. Macken gasped in pain.

'Dear God! Sorry, Jolly,' said Bull. 'Are ye alright?'

Macken nodded, teeth gritted.

'Well come on then! Their truck is buggered. We can catch them before they reach the border,' urged Bull, suddenly full of energy and purpose.

Cedric stepped back, putting up a warning hand to Bull.

'Don't come between me and this Judas.'

Macken shook his head sadly. To have survived so much, and then for it to end like this.

Cedric's hand was shaking. Macken was surprised to witness, for the first time, Bull display passionate anger, as his comrade levelled his own weapon at Cedric.

'You'll have to come through me then, Cedric. You and Gracey both.'

Cedric dipped his gun arm in surprise.

'I've just seen this man slaughter those bastards with my own eyes,' Bull said. 'They thought they had us blown to buggery. And so did I. Till Jolly took the fight back at them.'

Cedric frowned in confusion.

'If he hadn't been shot himself, he'd have killed them all.'

'What?' broke in Cedric. 'You're telling me he was shooting *at* them?'

'Mandear! I doubt there's one he missed. I had a go myself of course, once I'd found my feet again, thanks to Jolly here.'

Cedric peered closer at Macken, taking in his bullet wound and exhausted face, streaked brown and black.

'I really didn't know anything about it,' said Macken wearily.

Confusion fought with suspicion across Cedric's face. He glanced over his shoulder.

'You could be right about Armagh,' conceded Macken. 'Was there no raid after all?'

Cedric shook his head. 'Well, maybe it was a diversion. But that was the information I was given. I had to pass it on to McReady.'

'But you sneaked off...'

'He sent me away, Cedric. I was a wreck. With that drunk bloke in the square... I was thinking every step could be my last.' Macken laughed bitterly. 'He even pissed over me for my trouble.'

Macken dropped the Bren. Then, whether it was from his wound or that his adrenalin had finally run out, he slowly sank to the ground, crunching on broken glass and masonry.

Cedric watched, with a horrified expression. Macken looked up as Bull rushed to help him.

'Even before that drunken eejit tried to get us both killed, I expected a bullet in the back from you or Gracey. Would have been easy. Chalk it up to the IRA.'

'Hey, hey, you're alright,' said Bull softly. 'Nobody's going to be shooting you.'

'What about the motorbike?' snapped Cedric.

'For God's sake, Cedric,' said Bull angrily.

'He linked up with an accomplice, a fella pretending to be drunk, to get him offside and pass the keys to his motorbike. That's how you got such a start on me.'

'He was just a drunk,' sighed Macken. 'Too drunk to ride home. I took his bike. Stole it. I had to get away.

'And then I walked into all this.'

Macken shrugged at the destruction around them and grimaced in pain.

'And this,' he nodded towards Cedric and his gun.

Cedric looked from Macken to Bull and back again. He lowered his pistol.

'Well, I don't know. You can explain it to the DI. Or Gracey, if you dare.'

'Good, so,' said Bull. 'Now, do you plan on waiting here till his master's voice turns up, or are we going after those boyos who just tried to blow up Blackwatertown?'

'Just us? We should call for reinforcements.'

'Good luck finding the telephone in there,' muttered Macken, beginning to shiver.

'Aye, Cedric,' said Bull. 'Just us.'

Cedric pointed to Macken: 'What about him?'

'I'm fine. Just give us a hand up.'

Both men reached out, but Macken took Cedric's hand.

'Hey, Jolly, I'm sorry. I would never have...'

Macken whispered back: 'Oh, would you not have? Like you didn't with Danny?'

Cedric froze, gripping Macken hard.

'Aye,' continued Macken. 'Some accident. Bad luck getting another Fenian to replace him.'

'Is that what...'

'Bit risky to do me the day I arrive though. Is that what the play-acting in the woods was about?'

Cedric shook his head.

'Gracey chicken out at the last minute, did he?'

'No.'

'That's something else you'll want to tidy up. Though you'll need to get Bull out of the way. He may not go along with it in the mood he's in tonight. With the IRA blowing up his kettle an' all.'

Macken laughed bitterly at his own joke. May as well, he thought. But at the same time, he felt a gap inside him yawn wider and wider. The prospect of never seeing Aoife again sapped his energy. His legs gave way and he slumped beside the car.

Cedric shouted his name as he caught him. He pushed him against the car door.

'You've got it all wrong, Jolly,' murmured Cedric.

'What then?'

Cedric smiled uncertainly, but then shook his head.

'Let's get you in.'


By the time they bumped out of Blackwatertown, the truck was gone. The blasted village was still dim. Macken had not seen a single curtain twitch nor light come on during the entire episode, even though there were windows broken along the street. We know when to keep our heads down, he thought. If only I did.

Bull was excitedly regaling Cedric with the blow-by-blow of the battle, and ridiculing the banjaxed getaway truck. After surviving having the wind knocked out of him, the exhilaration of actually opening fire seemed to have unlocked a hitherto unseen vigour in Bull. He had become fearless, eager for the fight. Macken wondered if it was shock, and if he'd undergo another transformation when the momentum died.

Cedric was concentrating on wrenching the car round bends.

Macken's gun slipped to the floor, as he braced himself with his good arm.

Bull clung to the door handle to prevent himself from sliding into Cedric.

'Cedric, you great glipe,' puffed Bull in exasperation, 'you'll cowp us into the ditch at this rate, so you will!'

'Or into the back of the truck round one of these bends,' added Macken.

And suddenly there it was – abandoned across the junction, its tipper raised in salute as if discharging a final graveside volley.

Cedric stamped on the brake, sending the car slewing into the grassy bank. Cursing and ducking, the three men scrambled out through the unblocked doors, risking fire from the truck until they made it behind their car.

But no shots came.

'They're waiting for us to step out,' panted Bull.

Cedric peered round the side. 'I can't see anyone.'

'It's a trap, so it is,' said Bull.

Macken was on the ground partly to avoid getting shot, but mainly because that's where he'd landed.

'They've gone, I think.'

Looking between the wheels of the car, he could see no movement at the truck.

'I think they've dumped it. Or it dumped them.'

'I'm telling you it's a trap, so it is!'

'Maybe,' answered Macken. 'But they'd have opened fire when we stopped, surely. They must have gone on already.'

Cedric stepped out. Nothing.

'Jolly's right. They're away. But we'll definitely catch them now, unless they're off over the fields.'

Macken held onto the rear mudguard and heaved himself up.

'Wait, Jolly,' said Cedric. 'That big Bren's too heavy for you.'

He delved in the boot, handed him a Sten gun and gave another to Bull. 'Now we're cooking with gas,' he said.

'Better take a side of the lane each, just in case,' said Macken, as they approached the truck, eyes flicking between it and the hedges.

'Watch our backs, Bull.'

The wind seems to be going out of his sails already, thought Macken, noticing he was bringing up the rear. May as well make a virtue of it.

Bull's hesitation oddly strengthened Macken. It was simpler, knowing you had only yourself to rely on. Cedric seemed different too. Immaturity had been stripped away from his skinny frame, leaving something wiry, harder.

They circled the truck. They found no one. But the signs of human hurt were vivid in the first hints of dawn. Dark stains on the seats. Blood pooled on the floor of the cab, speckled with glass. Litter of discarded clothing, bandoliers, a flat cap.

There was a drift of cartridge cases round a pair of stained brogues inside the tipper. Also a jacket, discoloured and torn.

'No heavy machine gun,' said Macken.

'Probably fell out,' said Bull, who'd by now joined them. 'Or they dumped it.'

Nobody mentioned the third possibility, that they'd kept it to punish overhasty pursuers. The policemen looked around, almost superstitiously. Macken's pulse raced for a moment when he glimpsed movement over the thick hedge. The motion of light and shadow became a flapping. He relaxed. Just a scarf caught in branches. More signs of flight.

'No weapons and no bodies.' Bull shook his head in puzzlement. 'It looked like a butcher's shop in there before. There's no way they're in a state to run off anywhere.'

'Must have had cars waiting,' said Cedric. 'They'll be well on their way to the border by now.'

He looked at Macken.

'Did you do all that?' asked Cedric, taking in the damage

and signs of bloodshed. He seemed to be adding it to his reassessment of Macken's character.

'Still, it's nearly daylight. They'll have to take it handy in case they run into a patrol. Not everyone is in Armagh. And with wounded men on-board…'

He turned to Macken and Bull.

'We might catch them,' said Cedric, stepping back into the role of leader. 'Before they make it to Tycross and beyond.'

They looked along the road that took itself over the county boundary into Monaghan and the Irish Republic. Something was trying to push itself to the front of Macken's consciousness. Something that Cedric had said.

'Aye, if our car's still going,' Macken heard Bull remark.

They walked to their car and pushed it back into the road. Cedric started the engine.

'We'll catch them rightly,' he shouted.

Cedric roared up to the junction and turned right, heading for the border. There was something about the place that seemed familiar to Macken.

'Wait,' called out Macken. 'Stop the car!'

It immediately screeched to a halt, the front dipping and throwing them all forward. Cedric and Bull grabbed their weapons.

'What is it?' cried Cedric. 'Where are they?'

'We're going the wrong way.'

Cedric looked back at him.

'No offence, Jolly, but you're dead wrong. I've been here a brave wee while longer than you and I know my way around.'

'You put the heart across me there!' added Bull. 'This is the road for the border.'

'They're not driving to the border.'

'Well, they're not walking either. You shot the shoes off one of them,' said Bull.

Macken tried to arrange it in his head. It was what Cedric had said about the cars. Cars waiting.

'Listen to me. You're right. There were cars waiting. But...'

'And that's the road to the border,' interrupted Cedric sharply, a shadow of his previous suspicion passing across his face.

'I saw them. I saw the cars.'

'Where?' The question from them both.

'It's a dodge. They left the truck pointing towards the border. The way they want us to go haring after them.'

Macken looked for a sign. There must be something, he thought.

'The cars were waiting. But they're planning to cross on foot.'

'That makes no sense at all, sure it doesn't,' said Bull.

'I know this place,' said Macken. 'Back up. C'mon Cedric. Back her up. That other road must run close enough to the border.'

'Near enough I suppose.' Cedric looked unconvinced. 'But there's no crossing till you reach Caledon. They'd be mad to try that way.'

Macken got out and trotted back to the truck.

'Lord God,' shouted Cedric. 'What's wrong with him, Bull? Was he hit on the head as well as the arm?'

Macken did not know what he was looking for. But he'd know when he saw it, he told himself. Ignore the truck. That's not it. Look around.

Cedric was calling him to come back. That they would leave him there if he didn't catch a grip.

Macken saw hedge and branches and leaves and road. The empty tipper open to the empty lane curving away ahead of him. The flapping scarf caught his eye again. Ignore it, he ordered himself, now that he'd identified it. Concentrate. But there was nothing. Cedric and Bull caught up with him.

Macken walked away from the truck along the left-hand fork. From the corner of his eye he saw another piece of clothing caught in thorns. Ignore it!

A hand fell on his shoulder, stopping him.

'That's enough now,' said Cedric, quiet but firm. There's a man inside him after all, thought Macken. But I didn't see it, only the fool. Only the threat.

Macken resigned himself to failure. He saw more scraps caught on the long thorns. Small, stranded, frayed patches.

Macken blinked and then grasped Cedric's sleeve, pulling him round the curve. 'There it is!'

Cedric and Bull stared where Macken was pointing the spiky criss-cross of hawthorn along the lane which clutched at vests, shirts and children's shifts. White or faded to white. Pathetic and oddly disturbing at the same time.

Macken had not appreciated the site's true nature when he'd seen it before. They were rags alright. But they hadn't been thrown away. They been placed deliberately. It was a raggedy bush.

Desperate people were drawn to them as markers for springs or holy wells. Sometimes they bathed in the water. Sometimes they drank it. Superstitious country folk, thought Macken. Or was it that they simply had faith?

St Patrick had incorporated the pagan practice into the Christian Church when he had converted Ireland from the old Celtic religion. People still visited holy wells to leave garments associated with their own ailments or with those of their sick children. Sometimes it would be a calliper, an unravelled bandage or an old pair of spectacles. Usually it was clothing, rising and falling in the breeze. As the material faded and fell apart, so too, hoped the pilgrims, would their illnesses fade and disappear.

Macken had shied away from the place before. Now he was relieved to see it.

'We see the bush,' said Cedric. 'And the question is: have you lost your mind?'

'What Cedric's getting at, Jolly, is... what's the point?' asked Bull. 'Personally, I'm not too bothered, so I'm not, by whatever heathen practices you Catholics get up to. But I see no IRA men. No tricolours either.'

'I've been here before,' said Macken, with conviction now. 'There are farms along this way? Long before you get to Caledon?'

He was receiving guarded nods at best.

'The Penny farm? Am I right?'

Cedric frowned. 'There were cars hidden under tarpaulins. Cigarette butts too.'

Macken realised they weren't persuaded.

'The cover slipped. I saw them,' Macken lied. 'The same cars I spotted at the Big House the day of the attack there.'

It struck Macken that he could have accidentally stumbled upon the truth.

'The border runs behind Paddy Penny's farmyard. I chased a shooter there.'

'Jolly, we know you have a fancy for yon Penny girl,' said Bull. 'Are you saying she's part of this IRA gang?'

Macken realised he couldn't answer that, even to himself. He put it to one side.

'McReady sent me to spy out information after the ambush.' Macken turned from Cedric and looked at Bull. 'After Cedric, Gracey and myself were shot at, I came here to meet my contact.'

'Aoife Penny?' asked Bull, disbelieving.

'No. Well, yes to see her as well. She was my cover story.'

Macken paused for a moment, disgusted at how he had used her.

Bull nodded. Macken could not tell if it was in approval or the reverse. 'So that was what she was.'

'Look, she's got nothing to do with this. But her father…'

'Bad Paddy Penny, you reckon?'

'Could be,' said Macken. 'Maybe against his will.'

'Do you reckon they've got a hideout there?' asked Cedric.

'Probably using it as a staging post to the border,' said Macken. 'The line cuts through Penny's land.'

The three men considered it.

'That would throw us off the track alright, so it would. We'd not expect them to head that way, sure enough.'

'Which means,' said Macken, 'they may not be expecting us to appear on their tails so soon.'

Bull looked to Cedric expectantly. Cedric gave a grudging nod.

Soon they were twisting along the narrow lane. Macken remembered how Greenard had blocked the road on a blind bend, and warned Cedric to take it handy round the corners.

'You said yourself they're running for the border. Right?'

'Aye, I think that's their plan,' agreed Macken.

'Well then,' shouted Cedric over the engine noise, pressing his right foot to the floor.

So much for sneaking up on them, thought Macken, as he held on for dear life.

# CHAPTER 36

'Is this it?' asked Cedric, as they skidded into the dark farmyard. 'Looks all quiet.'

Macken stared into the open-fronted barn. Whatever had been concealed was gone. No tarpaulins even.

The barn was now full of hay bales, stacked right to the edge. Loose hay was scattered in front. Macken hesitated. He had been so earnest about the concealed cars that he had even convinced himself. What would he say to Cedric and Bull?

'So where would they be, Jolly?' whispered Cedric.

Of course, I never said exactly where I saw them, remembered Macken with relief.

'Let's look around,' said Macken firmly. 'Take it handy though.'

Macken walked towards the barn, reluctant to admit he had it wrong. The other two split up, Bull towards the house and Cedric to the far side of the yard.

As Macken got closer, he sensed a presence hidden in the shadows.

'Lads!' he called out. 'This way.'

The three converged on the barn, weapons raised.

'Come out,' shouted Macken. 'With your hands up.'

Silence. A long barrel emerged from the back of the barn.

'Watch it, Jolly,' shouted Bull. 'He's got a gun.'

'Throw it out in front of you,' ordered Macken. 'Then follow slowly.'

'Alright. I'm coming out. Don't shoot. I'm not armed.'

The weapon was thrown onto the scattered hay. Then, into the half-light, shuffled Paddy Penny.

Macken kicked the weapon aside. He frowned. The 'gun' was a broom.

'What's going on?' barked Macken. Then, a little more gently, 'You had us worried there, hiding in the shadows.'

Penny took in the three policemen, who were looking less sure of themselves than before.

'I wasn't hiding from anyone,' said Penny. 'Do you mind?'

He indicated his raised arms. Macken nodded.

'Thank you,' said Penny, ostentatiously rubbing them, as if to provide relief.

'I take it, Mr Macken, that it's not a social call this time? I would have expected more manners. Driving like a mad man into my farmyard, scaring the life out of us all.'

'Who all is that then?'

'There's myself for a start. Tidying up, as you see. The pigs. The chickens. The cattle. And Aoife – if you haven't forgotten her entirely.'

'Aoife,' said Macken sharply. 'Where is she?'

'Aoife?' He considered for a moment. 'Oh Aoife's around somewhere. Hiding from you marauders frightening decent people in their homes. Maybe she'll be glad to see you, even with your friends here.'

Mr Penny went to walk them towards the house.

'Hold on a minute,' said Cedric.

Penny looked at him, sizing him up.

'Is that it?' Cedric asked Macken. 'We didn't come here for a cup of tea.'

'I didn't offer any,' responded Penny sourly.

'What he means is,' interrupted Macken. 'Have any cars come by?'

'Hah?'

'Cars, or men on foot. We're chasing a gang of fellas for an attack on Blackwatertown.'

'Eh?' said Penny in a shocked voice. 'More trouble is it? That's terrible.'

Penny narrowed his eyes and studied Macken more closely.

'Is that you hurt, Mr Macken? Jesus, Mary and Joseph, it is, isn't it?'

'Aye. I took a bullet earlier. But it's not too bad.'

'Ah, Macken. You should've said. Let's take a look at it and have Aoife clean you up. She'll be very upset.'

Penny turned to the other policemen and made an effort to be more conciliatory.

'Sorry about before. You gave me a fright, is all. It's a bit early for all this excitement.'

Penny leant forwards to look more closely at Bull too.

'You're another one, aren't you? Jesus, you've been through the mill, alright. A cup of tea will set you rightly. You won't know yourself.'

Penny continued ushering them to the farmhouse, but then held up a hand to stop them on the threshold.

'I'd better warn herself. Don't want to be startling her with strange men appearing unannounced at a time that's neither decent nor Christian.'

He gave Macken a significant look, as if to say, 'Like you have a habit of doing.'

'Aoife,' Penny called out. 'We've some unexpected visitors from the police. The police, Aoife!'

Penny smiled back at them, then shouted in again.

'You might want to clear the table and put on some fresh tea.'

And then to the three policemen: 'Women and their kitchens, eh? Jesus, you wouldn't want to put a foot wrong there.'

Having neither wives nor the patience for Penny's forced bonhomie, none of them smiled back.

'Have we time for this?' asked an uncomfortable Cedric.

'Ah now, Constable. A decent start to the day will stand to you. And what was that business in Blackwatertown? Was there bad trouble?'

'Bad enough,' said Bull. 'Bad enough.'

Penny tutted again to himself.

'Is the damage bad, then? Was anyone hurt?'

'Some of them boys was badly hurt, I can tell you that,' said Bull. 'And they'll be more hurt when we catch up with them, so they will.'

'Right, right,' nodded Penny. 'I'm holding you back gabbing on, am I? Another time though? You'll be welcome. Ask Mr Macken here, he'll tell you.'


Without being conscious of having made a decision, they found themselves walking back to their car. It had been a waste of time and they were keen to continue the pursuit. Though by this time, they would almost certainly be too late.

Macken knew they would blame him. But they'd blame themselves too, for letting him persuade them – too easily probably – away from the obvious route. In the policing they were used to, the obvious answer was usually the right one.

Tiredness wrapped itself around him. He needed to let his brain catch up with events. Moving too fast had almost got him blown up at the barracks. And he had almost missed the lane leading here. Which really was a shame, he reminded himself, because if he *had* missed it, they might have caught the attackers.

Yet another bad decision to add to the long list. They'll not be slow to discharge me after this latest fiasco, he thought. It wasn't how he'd hoped to go.

And he hadn't even seen Aoife after all the fuss about coming here. Maybe it was because he was with the others. She'd not want to make a show of us in front of them, he thought.

'Jolly, come on!'

He heard the car doors slam. Cedric revved the engine to hurry him up. It feels like the last time I'll ever see this place. The idea surprised him, but didn't upset him. After all, he thought, we'll soon be leaving forever. That must be it, he reassured himself. He took a last look to fix it in his mind.

Macken smiled at the memory of himself cowering in the corner the last time he had been here. Literally caught with my trousers down, he thought.

As his mind ranged back in time, the engine noise and the shouts gradually faded. Macken hesitantly took a step forward. Then another. He kept his eyes down, trying to block out the world around him, going back in his memory. Trying to see.

Cowering in the shadows. Off balance. Quiet. He had been feeling around for his boots. Wetness.

He rubbed his thumb against his fingertips. Oil, he thought. And the cigarettes.

He walked into the barn. He could not go far now that it was full of hay. He slung his Sten gun over his uninjured shoulder and pulled down one of the higher bales. Using it as a platform, Macken stepped up and pulled more down.

He now saw the wall of bales was only double thickness. It

did not go all the way back. It's the same hay as the other day, he thought, just rearranged. So what's hidden here?

In the dim light, he could see... more hay. He closed his eyes. So tired.

Then Cedric was calling him, closer now, breaking back into his consciousness. He was nearing the end of his tether with Macken's bizarre behaviour and only tolerating him because of Bull's account of the barracks attack. But Macken was beyond listening, he just wanted to lie down.

He felt a sudden jab in his side and reached to his wounded arm. But the pain was on his right. He gasped. There it was again. Macken opened his eyes and saw Cedric holding Paddy Penny's broom.

'Do I have to poke you again?' asked Cedric. 'Or are you coming quietly?'

Macken grabbed the broom. Cedric stepped back, anticipating retaliation. Instead, Macken turned and thrust it into the heaped hay behind the bales.

Before his eyes, the loose hay fell away to reveal a tarpaulin.

'They're here,' said Macken. 'They're under the hay. Help me.'

He shoved more bales aside, destroying the wall. Then he climbed through the gap and brushed away the loose hay with his hands, all pain forgotten. Gradually the shape of something large showed through. Cedric was through the gap now too, grabbing handfuls of hay, till they could get at the tarpaulin underneath.

They looked at each other. This is it, thought Macken. If it's a tractor under here, that's the end. They each took a corner and raised the edge of the cover.

'Well now,' said Cedric.

Paddy Penny rejoined them, looking worried.

'Lads, lads. You're wrecking my hay.'

'What are you hiding?' shouted Cedric.

'Hiding? That aul' junk? Jesus, lads, I wasn't hiding them at all. Just trying to keep them smart. We're on a farm. No matter what you do, the chickens get into everything. You know yourself.'

They removed the tarpaulins. There were two cars, the same as before. Bull let out a low whistle as he took in the bloodied back seats and the stench of piss and pain.

'I think Mr Penny hadn't quite finished tidying up when we interrupted him,' said Macken. 'But, now he's had time to think, he's going to give us the full picture.

'Isn't that right, Mr Penny?'

'Ah now, Macken, that's just chickens...' blustered Penny, doubling over as Macken suddenly drove the butt of his Sten gun into the farmer's stomach.

'It's like a butcher's van in there, Mr Penny.' Macken registered a curtain twitch in the farmhouse. If Aoife sees this, he thought, and almost faltered.

'Where are they?' he demanded.

'Yes, alright, they were here. But I had no choice,' he pleaded. 'They said they'd kill us if I didn't help them!'

'I asked you where? Where are they?'

'They said they would kill us...'

Standing over Penny, Macken sensed someone rush towards them. He turned to see Aoife tussling with Cedric. But with only one free hand, he could not hold onto her. She ran at Macken and shoved him hard.

'What are you doing to my Daddy?' she shouted at Macken.

'Aoife...'

'How could you do this?' She was crying now and outraged

at the same time, hitting out at him. He turned his uninjured side towards her so he could take her pummelling without defending himself, and tried to get through to her with words.

Her father was shouting too, at his daughter, for her to get back into the house and leave them to their business.

Then she hit Macken's wounded arm, and he grabbed one of her wrists to restrain her. The fight seemed to seep out of her, but the tears still flowed.

'How could you, John?'

'Aoife, they tried to kill us. We know they came here.'

'Why did it have to be you?' she wailed. 'I knew they'd never leave us alone!'

'Who, Aoife? Who is it?'

'Everyone,' she cried. 'You said we'd get away from here.'

'We will, we will.' Macken tried to calm her down. 'I'm sorry. I'm sorry about your father. We're all on edge.

'Look, he's fine. Aren't you?' he said to Penny.

Paddy Penny grumbled his assent as he got back to his feet.

'He's fine. It's alright. Some of the things you told me before. They were building up. I was angry. I shouldn't have lashed out like that. I'm sorry.'

She was calmer now, but still angry and confused. Macken smiled weakly at her.

'I got hurt earlier. It knocked me off balance. I wish you'd never seen me like this.'

Revealing his own vulnerability immediately defused her remaining anger.

'Oh no – where…'

He raised the injured arm slightly. She clapped her hands to her mouth in horror.

'And I've been battering you there. Oh God, I'm sorry…'

'No, it's fine. I'll get it sorted out when we're done here. I'll be right as rain.'

Her stricken expression reassured Macken that her feelings for him were still strong. Yet he was puzzled she had been so quick to stand up for the man who had sold her into slavery. Still, he supposed, it spoke to her character that she could still honour her father, even if he didn't deserve it. She understood loyalty.

'Look, Aoife, you and me, we'll sort this out later. Myself and the lads here just need to take a wee look around before we're on our way.'

'You'll find nothing,' said Penny, reasserting himself. 'I've admitted they were here. And you have their cars. But they're long gone. You know yourself, it's only a hop, skip and a jump to the border.'

'We nearly had them, so we did,' sighed Bull.

Macken assessed his comrades. Bull was ready to accept defeat. Cedric still itched for confrontation.

'What about this fella here?' demanded Cedric.

'We were feared for our lives,' bleated Penny. 'They didn't give us any choice.'

'I'd like to give you the same choice,' snarled Cedric, stepping forward.

'Hey, hold on now.' Macken stepped between them. 'Bull, take Mr Penny inside. He can show you the rooms and put our minds at rest. See if they left any evidence.

'Cedric, you may as well turn the car round. And I'll have a quick juke round the outbuildings. Aoife can give me the tour.'

He gave her what he hoped was a reassuring smile. But she was looking at her father. Macken saw fear in her eyes.

'No,' said Paddy Penny. 'Let her back inside. Don't be dragging her into all this!'

'Calm yourself now,' said Macken, but with the hard edge clear in his voice. 'I want a wee word with your daughter anyway. We'll just take a quick stroll.'

The farmer grabbed Macken's forearm.

'I'll take you. She has chores inside.'

Macken looked pointedly at Penny and at where he was holding his arm. Penny let go and Macken sized him up.

'Mr Penny,' he began, 'I realise we're on your farm, and that Aoife is your daughter. But listen closely to what I'm telling you now.

'I know you have some role in this, and we'll come back to that. In the meantime, do not hinder us any further in the carrying out of our duty.

'As for your daughter. You have no power over her any more. Do you get me?'

Macken was aware that Cedric was ready, hoping for the farmer to put up a fight. Penny's cheeks bulged, but when he spoke, his words conveyed not rage, but anguish. Macken did not understand at first, because the tone was so unexpected. Not hectoring, but pleading.

'Please don't take her. Please.'

Macken had not expected such an emotional reaction to what he still thought of as a secret romance, especially not from such a dour character. He was disconcerted for their relationship to suddenly be laid bare so publicly. This isn't how I wanted it to happen, he thought. To take her away in the middle of such violence and harshness.

He stole a glance at Cedric and Bull. They seemed to be taking Penny's latest outburst in their stride. Maybe they don't realise what he's really talking about.

'Please, take me instead. Let her go back in.'

Why on earth would I want to take him? thought Macken.

Penny was pushing Aoife back towards the farmhouse. Macken was impressed by his strength of feeling for his daughter, even knowing how badly he had treated her. Maybe it was true what Aoife had said, that her father was truly sorry.

But am I so bad myself? thought Macken. Am I such an appalling alternative that he feels he needs to save Aoife from me? Now's probably not the best time to reassure him that I'll not be a policeman forever.

'I'll go with you instead,' Penny repeated.

Macken finally understood. Penny wasn't scared of the future, but of the here and now.

'That's enough,' growled Macken. He looked round the yard. Cedric and Bull detected his new wariness and raised their weapons.

'You're some cool customer,' said Macken grimly. 'They're still here, aren't they?'

Penny shook his head.

'Bull, take them both inside. Cuff him to something heavy. Then the three of us will sort this out ourselves.'

'What about her?'

Aoife and Macken gazed at each other. She was still frightened.

'Not her,' said Macken. 'But you have to promise me, Aoife, not to come out that door till I come back.'

She protested, but Macken spoke over her. 'I'll be fine, as long as I don't have to look over my shoulder worrying about you.'

Penny took a breath and then shouted: 'Look out, lads, the peelers are onto you!'

Macken shoved him backwards, shouting at Bull to get them inside for Christ's sake. Cedric and Macken followed them, taking cover from the gunfire they expected at any moment.

Bull roughly cuffed Penny's hands behind him round a wooden upright. 'You can stand or sit,' he told him. 'But if anyone comes through the door you'll be the first to get hit!'

Macken gently but firmly pressed Aoife down to a crouch behind the big kitchen table.

'Aoife.' He forced her to meet his eyes with her own. 'Is there anyone in the house?'

She looked for help to her father, but he was busy straining against the handcuffs.

'Aoife. Are they inside? Is there anyone upstairs?'

'Oh! No.' It was as if he had been speaking an obscure dialect she was suddenly able to understand. 'No, there's no one in here.'

'Right. Good. That's good. You have to stay here and stay low. Just in case.'

The other two policemen watched the doors and windows, while Macken went up.

'You turncoat!' snarled Penny. Macken accepted the abuse as a sign of Penny's impotence, that he had played his last card.

Despite Aoife's assurance, Macken took the steps carefully. Once again, the long, low room was empty of people. He crept past a small wooden crate padded with blankets. Like a miniature of the bed beside it, thought Macken. Penny must sleep below. His fingers stroked the cloth in the box. It was surprisingly soft. He wanted to press his face into it, to smell it, and feel the fibres scratch and caress his skin.

But he slowly pulled back, feeling as though he was trespassing. The aroma was coarser than he had expected, more the rich, dense pungency of the farmyard than the scent of a woman. His nostrils flared at the thought that he was, at last, learning that heady, intense smell.

He moved to the small window. Light filtered weakly round the edge of a thin curtain. He drew it slowly aside, not wanting to attract attention from any lookouts. It did not make much difference. Grime on the glass kept the light out.

Macken rubbed a space clear of dust and dirt. He could see over the pigsty. Nobody lying in wait there. Then movement in the fields caught his eye. He squinted and saw bobbing lines of shadow against the brighter green. As he watched, the small, dull shapes began to look like people jumping up and down. Or running.

# CHAPTER 37

Macken clattered downstairs.

'They're running for the line,' he gasped. 'Come on!'

Bull hesitated. He pointed at Aoife. 'What about her?'

'Leave her as she is,' said Macken. There was no way he was letting her be handcuffed like her father.

'Stay with your father, Aoife. Don't go through the door, no matter what.'

Macken wanted to put down his weapon and embrace her, to bring her comfort and tell her that everything would be fine.

Instead he implored her: 'No matter what. Do you promise me?'

Pale and at bay, she slowly nodded.


Macken paused on the threshold: 'Ready?'

After a beat, he burst out the doorway. Bull and Cedric crunched after him. Past the police car and into the cover of the barn.

'We go past the pigs,' said Macken. 'Then as fast as we can across the fields.'

'Then what?' asked Bull.

'Then get close enough to open fire. We don't need to hit them, just pin them down.'

'I'll not be shooting to miss,' put in Cedric, his jaw set.

'They won't be either,' warned Bull.

'Don't worry; they'll be tasting the border. They won't turn and fight till we make them,' said Macken. 'C'mon!'

Their hearts and boots hammered along the passage – easy targets for a gunman, if one was to suddenly appear ahead. Then they were out in the open again.

'There they are,' panted Bull. 'They're brave 'n' far ahead, so they are.'

Macken hacked and spat, running on. The ground got softer and the going slower.

'They can't move fast. They have wounded.'

He led the way through a gate left open, cursing at curious cattle who had begun wandering up to take advantage of the gap. They seemed to be closing slightly on the figures ahead, but not enough. The moist soil briefly clutched at them with each stride, holding tight, before releasing them to jerk forward.

'We have to slow them down!' shouted Macken.

He fired wildly, half stumbling over the uneven ground. Careering ahead of his partners, for once oblivious to the risk of stopping their bullet spray with his back.

The men ahead seemed to stop and fall. Macken knew they'd probably just taken cover. But they were slowing.

How far is the border? he fretted. Jesus, it must be close. Keep on moving.

'They're up again,' called Cedric, letting out an unearthly yell.

The ground had become damp and foot-sinking. Macken tried to take his bearings. A stream marked the border, Aoife had explained, when she had taken him to lie out on the grass. They had not been on damp ground like this.

Cedric passed him, letting loose another burst of fire. The group ahead fell to the ground again, but this time did not rise up in renewed flight.

Suddenly, Macken felt the shock of bullets coming the other way, zinging towards him. He swayed, boots anchoring him in the squelch of the boggy ground, like a man teetering on a precipice. Cedric pulled him down.

'They've stopped running!'

Macken experienced a sharp, stabbing sensation. Christ! They'd hit him. He let out a low moan.

'Sorry about that,' said Cedric, surprised. 'You were too exposed up there.'

Macken realised the pain was from his earlier wound. He batted the apology away. Cedric leant closer to exclude Bull and winked.

'Gracey said we'd started our own wee war,' he said. 'About time I played my part.'

They pressed themselves into the soil as more bullets passed over. Macken was alarmed to realise that Cedric was enjoying himself.

'They'd not hit a heifer if they were up its arse!'

Cedric returned fire, then ducked, waiting for the response. Instead, there was shouting. They looked up and saw one of the fugitives waving.

'What's he saying?' asked Bull.

Macken listened hard, and then slumped down.

'He's waving goodbye. He's saying they've crossed over.'

'Cheeky bugger,' snapped Cedric. 'I'll wipe the smile off his Fenian face.'

'It's no use, Cedric,' said Macken. 'We can't follow them over the border.'

'Fuck the border! We'll hunt them down and finish them or bring them back!'

'No. We've no authority there and they've stopped running. They're retreating in good order, covering their backs. We'd have to fight all the way.'

'But…'

'Leave it. They could have mates waiting. We can quit with all of us in one piece. And anyway, the Free State police may scoop them up.'

It was feeble and Macken knew it.

Cedric uttered Old Testament imprecations under his breath. Bull sighed with relief.

'Still,' he said, breathing heavily, 'we sent them packing, so we did. The three musketeers. Eh, Cedric?'

There was a grunt in return.

'Fair play to them though,' he continued. 'I thought the damage you did to them in Blackwatertown would have slowed them down more.

'They must have made the dead arise and run, never mind walk.'

'Shame we don't have more to show for it,' said Cedric angrily.

'Aye,' answered Bull. 'Though we've their cars. And Jolly surely wounded some of them bad. Maybe very bad. All in all…'

For Bull, the night's nightmare had taken a sunnier turn. Bruised and battered. Clabbered with muck. But he had seen action and come through it. Acquitted himself well. A wee cup of tea now, he considered, would be just grand. Which reminded him…

'So what about them?' Bull jerked his head back towards the farmhouse.

Macken thought for a moment. He was back in charge.

'We should search the farm. I didn't hear their big gun. Maybe they stashed it.'

Anything to postpone having to face Aoife after assaulting her father right in front of her, he thought. He knew he had diminished himself and taken a step away from her and a step back into the world from which they wanted to escape.

The prospect of another trophy put renewed spring in Bull's step. He strode ahead. Macken's eye was drawn to the farmhouse. He saw the curtain waving lazily out the kitchen window.

'I reckon they're both in on it,' said Cedric. 'Danny used to come here. He must have known there was something going on.'

Macken looked at him sharply.

Cedric looked back confidently at first, but then seemed to wonder.

'No, not Danny.'

'Is that why you did it?' said Macken in a low voice. 'And took this?'

He opened his hand to reveal the chain and medal he'd received from Gracey.

Cedric gasped in horror and reached for it. Macken closed his fist.

'How'd you get that?' hissed Cedric.

Macken threw the same question back at him.

'He gave it to me,' said Cedric, turning away.


Macken and Bull went to check out the chicken run – a large cage of wire mesh and wooden struts, not quite as tall as Macken's shoulders. Inside was a water butt, some feed trays and a broad, low shed where the chickens roosted.

It struck Macken how little impact the shooting appeared to

have had on the chickens. They were paying himself and Bull no attention at all, as they rooted and bustled and pecked and bickered.

'Aye,' said Bull, reading his mind, 'but if you rattled a bucket they'd notice you.'

Macken wrinkled his nose against the pungent smell of chicken shit.

'We should...' And he nodded to indicate the low shed inside the cage.

For a moment, Macken thought he heard that odd sound again. It was difficult to pick it out amidst the general chatter from the hens. But there it was. A louder screeching signifying... Signifying what, thought Macken? Alarm? He had the odd feeling that he was being watched again, this time from inside the cage.

Suddenly, with a rush of skirts, Aoife was in front of them.

Macken and Bull instinctively jerked up their weapons before realising who it was.

'No,' she said, loud and clear. 'Leave them be.'

'Aoife,' began Macken, 'what are you doing out?'

'Just leave them alone.'

She faced Macken with an implacable defiance he had never detected before. Her arms under a green stole, crossed in front like a barrier. Her breathing fast, the swell of her breasts straining against her shirt. Macken could see colour rising in her cheeks, the ends of her long curls flickering in the breeze like small tongues of flame. Then it came to him.

'It was the window, wasn't it?'

'I never broke my promise to you. Now just leave.'

Macken shifted his weight to step forward.

'Aah now, Aoife, we just have to check...'

She stopped him with an outstretched arm, her palm facing him.

'No.' She was almost shouting now. 'Get back!'

Her command was followed immediately by a cry of alarm from behind them. Someone else was shouting at them to get back, or get down, but Macken was too confused by Aoife to take it in.

He saw her eyes suddenly widen, and looked behind him.

The door of one of the sheds they had passed but not yet investigated was swaying open, and Cedric was running towards them. His mouth was opening wide and closing. He's shouting something, thought Macken. Cedric's motion seemed to slow to match the grinding gears of Macken's brain.

Macken saw him leap into the air and dive to the ground before them. Onto a small object that had just landed. Been thrown, thought Macken, from over...

Thought ceased as he was thrown into the air himself, amidst a roaring rush, which blasted all other sound from his ears. It hurled him against the wire mesh of the chicken cage, smashing the wooden struts behind him, sending the chickens into a clamorous frenzy. Oh, you notice me now, he thought, as the wire sprang back, dumping him onto the ground and into oblivion.

*He scuttered round in the gloom, hunched over against the sharp edges of alarm clawing and cawing all around. Panic at strange noises and hard, angry, new voices from outside.*

*Then, for an instant, he and everything around him flinched as one. The ground jumped at his feet. A rushing sound broke over him. His ears filled with pain, then seemed to snap into emptiness. The air was filled with the gritty sediment of scurf and shit that littered the floor. He was thrown and stuffed into a corner. Other bodies piled around him, while the world cracked and shook.*

*Then the gloom gave way to darkness. But this time, night was falling inside his head.*

# CHAPTER 38

Macken hit the ground. Dirt and stones in his eyes and his nostrils and his ears and his hair. His fingers clawed at the ground. A huge emptiness in his stomach. He felt hot and shivery at the same time. It was totally silent. No voices, no sounds of movement, no hum of activity. Was he the last person alive? Or dead already?

Then the silence gave way to a hammering in his ears. And there's Cedric. Why's he lying there? Get up you strange, diving fool, he thought.

Macken tried to lift himself up and set off the searing pain in his arm. He cursed and felt wetness running down his cheek.

Jesus, I'm weeping now. I'm completely out of control, he thought, wiping the tears away with a dirty hand. Dirty red smears on his fingers. And dry eyes.

Shite, thought Macken. He felt round his face and head. Bleeding scratches from where he had been thrown against the cage.

The hammering in his head stopped, and then started again. Macken gradually realised it was not coming from inside his skull, but from the Sten gun in the hands of Bull, who was pouring fire into a shed. Macken watched Bull dance lightly backwards, his body making tiny hops as the gun jumped in his hands.

Macken was baffled. Thrust suddenly into this dream world, disconnected from where he had been standing just a moment before.

Then he remembered the hand grenade curving through the air. And Cedric diving on top. Suddenly, as if water had drained from his ears, it all came back to him in a rushing, deafening roar. The explosion. The pain. And Aoife!

He twisted round to find her. But there was no sign she had ever been there.

Bull was cursing at the top of his voice as his gun sputtered to a halt. He wrestled with the slide in frustration. There was no answering fire from the shed. Macken heard Bull bellow and rush inside, brandishing his gun like a club.

Macken struggled upright. He saw blood pooling beside Cedric. Macken felt dizzy. But the cries of rage from the shed, signs of life, drew him to stagger after Bull.

The policeman was repeatedly swinging down the butt of his weapon on a body slumped just inside the door, pulverising it. For a moment, it looked as if it were just a boy lying there, being hammered. Then Macken didn't want to look any more.

Bull moved onto another body and began hacking at it in a frenzy. There was no resistance. It was like beating a sack of sand.

There's no one alive in here, thought Macken. He tried to call Bull's name, but could only manage a croak. He could see the butt of Bull's gun hitting a head again and again, till it cracked. Macken's empty stomach heaved and he vomited up a thin dribble of bile. Sated for a moment, Bull moved towards the third body. The corpse lay back with both hands resting on his stomach, dampness darkening his pullover, as if hoping to slip unnoticed into a post-prandial snooze. But his expression was a grotesque contrast: mouth agape, lips pulled back, as if in horror at what had just played out before him; eyes wide open, but cold, dead and glazed over, unexcited by yet more pointless ripping and gouging.

Like an executioner bathed in blood, Bull raised his gore-smeared gun again. Macken shoulder charged him, knocking him aside, and screaming from the bolt of pain that surged through his wounded arm.

Bull snapped round, ready to slash at this new enemy. Maybe what saved Macken was his wail of pain. Bull paused, panting, nostrils flaring. His arms and chest and legs stained dark with other men's blood.

'They're dead, Bull,' gasped Macken. 'They're dead.'

They looked at each other, then remembered and hauled each other up. They stumbled out of the abattoir to where Cedric lay face down.

Macken realised he was muttering to himself. Just 'Oh God, Oh God…' over and over. He crouched and touched Cedric's shoulder. There was a small groan.

'He's alive, Bull! He's alive!'

Macken knelt at Cedric's shoulders and tried to roll him over. The groan was louder this time, and deeper. Wetness seeped through the knees of Macken's trousers. He realised the dark pool under Cedric was spreading.

He carefully eased Cedric's head to the side and lay down beside him.

Cedric's cheek was smeared with dirt. There was grit in his hair. But his beautiful face is undamaged, thought Macken. No scars to mar him. Macken curled up beside the young man. He slipped a hand underneath Cedric's cheek to cushion his face, and pushed back the hair that had drifted over his eyes. He could be sleeping.

'Cedric,' thought Macken, or maybe he whispered it, 'what were you thinking, going and doing something like that?

'I thought you wanted me dead, you poor, wee, beautiful eejit.'

Macken saw Cedric's pale eyes slowly open halfway. They were not focusing on him, but on somewhere faraway. A tear welled and rolled from one corner, washing a clear path through the dirt on his skin. His lips parted, and whispered something. It sounded like 'Da'. Some small pink bubbles appeared at the side of his mouth, then disappeared one by one.

Macken sensed a change in Cedric, as if his body had given a sigh. The weight of his head was pressing Macken's hand into the ground. He put a finger to his carotid artery. There was no pulse.

Macken carefully withdrew his hand and hugged himself. He drew his knees up to his chest and leant into Cedric's corpse, eyes closed, weeping inside.

*Still no light. Not even a distant gleam. The darkness had moved back outside his head. But so close it pressed against his spine; he could touch it with his forehead and feel it on his cheek. It felt different from before.*

*He was alone. Safe from them piercing or tearing his skin. Away from the dirt and dust. It felt strange. Snug. His shallow breaths took in clearer air, though the boundaries of his world were tighter than before.*

The clucking and scratching gradually penetrated Macken's consciousness. He was used to the pungent musty odours in the darkness now and the faint rustle of feathers past his face. Then

a new pressure on his thigh. Something moving. Thin, bony
fingers gripping him. Or claws. And a loud, hoarse crowing.

Macken screwed his eyes closed more tightly. He felt the
jarring of running boots pounding the ground on which his
head lay. Then shouting.

'Get the hell out of that!'

Macken shivered. His eyes fell open. For a moment he just
gazed into the memory of those gentle eyes beside him, and
then started. They were gone. He was looking at a dark lump
beside his head on the ground.

'Jolly, you're back,' said Gracey. 'Bull said to leave you for a
bit. He said you were done out. But you're not done yet, are
you?'

Macken found himself shakily upright, with one of Gracey's
strong arms wrapped round him. At his feet, a police greatcoat
covered Cedric's head and shoulders.

Macken staggered back, almost doubling up, gasping for air.

'He's gone, Jolly. He's gone,' said Gracey, keeping him
upright. 'We covered him up. Didn't move him. Didn't want
to disturb you.'

Gracey's mouth zipped shut, as if he had already said too
much.

'How long have I...'

'Not long,' said Gracey. 'I heard the shooting. Bull told us
what happened.'

'He saved us.' Macken pointed to Cedric lying in the dirt.
The chickens advanced again, enjoying their new freedom.

Macken noticed other policemen moving round the farm,
occasionally calling out about small discoveries or after
stepping in something unpleasant.

'Where's Bull?' asked Macken.

'In the house. Having a wash.'

Macken shuddered.

'What do *you* say happened?' asked Gracey, an odd note in his voice.

'It's true. Cedric was annoyed. I stopped him from chasing over the border.'

'It sounded like a regular war you had going on.'

'Aye, but they left their big machine gun behind, I think. It's probably hidden round here. We were just going to check inside the chicken run. And then...'

Macken held his head in his hands. And then...

'Cedric was behind you, was he?'

'Cedric. Aye. He shouted. He must have seen it. We had no time to react. He dived onto the grenade. They must have thrown it from the shed. And then the explosion.'

'You're hurt bad, aren't you?'

'No, just dazed. Scratches. Looks worse than it is.'

'But your arm...'

'Oh, that. That was from earlier.' Macken took a long breath. 'I'm tired.'

'Aye, we'll have you looked at by a doctor and sorted out rightly,' said Gracey. 'Bull wasn't looking too good.'

'Bull's tougher than we thought. While I was blacked out he was emptying his magazine into the shed.'

'They must have put up a hell of a fight,' said Gracey. 'He looked like he'd been sheep-dipped in blood. And it wasn't his own from the way he was up and walking.'

Macken thought back. He tried to turn the pounding and pounding into an out of focus blur and see past Bull to the bodies in the shed.

'Two could have been long dead. There wouldn't have been much life in them before Bull got to them.'

Macken bit his lip.

'We were too close behind for there to be time to carry them across the border.'

'What about the young one?'

'The young one?' asked Macken. Then he remembered the long, slow grace with which the boy had lobbed the grenade through the barracks window. And the vision of Bull's gun crushing in the side of that young face that had caused him to...

Macken gagged, but kept control of himself.

'I think I hit him back at the barracks, but he mustn't have been as far gone as the other two. He was maybe guarding them.'

Macken remembered another detail.

'One of his arms was in a sling, I think. I suppose he couldn't hold a rifle. Just a grenade.'

Macken shook his head.

'That's what they left him with – two bodies and a hand grenade... And Bull. He was in a frenzy. Like he was possessed.'

Macken shuddered again. He felt too weak to even kick at the chickens strutting round his boots.

'The barracks is a shambles,' said Gracey. 'It's a wonder you drove them off the way you did.'

'We got lucky. The stairway shielded me from the blast. Maybe their explosives didn't detonate properly.'

'The way Bull tells it,' said Gracey, 'you acted with courage. And intelligence.'

'Ach, I was just a wee bit cross, you know. I was cross anyway. Then they came along, making demands and blowing in the door.

'I just wasn't in the mood for it.'

Gracey raised his eyebrows.

'Dear God, Jolly.' He laughed and slapped him on the back, knocking him forward. 'Sorry. Come here to me now. You're some pup! I'm glad I left that Bren gun behind. The whole

Armagh affair was a damp squib. I expect it was to draw us all away.'

Macken nodded.

Gracey put a hand on his good shoulder and looked into his eyes, searching for something.

'Got your bearings again, have you?'

Macken coughed and winced and shook his head.

'To be honest, I haven't had my bearings since I got to Blackwatertown. If it's not you threatening to plug me, it's been Cedric creeping around. Fake attacks, the IRA sending me on wild goose chases and then trying to blow me up.

'Last night I expected a bullet from Cedric. This morning he took a grenade for me. So I'd say that getting my bearings is some time off. Since you ask.'

Gracey screwed up his face and looked to the side, slightly ruefully.

'Aye, well, sorry about all that. We were a bit anxious about you, you know?'

'How come?'

'You come dropping in all mysterious. Like you were sent to snoop. We were getting on fairly happily in our own quiet wee way till....'

'Till I came along? Fucksake, Gracey, I wasn't the one who set it all off by shooting up my own fucking car!'

'No. Look, we were scared of you. You're sharp. I was scared of what you might do to Cedric.'

Macken staggered slightly.

'I'm more lost than ever now. You were scared of me! I was the one skulking around with that tickly feeling between my shoulder blades.

'Jesus, you even put me in Danny's bed. I've been wondering how long I'm to be left dangling before I have an accident of my own, or wander into a crossfire. Especially as you can lay on both sides of any crossfire yourself.'

Gracey stared at him, puzzled.

'It was almost a relief when they attacked the barracks,' Macken went on. 'I was thinking: At last, someone is coming right out with it and trying to kill me properly. We can finally get on with it.'

Macken barked a harsh laugh.

'I'm almost sorry for them. They caught the brunt of my frustration with you and Cedric.'

Gracey darted a quick glance about him.

'It's alright,' said Macken. 'There's nobody else listening. Only ghosts. And I'm so tired, I think I'm turning into one myself.'

Gracey looked down at his boots and then squarely at Macken.

'I suppose I'll have to tell you. Whether I can trust you or not, I don't know. But it's either that or kill you – and with Cedric gone... Well, I don't have the appetite for it. So I'll tell you and you can carry it too.'

Gracey turned to look at where Cedric lay. He closed his eyes.

'You're right about Constable McMahon. It wasn't an accident.'

Macken drew in his breath sharply.

'I knew it–'

'But we didn't kill him.' Gracey spoke over him. 'It may surprise you to hear that we don't automatically kill every Fenian we meet, even if they're as irritating as you.'

Gracey paused.

'McMahon shot himself. We didn't want it to go down as a suicide. So we covered it up.'

'What? Why? And why did you hide it?'

'Well, it looks bad, doesn't it? Somebody under your command deliberately killing themselves. Embarrassing.

'And it's a sin, isn't it? Taking your own life. No salvation on the other side. That's something we have in common. With Catholics, I mean. It's not something you want to load on top of his family. Bad enough as it is.'

Macken searched for a response. His brother must have been so lost. So alone. But to take his own life? Macken didn't want to believe it.

'Is that all it was for you?' he asked Gracey. 'Embarrassing?'

This was a side to Gracey that Macken was finding hard to believe – that he would all of a sudden reveal the truth, the whole truth.

'Very convenient – their embarrassment, your embarrassment – everyone is saved a lot of embarrassment.'

Macken gave Gracey a smile devoid of warmth.

'But why would Danny cause everyone so much embarrassment in the first place?'

Gracey did not respond.

'I suppose you'll say that the inner workings of a tormented mind are just a mystery.

'You could also say that it's far below your usual standard of making stuff up. I'm disappointed. I would have expected better, going on your past performance.'

'No,' said Gracey, slowly shaking his head.

'So I'm left guessing,' said Macken. 'If no less than a man than our prime minister won't have a Catholic about the house, why should you? God knows, Danny might have been one of those particularly irritating Fenians you mentioned before. Maybe you had Cedric do your dirty work.'

'Cedric didn't kill him,' said Gracey, with more force now. 'He'd have died for him.'

Gracey's words dwindled into a hoarse rasp.

'Now he's dead saving you. Bloody fool.'

'What do you mean?' asked Macken, narrowing his eyes at this latest feint.

'That's the trouble with you,' said Gracey. 'I knew as soon as you arrived. You're clever. An eejit all the same, but clever enough to ask questions. And to see things. That's why I was scared of you.'

'Back to that is it?' deadpanned Macken.

'Look, neither of us killed him.'

'So you said.'

'Cedric loved him.'

Gracey shrugged as if acknowledging something beyond his ken, but real all the same.

'I mean, really loved him.'

Macken frowned.

'Aye,' said Gracey. 'It was like that.'

'You mean he was... they were...'

'Yes. No. Maybe. I don't know the details. But they were on that road alright.'

They were silent for a moment. Gracey grimaced.

'How am I doing? Is the performance up to your expectations so far?'

He lowered his eyes again.

'I used to tease them about it. Before I knew there was anything to it. They were always mooning around together off duty. No trouble at all. No drinking to speak of. Especially McMahon. Quiet. Disciplined. They worked well together. In tune. I never realised...'

Gracey puffed out his breath as if expelling the secret he had been carrying.

'Well, you wouldn't, would you? It's not what you come up against every day, is it?

'It was one night; Cedric had been out for a drink. Off duty, mind. But unusual all the same. He came back and I made some silly comment. That Danny would be missing him. And he just came out with it. He told me.' Gracey looked down again. 'I wish to God he never had.

'It took a while for me to take him seriously. But all those wee jibes had been getting to him. He must have just wanted to tell someone.'

'Hadn't he told Danny?'

'I don't know. I'd say it was plain enough, even if they hadn't said it out loud. I don't know the details. I didn't want to. I still don't.'

Macken was staggered at how little he had known his brother; how much he had missed. It was almost too much to take in.

'But why would Cedric tell you? You were the one tormenting him. And you were his boss. He was admitting a fairly serious crime. Never mind being...'

Gracey screwed up his face again, and he finished Macken's sentence. 'Never mind being disgusting and unnatural? Yes, Macken. I am aware of all that. He was telling me that he was... well, a sodomite. There it is. Or at least that he was intending to become one.'

Gracey paused. Macken waited.

'You're wondering how I reacted? How would you react if it was someone close to you? I was angry. I threw him across the room. He got a sound beating that night. It was lucky he was drunk. He didn't feel it till the following morning.

'Of course the ruckus brought Bull and McMahon downstairs. I cursed Bull to get away the hell out of it. Then I put my hands round McMahon's throat and told him that I would throttle him if I heard any more about this filth.'

Macken looked away, feeling complicit. He was all too aware that he might have reacted the same way, horrified at his brother being led astray in such a fashion. Gracey plunged his hands deep into his pockets and drew his head down inside the collar of his greatcoat.

'I took a day away on my own the following morning. I didn't trust myself to be around them till I calmed down.

'I had a drink or two and received my own punishment for that the morning after.'

'So...' Macken began, but Gracey dismissed the interruption.

'I'd always been someone Cedric looked up to, God love him. I looked out for him. I suppose I thought of myself as a bit of a father to him. Maybe that's why he told me. Maybe that's why I took it so personally.

'Fair play to him though. He wasn't looking for approval. Or permission. Because when we'd all calmed down he told me it was between himself and Danny. Nobody else's business. He had just wanted me to know. God knows why. Maybe he trusted me.

'So, I very calmly sat Cedric down and explained a few facts to him. All very sober and reasonable. I told him that it was something neither I nor the rest of the world would tolerate. That it was a road he had to get off immediately, before it caused him great harm. I apologised for the beating, but said it would be nothing to what he would get in future.

'I said I'd get McMahon moved on. No blame would be attached to either of them. Not that I cared about that Fenian sodomite. But there would be no scandal. He could carry on as if it had never happened.

'The alternative would be disaster. There was no way something like that could be kept secret. Nor should it. A crime against God and nature and everything else.'

Gracey paused for breath.

'Did he agree?' asked Macken.

'Not at first. He said it was just the way they were, and there was no denying it. They shouldn't be made to feel there was anything disgusting about...'

Gracey's voice descended into a mumble.

'About... being in love.'

Macken screwed shut his eyes. They were talking about the wee boy who had dogged his steps in childhood. The young man who had admired him and followed him into the police. How had he never realised, never understood? How much else had he missed? 'I forbade him from coming out with any more of that nonsense ever again,' said Gracey. 'He agreed to think about it. I think I convinced him. But it was hard to stop the red mist taking over, you know?'

'But what about Danny?' asked Macken.

'I knew that sly, wee snake in the grass must have sucked Cedric into all this madness. I confronted McMahon. He was full of the same auld rubbish about love. All woeful and pious. Hypocrite. Thankfully there was no need to beat about the bush with him.

'I told him he was scum. Alright, Fenian scum. Sorry.'

Macken shrugged that no offence had been taken. He was impatient for more information.

'Then I told him that I would personally cut off his cock if he showed any sign of putting it to disgusting and unnatural uses, or gave Cedric any encouragement.'

They stood in silence. Macken heard Gracey's words as if he had said them to Danny himself. He winced at the hurt they must have caused. But at least Gracey had been here to say them. Macken had been oblivious to everything important about his own brother. Guilt consumed him. He hadn't known his brother, hadn't cared, hadn't been here when he was most needed.

'Was Danny persuaded?' asked Macken.

'I think the message got through alright.'

'How do you know?'

'He went and shot himself in the fuckin' head.'

Macken doubled up in pain that felt physical. Gracey patted his back.

'What a mess, eh? And it really was a mess.'

Macken forced himself upright again.

'But you managed to hush it up?'

'Aye, Jolly. You've got me. I hushed it up. Would you have preferred me to have told his family that their boy, the disgusting sodomite, committed suicide? They'd be sure to welcome a double helping of shame on top of the pain of having just lost him.

'Not one, but two mortal sins.'

Macken pursed his lips and said nothing.

'I got that from Cedric. McMahon told him in advance. Not in so many words. But he said he couldn't go on without him. Something like that.

'He told Cedric he was doomed already because of the mortal sin they had committed.'

Macken went to interrupt, but Gracey put up a hand to stop him.

'Apparently with you lot it's just as bad if you only intend to do it, so who knows. Maybe he thought one more mortal sin was neither here nor there.'

'So he *did* shoot himself then? It wasn't you or Cedric?'

'Fuck you, Macken. You're either a stupid bastard or just a bastard. Neither of us laid a finger on him.'

Gracey winced.

'I never touched him. I threatened him for sure. And they weren't empty threats.

'But if you ask me whether I pushed him to put the gun to

his head… I wish I'd never seen the fuckin' eejit. For all the trouble it's caused. For what it's done to Cedric.'

Gracey's guilt was turning to defensive anger.

'I suppose you would have let Cedric be thrown to the wolves too. Let the world know what unnatural crimes they were up to together.

'You have your chance now,' snarled Gracey. 'He's at your feet. But if you do, I *will* seek you out.'

'Hold on,' protested Macken. 'Then why were you always at me with the sly digs? And Cedric spying on me. I thought you were setting me up to be your next candidate.'

'Next candidate?' muttered Gracey. 'Don't flatter yourself.'

Macken tried to process this new information, to find a reason to disbelieve it. To find the slip that would let him unravel yet another of Gracey's elaborate deceptions and turn the clock back to the Danny he thought he knew.

'We had you pegged as a right wee snooper from day one,' said Gracey. 'All pious one moment, but not shy about bending the rules when it suits you.

'And that demotion bollocks. Didn't ring true. You were sent here for a reason.'

The two men weighed each other up, neither knowing where they'd go next, as enemies or allies.

'So here's the question, Jolly. Where do you stand? No one really knows with you, do they? Cedric died for you. What's McMahon to you?'

Macken pointed at Gracey, his hand in the shape of a gun, then touched him on the chest.

'Who was Danny? My brother.'

Gracey recoiled.

'I lost him. Left him. And then he followed me. Now I've lost him again.'

Guilt blinded Macken. This was the result of his selfishness.

369

Of his abandoning the wee brother who'd always looked up to him. I should feel more, he thought. More than guilt.

So where do I stand in this darkness? Then a tiny glint in some distant corner of his mind began growing in intensity. With Aoife, of course, with love.

'So Cedric and Danny were lovers?' said Macken.

'Love,' grunted Gracey. 'It's what makes the world go round.'

And he spat.

# CHAPTER 39

Macken gazed at the destruction. The splintered doorway where Bull had wreaked his havoc. The heap at his feet that once was Cedric. He bent down and entwined Danny's chain round the fingers of Cedric's right hand and squeezed them closed.

The chickens roamed free. Their cage was crushed in on itself, as though punched by a giant fist. That'll be the cause of the pain in my back, thought Macken.

He noticed that though the mesh was bent and distorted, it was unbroken. But the chickens had found a way out somehow. Macken retraced his steps to where he had been standing when the grenade exploded. The cage door itself was jammed open, the free corner dug into the dirt.

They got out the easy way, Macken realised. There you go as usual, always looking for the twisting path when the straight road is clear ahead. He smiled to himself, and finally remembered Aoife.

'Aoife. Where is she?'

Gracey raised his eyebrows.

'She was here when... Oh, God!'

'Hey, don't worry,' said Gracey. 'There was no sign of her when I arrived.'

'She's probably in the house.' A shadow passed over Macken's face. 'I made her promise not to set foot out the door, but I think she climbed through the window.'

Gracey shook his head.

'You never cease to surprise me. What about her Da, the bad Penny himself? Did he finally take himself away south with the rest of the boyos?'

'Penny?' said Macken. 'No, we cuffed him inside the house.'

'I sent Bull there to get cleaned up,' said Gracey. 'I didn't know you had Penny and herself inside.'

They ran to the house, sending chickens flying either side. Gracey burst in first, to be faced with a scared Paddy Penny still cuffed round the post. He said nothing. No need. His face, pale with shock, said it all. A livid bruise round one eye. Jaw tight. Not knowing whether these new arrivals meant rescue or something much worse.

Bull was slumped over the sink, his shoulders heaving. He did not turn round. Macken saw no sign of Aoife. He stared at Penny, questioning. He saw a moment of relief, and then renewed fear in her father's eyes. Penny shook his head slightly. Macken tried to speak, but Gracey beat him to it.

He spoke as if nothing special had occurred, and he had just encountered Bull amidst the comings and goings of a normal day filled with activities conjured up for the sole purpose of filling it.

'Sure there you are, Bull. How's the man?'

He continued in this soothing tone as he approached Bull from behind.

'Having a wee spruce-up? Good stuff.

'Jolly's with me. Not looking too pretty, but when did he ever, says you?'

Gracey forced a light laugh and put a hand lightly on Bull's shoulder. It tensed and then relaxed. As Bull turned, Macken could sense Penny freeze against the post.

Bull's face was pale and dripping. His temples and under his chin were dull red from the blood he'd missed. His hair shoved back, stood on end, wet from the water or stiff from drying blood. His hands seemed larger than normal, great hunks of flesh and gristle, dripping onto the floor.

'Alright then, Bull?'

He nodded.

'Has the master of the house been behaving himself?'

'Not at first,' murmured Bull, and then raised a paw to point towards Paddy Penny. 'But now he knows...'

Penny pressed himself back against the post.

'Aoife,' said Macken.

'Ach, sure that's right,' continued Gracey, maintaining his tone of easy chat. 'Where is the lady of the house? By God, we could do with a drop of tea right about now.'

The constable shook his head.

'Aoife isn't it?' carried on Gracey. 'Now where is she after getting to, I wonder?'

'She's not here,' said Bull, speaking slowly.

'Not here, Bull?'

'Jolly told her to stay, but she didn't.'

'She won't have gone far,' said Gracey, patting him on the shoulder. 'Probably frightened by the commotion.'

Gracey thought for a moment, then gestured towards Penny.

'Jolly, why don't you take yer man and have a wee gander round for her? Myself and Bull will forage in here for some tea. No better man for the job, eh Bull?'

Gracey gently turned Bull away. He jerked his head towards Macken and then to the door. Macken frowned at Penny's eye to keep silent. He quickly unlocked the handcuffs and helped him up. They slipped away, leaving Gracey to restore Bull the berserker to the man they had thought they had known.

Outside, Macken shoved Penny against the wall.

'Where is she?' he hissed.

Penny was a big man, but shrank into himself, like a dog cowering before yet another blow. Macken repeated the question, and then added: 'Was it Bull?'

'No,' said Penny. 'She was gone before he came in.'

Penny closed his eyes. Macken felt they were sharing a prayer of thanks.

'Was she not...' began Penny.

'She was there,' said Macken. 'But she disappeared.'

Penny looked confused.

'Bull said one of your boys was killed.' Penny looked down. 'I hoped it was you.'

Macken grabbed him by the hair: 'Shut up!'

'You've brought us evil from the day I set eyes on you.'

'You've no one to blame but yourself for brawling in pubs,' growled Macken.

Penny laughed bitterly.

'I was drunk because of you. I saw what you did in the woods. Would you have finished me off as quick as you did my dog?'

Macken let go of him.

'You were there? It was an accident.'

'He was innocent. You're worse than that mad ox inside. You showed no mercy.'

'I'd keep quiet about that,' advised Macken, 'or Gracey will kill you.'

'And to think you were trying to ensnare my Aoife...'

Macken started.

'Where is she? She saved my life.'

Penny looked away. Macken pushed him back against the wall.

'She could be lying hurt somewhere. Your daughter. Where would she go?'

'I don't know,' Penny shouted back. Macken banged Penny's head against the wall. Again and again, shouting the question in Penny's face. He did not hear the answer at first. It came in a whisper.

'The hen house.'

Macken stopped and stared at him.

'That's where I saw her. What do you mean?'

Penny's legs gave way. Macken let him slide down the wall. He saw he wouldn't get anything else out of him.

'Stay there,' he barked at the slumped man. 'And keep your mouth shut.'

Macken ran back to the hen house. She'd been here. Warned him. Then she'd gone.

Macken avoided looking at where Cedric still lay. He would not be moved till the farm had been properly checked. Forgive me, he said to himself.

The distorted cage was still vibrating slightly. Macken played the encounter over in his mind. But he still couldn't see it, whatever 'it' was. Wherever he looked, he saw only Cedric, cold and growing older. A chicken began to strut self-importantly over Cedric's corpse.

'Get out of that,' shouted Macken. Then he remembered. There had been no chickens outside. They had been inside, ignoring him, until he had crashed in on them.

They got out afterwards. Right, Macken told himself, because they walked out the door. Which must have burst open with the blast. So what?

So why was Aoife there? It was obvious. She'd come to warn him. Even after what I did to her father, thought Macken. She'd risked her life to warn him. He remembered it exactly. She'd told him to leave. And then… And then she'd stopped. She'd seen it. He had seen her face react the moment she saw it, and then… And then nothing, thought Macken. That was it. Or would have been if it hadn't been for Cedric. No time for him to shout a warning, just to act.

Macken realised he could not take much more. He was exhausted, mentally and physically. But he had to find Aoife. To explain. To make sure she was alright.

She can't have gone far, he thought. This is worse than that night in the forest. Another waking nightmare. But this time there's no pretending it'll end at the dawn.

He looked towards the border. Would Aoife have followed them? Or would she be nestled into the hollow where she took me before? Watching, waiting till it was safe to return. Safe from the madness and blood and wrath. Safe from him.

Macken was finding it difficult to take the next step, fearful it would take him in the wrong direction. He felt scared of doing something that could not be undone, or of pushing her into a corner from which she would lash out at him like he had at her father. Macken knew he would have to find her. What tortured him was that she might see him and burrow deeper to hide from the man he had shown himself to be.

A last glance around. Then, just as he made to leave, a small corner of bright green caught his eye.

It was out of place, protruding from the shelter inside the cage. A rich, emerald, mossy shade, clean and clear amidst the scurf of earth, feathers and shit. Macken stepped into the cage to look more closely.

He had to crouch down under where the wire was bent out of shape. She can't be inside, he thought, it's too small. She wouldn't fit. But as he bent to look inside the low doorway of the shelter, he knew that if she had crawled, she just might.

It was dark inside. Macken waited till his eyes adjusted. He began to make out the walls, where light pierced through cracks between the boards and round the edges of a sliding shutter. The small space was empty of any shape that could have been a human, living or otherwise. She's not here, he thought, and exhaled in relief that he had not discovered her lying dead. His breath stirred up the dust and feathers from the floor, making him cough. He squeezed his shoulders through the door a little further, so as to be able to reach the shutter and slide it open, letting in more light.

It was just a box really. Not high enough for even a child to stand upright. On the floor were a trough and some bowls. An old spoon lay in a corner. It looked like it had been used as a spade rather than for eating. Both options equally unlikely given the residents, thought Macken. The bowls, like the floor, were covered in grit and fluff and debris. It looked like one bowl had been covered over by a second, as a lid, which had slipped sideways. Maybe in the blast. Or thanks to an inquisitive hen. Inside the bowl were two thick pieces of bread, generously spread with butter. Macken raised his eyebrows. She really spoilt her chickens.

Macken twisted his shoulders to extricate himself and pulled the green cloth out with him. It looked like one of Aoife's scarves. She must have dropped it while feeding them, he thought. He held his nose against the stench.

Macken ducked out of the cage and walked down the gentle slope to where the gunmen had fled. I'll be an easy target for anyone still lingering, he thought. But he kept up a slow, deliberate pace, so as not to miss any clue, nor startle Aoife. He raised her scarf to his face. The stench of chickens was fainter than he'd expected. Mustn't have been lying there long, he thought. But the dark, rich smell was familiar. He was sure he had encountered it before.

That was another mystery, he thought. That Aoife herself carried no trace of the hen stink. Nor much of the farm at all. Did all women have an invisible layer that repelled the decay of the world, and preserved what was fresh and beautiful? He thought of the phosphorescent gleam of Aoife's skin from his dream. Maybe her secret is that she can live in the wickedness of the world without being corrupted.

An engine burst into life back in the farmyard. They won't leave without me, he thought, and plodded on. Then he heard shouts and a shot.

Macken began running back. He realised that there must have been more men in hiding and they'd stolen a car. Which meant he would never reach the yard in time. But he might catch them at the bend. No time to worry that he was unarmed.

Macken heaved himself over the gate. He staggered into the road and looked up to see the police car swerving in front of him. He saw Aoife wrestle to control it. The brakes shrieked as she tried to avoid him. He leapt into the hedge.

The car hit the ditch. Aoife was thrown against the steering wheel. Macken found his voice at last and called out. She sat back, dazed, and reached for an old suitcase next to her.

Macken's heart and stomach and carefully guarded hope all plummeted. He recognised the suitcase as the one she'd had by the lake when they'd first met. She's really leaving, he realised. She's going for good.

He called out her name again and pulled himself free of the brambles. She turned to him. A torn, anguished yearning seemed to be reaching out to scoop him up. Then she wrenched the gears into reverse to jerk the car free from the ditch.

Macken ran and grabbed the door handle. Inside, Aoife worked the gearstick.

'Don't go, Aoife!' cried Macken. 'It'll be alright. We can go together.'

She looked at him again. Their faces inches apart. Her lips parted slightly. Macken leant in to hear her answer. Or to communicate without words. Her lips on his.

Other voices began to filter through. Men shouting. Then a veil seemed to pass over her eyes, replacing her expression of confused indecision with an unreadable urgency of purpose. Macken had a sensation of falling, as if a great distance was rapidly opening up between them, though they remained close enough to touch.

He leant forward to touch her. To feel the soft skin of her face against his. His eyelids half-closed. Suddenly, his body was snapped back as the engine roared.

Macken felt the one arm still holding on almost wrench from its socket. For a moment his vision went white with the pain. He banged against the car, his feet scrabbling for purchase on the running board.

Turning his head against the rushing wind, Macken saw Aoife hunched over the steering wheel as if focused on the twisting lane ahead. But he could tell she was staring into the face of something else that only she could see. He realised she might not even know he was still there. But he could not communicate with her. He was putting everything he had into just holding on.

The sensation in Macken's fingers began to dull. He knew he could not hang on much longer. He would not even know he had lost his grip till he hit the road.

Aoife suddenly slowed to take a tight bend to the left. For

a moment, the wind eased and as the car took the curve, his body was pressed against the bodywork. Macken screamed as he put all his energy into one last heave. In a single movement he twisted back round to face Aoife through the passenger window. He was holding on with both hands now, though only one of them was much use.

He shouted her name. But it was as if her mind had already left this world. Macken kept calling for her to slow down, to not be frightened.

He pressed in closer to the car door as brambles from the ditch raked his head and back. I've got to get inside, he thought.

Macken reached in to unlatch the passenger door. It swung out, sweeping him off the running board. He held on, his feet running in the air and rapping off the roadway. A thick bush leant into the lane on Macken's side.

'Christ, I'm going to hit it!'

Aoife slowed into another left curve and the door swung back in. Macken lunged towards the roof post. He caught hold before the door swung out again, and hooked a leg round behind the door. Now, if he could wait for the right moment to heave himself in, he would be able to grab the steering wheel and stop the car.

Aoife's suitcase was in the way. Macken didn't want to bounce back off it and out the door again. He shifted his weight to his back foot on the running board. Then he slowly raised his left leg and hooked his foot round the corner of the suitcase, to pull it towards him and out of the car.

Aoife's body seemed to jump, as if she had suffered an electric shock. Her head jerked round for the first time, but not towards Macken. She put out a hand to steady the suitcase.

'It's alright,' shouted Macken. 'I'm coming in.'

Her face showed confusion. Macken smiled. 'You don't get rid of me that easily.'

He felt the car slow. It was easier for him to get a hand to the suitcase now. One more heave and it would be out and he would be in. Aoife glanced round as he stretched to slide out the case.

Her mouth formed the shape of a horrified 'No'. She tugged at the suitcase and stamped on the accelerator. There was nothing for Macken's fingers to fasten round, and therefore no resistance as he pulled back. As the car jumped forward, he felt himself falling backwards. Then the slow, weightless moment ended as he smacked into the road and bounced through the hedge.

*The walls of his new, small world bumped him back and front, shielding him from the shouting and rasping, rumbling, growling, roaring outside.*

*He lay on his side, the floor shifting continually, slipping to and fro, back and forth in darkness.*

More pain. He knew it was coming. One thing at a time, he thought, it's all I can cope with. Macken felt pinned in place. His vision swam into focus to reveal the sky fluttering above him like a torn, dirty nightdress. So low and opaque he almost felt smothered. Then it dipped and flapped across his face. He recoiled and then struggled in panic and pain as spikes pierced his skin.

The ghost world above him was filled with pale, soiled, waving flags. Some began to take recognisable shape – a torn shirt, a slip. Something brushed against his cheek. A sock. Small and dirty. A child's sock.

Macken was still bewildered, but was gradually coming to accept that he was still earthbound. He had not bounced off the road into some bizarre afterlife.

Right, he thought, I'd best get up. Then he heard a scream. And felt those sharp, piercing pains in his arms and legs again. He realised the scream was coming from his own throat. He was caught in thorns. A hawthorn hedge.

Gingerly and painfully, he began to extricate his battered and punctured body. With his first free arm, Macken batted away dangling shreds of clothing. He could see pairs of spectacles caught in the thorns. There was a shoe. And another. Walking sticks. Crutches. A complicated apparatus of leather straps and metal.

It dawned on him. He had been thrown into the raggedy bush. It gave him the creeps. He struggled free and blundered back into the lane.


Macken lay winded and heartsick. He tried not to think about the vast, howling emptiness inside him after his violent rejection by Aoife. Nor the inevitable physical agony he knew was galloping towards him. He had been fighting through the pain of the wounds he had picked up at the barracks and since, and the accumulated strain and lack of sleep.

Now, on his back in the roadway, this must surely be the end, he thought. No denying that the whole idea of running off with Aoife, of finding a better life, had been just a ridiculous, impossible, childish fantasy.

He gazed upwards. No ghosts this time. No waving phantoms. Just a clear pale blue. No clouds, no dark corners in which to hide or harbour false hopes. It's about time I saw life the way it really is, he thought. It's a hard sentence. Hard hearts and hard faces. Maybe if you accept it for what it is, he thought, there may still be small mercies and simple pleasures to be found.

Dull pounding began to reverberate up from the road surface through the back of his skull. His eyes moistened with the knowledge that this was the point of no return, that once he emerged from the purgatory ahead, he would be wiser and irredeemably sadder. No more blue skies, thought Macken, and he closed his eyes.

# CHAPTER 40

'So, is he dead? Or just out for the count?'

'Hauld on till I see.'

'Ach, look! That wee bitch must have clipped him.' Bull shook his head in regret. 'I wish I *had* hit her now. He's beyond caring by the looks of it. You shouldn't have stopped me.'

'Jolly!' It was Gracey, shaking his good arm. 'Are you right?'

This wasn't how Macken had expected things to play out. He opened his eyes to see Gracey blocking out the heavens.

'Ach, I knew it,' said Gracey with satisfaction. 'Sure don't we know you're the hard man to kill?'

Gracey eased himself back up.

'He's still with us, Bull.'

Macken saw the sky still clear and blue above him. Bull and Gracey lifted him up.

'Lord, Jolly, I thought you were another goner,' said Bull. 'Did she run you down?'

'No, she swerved to miss me. Then I jumped on.

'But I didn't stay on.'

Macken looked back along the lane. A car was wedged sideways between the ditches on either side. Hissing came from beneath the bonnet.

'What happened at the farm?'

'Looks like she was involved all along,' said Gracey. 'The first we knew was when we heard the car start. We ran out, but she was away too quick.'

'Did she shoot at you?' asked Macken.

Gracey looked a little defensive.

'No, that was Bull. Heat of the moment.'

Bull shifted uncertainly. 'Sorry, Jolly, but she tried to run you over.'

'She didn't,' sighed Macken. 'It doesn't matter. She's gone. What's up with the car?'

'She stole mine,' said Gracey. 'And she'd sabotaged the others to stop us following.

'We ran after her. Nearly caught up when she crashed into the bank. You were on the ground. The next moment you were gone.

'Then Bull remembered the cars hidden in the barn. She must not have had time to mess with them.'

Gracey nodded at the car blocking the lane. 'That one's a bloody mess inside, but it started fine. Not sure if it will now. It's wedged in.'

'We'll need the other one to pull it clear,' said Bull.

They stood, bottom lips out, sizing up the vehicle like farmers assessing cattle at a mart. Macken turned away. He focused on the small wildflowers growing on the bank. Gracey seemed to pick up on his mood.

'Aye, it would be a lovely wee place this, Jolly. If it wasn't for the likes of them and us wrecking it, eh? That what you're thinking?'

Macken said nothing. Bull clucked round the stranded car.

'It's the sort of quiet place Cedric might not mind resting in,' Gracey continued. 'Not that there's been much quiet lately.'

The sergeant suddenly looked bleak, as if his face had been stripped away to the rock beneath.

'But we'll not leave you here, Cedric,' he said quietly, almost to himself. 'You'll be coming back with us, Son.'

Macken watched Gracey shrink into himself, as if against a chill. Macken felt it too.

Gracey spoke quietly.

'I'll take Bull back for the other car. You'll be alright here, won't you? Just make sure no one else crashes into that heap.'

Gracey patted him on the shoulder.

'Then we can deal with Cedric.'

'What about…'

'She'll be long gone over the border, Jolly. You did your best, eh?'

Macken looked down. There had not even been a goodbye. His last glimpse of her had been that hunted look. He knew her fear would fill his dreams, erasing all the joy and all the hope they had shared.

As he began to walk towards the junction, Macken recalled something else in Aoife's final glance. Not just fear, but pleading. As if she had been asking something with her eyes that could not be put into words. To not give up on her. Whatever happened, she was as much a victim as anyone. No wonder she ran. It doesn't matter whether I understand or not, thought Macken. I just have to trust her.

He went over his options. Gracey had said she'd be running for the border. But which way? The short road to Tycross or some less predictable route? I've only one chance, he thought. It has to be right. Once she gets across…

Doesn't matter, Macken nodded to himself. If I'm on the right road behind her, I'll not stop at the border. This is personal. Nothing to do with lines on maps. So, the short way to Tycross then, he decided. She has her bag packed and she wants out.

God knows when I'll get after her though. He sighed in exasperation.

Suddenly Macken caught his breath. The truck.

Macken swivelled round. He saw Gracey and Bull clambering over the wedged car. He waved and shouted: 'The truck! There's still the truck!'

He did not wait for a response. He began hobbling faster. New hope drove out the crippling despair and pain. Would it work?

He climbed inside. The windows were shattered. He brushed glass off the seat and tried to start the engine. It caught and turned over.

As the cab shuddered in time with the engine, Macken saw Gracey and Bull running towards him. He waited. Not for them, but because it was still not quite clear to him. It was right to follow her, he was sure of that. But the border felt wrong. If Aoife was running from him, there was no need to leave the state. She could go wherever she wanted. Lose herself in the city maybe? But did that mean Belfast or Dublin or somewhere else? Derry? Macken swore. She could be going for a boat. Didn't have to be for England. Scotland even. Or straight to America like they'd discussed. Somewhere far away without him.

But she knew no one in any of those places. They'd all be strangers. Maybe that's what she wants. A fresh start. Somewhere safe. Macken squeezed the wheel in frustration. Think!

Macken noticed Gracey at the back of the truck. It was still raised. Macken pulled the tipper lever. It was stiff, but it moved. The mechanism was working. Gracey gave a thumbs up, but then the truck shuddered and he put up a hand and shook his head.

'It's not staying down,' he called up.

'Didn't I tell you he banjaxed it,' said Bull, memories of the battle sparking fresh excitement in his eyes.

Macken could tell Gracey was calculating the odds.

'That's that then,' said the sergeant. 'We'll never catch her in this.'

The knot in Macken's gut reminded him that this was his one chance. There had to be some special place set apart from the whole rest of the world where she would go. He realised that if he could not come up with the answer right here, right now, all he deserved was to have her as a beautiful memory.

His mind wandered back over the brief times they had had together. He tried to resist this defeatist tumble into reminiscence. It's not over yet, he urged himself. Come up with something or drive yourself into that lake and finish it all. Christ, he railed bitterly, it started there so it may as well finish there.

Macken put his head on the steering wheel. Then a spasm coursed through him. He knew where she was going, but the awareness that he had been so slow, and might yet be too late, was agonising.

Macken stuck the truck in reverse and backed up to give himself room to turn.

Gracey put his foot on the step to climb into the cab. But Macken knew he was going after Aoife on his own.

'Out of the way, Gracey,' shouted Macken.

'You're going the wrong way, man!'

'No passengers,' Macken shouted back. 'It's for me to sort out.'

Gracey jumped off. Whatever he shouted was lost in the

clamour of the engine as the truck surged back towards Blackwatertown.

Macken gave up trying to work the tipping mechanism, and left the bed of the truck pointing skyward. As he rattled along the narrow roads, the top edge of the tipper tore off overhanging branches. Driving so fast with it raised made the truck unstable. Macken gouged chunks out of the grassy banks on either side.

As he approached Blackwatertown, Macken saw people clearing the street of debris and beginning to fix up their homes. Some were knocking out the remains of broken windows. He spotted Molly, the barracks housekeeper, shaking her head at the remains of the barracks doorway.

Macken leant on the horn. The locals seemed to jump en masse, and then leap off the road as it became clear he was not stopping. Lena Williamson was out with her bucket. She dropped it in surprise. Macken sped past the bombed barracks. Then he was over the bridge and leaving them all behind.

The first time they had met by the lake, Macken remembered, had been far into the Brookemartin demesne, amongst the rushes. He guessed she would most likely go via the back gate and then swing off to the lake, like she had shown him before.

He recalled that this end of the lake was more manicured. A mown grassy slope, with a small cliff bordering the open water. Specially built and landscaped for His Lordship no doubt, the better to survey the geese splash-landing.

Macken turned in between the stone gateposts, and then gunned the truck down the track to the lake. Branches smacked and snapped across the cab. As he emerged at the lakeside, he saw her car perched on top of the viewing point. He followed the muddy ruts up the slope.

# CHAPTER 41

The truck slowed and settled into the fresh grooves. The wheels spun as Macken pressed the accelerator, and dug in further. He saw a head bob over the bonnet of the parked car.

Macken cut the engine and got out. He called out to Aoife to wait. To not do anything. That it would be alright.

And he felt relief that what he said could still be true. He was not too late.

Aoife stepped out and calmly appraised him. There was still that look of purpose on her face, which had put distance between them before. She put her hands to her hair, as if to adjust a scarf, and then let them fall to her side.

She raised a hand in a gesture that told him not to come any nearer. Macken recognised it was the same warning she had given back at the farm. Instinctively, he looked over his shoulder for danger. There was no one. Just the lines he and Aoife had carved into the grass.

Aoife ducked behind her car. He did not understand how, but Macken knew that by looking away he had broken the spell. He lumbered up the slippery slope.

Then she was at the cliff edge. Macken shouted: 'No! Don't!'
He saw her test her footing and then pick up her suitcase.

Her back arched like a bow as she took the strain of the weight. She swung it forward a little, then back, and then hefted it forward again. Before her arms reached full stretch, the weight of the case seemed to tear it from her hands. It plunged beneath the lake's surface with a gulp.

Aoife gave a small grunt, swaying on the edge, unable to prevent herself following through on her swing. Macken caught her. She gasped in surprise as he wrapped his arms round her and smothered her with reassurances.

He felt his eyes moisten and he brimmed over with too much emotion to say anything coherent. No need for words, he told himself. He held her and kissed her auburn curls and her cheeks. He could not tell if she was crying, or if his own tears were wetting them both.

'I thought I'd lost you,' he told her aloud, regaining the ability to speak. 'But it's over. And we're fine, aren't we? We're fine.'

She smiled uncertainly. Macken beamed back. 'Don't worry about any of that,' he answered the question he thought she was asking. 'It'll all be sorted out. And I'm fine. Look at me.'

He released her and stepped back a little, opening his arms to reassure her. She looked on, eyes wide, as if not quite believing him. Then she noticed him wince as he raised his wounded arm too high. At once, her eyes creased, and that familiar, mischievous light crept back into them, as she slapped a hand over her mouth to hide the inappropriate smile his misfiring gesture had provoked.

Macken grimaced and then made an effort to turn it back into a smile.

'Well, mostly alright. Bit worn round the edges.'

Aoife stepped forward and hugged him.

'Gently,' warned Macken.

'You're impossible,' she answered. 'I can hardly believe we're both here. I can hardly believe you're alive at all. Is it a dream? Can I pinch you to be sure?'

They laughed, and Macken drew a deep breath, sucking life and vitality back into his bruised body. He wanted to explain, and to make her understand how sorry he was for the terror he had brought into her life. But he realised how unnecessary apologies were. How pointless when set against the reality of the two of them holding each other in the here and now. Plenty of time for explanations later.

'I'll always remember our time here. In my dreams too.'

'Is that how you found me?' Aoife arched an eyebrow. 'You dreamt your way?'

He nodded and she touched him with a fingertip, lightly on the tip of his nose.

'We'll have to keep dreaming, so.'

Macken spotted the suitcase crest the surface of the water with a fringe of bubbles. 'Shame you'll have no clothes though,' he said, nodding towards the floating case.

Aoife stiffened in his arms. 'Don't worry,' he said, kissing her lightly on the tip of her nose. 'New clothes, new beginnings. It all goes together. I'll need some new clothes myself.'

He pretended to consider his tunic. 'What do you think? Something in a lighter shade?'

Her smile returned, though weaker than before.

'You're weren't going to, were you?' asked Macken. 'Just now?'

She thought for a beat, then shook her head.

'Lucky I caught you then, before you had a dip by accident,' said Macken.

'Sorry,' he added, when he saw she was not enjoying it.

She pushed her face into his shoulder, like a small bird tucking its head under its wing. Macken closed his eyes, enjoying her body pressed against him. Her heart beat against him. Once again he felt transported by her presence far away from the dull, sordid realities of life.

Aoife withdrew from the burrow she had nuzzled into his armpit.

'Can we leave?' she asked. 'Right now?'

'Yes,' said Macken. 'I'll have to make my report. And then tender my resignation.'

She frowned.

'Just loose ends. So we can make a clean break.'

He smiled.

'Well, what'll it be? Your car or mine?'

'I think yours is stuck,' said Aoife.

He shrugged.

'Sure about your clothes? They've still not quite gone under. Shall I rescue them?'

'No, leave it.'

'Seriously, they're not far out. And you know I enjoy the occasional swim. You can warm me up afterwards.'

'Leave it be,' she said, steel in her voice. 'I've thrown away the past. It's the only way for us to have a future.'

Macken was struck by the bitterness in her voice, something he had never detected before. Though God knows, hadn't he been bitter himself sometimes about the hand life had dealt him? And that was little compared to what he knew she had endured.

'It's difficult to understand what you've been through. But I am trying. I don't mean to treat things lightly. I know the clothes meant a lot to you. They were all you took with you when you made your break for freedom.'

Colour rose in Aoife's face. It seemed she could not contain herself any longer.

'You talk about freedom!' she said angrily. 'Well, let's take it!

Stop trying to wrap me up in the past. I'm free of it, d'ye hear me?'

Her voice caught and she fumbled at her neck for something to wipe her eyes.

Macken reached into his pocket and pulled out a crumpled green wrap.

'Here, use this.'

She took it and dabbed her eyes. Then, in a well-practised movement, she opened it out and wrapped it round her head, knotting it under her chin. Macken watched her suitcase slowly sink below the surface a second time.

# CHAPTER 42

'It's the guns,' said Aoife. 'I took them to get rid of them.'

Macken's expression showed he didn't understand.

'From the boys that attacked Blackwatertown.'

'You were part of it?'

'No,' she shook her head sadly. 'My Da was. A little. They exploit him. But not me.'

'But why?'

'Why tell you? I can see that you won't leave it alone. And we're supposed to be honest with each other, aren't we?'

'Yes. But I mean, why did you take them?'

'It's evidence. Guns stashed on our farm. Wouldn't look good, wouldn't it?'

'But if they're nothing to do with you,' said Macken.

'No one would believe it.' She pointed to where the suitcase was disappearing. 'That's our freedom.'

'It's not your fault,' protested Macken. 'I'll explain.'

'No,' she put up that warning hand again. 'There can be no explaining.'

'I'll tell any lies I have to,' he promised.

'The best you can do is to have never seen it,' said Aoife.

'Alright, if it's that important we'll leave them for now,' Macken agreed. 'I'll tip them off later.'

'No,' said Aoife.

'When we're long gone,' he reassured her. 'When I'm out of the force and they're rusted away. An anonymous letter from America. Or Australia.'

'No. Never,' she said, shaking. 'Listen to me now. It's what you promised. How you said it had to be. Just you and me. No baggage. Nobody else.'

She held his gaze with her own beautiful, clear, green eyes.

'We can have a life together. A family. But it starts now. Or never. Leave the suitcase. Never look back.'

She saw his confusion but did not waver. It felt wrong to Macken. That nagging feeling again. He had been told often enough that some things were better left alone. Maybe it was time he learnt the lesson before he threw away the best thing that had ever happened to him.

Macken felt he should be able to make Aoife understand that he would be able to smooth it all away. There was no need for this all or nothing business. But maybe that was the price of something special – total commitment, proving it was more important than anything else.

Anyway, what did it matter, he thought? A moment ago it was old clothes. Now it's guns. I'm no better off knowing. He closed his eyes, just now piecing together the discarded scarf in the hen house with her warning before the explosion. She was after the guns all along, he realised, hidden in the hen house. All that was left for him was an old spoon and a sandwich. Time to move on.

Aoife detected him relaxing. She could tell he was weakening. She had won. Macken replayed their confrontation before the explosion over in his mind. And Aoife's expression of surprise. It made sense. She'd been trying to stop him searching. Christ, he thought, squeezing her to him, Cedric saved her too.

Macken felt he had scratched the nagging itch long enough. Why shouldn't he choose happiness?

'We'll let them rust, so.'

He cast a last glance over the water. The suitcase was gone. Just a faint eddy from the last few bubbles streaming up from air pockets betraying its presence below.

'So that was why Danny gave you his wee medal,' said Macken. 'For protection. He knew there was something up.'

Aoife recoiled.

'It's alright. I know you lied about knowing him. I don't care,' said Macken, shaking his head. 'Was he in with the IRA too?'

'No,' said Aoife vehemently. 'He had nothing to do with it. He just cared about me.'

'You and my brother?' asked Macken.

Aoife looked away and only spoke with reluctance.

'Yes, but it wasn't like what we have.'

Macken closed his eyes – sad she still couldn't be honest with him. He didn't want to see her lie. There was no need.

She tugged his sleeve. He felt that misgiving again, stronger and more urgent. Still nagging him. Almost as if it too, like Aoife, was confronting him with a now or never ultimatum.

Odd, he thought, that the gang had not left the weapons with their wounded. Unless the commander had known they were already at death's door. More sensible to stash the guns until it was safe to retrieve them. Leave the wounded with a single grenade. Something to cling to. An illusion of control. An exit strategy. Martyrdom.

It didn't mean they gave them to Aoife, he thought. She maybe just swiped them to protect her family. She must have hidden strength in that wee body to lug the big gun around.

Macken knew he might not be fitting it together exactly right. But these were just details. Did it matter? Not many bubbles now, he thought. It was taking a long time to sink, for such a heavy weight.

'They'll not be safe here,' said Macken. 'Our tracks lead straight to them.'

'No!' exclaimed Aoife. 'We agreed.'

'If they find nothing at the farm, my sergeant will suspect we dumped them here. The estate staff will help him look. Most of them are in the Specials.'

'No, leave it, John! Leave it!'

'I have to move them, Aoife. They're not safe here. Not safe for you.'

Macken patted her arm; knowing nothing he could say would reconcile her to his chosen course of action. He slid and teetered down to the water's edge. Better get it over with quickly, he told himself. Gracey could be along any minute.

His mind churned over the options as he untied his boots. Dump the guns over the border. Or bury them properly.

Macken removed his belt and tunic. He looked at Aoife. Her expression stopped him. Something he had never seen before. Terror.

He wobbled. Then somehow he knew he had to act fast before his resolve faltered. He strode into the dark water and dived forward, gasping with shock as the cold clamped itself around him.

*He felt weightless. All movement was slower, smoother.*

*No ripping claws. No screeching. Quiet wrapped round him. Damp seeping. He stayed curled up. Awake or asleep? He did not know.*

*Alive or dead? He did not know.*

*He had finally taken flight from the world he had known.*

*Neither alive nor dead meant anything to him. Only light and dark.*

*But no light at all now.*

*Gasping for air.*

*Growing clammy, he felt the darkness and the cold pressing in on him now like never before.*

Macken swam till he gauged he was where the suitcase had sunk. He couldn't see if Aoife was watching.

He treaded water for a moment, then bent forward and dived down, kicking his legs and pulling with his arms. The turbulence sent up swirls of silt, making it hard to see through the murk. He flailed around blindly, the water seeming to thicken to a viscous tar sapping his strength. Macken realised his eyes were squeezed closed. But when he opened them, he was as blind as before. The pain in his chest grew into a fist, and he clawed his way back up to the surface.

Macken gasped, trying to suck in as much air as quickly as he could. He knew that every breath let the suitcase sink further. Down again. Reaching for the bottom, scrabbling with his hands, kicking with his feet to keep him down. Snatching at weed and mud and stones. The pounding in his chest growing. Fingers raking along the bottom. Catching a root. No, something less yielding. The handle of the case.

He hooked his fingers round the handle to anchor himself to it. No movement. It was wedged into the muddy lakebed. The remaining buoyancy in his body was dragging him up. Macken winced at the pain shooting through the arm holding him to the case. More of his air leaked out. The case was not shifting. He pulled again, both hands clenched round the handle. One last heave with all his strength.

Then, amidst a cloudburst of silt, the suitcase moved. The

mud released its catch, slightly, for a moment, before sucking it back down.

Too heavy, thought Macken. Too heavy. Letting go with one hand he crawled his fingers over the case to find the straps holding it closed. One buckle. Undone. The pressure in his ribcage now a deafening alarm bell ringing inside his head. He felt for the other strap. Screaming silently in rage and desperation at the fingers hooking him round the handle, that they not go numb and loosen.

He traced the line of the other strap to its buckle. Macken was dimly aware of the sharp edges cutting through his skin, but felt nothing. The second buckle came undone. He moved to unclick the catch to open the case.

It would not slide. He would have called on God, begged Him, cursed Him – if he'd had the breath or consciousness. His mind was beginning to wander, preparing to jump ship along with his last breath. Despair. Acceptance. He was on the verge of his last gasp, that would bring water rushing into him, overpowering him. Making his eyes pop.

He could not remember where he was or why. He was stripped to the core of his being. No thought. Just an existence. A faint spark that the endless black water was pushing, pushing to extinguish.

Macken forced the fingertips of one hand between the lid and body of the case. Squeezing the handle as tight as he was able with the other, he pulled his hands apart as hard as he could. The lock broke. The clamshell opened.

# CHAPTER 43

Silt clouds billowed round Macken. His last air escaped. Tendrils of underwater weed, thin as hair, twined round his fingers.

He struggled to free himself, and with the panic came rushing back consciousness of who and where he was. He realised that if he did not untangle himself he would be down there forever. He yanked his arm back, and kicked for the distant light above. The delicate fibres did not snap. Instead, the whole clump followed him.

As if in a dream, Macken climbed away from the sucking mud. But it was still so dark, and so far and he had no strength left. The weed was holding him back, dragging him down. He tried to unknot it. Through the gently waving filaments, his little finger touched something solid and soft.

This must be what death is like, thought Macken, as he felt his little finger gripped by what seemed like an even smaller hand. I never knew it would be so gentle. It's like a child taking me, reassuring me not to be frightened. It's Danny welcoming me. He smiled as the melodies of classroom hymns came back to him: 'Suffer little children to come unto Me, for theirs is the kingdom of heaven.' Dear God, he thought. I really did try.

Macken burst through the surface, retching for breath, wracked with pain. There was a deeper pain too, of abandonment. The door to paradise had been slammed in his face. The promise of no more suffering snatched back. He cried out at the loss of that gentle guiding hand.

Then he felt it. Still holding him tight.

Macken shivered violently. He drew the hand towards him and lifted the sodden bundle into the air. He couldn't take in what he was seeing or what it meant. He swam until his feet could touch the bottom. Then he staggered onto the grass, with the bundle in his arms. He set it down carefully, but detected no signs of life.

Macken heard a high-pitched wail, a keening, from above. And shouts, deeper, coming closer. He saw Gracey running towards him. Bull and other men close behind.

He looked at what he had brought up from the deep. It was beyond his comprehension. Almost like a child. But curved in on itself like a small animal. Like a foetus bent double in the womb. Macken touched the hand that had grasped his finger. It has hands, he thought. Tiny, gnarled fingers twisted together into bent scoops.

He dripped over the creature. His eyes followed the tightly curved spine from the hunched shoulders down to a – Macken spasmed in shock – a little pair of short trousers.

He flicked his eyes up to what was unmistakably a tiny face, pinched and blue from the cold, crowned by thin wisps of pale, copper-coloured hair.

Macken swept the small body into his tunic, then laid it back down gently.

'Jolly! What the hell?' Gracey panted, bent over double. 'Is that a child? Jesus!

'Is it dead?'

Macken looked up.

'I don't know.'

'Come on then!' roared Gracey.

Macken gently pressed on the child's forehead to push its head back and open its airway, but it seemed the small body could not be straightened. He gently opened the tiny mouth with his finger. He felt round for any weed inside, but it seemed clear.

Then he placed his mouth over the small opening below. He blew softly and then lifted his mouth a little. He repeated the action. And then again. He lowered his face close to the child's mouth to feel any air moving. Nothing.

It suddenly struck Macken: was this what Danny had known, or suspected? The reason he had given Aoife his medal – and why she'd refused it? He prayed: 'O Mary, conceived without sin, pray for us who have recourse to thee.'

He felt Gracey's hand on his shoulder. 'Let me take over. You're perishing with the cold.'

Macken shook him off, and bent down again to try to breathe some of his own life into the tiny water baby. For a moment he felt the skin under his fingertips tauten, and then a small movement. Macken heard a small cough. He put his face close to the child's mouth, just in time to feel it gasp for breath on its own.

Macken threw back his head and let out a cry of relief.

'It's alive, Gracey!'

He rocked back on his heels as Gracey gathered up the child. The small creature gave a bleat of distress, and then let rip with a long, shrill, squawking cry that chilled everyone who heard it.

*He gasped. The walls were gone. The light was so bright it hurt his eyes.*

*He felt arms around him. But not hers. Bigger. Rougher. He was frightened. Cold.*

*A strange giant stared down. And beyond him, sky and space. So much space all around. He opened his heart and finally found his voice and screamed louder than ever before.*

# CHAPTER 44

Gracey held his bundle at arm's length, as if suddenly frightened by the delicate package. The other men seemed turned to stone. Macken's own heart skipped a beat at the inhuman cry.

All eyes were on the creature in Gracey's arms. Except for Macken's, who turned now to search out Aoife. Her wailing had ceased just as suddenly as the child's shriek had begun. She was staring at it. As he watched, he saw she was transformed. Where once had been light, and softness and joy and mischief, was now only the scraped-out shell of a women, drawn and ravaged by deep distress. She felt his gaze and turned her own deep, dark eyes on him. He saw guilt, terrible guilt. And he knew that, somehow, he shared it.

Macken rose to go to her. He called her name. She hammered her fists on the car bonnet.

'You've killed us,' she shouted. She shook her head slowly, as if baffled and saddened at his failure to understand. And then more quietly, almost to herself, she repeated it: 'You've killed *us.*'

One of the estate workers took her arm. As soon as he touched her, she screamed and pushed him in the chest, knocking him over. She twisted towards the edge of the cliff, but another worker caught her and held on. With more assistance, they hustled her off through the woods and out of sight. Macken heard her shouting 'No!' over and over.

Then Gracey was beside him, empty-handed.

'Bull's taking it to the doctor. It, he, she? We'll know soon enough. I need to take you there too. Don't worry about Aoife Penny for now. It's shock. She's just hysterical.'

They stood shoulder to shoulder, saying nothing, looking out over the water. Macken's mind roamed beyond where they could see, to where he and Aoife had watched fish dart below the surface, and to where bulrushes had hidden their lovemaking.

'Too neat and tidy for me,' said Gracey eventually. 'Though they say you can pick up a good bird or two in the wilder parts further up.'

'I've heard the same about the fishing.' Macken accepted the conversational lifeline back to normality. 'Though you have to keep an eye on your catch. You'd never know who'd be wandering about after dark.'

Gracey looked at him. Macken raised his eyebrows in innocence.

'That's one mystery cleared up,' laughed Gracey. 'You got the drop on us that night.'

'Naked,' added Macken, 'with only a stick.'

Gracey turned to him again, a pained expression on his face.

'Thank goodness it was a stick.'

Gracey nodded to himself.

'Cedric loved it here.'

Macken murmured agreement. Then they turned their backs on the water and began to walk towards the trees.

'I've one question for you,' said Gracey. 'And I'd like you to think carefully before answering.

'What I want to know is this. Are we finished for the day now? I mean, is that it? No more excitement? Because I'm bleedin' starving. Never mind the rashers; I could eat a whole pig.'

He put an arm round Macken, as they strode together under the trees.

'I'm not joking you, Jolly. Just put the whole pig on the pan!'

# Some months later

# CHAPTER 45

It was the day Macken had been dreading. He was going to have to face in the flesh the two spectres who haunted his dreams. Every night since he had dived into the black water, one or other found him.

The dream always started the same. The dark lake rippling around him. More like oil than water. Somehow he was standing on the surface. Aoife would gradually rise from the water, naked and glistening. Not brazen but beautiful. Glowing like the Virgin Mary. Phosphorescent. She moved towards him slowly, so slowly, arms outstretched. At first, they offered an embrace, a haven. Succour from his mental torment and recrimination. Then her placid smile would subtly tighten into a mask of anguish. Her arms begging him not to abandon her.

Macken was never physically able to respond in the dream. Each time his arms hung slack and helpless. Her silent entreaties would become more and more wretched. Every time it ended the same. Her fingers would almost reach him. Her face would come breathtakingly close. Then she would slowly sink back into the darkness. Each time he would be consumed with regret and self-loathing.

Some nights it was different. The dream began with the same oily water and a glowing figure breaking the surface. He could not see who it was. The head was bowed down. The face hidden behind a veil of long, fine hair. A slim arm would reach towards him. Once again Macken was paralysed. But this time he was struggling to flee in dread. The strange head would rise, the wispy curtains of hair part and...

He always woke at that point, in a pool of sweat. It was time to confront his demons. He had no choice. Aoife was on trial. He was a witness for the prosecution.

Mad or bad? That was what the newspapers were asking, and what several months' detention at a local mental hospital were supposed to establish. The delay did nothing to dampen public interest in Aoife's trial. Macken waited outside the main chamber of the grand Victorian courthouse on Belfast's Crumlin Road. The door opened and an usher beckoned him in.

The public gallery was full to bursting. Macken looked neither right nor left. He particularly did not want to catch *her* eye, afraid it would paralyse him.

He put his hand on a thick Bible and tried to speak, but nothing came out. Macken cleared his throat and this time managed to lie properly. He knew he was expected to give evidence only about finding the child and events immediately before that. The authorities had decided to draw a veil over the whole truth, including what might have been his relationship with the defendant. Risked muddying the waters apparently. And neither side wanted the political aspects complicating matters.

The prosecution barrister had been briefed not to ask how

he had known where to find Aoife. He led Macken through seeing her car and what happened next.

'I witnessed the defendant struggling with a suitcase. It appeared to be heavy.'

'Please confirm for the court that the defendant is the woman you saw that day.'

This was the moment he would have to face her, thought Macken. The woman of his dreams. And nightmares.

He felt as though he was in the dock – should be in the dock – for betraying her and the future he had promised for them both. The court was silent. Macken heard the creak of the judge's chair as he leant forward to see what was causing the delay. The prosecutor cleared his throat. Macken knew he could put it off no longer. He raised his head and looked towards the dock.

He hadn't known which incarnation to fear more – the moonlit siren who stalked his nights, or the living, breathing bundle of mischief and energy who had first opened his mind to the wonder of the world. An accusing finger or a reminder of the beautiful, beguiling woman who had breathed new life into him?

He saw her. Paler than ever. Her face thinner. The springing cascades of auburn hair now flat and dull. Dark shadows under dead eyes.

'Yes, sir. That's her.'

The public gallery let out its collective breath and began to mutter. Macken gripped the edge of the witness box, keeping his face expressionless. Aoife was not permitted to speak at this point in the proceedings, but Macken cowered inwardly in anticipation of her reaction. If not a word, then a look. A pleading or accusing stare would be enough to send him rushing to her or fleeing from the court.

But the small, defeated figure averted her face, like a crippled bird turned away from a predatory cat, some vestige of dignity preventing it bowing to the inevitable.

Macken's statement threw doubt on whether Aoife had intended to throw the suitcase into the water. He told the court that she had been moving away from the cliff edge when he had startled her and that the heavy case had slipped from her hands. So the attempted murder charge had been dropped, but not forgotten by anyone present.

The defence counsel had no questions. No reason for him to pry into what I've said under oath, thought Macken. But even he, who had been there, was having difficulty choosing between the truth of his eyes and the truth of his heart.

He snapped to attention as he realised the judge was addressing him directly, commending him for his bravery. He could only see Aoife's face in profile but noticed for the first time a small gleam in her eye. Macken focused on this sign of life, suddenly willing her to give him some sign of recognition on what could be the last time they saw each other. As he watched, the light left her eye and became a single, fat tear running down her clenched face.

Macken sensed a hand on his tensed arm. It was the usher. He let himself be directed to the back of the court. He waited for a moment, a pain in his chest from willing her to look at him and give a sign of the bond he knew they had. But he was also terrified of the verdict she might pronounce from the dock. One word. *Judas.*

Macken left the court and bought a newspaper to hide behind. There was now nothing in the way of the other confrontation he had been avoiding. A new knot grew in his stomach.

Hunger, that's all it is, he thought. He had been too nervous to eat breakfast. He rolled the newspaper into a baton and set off downhill to the city centre. Perhaps he could lose himself in the crowds, until the myriad voices trying to be heard blended into a hubbub easy to ignore.

Even out of uniform, Macken had the long, steady stride of a policeman. And the mindset to go with it – detachment from the crowd, be it Orange or Green. Locals turned away, assessing that this stranger who displayed neither fear nor curiosity was probably best left alone.

Only a mongrel darting out from a side entry paid him any overt attention, barking at his heels. Dogs can always sniff out policemen, he thought.

Without slackening, Macken flicked his rolled-up paper at the dog's nose, and it retreated. Aoife's story was on the front of the early edition. Sex, crime and family secrets. Two photogenic stars, Aoife and the mysterious child. The malevolent beauty and the pitied beast. Leader writers asked of Aoife: Is this the face of evil? It fed other agendas too. Proof for evangelicals of the darkness lurking under all that Catholic piety. Politicians pointed to the Penny family's links to the insurgency – a salutary reminder of the dual threat from Dublin and Rome.

There were no quotes from Macken. 'Whatever you say, say nothing.' That was the Ulster motto he'd finally learnt to live by.

And nothing had been printed about his connection with Constable McMahon, nor what he'd reported to senior officers. Yes, it looked like a tragic accident. Yes, Blackwatertown was a happy ship. The community had pulled together, as communities do, and so on. And then it was onto the attack on the barracks and afterwards. Yes, sir, a privilege to serve with Constable Andrews. Cedric had been posthumously honoured. That at least was deserved, thought Macken.

Meanwhile, the insurgency dragged on. Every time it

seemed to be petering out for lack of Catholic support, there would be another incident. A police constable had been shot dead. Four IRA men had blown themselves up making a bomb. If you believe the papers, he reminded himself.

Accustomed to disappointment and wary of provoking the Protestant state into lashing out, as in the past, Catholics in the North clung to their bitter isolation, rather than trust in the latest generation of would-be saviours.

The funerals of the 'heroes of Blackwatertown' gave the IRA a boost down south. Small comfort for Peadar Greenard, who had been scooped up after the introduction of internment without trial on both sides of the border. The resolve of the Dublin government had caught Republicans by surprise and seemed to have broken the back of their campaign. We'll soon settle back into our peaceful existence of paranoia and resentment, presumed Macken. We're bored of the border now, he thought sardonically. They need Aoife to sell newspapers.

As he reached the city centre, Macken accepted that only a proper drink would do. A quiet bar. No clinking china. No women. A pint through which to contemplate the world.

Belfast's centre is threaded with alleys into which men disappear without emerging at the other end. No mystery. They lead to hidden bars, refuges from the world of drudgery. Havens of polished, curving, wooden flourishes and secular pews. Rust-spotted mirrors and spirit bottles reflecting light from the reredos behind the counter.

Macken sought comfort in one of these shrines to procrastination. He found the streets too big and busy. He had never shaken off that childhood feeling of threat from the city. The ducking and weaving of everyday life seemed sharper here, more likely to cut you – like a flash of expensive lining inside a plain jacket.

The barman was perched on a stool at the far end of the counter, hunched over a radio at low volume, but switched it off as Macken approached.

'Sorry about that,' he said, looking hopefully at Macken. 'Not much craic in here today. What'll it be?'

Macken ordered a pint of stout and a sandwich from the glass case on the counter. The barman chattered on as he served them up.

'We've never had it so good. Did you hear?'

Macken said nothing

'It's not me saying that,' protested the barman. 'It's Mr Macmillan and he should know, like.'

Macken put some coins on the counter.

'Well, I was just making conversation. It was on the wireless just now.'

Macken took his pint and sandwich to the most remote corner. The barman returned to his radio. Macken contemplated the dark liquid settling in his glass. The sandwich was more of an alibi than to be eaten. He spread his newspaper over the table to deter other drinkers looking for conversation.

The headline shouted: 'Hen House Boy'. The strange, stunted foundling had turned out to be a he. His trailing, wispy hair was paler than Aoife's rich auburn gold, but there was little doubt that he was her son. She would not identify any father, so suspicion had naturally fallen on Paddy Penny. Why else would a child be hidden?

However, Aoife was steadfast in denying that her own father was also father to her child. And he said little, except to agree with Aoife. Neither repeated the tale she had told Macken, about her being sold into marriage.

That puzzled Macken. Why not tell that part of the truth? If it did not prompt sympathy, there might at least be understanding. Perhaps silence was the deal between Aoife and her father. They kept each other's shame secret. His shame at selling his daughter. Hers at running from a marriage, however it was arranged. And the shame of a deformed child. When in doubt, knew Macken, folks in these parts turn to the Bible. 'Whosoever hath any blemish, he shall not approach: a blind man or lame. Or brokenfooted or brokenhanded. Or crookbackt or a dwarf.' That's good old-time religion for you, he thought.

But Macken knew there could be another reason for their silence. Perhaps her story had been for his ears only, because it was just another convoluted lie to explain why she was single and available. With hindsight – too available. He had been so easily persuaded that she was a wounded bird needing looking after.

He had argued it out with himself over and over. In his hurt, he hardly knew what was true and what had been wishful thinking. Was he to recast it all as lust and deceit? Or had there ever been love and honesty between them?

Macken took a long swallow. The first was always the best. Leave it sitting too long, and it would turn from cool to sour, the white head becoming brown scum round the glass. He put the glass down on the newspaper to cover Aoife's face.

Apart from the attempted murder, which had been dropped, she had been charged with wilful neglect and wilful ill treatment of the boy. He was always referred to as 'the boy' or 'the child' or sometimes, when it served to emphasise the cruelty, 'her son'. Neither Aoife nor Paddy Penny divulged any name the child might have gone by. She merely shook her head when questioned. Her father said they had begun by calling him 'the child' and that there had not seemed any need to change it.

That revelation had been another turn of the screw of scandal. No name suggested no baptism. For some the possibility that he could have died unbaptised was worse than the physical abuse he had endured while in hell on earth.

Doctors working with the National Society for the Prevention of Cruelty to Children had testified to his subnormal physical and mental condition. They said they had been horrified to find that he weighed only two stone. He was only thirty inches high. They admitted that the curvature of his spine could have been a birth defect, but said the cramped conditions of the hen house could have contributed too. He had also been suffering from rickets, they said, due to continual denial of sunlight.

Aoife said she had confined the child for his own safety for short periods while she was getting on with her work. Such an abnormal child needed somewhere secure and safe, she explained, with no fire or stairs. As for the darkness inside his little shed, it was to keep him calm and help him rest. The lawyers dropped their eyes in embarrassment, but the snarls and catcalls from the gallery were clearly audible.

An NSPCC inspector testified that the boy's arm and leg joints had been swollen, and that his shinbones were concave in shape. When helped up, the child had been able to remain standing without assistance for only thirty seconds before collapsing.

The defence leant heavily on Aoife's youth and vulnerability, hinting at mental instability and victimhood. They hinted that she had herself been abused and possibly held in thrall to the father of the child. But Aoife's denials undermined any attempt to drum up sympathy.

She pleaded guilty to wilful neglect, but denied ill treatment and the Crown entered a nolle prosequi on that charge. Macken had not waited for her sentence.

The last he had heard before escaping the court was the judge summing up. He had said that, despite the child's possible pre-existing condition, he couldn't hide from himself the fact of the confinement in darkness.

'Your child lacked sunlight. You deprived him of something God gave him. You deprived him of something the State was prepared to give for nothing – medical advice and attention.

'Perhaps you were ashamed of the child. If you were it seems a sad thing that you should try to penalise him.'

The question everyone was asking, but to which she would never respond – why had she done it? The question Macken had been too scared to ask her, in case she had given him an answer too awful to hear.

Aoife asked quietly for the mercy of the court. The judge was discouraging.

'There may be some Divine providence who will provide mercy. I cannot.'

Paddy Penny had subversion charges hanging over him and failing that, the prospect of internment, so he would be locked up one way or another. He kept quiet about the faked ambush, fearing that the truth might cost him his life.


Macken felt tired. He prodded his sandwich. It felt tired too.

We're all tired, he thought. There's no appetite for martyrdom for Mother Ireland any more. We're stuck with each other. Twenty years from now we'll have outgrown this nonsense. By then it'll not just be dogs in space. We'll probably be sending people to the moon. Give us some new territory to scrap over. Orange marches on the moon, thought Macken. That would be a sight. They can chuck moon rocks at each other.

He lifted his glass and drank till it was empty. It no longer hid the faces beneath. He couldn't put it off any longer.

'Time to go,' he told himself. 'Time to meet the child.'

## CHAPTER 46

As Macken grasped the large knocker on the nuns' side door, he regretted the pint of stout. Meeting nuns was enough on its own to spark insidious feelings of guilt. Booze on the breath was like confessing that he was no more than a worthless corner boy.

The face that answered was benign and only mildly curious. No nose-twitching or pursed lips as Macken identified himself. He followed her along quiet corridors smelling of polish. Sepia-toned pictures of, presumably, dead nuns looked on. Or saints, he supposed. Or both. Looking pale and pure like Snow White, thought Macken, waiting for... He banished the inappropriate thought, as the swish of black and white ahead of him paused at a door.

He could hear faint music. The sister raised her eyebrows and smiled.

'Are you ready?'

He nodded.

She led him to a cloister, which opened onto lawn and flower beds. Beyond were vegetable plots and sheds and greenhouses and sounds of pottering. They sat at a table in the sun, set with a jug of water and two glasses. A rust-spotted old tin box decorated with Disney characters rested on a stack of foolscap paper. Classical music was playing on a gramophone set back under the cloister.

'You're very welcome,' she said, pouring him a glass. 'Thank you for coming.'

His mouth suddenly felt dry, and he took refuge in the cool drink.

'You're the officer we have to thank for bringing us Kevin.'

Macken coughed as some of the water went the wrong way.

'We decided on "Kevin",' she explained, 'because his saintly namesake had difficulties with women too and spent a lot of time in isolation and discomfort.'

'Kevin?' echoed Macken, trying out the name. The music wove around him in the calm of the garden. It seemed as though time was slowing, that they had travelled far further from the city than the length of the corridor.

'And how is he, Sister? How is... Kevin doing now?'

'He's made great steps, thanks be to God. And what about you?'

Macken looked away. He saw two backs bent over a flower bed.

'You're not in uniform,' she continued. 'Off duty? Or did you leave after all?'

Macken was surprised at how much she knew. But before he could answer, she raised a hand to stop him.

'No, that was very wrong of me. You came looking for answers, not to be – how would you put it? – not to be interrogated.

'I'm an inquisitive old woman, God forgive me, who should know better.'

She settled herself more comfortably and Macken saw her drift off with the music. Strangely, he did not feel at all impatient.

'Kevin is a lovely boy,' she said. 'He's so loving it's easy to forget he's known so much sadness.

'He loves being in the fresh air. And, like myself, he enjoys a little Mendelssohn. So we try to combine the two.'

She smiled to herself. 'His Violin Concerto in E Minor.'

She caught Macken watching her and nodded towards the waggling backsides across the garden.

'When he first joined our family here, he was a scared little boy, very mixed up. He wasn't used to sleeping in a bed. When we found him a cot, he would perch on it and caw like a hen. For weeks.

'But you can see how he's grown and responded to love and attention,' she nodded towards the gramophone, 'and music.'

'Has he said much about...' Macken's question petered out.

'He doesn't speak.' The nun reached over to the table and lifted the Seven Dwarves tin off the pile of paper. 'But he does communicate.'

She handed the pages to Macken.

'And he loves his crayons.'

Macken looked at the sheaf of drawings on his lap. Each page almost covered in heavy, dark scrawls, sometimes with a narrow letter box slit in the gloom with a yellow ball inside.

'Not very cheery,' said Macken, frowning as he considered the life experience at which the drawings hinted. 'Is that the sun?'

'Maybe,' said the nun. 'It's a comfort, isn't it, to think that even then he had some kind of light or hope.'

'What about these?' asked Macken, pointing to the large brown shapes with stick legs, spike toes and sharp, pointy faces. Threatening-looking. Sometimes almost filling the page. Macken didn't want to think of them as monsters.

'Yes, poor little lad,' said the nun. 'I think he must have spent a lot of time confined with the chickens, in the dark.'

She closed her eyes, her hands clasped in her lap, and they were silent together for a moment. Then she smiled gently again and suggested that Macken look further through the drawings.

He noticed the colours changing, brightening. Greens, blues. Big yellow circles at the top. Reds and purples and oranges.

'He loves flowers,' said the nun. 'But there's one picture in particular you should see. Right at the bottom.'

Macken drew out the last page. On it he saw a big yellow sun shining on a small stick figure, with a round head, dots for eyes and a carefully drawn crooked smile. It was holding hands with a giant, a wide, curved smile also filling its big, round head.

'All his faces have smiles these days. But we were not sure who this was,' the nun said, pointing at the happy stick giant. 'I think we know now.

'I'm sure he'd like you to have it.'

Macken blinked down at the crayon drawing, unable to say anything.

The nun rose to lift the needle arm from the disc and stop the turntable.

'Oh, Kevin,' she called across the garden.

The smaller of the backsides stopped waggling and began to rise, slowly and jerkily. The little figure leant on the shoulder next to it and accepted first one crutch and then another. Macken held his breath as gradually the wee bent boy turned and inched towards them.

'Shall we meet him halfway?' encouraged the nun.

They strolled unhurriedly to where the boy was determinedly advancing. She put a hand on Kevin's shoulder. The face that looked up was more innocent and full of joy than anything Macken had ever seen. He felt a great pain welling up inside, as the nun chatted lightly to the boy.

'That's great walking you're doing, Kevin. Just wonderful.'

Kevin smiled back. The sounds from his mouth were not recognisable as speech, but it seemed to Macken that he was trying to talk.

'And what about those roses?' asked the nun. 'Are you looking after them for me?'

Kevin dropped his head as he manoeuvred himself to lead them to the flower bed.

'He understands a lot,' said the nun more quietly to Macken. 'We're a long way from getting him to express himself in speech, but we're making progress.'

They followed the boy, his auburn hair cut short, thicker and healthier. Macken felt as if he were lifting the crutches himself each time Kevin moved forward, he was willing him so fervently not to stumble. The boy's back was still severely curved, and he clearly found it difficult to move and keep his balance.

'He's needed a lot of medical treatment on his legs. Operations. And more to come. I'm afraid his back may be beyond us. But, God willing, he'll eventually walk.'

'Where will he go?' asked Macken.

'Oh, we'll always have a place for him,' said the nun, and then more loudly as they covered the last few inches to the rose bed, 'and sure who wouldn't be delighted with such a talented gardener?'

She hitched up her habit a little and crouched down by the flowers. Macken went down on one knee beside them to join in. He felt a gentle pressure on his shoulder as the boy leant on him. Macken slowly turned to gaze on Kevin's small face. Pale and pointed, as though it had been drawn to a tip, longing for distant light glimpsed in darkness. He's like a small animal you could sweep up and put in your pocket, thought Macken. Almost weightless, lost in those clothes.

Kevin turned his large soft eyes onto Macken, who felt his own welling up, as the boy revealed a small, snaggle-toothed beam of happiness.

'To think,' Macken stammered. 'To think that she would have...'

'Ah, now,' the nun gently interrupted, 'didn't she keep him all those years? It wouldn't have been easy. Only God knows what is in people's hearts.

'If you look hard enough, you can always find goodness.'

Macken felt Kevin take his hand and carefully guide it past the thorns to touch the soft underside of the rose.

# Acknowledgements
# and a Note on Sources

Lots of people have helped, supported and encouraged me in the writing of this book and I want to thank them.

Blackwatertown is dedicated to Oliver and Helen. Whatever you say, say nothing – that was the motto I grew up with in Northern Ireland. We did not discuss the madness unfolding outside our front door. Except for Oliver. He shared stories. I listened. Later on, Helen gave me some of the space I needed to make up and tell my own stories. Thank you both.

Never offer to read someone's work in progress unless you really mean it. Because they'll be waiting, and waiting, impatiently and anxiously to hear your feedback. And as we're all busy, no time to read, don't really read much these days, it's better to offer encouraging words – or a pint – instead. But to those who did offer to read and actually *did read* versions of *Blackwatertown*, and even went on to give me detailed and sometimes heartfelt feedback – Helen Jones, Su Verhoeven, Kirsty Canning, Barry Turley, Colleen Jones and Clare Waters – I thank you very much. It was a huge help – very useful and very encouraging.

Since I began writing *Blackwatertown*, several people have helped me. Thank you Colin Cameron and Jesse Quinones for early encouragement, and Tim and Kate Jenkins for early and sustained support. Stan Burridge – you've been a constant support through ups and downs, writing-related and otherwise. (Your book will be a must read, when you write it.) Thanks also to my children Aidan and Erin for plot suggestions and for putting up with me writing. Pete Richmond, Angela McMahon and Parmjit Singh – thanks for the contacts and suggestions.

Thank you also to Andrew Paul Smith and Zoe Page for holding me at gunpoint, Andy Rolfe for the guns, and Mark Page for shooting it all, on video. And for the pictures. (If it's atmospheric photos you want – go to the award-winning Mark Page.)

Writing a book is one thing. Getting it published can seem like a whole other increasingly remote prospect. Endorsements and reviews from Frederick Forsyth, Rev Richard Coles, Peter Taylor and Gerard Brennan came at just the right time – thank you all.

I'm lucky to live near the small but beautifully formed Milton's Cottage Museum in Chalfont St Giles in Buckinghamshire, where John Milton lived and wrote *Paradise Lost*. The curators there are surrounded by the artefacts of great literature, but they opened their doors to me too. Thanks for your support. (I highly recommend you pay a visit yourself.)

Thank you to all my pledgers, including the anonymous ones whose names do not appear on the list. Especially Alena Doll and Deb Mowers for naming characters. And Janice Staines for naming a mischievous mutt and other support.

Nearly done. I write because I love to read. The credit for that goes to my parents – and teachers who didn't stop me. I also had a welcoming public library within walking distance.

And I benefit from the support of my very cool siblings, nieces and nephews.

A few people helped me to the finish. Stevyn Colgan – the very funny writer and my partner in chat on the *We'd Like A Word* podcast – thanks for your guidance. Author Russel D McLean – thanks for your great structural edit advice. Anita – your last minute advice was very useful and delivered at astonishing speed. And Aneysha, thank you for digging in and helping me over the line.

## HISTORICAL NOTE

Blackwatertown is a real place, on the Blackwater River, on the Tyrone-Armagh border. If you know it, you'll notice that it's not exactly the same as my fictional version. You can visit the real one and have a pint and a meal in The Portmor.

The story you've just read is inspired by two historical events. Firstly, the case of Kevin Halfpenny, a child who was kept confined in a hen house on a farm near Crossgar. I've changed some of the details. Seamus Heaney wrote about him in his poem 'Bye-Child'.

The second is the IRA border campaign, Operation Harvest, in the 1950s and action by other Republican groups at that time. Though Jolly Macken didn't really provoke it. How could he? I made him up.

However, I was keen to be true to the spirit of those times – the attitudes and behaviour. I found the book *Portavo – An Irish Townland and its Peoples* by Peter Carr particularly useful.

Unbound is the world's first crowdfunding publisher, established in 2011.

We believe that wonderful things can happen when you clear a path for people who share a passion. That's why we've built a platform that brings together readers and authors to crowdfund books they believe in – and give fresh ideas that don't fit the traditional mould the chance they deserve.

This book is in your hands because readers made it possible. Everyone who pledged their support is listed at the front of the book and below. Join them by visiting unbound.com and supporting a book today.

Jamie Adamberry
Adrienne Aiken
Andrew Al-Wagga
Jean Alderman
Kirsty Allison
Patrick Altes
Kwesi Andoh-Korsah
Liz Apedaile
Musty Aziz
Julia Baber

Martha Backshall
Jason Ballinger
Layil Barr
Philly Beaumont
Alan Bell
Gareth Bellamy
Simon Bendle
Howard Benson
Terry Bergin
Julia Betancour-Roth

Helen Blaby
Megan Bonhomme
Lucinda Borer
Grainne & Steve Bourne
Ian Braidman
Ethna Brennan
Wendy & Robin Bretherick
Stephanie Bretherton
Madeleine Bridgman
Damian Brown
Fiona Bugler
Peter Burroughs
D C
Douglas Canning
Julian Cattle
Joe Cawley
Sue Cemlyn-Jones
Megha Chand Inglis
Andrew Chaplin
Jean Clark
Sue Clark
Amelia Coffen
John Colgan
John & Di Collins
Alan Conchar
Tanya Conyers-Silverthorn
Louise Cotton
Nick Couldry
Matt Cox
Lesley Crooks
Helen Cullen
Em Cummins
Brian Cunningham
Aidan D'Abet
Carl D'Agostino
Helen Dafedjaiye
Steve Daish
Richard Dallyn
Ed Davey
Andy Daymond
Fabio De Robertis
Jo Deahl
Sim Dehra
Neil Denham
Dave Dixon
Sue Dodd

Gary Duffy
Gill Edmonds
Daniel Emery
Tracey English
George Eykyn
Natalia Fernandez
Dave Ffowcs Williams
Jude Flashman
Brenda Floyd
Nuala Fox
Anne-Louise Gallagher
Malcolm Galloway
Michelle Gaskin
Mark Gentry
Ben Geoghegan
Jonathan Glover
Angela Goldson
Lucy Gow
Phil & Mary Green
Josephine Greenland
Cathy Grieve
Jason Grubbs
Conrad Hake
Thanatip Harrison
Priscilla & Richard Hazell
David Heath
Phil Hertel
Chris Hiley-Payne
Richard Horton
Daniel Hughes
David Hunter
Husain Husaini
John & Maureen Huxtable
Clare Isdell
Al Jackson
Shaw James
Suizan Jefferson
Jolly Cricketers Landlord's Question
Mike Jones
To lovely Joy
Dhiya Karwal
Julian Keane
Mary Kelly
Joe Kent
John Kevan
Dan Kieran

Philip Kimberley
Melanie Kimble
Juliet La Marque
Matthew Langley
Giles Latcham
Dominic Laurie
Julian Leach
Drew Leckie
Sarah Leslie
Hugh Levinson
Paul Lewis
Gary Lonergan
Graham Louer
Gillian Lyle
Gerry Mackin
James Macleod
Anoop Mangat
Simon Mann
Mark Marmur
James Martin
Louise Martin
Bernard McGuinness
Catherine McGuinness
John McGuinness
Peter McGuinness
Anon McL
Oscar Midgley Masters
Huw Miles
John Mitchinson
Jane Moore
Stefan Mork
Charlotte Morrison
Carlo Navato
Anthony Newman
Zoe Newton
Rudy Noriega
Pól Ó Duibhir
David O'Connell
Sandra Offord
Peter Orton
Sarah Parfitt
Haydn Parry
Aleksandar Pavlov
Lizz Pearson
Katie Phillips
James Pierson

Justin Pollard
David Potts
Sally Powell
Alan Powell(Baggies)
Linda Pressly
Sean Prior
Elena Prokopiou
Rob Quick
Jesse QW
Kush Ramjee
Marion Richmond
RKI
Richard Roy
Chris and Jules Rumsey
AS
Yoko Saito
Harry Salvidge
Nimesh & Neeta Samani
Tim Samuels
Andrew and Lynda Scott-Priestley
Pamela Seaman
Zanna Sebba
Nick Sharwood
Clare Sherman
Jennifer Shilleto
Ian Shoesmith
A Shrestha
James Silver
Harjit Singh Sagoo
Bidisha Sinha
Corinne Smith
Mandie Smith
Michael Smith
Dino Sofos
Eamon Somers
Jamie Stangroom
Janice Still
Richard Swede
Carmen Taylor
Thalia, Elodie and Theo
John Thorne
Rachel Toft
Sue Toudup
Emma Tracey
Andy Tsoi
Rupi Ubi

Mihai Udrea
Richard Vadon
Amali Valan
Vibeke Venema
Su Verhoeven
Wink Verhoeven
Sonja Verma
Ciaran Ward

Stefanie Wareham
David Waters
Erin Waters
James Watson
Megan Whittingham
Carien Windell
Jackie Wixon-Jones
Matthew Yalden